ARCANE KNIGHT

ARCANE KNIGHT

AN EPIC LITRPG FANTASY

ORDER & CHAOS
BOOK 4

TIMOTHY MCGOWEN

ILLUSTRATED BY
RICHARD SASHIGANE

RISING
TOWER
BOOKS

Fantasy / LitRPG / Gamelit

BIBLIOGRAPHY OF TIMOTHY MCGOWEN

Haven Chronicles
Haven Chronicles: Eldritch Knight

Short Stories/Novellas
Dead Man's Bounty
Exiled Jahk (https://dl.bookfunnel.com/c10uz8peaf)

Last Born of Ki'darth
Reincarnation: A Litrpg/Gamelit Trilogy
Rebellion: A Litrpg/Gamelit Trilogy
Retribution: A Litrpg/Gamelit Trilogy

Order & Chaos
Arcane Knight Book 1: An Epic LITRPG Fantasy
Arcane Knight Book 2: An Epic LITRPG Fantasy
Arcane Knight Book 3: An Epic LITRPG Fantasy
Arcane Knight Book 4: An Epic LITRPG Fantasy

The Elemental Realms
Nexus Guardian Book 1: A Fantasy LitRPG Adventure
Nexus Guardian Book 2: A Fantasy LitRPG Adventure

Arcane Knight Book 4: An Epic LITRPG Fantasy

Order & Chaos

Paperback ISBN: 978-1-956179-23-1

First Edition: July 2023

Published By: Rising Tower Books

Publisher Website: www.RisingTowerBooks.com

Author Site: AuthorTimothyMcGowen.com

REVIEWS ARE IMPORTANT

Every review matters, get your voice heard.

Follow me on Amazon to get informed when my next book is released!

https://www.amazon.com/stores/Timothy-McGowen/author/B087QTTRJK

Join my Patreon for early Chapters!

https://www.patreon.com/TimothyMcGowen

Join my Facebook group and discuss the books

https://www.facebook.com/groups/234653175151521/

SPECIAL THANKS

I wanted to give a special thanks to those that helped bring this book to its current state.

Candace Morris - Alpha Reader, Beta Reader, Editor, and Proofer

Dantas Neto - Editor, Proofer

Sean Hall - Proofer

I would also like to mention my patreons and thank them for their extra support!

Jesse Butcher, John Percival, Brad Gibson, Destin McMurray, Eric Letcher

Thank you.

I dedicate this book to my friend Stephen and thank him for all the help to make this novel possible.

CONTENTS

LEAVE A REVIEW & CHECK OUT MY WEBSITE

Don't forget to leave a review! You can follow this link to do so after you finish reading! My Book

Get an exclusive short story to read if you subscribe to my newsletter at https://authortimothymcgowen.com/

PROLOGUE

"In light of the changing tide in the human nation, we have no choice but to act." I pleaded my case before the queen, but despite my many years under her service I still had no indication of her demeanor. Surely, she must see that with the power the humans have unleashed, finding a foothold elsewhere is the only prudent course of action.

"And you'd have us act as transport for Elkor's kin as well? My many ears within the kingdom say he is the mastermind behind this great new destruction," Queen Elsena said, her smile going into a tight line.

"Then would it not be prudent for us to take this young inventor into Eldah'ren and help mold him into a suitable champion for all?" I countered. Though I felt my argument was poor, I knew of the weakness my queen had for Elkor and the deeds he'd done for her.

"Or contain him as we have Lady Alayna Variyn," Galdr'ten said, making me cringe at his mention of the girl.

We'd all but locked her away in a very elven fashion, making her think she was a guest while also barring any attempt to leave by means of everything other than force. We'd set her to help us put her inventions to use within our ships. We of course had tried a similar form of rune work before, but none worked as elegantly as what she'd brought us. Though I suspected she held back more than she was freely giving, it wouldn't be wise for her to do anything but that.

Several times she'd attempted to leave, saying she was needed at the front, but we'd manufactured emergencies that required her close care and inspection. We elves are wise in the ways of manipulation, but it stung to hear Galdr'ten so casually mention our methods in polite conversation.

"A fleet of ships will be constructed," the Queen said, with fire in her voice. "We will venture out into the old lands and reclaim the islands that were once ours. Gather the strongest of our kind and give them the promise of old dungeons whose depths haven't been plundered in a thousand years. Make it so, Adathren Valamin."

"As you command," I said, turning to leave.

My son, Adathin, awaited me outside the chambers.

"It is not right that we hold a companion of Caldor Miles under lock and key," he said, for what felt like the millionth time. His passion as an adventurer was to be commended, but he felt too deeply for those he'd met on his adventures.

"The time of holding her has ended, it is now time to gather forces together," I said, then going into more detail I set him to task to writing a decree that would go out to all the nations under elven control. The strongest and most powerful adventurers we had to offer would be summoned together and old lands would become new again.

***

Approaching the door where Alayna Variyn slept, I expected to receive a cold reception. What I didn't expect was the state of the room. As the doors opened, I saw that all of the smaller tables we'd given her to use had been pushed together and covered in notes. She was an intelligent girl, and it appeared she was too concerned with her work to have noticed she'd been imprisoned.

"Adathren, it is good to see you, I believe I have worked out our latest hang up with the thrust controls. If we can..." she spoke in a rapid pace, and I smiled hearing her words. We'd worked out the issue days before, but she was spot on in her calculations, coming to the same conclusion we had.

"We will implement your changes right away, but I believe I have good news," I said, smiling down at her as she bent herself over her papers, shuffling through her notes.

"I'm finally going to be allowed to leave?" Alayna asked, a smirk on her face.

Perhaps not so aloof as I previously thought. This girl had a fire that burned inside her and a mind as sharp as any elf's.

"You have always been allowed to leave," I lied, keeping my smile as firm as ever. "However, we believe we finally know enough to construct a prototype or three. It would be best that you gather your forces together while we do the same."

"So, you'll agree to the expedition to Avalon?" Alayna said, standing in her excitement.

"Indeed, we shall. However, the journey will be a long one and we plan on stopping on many of the islands along the way to search through ruins of old, this won't be a problem, will it?" I asked, knowing full well that Alayna loved rooting through ruins and discovering lost secrets.

"If we must," she said, barely containing her enthusiasm. "I will get Caldor and return at once."

"Three months will be needed to retrofit the ships we have available," I said, giving her a firm look. "Be sure that your friend and your father know of the favor we are doing for them. I would hate to bring our nation under their ire."

Alayna looked at me oddly at that, as was expected since she hadn't been told the news of what had happened to House Blalor. I nodded down at her and gave her my best wishes. It would be at least a month before we were ready to leave, but the queen insisted we tell them that we require three. What she had planned I couldn't say, but I knew my queen to be honorable, so if she said she'd take them, then she would. I just wondered if an advance group of ships would be leaving sooner to act as scouts. Yes, I decided, that was the likely path forward.

CHAPTER 1
RIGHTING WRONGS

Standing outside Cam's modest home I watched as chickens pecked away at the ground while a rooster announced the beginning of the day. It was early morning, much earlier than would normally be proper to visit a friend, but I came bearing gifts that couldn't wait. Kora stood beside me with two gifts wrapped up in her arms in tight cloth bundles. I'd sent for her days after getting back to my home, as I had an idea of how we could help Cam. I had the ability to help him in a way that I couldn't help the others I'd failed, so I needed to.

My sour mood persisted, despite the good deeds I'd tried to do, and I wondered if I'd ever be the same again. Likely not, but I refused to let myself become the dark brooding person I was turning into throughout the war. There was a happy middle ground somewhere, and I'd find it. It was like my father always said, 'Take the good with the bad, but never let the weight of the bad make seeing the good impossible.' I hadn't really understood what he meant back when he'd told me that, but I knew now.

It took great effort to see the good of it all, but it was possible. This act for Cam was the start of my deliberate action toward good. It was with much trepidation and hesitation that I did this for him, but I knew that it would be a welcomed gift. Before I reached the front steps, the door opened and Tyrza stood in the doorway.

She had the same sweet smile and kind demeanor that I'd first seen on her when I met her some days before. Despite it being wholly my fault that Cam had gotten into the condition he now found himself, she held no malice in her gaze. In fact, quite the opposite, she beamed with pure joy upon seeing me walking up to the front door.

"We are so happy to see you," she said, her voice like a sweet cool drink on a warm day. "Cam is just getting ready but come in for a spot of tea while I help him get ready for the day."

"We can wait outside if you'd like?" I offered. Their small cottage home had no more than two separate rooms, one being a kitchen. I heard the cry of a baby from inside and was reminded of their newborn baby.

"Please, come in and rest your feet. I'll only be a moment," Tyrza pleaded, her lower lip pouting as she stepped aside for us to enter. She was being playful, I knew, she was like that. So, I obliged her and entered into their modest cottage.

I'd spoken with Cam before and had tried to force a sizable sum of gold onto him so he could buy a much nicer place, but I'd failed to convince him. He refused to what he called 'hand outs' and I couldn't blame him for wanting to hold fast to a bit of pride. Instead, I gave him a small sum of gold, still a fortune by Creeshaw standards, and assured him that this was the same amount all injured in my service received. In that, I was honest, though it cost much of the blood money I'd received, I no longer cared for what else the money could be used for.

Tyrza brought me some tea and turned to Kora, saying, "I'd offer you some, but I wasn't sure if you could drink tea." She seemed flustered at not knowing how best to show hospitality to Runeforged, but Kora was quick to put her mind at rest.

"I'm fine as I am and need nothing. Thank you for your thoughts, however, it is nice to see humanity showing care where others might simply ignore my presence as a mere tool of Caldor's," Kora said, a hint of amusement in her voice.

I smiled at Kora, war had done nothing to diminish her unique view on the world, despite her losing several Runeforged permanently. Suddenly I saw flashes of Ignis's death and the tremble that had been in her voice at the time of her parting. She hadn't wanted to die, she had a great will to live, and yet she'd perished like so many of those under my command.

My grip tightened around my cup as I focused my mind elsewhere, trying to leave the war behind or at least out of the forefront of my head. I knew by experience that if I didn't, the images and the feelings that came along with them would continue to haunt me until I broke. Too often as of late, I struggled to keep my mind intact against the horrors of war I'd witnessed. You'd think being an Awakened would have prepared me, but monsters rarely begged for their lives or screamed in such a way that it left a mark on your soul. But I would remain strong and stay focused on what needed to be done.

It was this focus on righting the wrongs, in some small part, that helped me hold on. That, and the comforting words of my mother. It had been like she expected that I would crumble under the pain of my ordeal, and she was ready with words and reminders of my father's and hers. She spoke of honor, responsibility, and the nature of grief. Then she surprised me by telling me that sometimes my father would come home from his adventures and cry in her arms at the things he'd witnessed. She told me to be strong and not see my own emotions as a weakness. But to see it as a reminder that I too was human, and it was okay to grieve and struggle.

All the while, as my emotions stirred and moved like a hurricane inside of me, my outer calmness stood in stark contrast. So easy it was to hide the pain within when the moment was right, so hard for others to see the pain hidden within.

"Here I am," Cam announced, walking into the room with a slight limp. The leg he'd been given worked perfectly, but the healing would take months before it worked as well as the original, despite the powerful healings he'd received.

I stood and saluted him, something I'd begun doing to all the injured soldiers under my command. Each of them deserved the respect and honor that came with being addressed by their Commander in such a fashion.

Cam just smiled and shook his head, gesturing with the stump of a left arm for us to sit back down. Only then did I notice that Kora had also stood, inclining her head toward the proud soldier.

"You are looking well," I said, seeing that more color had returned to his pale face. Several weeks on bed rest had stolen away a good portion of the muscle and color from his face, but he was swiftly getting the color back, if not some of the muscled tone.

"As well as I can," Cam chuckled, lifting his arms. "I've been speaking with Teland the Blacksmith about helping me make a harness that will allow me to grip onto objects, just a simple device so I can help out around the house or tend to the livestock. I won't be a scribe any time soon, but perhaps I can still be useful."

"You are more than useful just the way you are," Tyrza shot back at him the moment he paused in his speaking. "The fact that you returned to me alive when so many didn't, arms or no arms, you are enough."

My thoughts went to Dan Lion, one of Cam's close friends, who'd fallen in the last weeks of war. He'd been so close to making it out, but I hadn't been able to keep him safe, and war ate him up like it had so many others. I'd visited with his parents just a week before, one of the few fallen that I personally delivered the news of their fallen son. Much to my surprise, they'd received the news already. His mother wouldn't speak to me, but his father asked about Dan's performance in the war.

I told him truthfully that he was a soldier to be honored and his death was a great loss to our forces. I then gave them the gold I'd set aside for those who fell in battle, which included all their earnings plus a larger amount to help ease the burden of death. There was truly no amount that could pay for the life of one who'd fallen, but the amount I gave would mean that the Lions would never have to want again for the rest of their lives if they were smart with their gold.

Of all the things I'd done, I'd hoped that some of it would lessen the pressure I felt almost constantly in my chest from the results of the war, but it didn't. Instead, I knew I had to focus on doing what I knew to be right, if I had any hope of making it out of this darkness in one piece.

I'd let my mind wander and missed something Cam had asked, so I inclined my head as a signal for him to ask again.

"Still getting lost with your thoughts in the clouds, eh?" Cam asked, laughing. Since returning he'd become much more informal with me, and I didn't try to stop him. I felt like he was a good friend and I'd let him speak to me in any manner he wished, he'd earned as much. Clearing his throat when my only response was to smile in his direction, he asked his question. "What do I owe the pleasure of your visit? Not trying to hire me back on this season, are you? You might find I need more of a hand than I did last season."

My smile deepened and I wanted to laugh at his humor, but I couldn't. If anything, I was a bit jealous at how jovial the man could be, considering all he'd lost. I envied him then, and wished that for the barest of moments that I could trade places with him. But no, I had a great responsibility to see to and I would do what needed to be done.

"You've got your own little farm to tend to," I said. His cottage was on an entire arc of land, but he hadn't yet had a barn erected or used any of the land. All around the edge of his cottage and small potential farm, were neat rows of orchard trees, the prominent crop of Creeshaw. From what I'd heard, he hadn't tried to buy up any of the trees yet, but I think he ought to as he'd soon have the ability to work the trees once more. "I come bearing a gift that I will not let you turn down."

Cam rolled his eyes and looked at the bundle Kora held. "Well let's have a look then," he sighed the words, but I could tell he was intrigued by the way he looked at what Kora was holding.

Kora unwrapped the package, revealing what looked like two severed Runeforged arms. They had been hollowed out to just an outside frame all the way to above the elbow, so that they'd fit around his stumps. Each one was connected by leather bands that would be helpful in keeping them tight, but they had clamps around the connection point as well. The idea had been mine, but the execution had been entirely Kora's work. She'd worked out that, despite not being Awakened, she'd be able to create a sensor of sorts that would take the tiny impulses the body gave out when you tried to move your arms and transfer them into the arm, similar to how the elementals relayed their thoughts into movements as Runeforged.

I'd expected it to take her weeks, if not months, to figure it out, but she'd accomplished the impossible within three days of nonstop work. This would be the first test and the arms required a steady supply of Essence that would need to be provided by Monster Cores, but I'd had her fit in a half dozen into each arm in various places. It would give the arms, according to her tests, ten years of usage before the cores would need to be replaced. By that time, I hoped to have a better prototype for him that pulled from the essence in the air all around us. Kora knew all my research on the matter and assured me that with time it was well within the realm of possibility. I would leave it to her though, as my own responsibilities required that I focus elsewhere.

"I'm flattered, but I don't really know what you have there," Cam said while awkwardly rubbing at the back of his neck.

"They are your new arms," Kora said, answering before I had a chance to. "They are, in theory, able to take the signals from your body and translate them into movement. Allow me to put them on you so we can begin testing?" She posed the last bit as a question, and Cam just looked at her, then at me for a long moment before answering.

"This is," he began to say but his wife interrupted him.

"This is a wonderful gift that we accept," she said, then shot a look at Cam who still seemed torn. "I'm going to tend to the baby, you help my stubborn husband into his new hands, please."

There was a yearning in her voice, and I saw it battling against Cam's desire to stay stubborn and prideful. But in the end, as with so many others, Cam relented under the gaze of his wife.

"It's a wonderful gift," he said, his voice trembling a bit at the end. "What do I need to do?"

"Just let Kora set it up on you and we will see if they work or not. Mind you it might take some time, but she is confident that this prototype will give you close to a full range of motion and ability to lift, squeeze, and even feel," I said, inclining my head towards Kora, who stood and set the arms on their small table just to the left of us.

The room was small but had enough room for a table and four chairs that currently had been moved to sit around the fireplace, despite no fire burning in the hearth. Over the fireplace, mounted into the stone, was Cam's spear and shield. I'd helped him mount it during my first visit, a special request by him meant to show respect toward the means that got him the cottage in the first place. I didn't like it, but I wasn't going to turn down his request or comment on my true feelings.

I felt my hand tremble and I pressed it against my leg before anyone noticed. I'd been getting random shakes when thinking of wielding a weapon for a while now, but I needed to get over it soon, as I'd scheduled some training with Michael, as well as wanting to go over the twins' progress.

I watched as Kora gently took Cam's shirt off, showing his many scars and stiff skin. The healing and ointment I'd gotten him had done its work, but he'd be forever scarred by the powerful flames of the sorcery he'd gone up against. The light from the nearby window fell across his scars, making it look like a web of dark shadows and white lines.

It took several minutes but she'd gotten the artificial arms in place and the length was perfect, she'd been able to judge just by memory and had nailed every aspect.

"How does it feel?" Kora asked as she tightened the clamps around his flesh that would intercept the signals in his arms.

He cringed a little as the small, spiked receptors entered his flesh, but nodded without saying anything.

"The arms can come off whenever you'd like, but the receptors should remain inside your flesh, see here, you can twist this and it releases from the main section. Give it a few minutes and you should start to feel it begin to tingle as it tries to connect with you," Kora said, but Cam already had a look of astonishment on his face.

"I can feel it already," he said, then focusing on his left hand his forehead scrunched in concentration. The middle finger twitched, and my smile widened, not having to fake my joy this time. "It moved!" He exclaimed, and he caught Tyrza's eye as she entered holding their baby girl as she snoozed in her arms. He gave her an apologetic smile when he saw the child stir, but Tyrza didn't scold him. Instead, it looked like she was going to start crying.

She came over to me and offered the child. At first, I meant to decline the offer, not wanting to hold such a fragile life, but she insisted, giving me a motherly look that I knew all too well. I reached out and held the child in my arms, trying and failing not to hold her awkwardly. Little baby

Daniella, named in part after Dan Lion, Cam had said. If not for Dan, Cam claimed he'd never had made it out of the war alive. I believed him, having heard the stories of them working together and pushing back against even the most fearsome odds.

Little Danny girl had woken up, but she was a quiet and thoughtful baby, peering up at me with curious eyes. I didn't know her exact age, but she had grown much bigger than I'd have thought for such a newly born child. I peered into the innocence of the child I held, and a flash of panic rippled through me. How many little children had been killed by the monstrous weapon Lord Variyn had deployed? How much of their blood dripped from our hands? Lord Variyn needed to pay for his crimes, and I'd set myself up to be his judge, jury, and executioner.

The problem, I thought as I stared into the eyes of this innocent child, was that I had no idea how to accomplish such a feat. The first step was clear to me, I needed to be released from his service. That would end any oaths in place that became binding when I went into service under him. What did that mean for Blackridge Keep and the diverse population I'd gathered there? Perhaps I could use my significant wealth to purchase the land and allow them to live free, outside the rule of Newaliyn? It was a possibility that I clung to; however small it might be.

Tyrza sat beside Cam, stroking his metallic arms, while tears fell down his face. "I can feel it," he said, unable to control his emotions any longer.

Slowly, taking minutes of concentration at a time, he

began to move each finger. I watched in amazement at the creation that Kora had put together and the implications it had for any who'd lost a limb. Once more, I was at the center of a potentially world altering device. My thoughts immediately went to how this might be used for ill intent, but I struggled to see how until minutes later, when Cam tried to pick up a teacup. He'd gotten to the point that he could move all the fingers and wanted to test his dexterity, Kora agreed and Tyrza offered up her empty teacup.

He tried to close his hand too fast, and it shattered in his grip.

"You will find your forearm and grip strength is far superior to what you had before, this is because, unfortunately, a side effect of the Runeforged design and not something I can adjust easily. You will need to learn to be extremely careful in your interactions until you are in complete control. So, how does it feel to have superior arms now?" Kora asked, very proud to have 'improved' him by giving him metal arms.

"I don't know," Cam said, a sudden change coming over his face as he stared at the remains of the teacup in his hands. "What if I hurt someone by accident. Maybe this isn't a good idea after all." He began to move to try and remove them, and I was surprised at how his movements answered his mental calls seamlessly.

He also paused, looking down at his new hands and setting aside the remains of the cup. He opened and closed his hands, twisted his wrists, and made a fist.

"It will take time, but you will learn to control them as well as you did with your own hands. As you well know, weak or strong, any pair of hands can cause harm. You just need to be cautious, and your improved form will become second nature to you," Kora said, beaming.

"I suppose," Cam said, looking over at me holding his baby. "The idea of holding my baby isn't something I can give up on so quick. But keep clear of me until I am absolutely sure I can control these." He directed his words to Tyrza and flexed his fingers in front of his face as he spoke.

"You'll have to help around the house now," Tyrza said, a coy smile spreading over her lips. "Just try not to break any more of my mother's favorite tea set."

With that done and Kora promising to check up on him tomorrow, as well as telling him he should try working outside to help make the connections stronger, we stood ready to leave.

I handed over the baby to Tyrza and she pulled me into a side hug, kissing me on the cheek before whispering a soft thank you in my ear. I smiled at her, the hollowness inside feeling slightly less oppressive under the circumstances. Turning, I bid Cam farewell by saluting him as I had when entering and felt a warming in my chest, when he was able to return the salute.

The world wasn't perfect, but I'd done a good thing here today and I would continue to do good as long as I lived.

CHAPTER 2
UNTOLD STRENGTH

"I think he makes a good half-man," Kora said when we were several steps down the road.

I looked at her with a blank stare and shook my head. "Half-man?" I questioned her when she didn't elaborate.

"And half Runeforged, the superior race," she said, filling in the gaps. I knew that this was a mix of her sense of humor and her thinking that Runeforged were basically her children, so I let it go for now. However, she wasn't done. "I need to speak to you about our independence."

"Our independence?" I asked, giving her a skeptical look. Surely, she didn't think that I held her as some type of property. She was free to do as she wished, however I wasn't sure if I'd ever actually told her as much.

"Runeforged, those I've altered to more fully be that which they were before their enslavement. Surely, you know that they seek true independence after being forced to fight in a war they couldn't understand," Kora said, her words coming out like a parent explaining something to a child.

I knew she didn't mean to sound so condescending, but it stung as she'd been so casual yet respectful to me up to this point. I took a deep breath to steady my emotions and keep them out of my response. Turning to her, I stopped and put a hand on her shoulder. "I respect their sacrifice and acknowledge their need to grow, but do they really want to be considered independent, and what will they do if granted said independence?"

Kora shifted and her glowing gaze met mine, before looking up into the sky. "Each of their souls, or their Cores as you'd call them, seek freedom. For some, knowing that they are free is enough, but for others, they want to go explore and grow stronger. They want the ability to choose their own path."

What did I think about this sudden change in Kora? Is this why she'd been changing so many of the Runeforged into the new type, she'd done just about every single one by the end of the war. Did she intend to create some kind of indestructible race of beings that would eventually rival even the strongest of *Awakened*? I felt immediately suspicious and began to doubt all the previous encounters I'd had with Kora. As a dungeon core, she claimed to be old, wise, and knowing, but perhaps she had a different plan in motion.

"I don't know," I finally said, walking forward down the dusty road toward Creeshaw. She began to walk after me and made no attempt to stop me.

"You have united so many races under a banner," Kora said. "What is one more to you?"

I sighed. "This isn't a simple matter of me calling them citizens."

Kora waved her hands about. "No, but it would be a great first step if you said as much, showed them that you saw them as more than just weapons."

That made me stop again and I stared at Kora until she met my eyes. "You know I care for them. When Ignis died," I began to say, but my voice cut off. No, I couldn't do this right now. I didn't want to discuss this topic any longer. I began walking again, but Kora persisted.

"Some can feel your emotions for them, but not all. A show of goodwill is needed," Kora said, her voice insistent.

I walked for another half mile in silence as I thought over the consequences of my actions if I took the step of offering them a place as citizens within Blackridge Keep. As I'd been doing in the past few weeks, my mind went for the worst-case scenario first. What if, as citizens and not tools to be ordered around, they decided they didn't want to serve under me anymore. Perhaps they decide they want to wage their own war against the weak fleshy races? Could I stop them after they've grown to match even the strongest adventurers in strength and power?

That was the thing with Runeforged. They didn't age, but they could get stronger now. So even the longest-lived adventurer would pale in comparison to a race of metallic beings that could slowly progress to the point of near god-like strength and power. And once that happened, would their monster nature be what dictated their actions? For that matter, what if, given the freedom she says they so desire, they decide to go back to their monstrous nature of killing all that approach them?

As Runeforged, they had certain guidelines that dictated their actions, and as such, they weren't the monsters their cores had once belonged to. How much different was the process after Kora finished messing with them. I needed to know more about what she changed and what she didn't. I had to know what made them tick and where these desires came from, the wildness of their original selves or a new, more profound being.

I determined that I could get these answers well enough from Kora, if she was willing to share them. "Answer a few questions for me and I will consider it."

Kora nodded swiftly, ready to do whatever was necessary to get her answer.

"As Runeforged, they have to follow orders, they won't attack unless given an order, but after the changes you made, how much closer are they to the monsters they started out as? What I'm trying to ask is, what is preventing them from becoming monsters again that attack at the simplest provocation? They are much stronger now than many of them ever were as monsters, so you must understand why I'm worried about the potential freedom they seek."

Kora listened to my questions with a measured gaze and took time to consider all my words before finally responding. "Their natures are in question then." Kora nodded, seeming to take additional time to consider. "Do you feel Ignis was a monster before dying?"

"Of course not!" I shot back immediately. "I'd probably consider her a friend, and definitely a comrade in arms."

"Then why do you doubt the others who have the same changes wrought upon them?" She questioned, her tone sounding like that of a parent scolding a child again.

"Because I have to," I said, getting frustrated. "It isn't enough anymore to just see the good in people, there is always bad and if I don't consider it then who will? Imagine for a moment the worst-case scenario with me. What happens when they decide they enjoyed life more as monsters? What happens if they change from what I know them to be and get a taste for more? More wealth, more blood, more mayhem. It doesn't matter what they choose because if they get strong enough, who will stop them?"

"I will," Kora said, standing confidently in the sunlight of the morning. Where armor didn't cover, her neck and face mostly, she glistened beneath the sun of the early morning.

"And how long will you be able to enforce that? How long until they grow even stronger than you?" I asked, shaking my head. It just didn't make sense to take the risk.

"You have witnessed so precious little of my strength, my power," Kora said, stopping dead in her tracks and a look of determination appearing on her face. "Face me in single combat and if you can bring me to the ground before I do the same to you, then I will let the matter drop for now. But if I win, you will admit that I have the ability to keep them in check and you will grant them citizenship at Blackridge Keep."

I looked at her hard. She had power, and speed, but I doubted she could match me. I thought back to our last sparring session and how quickly she'd learned, how she got faster and faster as the fight went on. With the small bit of essence I collected during the last moments of the battle, I could infuse every action I did and easily bring her to her knees. This could be an easy way to end the argument, but where did she expect us to fight? I'd need space to not worry about harming those around me if I'd be infusing myself.

"Fine, but not here. We need someplace away from civilization, a place that is remote enough that onlookers won't be harmed." As I said the words I thought of a place. In the middle of the massive Redridge Lake was a small island that had just enough space for us to fight and boats almost never went out to visit it, as it was said to be bad luck. Something about, never any good fish around the island, in fact, most fishermen stayed a way's away from it. "Let's have our fight at Redridge Lake."

Ares appeared minutes later, giving up on her hunt where she was pursuing a nice-sized boar. I promised her a new hunting ground filled with tasty fish and she happily gave up on her hunt to give us a lift. More and more I realized she was truly her own person, loving the hunt and having preferences to different tastes like any animal, but also deeper than that. She preferred certain people, worried about me constantly, and had several people that she didn't care for. In an odd display of annoyance, she'd made several screeches at Breanna the Donkey when she'd seen her after the war. I tried to read her emotional state at the time, but I just got confusion and frustration from her, like she wasn't sure how she felt either.

Ole reliable Breanna didn't even seem to care, walking right up to the griffin and hee-hawing in her face. That had been enough to silence Ares and really compound the confusion she was feeling toward the pack animal. I needed to spend some more time with Breanna the donkey, but I'd made sure the twins had cared for her. Apparently, Gregory had made it his personal responsibility to keep her well taken care of, even taking the time to do what I used to do, walking her into town for goods while speaking to her all the while. If there was one thing Breanna liked, it was talking. I'm sure if she wasn't just an ass, she'd be speaking a bunch herself. Instead, she had to be content with others speaking to her.

We soared through the air, Kora holding me tight from behind while we circled the lake, slowly descending toward the small island. As I'd thought, there wasn't a single boat anywhere near the island and it lay mostly barren, not a single tree or much less a bush. Just dirt, rock, and what looked like a cluster of weeds at the water's edge. It was easily a hundred paces wide from the center and made a mostly equal circle, except for one edge that curved inward with three long grooves like an animal clawing out the dirt. It made for an interesting look, but one I didn't care to think about as I went over my plan in my head.

Already I had begun to slowly pump small amounts of essence into my muscles and prepared myself for the upcoming battle. She'd not see what hit her. I planned on using Speed Burst for the four seconds of increased speed, mixed with my infusion of essence it would likely grant even more than double speed. I would put her down with a swift leg sweep and a punch to her chest and it would be over. It was a simple and straightforward plan, but it was all I needed. Kora was fast, strong, and could summon monsters to aid her, but none of that would matter when put up against my own power. I may only be level 30, but I'd matched a level 50 in combat, and that was saying something. Old Ironfist hadn't been an easy fight, but in the end, I had been victorious.

Ares landed and we dismounted. Kora looked as confident as ever, stepping down and walking off a distance. "I have easily tripled my frame's capabilities during the war you humans forced my kind into. I say that, not to sound bitter, as it was a great growing opportunity for myself and my children but think about what you are about to face. I was nearly a match for you before and that was while I held back. You don't stand a chance now. I will give you first move, meatbag."

I smiled, appreciating her straightforward manner. She wanted to give me the first attack, that was fine with me. Surging more essence into my body I shot forward, activating Speed Burst halfway to her, surging essence into it as well. My body ached from the sudden speed, but I kept myself in control as I moved. One moment I was standing some twenty paces away, the next, I was kicking her feet out from under her. Her feet flew forward and I struck down hard, activating Swift Strike on my punch infused with essence, the two making my fist move so fast that it was impossible to dodge.

I felt her armor and metal body cave in a little as I punched downward, and suddenly I wondered if I'd gone too hard, too fast. But then she reacted with a speed that matched my own and left me wide-eyed. Everything seemed to move in slow motion as her body plummeted down toward the ground and what I thought would be my victory. She twisted in the air and barely tapped the ground with a couple fingers, the force enough to launch her back up. My Speed Burst ended, and I was hit with a punch to the face that sent me flying backward.

I summoned my sword to my hand midair and pumped it full of essence, increasing my attributes even further. Before hitting the ground, I stuck my sword in the dirt and used it to flip around, landing on my feet. This had all happened within seconds and I raised my gaze up just in time to see energy pulse all around Kora, before she seemed to disappear, then reappear right in front of me. Her speed was beyond insane. Slashing forward, I activated Swift Strike, then using my shoulder and the momentum I'd gathered—as I already saw my blade swing missing completely due to her speed—I threw my shoulder forward, hitting nothing but air.

Again, she'd moved, this time behind me and a powerful blow hit me in the back, sending me flying toward the ground. Activating Power Strike, I hit the ground and the blowback from my powerful attack sent me upward, giving me enough time to right myself in my fall. As soon as I hit my feet, I activated an Infused Mana Shell, as I couldn't see where Kora had gone and couldn't allow her another cheap shot. She was faster than I could wrap my head around and I'd already burnt through 35% of my total Stamina.

War had given her much more control over herself than I realized. I wondered why she'd held back so much during the final battles, just by herself she could have done some truly devastating damage. Instead, she'd focused on commanding her troops and doing what I had been forced to do, staying back to ensure battle strategies were followed, rather than a brute strength approach.

My Mana Shell shattered from behind, and I activated Speed Burst, throwing more essence into it and extending the effects while increasing the speed at which it increased. For the next eight seconds I would be able to see her move. Sure enough, as I looked over my shoulder, I could see her moving toward me in what appeared to be normal speed because of my own increased speed. I got my sword up, blocking her next punch, her hand shifted at the last moment and became a sword, clashing hard against my own. Her strength was immense, throwing me backward.

I cast Lightning Strike, infusing it as well, unwilling to accept defeat. I had seconds before we'd no longer be equal speed, then I'd have to wait three seconds from the end of the cast to use it again. In three seconds, she could surely beat me if I didn't act quick.

I stepped forward, filling up a Fireball and releasing it into the ground beside her, wanting to catch her attention more than I wanted to damage her. I closed the gap and hooked my sword behind her neck, bringing her down into my knee just as Speed Burst ended. She nearly touched the ground after my strike, but she caught herself with her hands, and spun around her entire weight on a single hand. Her kick came out of seemingly nowhere, striking me hard in the head. I wasn't wearing armor, or a helmet, and she was solid metal. My senses went dull for a second as my body struggled to repair the sudden damage, but it wasn't fast enough.

I hit the ground some ten feet away as the force of the kick finally allowed me to stop flying through the air. I rolled for several seconds until I stopped just at the shoreline of the lake, my feet wet from the water. I took a deep breath, awed at the amount of power Kora had just shown. She would only be getting stronger, and it would appear being a dungeon gave her access to incredible power, beyond just summoning monsters.

Kora stood above me with her hand outstretched. I took it and let out a heavy sigh. "You win, I'll make them citizens and trust that you will keep them in line."

CHAPTER 3
APPROACHING AWAKENING

K ora walked off toward the barn, she also liked speaking with Breanna the donkey, though in her case I didn't know why. The season had reached the time of early harvest already, the war taking up much more time than I had ever imagined. The twins were turning fifteen in a week, and I wanted to talk with Michael to see how their training was coming along.

Since it was still early in the morning, it looked like they were working on their cardio and reactions still. This involved a fair bit of running and, funnily enough, Michael throwing bags of sand at them that they tried to dodge. Grace was nothing short of graceful, no pun intended, weaving around each bag with ease. Meanwhile, Gregory seemed determined to get hit by each one, even managing to be hit by some intended for his sister.

"You make a damn good wall, but this exercise is meant

to test your reflexes, young man," Michael called out to the pair as they ran.

An entire space had been created beside the barn to aid with their training. A pavilion had been built and beneath it were weapon racks, weights, and even a small obstacle course. Sunlight poured through the pavilion's planked roof, and I wondered who had constructed it, but hadn't cared enough to ask yet.

Michael saw me and waved me over. "Will you be joining us, Master Miles?" He had been a fair bit more respectful to me since I returned. It bothered me that he treated me differently now, but I wasn't going to call attention to it.

"I've research to attend to, perhaps another day," I said, repeating the same excuse I'd been giving since arriving home. I secretly went out and trained my sword forms for hours on end, then came back to focus on my profession, needing more powerful gems to strengthen myself. So far, I'd made no significant advancements over the ones I'd been using during the entire conflict, but I was close.

"Then what can I help you with?" Michael asked, raising a curious brow at me and throwing a sandbag without looking, yet striking Gregory perfectly in the face. "That boy can catch blows better than any I've met before. The makings of an effective tank." He didn't even look in his direction, but I knew that somehow, he knew he'd struck home with his attack.

Unable to hold back any longer, I had to know. "How do you manage to see where you are attacking when you aren't even looking?" I asked, momentarily forgetting the real reason I wanted to talk to him.

Michael smiled and chuckled. "Against young Gregory, it isn't a matter of using skill, so much as throwing in the direction of his very loud breathing. I do have a skill that allows me to enhance my senses, but I didn't need to use it for that strike, only to confirm I had hit him. It is worth learning if you ever wish to do an extended training session with me. You are clever enough to work it out in a week or two. Or you could search and see if it is a skill that you have available. It is simply called 'Enhanced Sense'. It must be upgraded several times to reach the effectiveness that I enjoy with it. Was that all you needed, because I have students to attend to."

"No, sorry, I wanted to ask you about the two of them. They are turning fifteen soon, how close are they to Awakening, do you think?" I asked the question that had been on my mind since returning.

I sensed a fair bit of essence and mana off of each of them, interestingly enough my work with essence had made it possible for me to differentiate between the two on an individual. Gregory had more essence, but Grace had several measures more of potent mana potential than Gregory. Michael was probably right to say that Gregory would make a good tank, while Grace had a potentially higher mana pool and would do well as a hybrid or caster class. Though, with her reflexes, she'd not go wrong looking for a monk class. One thing was for certain though, neither of them should try to be an Arcane Knight.

Because of the system, I'm unable to warn them not to try if it is offered, but I held a hope in my heart that they'd take the path of a normal adventurer. I was also fairly certain just by feeling their power that each of them had a paragon attribute, though if I had to guess which, I wouldn't be able to. It was clear that they were different enough that they likely didn't share the same paragon attribute, but at that point I was just speculating.

Michael scratched his chin before responding. "Because of my training, they've gained a few months, but I'd put them in the next Awakening ceremony if it were my choice. Your mother feels like they ought to be at least sixteen before they attempt it, despite my warnings of the dangers of waiting that long. Perhaps you can talk some sense into her before she does more harm than good with her gentle parenting."

I sighed and rubbed at the back of my neck as I considered his words. "She means well. I think she worries that their age will make it harder for them, but she doesn't understand the toll it takes on the body when your spark is going wild. Find the closest Prime Mana Ceremony, Variyn city is out of the question, so perhaps a bit more south? Let me know where and when it is, I'd like to attend if I can."

"Yes, Master Miles," Michael said, inclining his head slightly.

"And Michael, one more thing," I said, considering my next words carefully. "What would you say to continued training for the two after they are *Awakened*?"

"I believe they will need it and I am more than willing to

continue in your employ," Michael said, his face serious as he regarded me.

"And are you willing to go with them on their Class Quest to ensure their safety?" I asked the question that was really on my mind regarding their *Awakening*.

He set me with a long look and held it for nearly a minute before responding. "I do enjoy an occasional camp out. Might I suggest that I follow them in secret so that they may gain the confidence of acting alone?"

I smiled. "Yes, that would be a good idea. Thank you for understanding Michael."

"Of course," he said, turning his attention back on the two running youths. "I suggest you tell Mrs. Miles of your plan to set her mind at ease, else we might find ourselves without the comfort of a hot meal for some time."

"I'll talk to her," I said, shaking my head at how close Michael and my mother had been getting. I wasn't worried about romantic interest, but it was odd for me to consider my mother making new friends, despite her being of a sound mind for over a year now.

CHAPTER 4
HOME

The once white, flaked paint of the house had been replaced with a fresh coat of light blue paint. It also looked like someone had replaced several of the boards on the outside porch. Looking closer, I saw several more upgrades and changes to the main house, including what appeared to be an expansion to my old bedroom, bringing it out another five paces and extending the roof into a less slanted angle. That, added to the finished workhouse that could fit all the workers we had, and it would be a wonder if my father would have even recognized the place anymore.

A sudden caw caught my attention and I saw a black bird sitting atop a branch of one of the few trees we had growing just outside the house. It was an oak, old and gnarled, but we kept it around as it hadn't died yet and with just a little care continued to grow strong. The bird was about three feet above where I could reach easily, but I walked up to it all the same and set it with a stare. It stared right on back and I wondered if my suspicions could be right after hearing what Warrick had said.

"Are you a messenger?" I asked it, my attention on feeling out any use of mana or magic but I felt nothing.

It cawed at me and fluttered its wings, but what it could mean by that I hadn't any clue.

"You are just a bird that likes to hang out around our house, aren't you? Well good luck avoiding Munster our faithful tomcat," I said, turning to leave the bird behind. As if summoned by the calling of its name, I saw Munster run out of the barn from across the way.

The bird cawed louder suddenly, and I turned back to look it in its deep black eyes. I felt something suddenly, a presence or something deeper, but it was so foreign it gave me chills down my spine. I took a step back from the bird and felt a childish fear to be away from the creature. I stepped onto the porch, it creaked underfoot, and I made it to the door. Checking over my shoulder I saw that the bird had gone, and I let out a relieved breath.

I didn't know what I'd felt, but it was powerful in a way I hadn't felt before. A distant memory stirred, and I thought maybe I'd had a nightmare that held the same feeling, but I couldn't remember if I had. Just a vague feeling, and by the time I'd entered the house and made it to the kitchen I'd all but forgotten about it, pushing the bird from my mind.

The inside of our humble home had been completely refinished. New plaster had been applied all over the walls, the old yellowing color I was used to was replaced by a bright white—though I could see several places already discolored from one thing or another. The basin in the kitchen had been replaced with one twice as big, and the cooking fire was just as I remembered it, at least something stayed the same. Just as the thought came to mind, my mother came in from the pantry carrying a sack of potatoes.

"Come to help me peel?" She asked, her sparkling green eyes flashing with a touch of humor. She knew I hated peeling potatoes.

I surprised her, pulling over a chair and producing a small knife from my inventory. "I'd love to peel a few," I said, smiling back at her surprised grin.

She looked around the kitchen, seeing that we were alone, and suddenly grew very serious. "How are you today? Ferdel says you were screaming in your sleep again. Are you sure I can't make room for you in the house, you don't need to sleep in the workhouse."

I cringed at that. Ferdel had told me I'd had a rough night in not so many words. Basically, he told me I was scaring the new workers and I should work out my issues while awake so they don't follow me to my sleep. I wish it were that easy. I had no control over myself while sleeping or the images that ran through my mind. I hated that I was losing control while sleeping, but there was nothing I could do. Ferdel had suggested seeing an alchemist and that there might be a sleep draught that would help me sleep deeper, but I'd been putting it off. Now I think I might need to go into town and see what I could purchase.

"I'm fine," I lied, not wanting to get into the war with

my mother again. She'd been supportive, but it was hard for her to truly understand the hellish nature of war.

She gave me a look that told me she wasn't convinced, but I just shook my head and changed the topic.

"I need to talk to you about the twins," I said, affixing her with my own parental gaze. She cut her eyes at me and I nearly broke.

"You've been talking to Michael," she said, rolling her eyes.

"I have and we both feel that the twins need to, not should, they *need* to Awaken soon, otherwise they'll be at risk of being gravely injured," I said, trying to stress the serious importance of what I was telling her.

My mother fixed me with a stare. "They are too young. If they go now, they'll die. So, unless you can tell me you'll be by their side the entire time, I don't see any alternative."

"I can do one better," I said, putting a comforting hand on her shoulder. "Michael has agreed to watch them from the shadows. They will think that they are independent and all the while they'll be under the protection of the greatest living weapons master I've come across."

She didn't seem immediately convinced so I kept going. "I don't have much longer that I can stick around, and I want to be there for their Awakening. I need to know they find Classes suitable for themselves."

Without looking me in the eye she shook her head, then let out a measured breath. "I will agree to it only if Michael swears that he will keep them safe. But they are to return immediately after doing their class quest for more training until they are seventeen."

I sighed; this was probably the best I was going to get from her. "They will need a way to gather essence and get stronger during those two years, but I'll agree to that for now." I held out my hand in a gesture of agreement and a smirk on my lips. Being around my mother was almost enough to push back the darkness that threatened to suffocate me on a daily basis.

Just then the door swung open, and I heard footsteps approaching. I pulled my mother into a quick hug and stood. Grace and Gregory entered looking much older than I remembered them from mere months before.

"Please tell me we've got cut kelt fruit," Gregory said, his eyes darting around the kitchen. "I'm pretty sure I'm more bruises than not at this point."

"Learn to dodge at least one or two and maybe you wouldn't be in such a sore condition constantly," Grace said, basically dancing into the kitchen and showing off her lithe movements. "He's jealous of me." She said as she passed by me and into the pantry. She came out with several kelt fruit, which she proceeded to juggle with like it was nothing.

Grace had certainly lost a fair bit of her shy manner and I liked the confident girl I was seeing in her now. Gregory, for his credit, remained the moody little man that I remembered, only he'd grown nearly as tall as me and began to fill out with rippling muscles that would soon give me a run for my money, at least by appearance.

Gregory's hair had grown long enough that he'd tied it

off in the back and recently, according to mother, he'd shaved the sides off leaving just the top bit of hair. He claimed it kept him cooler, but when I asked why he didn't just shave it all off, he proclaimed that idea madness. He had his female prospects to consider, he'd told me in confidence later that same evening.

Grace meanwhile, kept her hair at shoulder length, it acted much like my own hair when it grew long and fell in loose curls. She had clipped her bangs out of the way, and somehow kept her hair in pristine condition despite the training they'd been going through. That was when I noticed the basic training clothing they wore, a loose white tunic and tan pants. Gregory was covered in sweat and dirt stains, like he'd really been put through the ringer. Meanwhile, Grace had the slightest of sweat marks on her chest, but it was fading fast.

It would appear Grace was in much more control over her body in every aspect than Gregory was showing himself to be. This was fine of course, since Sparked learned to harness their latent power in subtle, almost imperceivable ways. For instance, Grace was likely strengthening her own body with her mana and essence without realizing, while Gregory was hardening himself against the potential attacks which caused him to react slower and his body to grow stronger than it normally would. This was just my own personal theories, but the more I spoke with Kora about the Spark the more I felt I understood it. She'd been a useful pool of information these last few weeks in isolation.

The twins were eating kelt fruit and visibly relaxing from

its regenerative effects. It made me wonder at the benefits they must be reaping from a lifetime of consuming such a useful fruit. Adding the study of the kelt fruit effects to my ever-growing list of things I'd like to do someday, I sighed at the sheer size of the list. I had a responsibility to battle the Chaos, but could I do that without first dealing with the wrongs wrought against my own soul? Could Lord Variyn be left to live and cause more pain and suffering while I went about adventuring like everything was normal?

I didn't have answers to my own questions, but I knew that I couldn't hide out here forever. With no plan in place to remove him, I settled with a single goal for now; fix the ley lines. But to do that I needed to know how Alayna's trip to the elves had gone. Alayna had been suspiciously absent during the entire conflict against House Blalor. The plan had been for her to pass along secrets in exchange for a ride to Avalon, but with her gone for so long, her father must be suspicious of her intentions or those of the elves.

Could she have returned already and be suffering in the grip of her father? Before the war, I'd have said he wasn't capable of imprisoning his own daughter, but now I wasn't so sure. So, my goals narrowed, finding Alayna being my next step among many.

"You awake in that big head of yours?" Grace teased, tossing a kelt fruit to me the moment I looked up. I easily caught it out of the air, and she grinned madly. "See, even Caldor has some dexterity, what's wrong with you, Gregory."

"Well, Grace," Gregory said, waggling his head mockingly at her. "I won't need much dexterity when I get the class I want," lowering his voice he continued. "I'll be an armored titan standing tall against the darkness of my foes!"

"How about a little exercise. I'm itching for a sparring session that doesn't end with me in the dirt," I said, butting in on their quips back and forth. I wanted to spar with them both and determine for myself what class they might be well suited for. Neither had studied classes or, at the very least they hadn't before Michael's training.

"Can we fight you together!" Grace said, showing a level of eagerness that I hadn't expected from her. Gregory seemed just as enthusiastic about the idea, grinning wide as he rolled his shoulders.

"Let's do this," he said, making an effort to appear bigger by flexing his muscles.

I would have to teach them an important lesson today, no matter how strong you get, there is always someone stronger.

CHAPTER 5
FRIENDLY SPARRING

Not only did Michael approve of my sparring idea, but he also gave the twins real weapons while giving me a wooden sword. "Be gentle, I don't want any broken bones," he said, his attention on me. I nodded and cracked my neck to the side.

I had enough control over my power to keep the twins in a fair condition, so avoiding breaking any bones should be easy enough. Kora had come out of the barn and stood beside my mother as we readied ourselves for the duel.

The twins put on armor, leather and pads mostly, but I opted to stay unarmored. It was already an extremely unfair match up, so it would be even more so for me to rely on armor. I decided to start at about ten percent of my total speed and strength, hoping that wouldn't be too much for them to handle.

Gregory looked like he was rearing to go, bouncing up and down on the balls of his feet. Grace, on the other hand, watched my movements intently, her keen mind likely trying to work out a way to catch me unaware. She leaned over to Gregory, and they exchanged a few whispered words, that despite my increased attributes, I did not hear.

I decided I'd let them make the first move, paying more attention to the nature around me. Bees buzzed, passing from tree to tree in the distance. The sun had risen to the mid-point in the sky, meaning we'd left morning behind and moved into the afternoon. A familiar, yet distracting, caw sounded from behind me, but I didn't look, instead sending out a silent prayer that Munster would rid us of that bird. The first attacks came so slowly as to be laughable.

Dust kicked up from Gregory as he charged like a bull toward me. I saw Grace slip off to the side, likely thinking she'd be able to flank me. I closed my eyes for a moment and almost went into the fight with my eyes closed as a practice method, but decided when live weapons were involved, it wasn't the time to innovate. Gregory had a massive two-handed sword, while Grace had gone with two daggers.

Lifting his massive weapon up over his head with practiced ease, I couldn't help but feel proud at how far Gregory had come. Using only ten percent of my speed I lurched forward and struck his weapon, testing his grip. I was surprised when he held firm, swinging down at me with speed equal to what I expected from him. I dodged it easily, twisting while using a touch more speed than I wanted, to avoid Grace's sneak attack.

She'd come all the way around and attacked through the cloud of dust Gregory had kicked up, trying to hit me head-on instead of from the side as I'd expected. She was clever and neither of them were ready to give up so easily.

I scored a strike on each of them, a light tap to Gregory's helmeted head and a slash across Grace's arm. Each of them shrunk back after the attack, circling me and looking for an opening. Back and forth we went, them striking as fast as they could, while I danced between their movements. At only ten percent of my speed and strength, Grace was almost too much for me to dodge, and Gregory nearly matched that amount of strength. However, it was clear that I outmatched each of them by such a degree as to make this sparring session nonsensical.

Grace came in low with a kick, then surprised me by throwing her dagger right at my face. I jumped over her kick and caught the dagger out of the air, redirecting it right in front of her feet. It stuck into the ground, and her eyes went wide with how swiftly I'd turned away her attack. Gregory took that moment to throw himself against me, I went with his momentum for just a second before planting my feet. I went rigid and he bounced off me like he'd just tried to tackle a city wall made of sturdy stone.

Grace had her daggers back in hand and struck for my midsection a moment after I planted my feet. This forced me to actually parry her attack with my wooden sword, which I did with little effort. But she kept the attacks coming, I weaved and parried as needed until she was huffing and puffing from exertion.

I glanced over to Gregory to see where'd he'd gone, only to realize he wasn't where he'd been a moment before. I felt the push of wind behind me, and I knew why Grace had been attacking me with such earnest. She'd made an opening for Gregory, and I was going to have to tap into a bit more of my speed if I hoped to avoid the attack. I did so, but suddenly power crackled around Gregory, and he matched my speed. I put my blade into place to parry his attack, while kicking out wide with my leg.

Grace was thrown back from my attack, my foot connecting just hard enough on her chest while not breaking any bones. She rolled several times while I deflected Gregory's attack and went a step further, disarming him. Then putting my hand on his shoulder, I moved my leg to the side and tripped him. He grunted as he went down, and I smiled at him before going to check on Grace. She was back on her feet and blue sparks surrounded her as well.

I could feel the more potent mana surging all around her and knew I'd need to tick up my speed just a hair. Sure enough, as soon as she lunged forward, she was at least twice as fast as before. She swung low, twisting and spinning in an athletic display of dexterity. I parried her attacks and kept backstepping to allow her room to move. At any time, I felt like I could strike out and send her sprawling, but I didn't want to crush her confidence.

Gregory made it back to his feet and was readying himself for another strike, but I'd seen enough from the both of them to get a feel for their potential, so I decided I'd end it. Being as careful as I could, I struck Grace several times in quick succession, her daggers falling to the ground as her muscles were likely screaming from the sudden strikes.

Then as fast as lightning I turned and added a few bruises to Gregory's collection, until his weapon fell free as well. I was careful to kick them out of their grasp before speaking to them.

"Very good," I said, and I meant it. They'd shown a level of control that I wouldn't have expected from a pair of fifteen-year-olds. I certainly wouldn't have been so even headed at their age, despite the responsibilities thrown my way. "Gregory, tell me again, what kind of class are you thinking about getting?"

"I want to be tanky and super resistant to damage," Gregory said, huffing and puffing as he still struggled to catch his breath. He was rubbing his shoulder so I hit him with a heal, not sure how much damage I'd inflicted on him.

"I think you'll make a fine tank, but I'd advise you to look for a class that balances damage and mitigation. It is useful to be a damage sponge, but being able to deal damage is also very important." I was surprised he didn't have a burning desire to be an Arcane Knight like my father and now me, but they'd been so young when he'd died so I didn't find it that unusual.

"Do you want to know what I'm going to pick?" Grace said, a bit of sass entering her voice.

"Sure, what class or role are you hoping to fill?" I asked, smiling at her. She'd already caught her breath and made sure not to show where she was hurt, but just from the way she carried herself I could tell I'd hit her a bit too hard. I cast a heal on her as well as it came off cooldown.

She relaxed visibly and cleared her throat. "I want to be like you."

I frowned at her words; I was honored, but the idea of her taking up the mantle of Arcane Knight gave me pause. Luckily, she elaborated, and I relaxed a little bit.

"I mean, not exactly like you," she corrected. "I want to be a mixed fighter that can use magic and fighting. I'm thinking a mix between a rogue and a mage, but I don't know what that'd be called exactly." She looked up at me with wide, hopeful eyes, as I considered the classes I knew.

In the end, I decided telling her an exact class wouldn't be all that helpful. "When the time comes to pick, just focus on that and you will find a decent hybrid class, I promise." I knew without a doubt that she had the potential to be a powerful hybrid, so I wasn't really worried that she wouldn't get the right class presented to her.

"Sounds like a plan," Grace said, walking over to pick her daggers up from where I'd kicked them. "You know brother, you are crazy strong. I thought for sure Michael had taught us enough to whoop your butt."

"Yeah, turns out we don't know anything," Gregory said, shooting a look at Michael.

"While your technique was questionable," Michael said, giving them both hard looks. "It is a manner of raw power when you go up against someone so vastly powerful. Rarely can you find a way to exploit their mistakes, when you move like the slowest of snails in their perception. Caldor was humoring you both that entire match, he could have ended the fight within a single second and still had time to begin cleaning his weapon. But do not fear, if you continue to train with me and strengthen your bodies, you will one day be a match for your brother. For you train, when he does not."

I didn't agree with Michael's assessment about them ever catching up to me, but the idea obviously lifted their spirits, so I said nothing. It felt good to move about and moreover, not be so outmatched by an opponent's speed. Flashes of my sparring session with Kora had me doubting my abilities, maybe I would borrow Michael for some intense training before I left.

With that on my mind, I pulled Michael aside and told him that I needed his individual attention for the next week. He agreed, but said he was skilled enough to keep the twins training and see to my training needs. I agreed but told him I wanted to do the training out of sight. He reluctantly agreed and the twins were left with instructions to keep training, while Michael, Kora, and myself went back to the island to train. Michael surprised me by summoning forth his own flying mount, a pure white pegasus.

CHAPTER 6
EMORY AND ISMENE RETURN

On the seventh day of training, I got word from my mother that Ismene and Emory had stopped by. They left a message asking me to meet them at Merlin's pub for drinks that night, so I washed up, thanked Michael for the intense training, and dressed in fresh clothing. Ares was happy to soar through the night air when I promised her that she'd be free to hunt while I drank, or she could get pampered at the stables. She told me in no uncertain terms that she preferred the latter option. I think she'd eaten an entire boar during my day's training, so she wasn't very hungry yet.

The town square bustled with activity, more than I'd have expected for the evening hour. Adventurers, townsfolk, and travelers moved from one place to another, visiting shops that hadn't quite shut their doors for the night. The air felt cool and refreshing against my face as I saw the signs of new life in the town. What exactly had been the cause of an influx of visitors, traders, and adventurers, I did not know, but as I pondered over it, a few reasons came to mind.

Of all the ideas that I could think of, I hoped the most prominent wasn't the cause, refugees from House Blalor. It seemed like the most logical answer, but it didn't explain all the adventurers. Perhaps the dungeon regulations Emory had spoken of last I'd seen him, was causing weaker dungeons to be more popular. We had several easier dungeons close to Creeshaw. That would leave the strongest dungeons to the Adventurer's Guild collection crews. It sickened me that they were using my discoveries to shut out adventurers from dungeons and collect massive amounts of essence for themselves.

Ares, as she always did, caught the attention of many adventurers, each of them ogling her and pointing. I heard the usual, must be a noble, or wish I had rich parents, as if the only way one could get a griffin was to either be nobility or extremely rich. I found the likelihood of that to be quite the opposite. Griffins were noble creatures that cared nothing for gold or social status. Ares and I were friends and companions by choice, not station.

She walked into the alley to where a thorough grooming awaited her, and I found my way past a small crowd outside of Merlin's. As I was passing by one particularly large adventurer, he shifted and threw his shoulder into me. I braced myself, causing him to stumble back instead of what he intended. I played dumb, looking up at him in confusion.

"Excuse me, I didn't see you there," I said, smiling up at

the giant of a man. He looked like he was in his late twenties and stood an impressive foot taller than me.

"The hell you think you are doing coming here, peasant," he said, his voice exactly what you'd expect from a low intelligent grunt who was used to throwing his weight around.

"Just here for a drink," I said, reaching out and ever so slightly pushing him aside so that I could pass through the door. I overestimated myself and he went stumbling back until crashing and falling over a female sorcerer in red and black robes.

What followed was several hushed whispers and everyone taking steps back from me. It was clear to them I was not just a peasant now, and my show of strength had quieted even the brute of a man. He stood and looked around, red faced, but unwilling to press his luck any further. He knew, like all those that witnessed my show of strength, that if I could casually throw him to the ground with two fingers, then I was an *Awakened* and a powerful one at that. I sighed and looked flatly in his direction, then shook my head before walking into Merlin's sturdy black oak doors.

The pub was as busy as it had ever been, live music playing away in the corner, every table filled to overflowing, and the fireplaces burning at full strength, providing both heat and light. At the bar stood the same lady as before, wearing the exact same tight black dress that cut low over her chest, and a simple silver pendant around her neck. Even from this distance I could see her piercing purple eyes, the eye makeup she wore heavily applied making them pop. I decided I ought to pay her to stable Ares first, so I cut through the crowd while keeping an eye out for Ismene and Emory.

I didn't see them by the time I crossed the distance, so I focused on the mysterious Mab and the wild look in her eyes.

"Caldor Miles, destroyer of cities, ender of lives, and all-around killer," Mab said, as if she were reading off great titles of mine. "How can I assist such a dedicated person as yourself today?"

I cringed under the titles she assigned to me, each one bringing visions of death and destruction I wanted no part of. But I kept my emotions in check, the time I'd spent with my family helping me greatly, but more than that I refused to take the blame for the horrendous actions, shifting them to Lord Variyn instead. It wasn't a foolproof plan, but it helped if only a little.

"Good evening," I said, through clenched teeth. "Here is the gold for a room and care for Ares. Please see that she is well taken care of."

"Of course," she said, doing a mock bow in my direction. "For the Lord of Death, I will oblige almost any favor."

She was really starting to piss me off.

Taking a deep breath and releasing my clenched teeth I spoke. "Have you heard from Merlin?" I had to ask, though I expected her answer to be either unhelpful or completely nonsensical.

Mab put a gloved hand to her face and tapped on her

cheek with her finger while making a show of thinking. "You know I did visit him recently, but I completely forgot to pass on your regards. Perhaps next time if I had proper motivation, I would be able to speak to him about you."

She decided to speak nonsense and be completely unhelpful, how wonderful. "And what would give you the proper motivation?" I asked, playing into her stupid game.

"What indeed," Mab said, letting out an exaggerated sigh and going back to polishing a glass, her eyes passing over the patrons and purposely ignoring me.

Grabbing the key she placed in front of me, I turned away, done with her stupid games and ready to find my friends. They were tucked away in a corner, with only a single empty chair next to them. On my way over, twice someone tried to grab it to take it over to their table, and twice Emory had to man handle the chair to keep them from taking it. One good look at the massive man was usually enough, but the last guy was being far more stubborn—I recognized him as the man from outside that I'd thrown aside with a few fingers.

I tapped him on the shoulder as he yelled down at Emory, who for his credit just grinned stupidly at the bumbling large man. The half giant turned and saw that I stood behind him and his face blanched white. While he still held a hand on the chair, I sat down in it and Emory released his grip on the leg. It took the man a few seconds for his brain to catch up to what was going on and when it did, he turned and shuffled away muttering apologies.

"Someone you know?" Ismene asked, laughing a bit as she spoke.

"Someone he beat the shit out of by the look on his face," Emory said, laughing even louder. "What'd he do, speak down to you M'Lord and you showed him which end was up?"

"Hey Emory, shut the hell up and give me a drink," I said, trying to smile and be as playful as I'd been before, but failing to quite match the tone.

It was great to be around Emory and Ismene again, but I wished I could banish away the dark weight that rested on my shoulders. Instead, I listened to them joke and make jabs at my expense while sipping away at my drink. After a few minutes I flagged down the attention of a barmaid and ordered a plate of food. If there was one thing I could still enjoy, it was a plate of steaming hot food.

What arrived could give Awakener's Pub a run for its money. The plate was twice as big as I remembered and on it was two proteins, a healthy portion of mashed potatoes, and a mess of colorful vegetables, all steaming hot. I dug into the first protein, a breaded steak of some kind with a light brown gravy. It was seasoned fantastically, each note of the dish singing in my mouth as I chewed. Next, I took a bite of the steak with a green drizzled sauce on top of it. It was tender but still had a touch of chewiness to it, this seared meat with the green sweet sauce on it melted in my mouth.

It was like placing butter on a hot pan, the meat just fell apart and the flavors were beyond description. Whatever seasonings were used had drawn out the flavor of the meat to a level that I'd never tasted. And the sear gave it a nice texture before it fell apart in my mouth, just heavenly. For the minutes it took me to eat the entire plate clean, I worried about nothing but enjoying the food. I ate the sides next, each one seasoned to perfection and cooked well enough to make this meal fit for a king of kings.

Between bites I caught Mab's eye and she winked at me. She did remind me too much of Merlin, but I preferred the elderly man to her any day of the week. Their similarities gave me a thought as I finished my final bite of the best meal I'd ever had the pleasure of eating. If Mab and Merlin were similar enough, perhaps she'd be able to take me to Avalon and help me finish my quest? Sparing a glance in her direction was all it took to abandon that idea. If she wasn't willing to pass on a message to Merlin without some grand favor, then I could only imagine what she'd want in return for taking me to Avalon. Hell, she'd likely let me die by the hands of the first powerful monster we encountered and say something like, 'Not part of our deal' then go on her way.

"So, you finally going to tell us why you are so out of it lately?" Emory said, and Ismene hit him on the arm.

"That's not how we planned it," she hissed, smiling at me. Her kind eyes and gentle smile put me at ease. Damn she was so beautiful, her purple irises glistening in the light of the nearby fireplace. "We barely got to interact with you while you fought in that stupid war and then the destruction of the city of Blalor. People are saying you were rewarded for your part in it?" She didn't try to hide her confusion at such a thought.

I leaned forward and practically hissed the words. "Lord Variyn is to blame. But I am not without sin." Taking a deep breath and casting my eyes down to the table I continued, I'd not been looking forward to this conversation, but it needed to be had. "My discoveries, like these bands," I gestured to where mine sat beneath my shirt, "have unfortunately given people the tools to make powerfully destructive weapons. Regina insisted that we sell rights to the discoveries and now I'm as rich as any king but covered in the blood of thousands of innocents."

I was probably being over dramatic, but it was how I felt, and they needed to know that I wasn't without blame. Emory and Ismene shared a look, each of them looking puzzled.

"That's it?" Emory finally asked, looking extremely confused. "That isn't your damn fault. Do you think the inventor of the sword should be blamed for all of those who had died by the sword? Come on man, even if that were true you didn't even invent the weapon, it is like blaming the person who discovered the means to make steel for all the deadlier weapons it produced. I don't want to be that guy but get the fuck over it."

"Emory," Ismene scolded, hitting him in the arm again.

"No, he's right," I said, shaking my head. "I'm not fully responsible, but you don't know the horrors of war. You weren't there at my side when so many fell all around me. Men and women that I was meant to protect. I can't ever just get over it, but I do appreciate you being a good enough friend to help me see where I'm overstepping my blame."

"I agree that you shouldn't blame yourself, but Emory is about as subtle as a minotaur running through a maze. Listen to what he means though," Ismene said, putting a comforting hand on mine. "You aren't to blame, not even a little. And we are sorry that we weren't around as much as we promised. With the dungeons having longer wait times we had to do more traditional monster hunting; finding queen spawns and roaming out into the wilderness for essence."

"Yeah, we got strong as fuck," Emory said, smiling wide and not at all put off by the scolding Ismene had given him seconds before.

"What level are you now?" I asked, expecting them to be in the low twenties at the most.

"I'm level 32 and Emory made it to level 31," Ismene said, clearly proud of herself.

I couldn't blame her; those were amazing gains. The essence bands were really changing the playing field for them. It also didn't help that I'd been doing nothing but burning away essence for the last two and a half weeks since the battle ended. Meanwhile, they stayed out killing monsters and clearing dungeons.

"You guys leveled higher than me," I said, letting that sink in as I spoke it. Obviously, they'd still be no match for me, my increased attributes giving me an almost double level equivalence. "Are you spending enough extra essence into attributes?"

"Two extra per level," Emory assured me, giving me a thumbs up.

That, mixed with the normal one or two attributes they get naturally, meant they'd be on par with other adventurers taking the same path as them, but people like my father and me would be in an entirely different league without even matching their level. I was certain by this point that my father had taken a similar path to me before the events of the Battle at Lynsteen pass.

"Good," I said, nodding my acceptance. "Keep it up and you might be able to challenge me in another thirty levels."

"Damn," Emory said, taking a quick pull on his drink and messily wiping away at his mouth. "You're just sitting on a ton of essence, eh?"

"I was, but I spent all of it to help out Fred, but it seems like I always am," I said, I collected essence so well between my band and my core, it was a bit silly.

The rest of the night wore away as Ismene and Emory went into detail about their adventures while I was at war. I told them in very vague terms about how the war went and how many soldiers and friends I'd lost. I also told them about Fred and how we still weren't sure what happened to him. Fred and Fran had gone to visit their parents, but they were due to return any day now. I told Ismene and Emory my plans to visit Blackridge Keep soon and check on their progress, the troops should have gotten back from their march by now.

They asked if they could come with, and I welcomed the idea. Ismene asked about Alayna and where she was these days, but I didn't have an answer for her, telling her as much. The night wore on and by the time we finished we were some of the last patrons in the establishment. After walking Ismene to her place, Emory and I went back to the pub and each took one of the two beds in my room, drifting off to sleep in mere moments.

What followed was a nightmare of a different kind that I'd been dealing with lately. Great black shadows moved through the space between worlds, and they'd set their sights on the Wyrd. With them, they brought destruction and endless torment beyond that of ordinary Chaos. It was as if pure evil moved against us, and I knew that this nightmare was more than just a dream. I needed to prepare the people of the Wyrd, but how?

CHAPTER 7
WHITE FLAMES

Two days later Fred and Fran arrived in town. I was visiting the magic shop, selling a few items I'd picked up but never had a chance to offload when I came across the pair just walking down the town square. Fred had a completely white outfit with golden flair, very uncharacteristic of him, with a hood covering all but the bottom of his marble white skin. Fran looked like her usual self, in armor and a sword at her waist. When she saw me, her face lit up.

"You just missed my parents," she said, slowly jogging up to me. "They really wanted to thank you for what you did for Fred."

Glad to have missed them, as I didn't want any awkward emotional moments more suited for Ismene to deal with. I smiled, though I'm sure it didn't touch my eyes. "Glad to have helped." I tried to peak under his hood and Fran noticed, chuckling.

"Any idea what you did to him?" She asked, nudging him with her elbow. "He's been even more solemn and quiet since it happened. Not even mother can work out what happened to him. I told them what you told me when it happened, that you infused him with essence and healed him, but Infusing essence is so new that we aren't really sure what that would or could do to a person."

"I'm only quiet to avoid having to explain that which I do not know," Fred said, his voice just the same as I remembered before. He lowered his hood and I saw that his hair and skin were white as ever, making Zander look like he was tanned. I stepped forward, catching his eye while holding my hand out. He nodded and I placed my hand over his heart.

Just like before, it beat only once every dozen seconds. Whatever I'd done to him it had altered him down to his internal organs. I leaned forward a bit and asked him a question that had been on my mind for a while. "Can you still cast your normal spells?"

He nodded. "In a sense yes, everything is as it was before, but my skills and abilities are different. When I use any of my flame spells they have that white flame, doing massive amounts of damage. And my basic flame control, like what I used on the battlefield, is measures stronger than it has ever been. I also burn through mana twice as fast and upgrading my skills, attributes, or levels have become four times as expensive. But I have the strength of someone three times my level, I even scared my mother when we sparred because my flames burn so hot."

"Interesting, I don't know how my Essence Infusion was able to revive you when my healing couldn't, but I suspect that your Core has been altered in some way. It would explain why essence values have been turned on their head, maybe. This is something that requires a brighter mind than my own. I'm just happy you are alive," I said, reaching out and touching him on the shoulder.

He flinched from my touch and lifted his gaze to mine. "Sorry, my skin is overly sensitive to touch now. Everything is so different."

"Are you up for a hunt? I need to start gathering up some essence and Emory said that there was a pack of Dire Wolves half a day away. They wiped out the queen but there are likely stragglers that need to be picked off. Maybe we can learn more about your abilities during some combat?" I asked, whether or not I believed my words was another matter. However, I did want to see what he was capable of and it might help me begin to understand the massive essence aura that pulsed around him at all times.

"Yes please," Fran said, jumping on the balls of her feet. "Mr. Ghost wants to come too, he's just not used to being so transparent about his feelings."

Fran snorted at her own joke, Fred didn't react at all, and I gave her a pity smile. Before I knew it, we were off, flying over the trees to the location Emory had marked. Me on Ares, and them on their hippogryphs. Ares kept focusing on Fred in his white robes as he billowed through the air, and I felt a curiosity there. She wanted to know what was wrong with him. I sent her an emotional communication that basically said, 'who knows' and we continued onward.

As we flew through the air, I had a thought. I'd not had the chance to speak with Kora in length about Fred and his condition, perhaps she would have some insights beyond what anything I could come up with. She was a dungeon and had been alive for hundreds if not thousands of years, surely, she'd seen a little bit of everything. I made a mental note to ask her the moment we got back and before we left for Blackridge Keep.

We spotted the first few wolves in a clearing as we flew above and, following my lead, we swooped low so I could get a read on each of them.

Adult Dire Wolf, Level 38
Dire Wolf, Level 28
Dire Wolf, Level 25

Spurring Ares upward and away from the dark forest floor, I eyed a location for us to land and begin our hunt. I didn't want to land right on top of them, as I wasn't sure of the battle capabilities of Fran and Fred's mounts, so we set down a little ways away. Shadowcrest Forest was technically meant for hunting by the Lords of Variyn, which whether or not I wanted to be one, I was, so I felt no qualms about entering the area of black barked trees. Ares landed gracefully with the two hippogryphs landing just behind us.

"Nothing we can't handle, a level 38, 28, and 25," I reported, to which they answered with nods of acceptance. We'd faced much stiffer odds together, so this was nothing. In fact, I had an idea that would make it even more exciting.

"Why don't you handle them by yourself Fred," I suggested. "We can provide support but see if you can kill all three without ruining their pelts. It'll be good practice to control your power."

"I have been wanting to test my limits on something other than my parents," Fred said, thoughtfully. He nodded and it was agreed.

"Get ready to kill anything that gets too close to him," I whispered to Fran. I wanted her to be ready, though I doubted anything would get past Fred and me.

The forest was much as I remembered it the last time I'd come through here. This time, however, I wasn't going to be facing off against a Baby Drake or, hopefully, any Chaos beasts. It wasn't long ago that I was the innocent youth running into danger to save someone whose father would eventually prove to be a mass murder.

What if I hadn't run to save her? Would it have changed my path forward enough to avoid my service or the discovery of the magic that made what he did possible? Doubtful. Even without his aid and titles I'd have earned my ability to infuse essence and if I hadn't found Regina, then it would have been someone else.

I had been too open-minded and hopeful about the future to have taken any other path. But I had to stop blaming myself, it wasn't like I'd made the device they used. My discoveries were but a small part of a great plan to cause death and destruction. That same discovery can and is helping adventurers grow more powerful, thus enabling them to protect more people by stopping greater threats.

I focused my mind as we approached, Fred at the head of the group walking through the shadow of the forest like a wraith in his white flowing robes. The aura of power around him was so immense that I swear I could taste it, but it was hard to truly identify if it came from his gathered essence or his mana. It was like the two had merged their auras and acted together in a unique way.

The wolves turned as we entered the clearing, the largest baring its teeth at Fred, while the other two took up flanking positions. Fran and I stopped at the edge of the tree line, far enough away to not be harmed by Fred's powerful magic, but close enough that a Speed Burst would get me by his side within moments.

Reaching out his hand, Fred said no words of power and made any recognizable sign, yet powerful bright white fire sprung forth. It was much less than the first time, but still there were at least half a dozen tendrils of fire rushing toward the wolf. It jumped to the side, but the fire didn't care, turning to match its destination.

The two flanking wolves dived forward, and their forms blurred as they activated a power of their own. Before I could think to step forward, it looked like one of them might be upon him. A flare of white fire revealed two scorched wolves lying in a heap, while the third wolf howled in rage just before the thinnest tentacle of flame pierced through it, slaying it a moment later.

He'd killed all three and that was fine and good, but something weird had happened. I didn't get a rush of essence; in fact, I barely earned a few hundred essence for that fight. It was like all the essence from the wolves had been burnt away when Fred attacked, absorbed almost fully into Fred, allowing none to reach the rest of us.

"Fran," I said, turning to her. She nodded, looking concerned.

"I barely got any essence," she finally said, her expression turning sour. "Son of a bitch, Fred you sucked up all the essence! You suck."

"It appears I did get a significant amount of essence from just three kills," Fred said, scratching at the top of his head and looking over to us with a look of perplexed confusion.

"How much is a significant amount?" I asked. There had not been a single essence that escaped those kills which meant he was able to absorb every little bit that wasn't locked away inside the cores.

"Just a little over a hundred thousand but that's not all," Fred said, his tone one of utter disbelief.

"What?" Fran asked, on the edge of her seat as much as I was.

"My spells burned away a good portion of my essence as well. I lost nearly two thousand just from that single attack. What happens when I run out of essence and don't earn more?"

I looked at him and wondered the same thing. If his new form burned away essence while doing simple castings, what would happen to him when he ran out? Would he simply not be able to cast or would something worse happen?

Either way, it was going to be important that we never find out. My work on essence collection would need to continue, but I just couldn't imagine doing it while Regina sold off all my discoveries to the highest bidder. Something would need to be done about that.

I checked my essence band and saw that it had just a small amount collected as well, so while helpful to get a bit more, not very useful at the moment. I bet that being in close proximity to Fred, his band likely collected even more essence than what we'd gotten. It was a disturbing thought to be around someone with a stronger Core pull than my own, especially when it hadn't been the case before his healing.

"You are going to be hard to take on dungeons now," I finally said, figuring any words were better to break the growing silence.

"What happens if he runs out of essence?" Fran asked. It was the very question I'd been grappling with, but I wasn't ready to tell her my theory.

"Let's just make sure that he never does," I said, matching my gaze with Fred's until he finally nodded slightly. Without saying, I felt like he understood the implications, he was quick when it came to deducing facts, but in this incident it seemed so was his sister.

"You don't think he'll die, do you?" Fran asked, her verbalizing my fear made it seem all too real.

"I think that whatever miracle brought him back is tied to essence and I can only see two outcomes when he runs out. Either he loses his ability to do any spells and other *Awakened* benefits, or his body just stops working." My words came out even and emotionless, despite the turmoil that swirled inside. "You should keep hunting, Fred. If wolves give you that much, then hunt them all and let's see how much essence you can retain before your Core pushes back. But be careful not to overdo it."

Fred remained silent, just nodding his assent.

Fran on the other hand, huffed out a loud breath of air, looking between the two of us. "Well, I'm going too. I don't care if I don't get any essence, this colorless Fred needs my help."

I smiled, her determination to protect her brother something I admired. There was no doubt in my mind that this turn of events had Fran scared, but she needed to be careful around him now. If she insisted on adventuring solely with Fred, she'd stop progressing and soon he'd need to protect her as she remained at the same level she was now.

"I'll tag along today as well, but in the future, it would probably be best for him to start hunting alone, at least until we find his essence limits," I said, then looking at the ground I muttered, "If he has any."

The rest of the day played out much like I'd planned, except I got very little essence as we hunted out the remaining Dire Wolves. We'd killed another nine and still, Fred had no end to the essence he was collecting. I noted that his aura increased as he added more essence, and I couldn't imagine what it would be like when he'd reached over a million essence. It seemed like an impossible amount, but he was well on his way with how much essence he was pulling out of these monsters. It wasn't all bad though, we collected four monster cores and split them between Fran and myself, each of us opting to wait until Fred wasn't around to use the essence within.

CHAPTER 8
UNWANTED CHAOS

We'd just finished the last pack of three when a roar split the silence, echoing through the forest some mile or so away. We exchanged a quick glance, before mounting up and taking to the sky in the direction of the scream. What we found was a curious sight indeed and I almost signaled that we should withdraw. But Fred was already going in for a landing, his aura pulsing around him, ready to be put to work.

I knew by description and experience what awaited us below, three massive ogres were fighting a huge Drake. This wasn't the little baby drake like we'd encountered before, and I immediately wondered if this was the mother of the one I'd killed. I'd grown stronger, but did I feel like I was a match for such a beast? Fred did and I couldn't allow him to fall prey to this chaotic beast.

Urging Ares forward I told her to slash at the beast from behind, giving Fred time to dismount and work his magic.

Ares was all too happy to oblige, and we darted downward, her claws out and ready. What followed was a confusing mix of flying through the air and pain. We hit the Chaos Drake on the back, but Ares's claws couldn't make it through its scales and its mighty tail slammed into the pair of us, throwing us aside.

Getting to my feet and cracking my neck to the side, I summoned my sword and bid Ares to fall back. She was reluctant to back off, but with some urging I got her to take up position behind me.

"This isn't going to be easy," I said, dodging a stray strike from a club as big as Fran from the ogre trying to hit the Drake. I hadn't inspected them, but they were fighting a losing battle. Three members of their party of six had already fallen and it wasn't looking good for these twelve-foot-tall behemoths.

"Get back!" Fred yelled, white flames dancing around him.

The ogres noticed him, one of them letting his guard down and getting one of the Drake's claws around his leg for his trouble. The remaining two stepped back, weapons held up before them, but the Drake wasn't finished yet. Fire filled its maw, and it roasted the injured ogre, then lifted its head roasting the final two while they screamed in painful agony.

I itched to step forward and attack, but I didn't want to get in the way of Fred's flames. He waved his hands around and fire covered him like a pillar of spinning white light. Then, just as the Drake turned its attention on the flames, he let it loose.

At first, I thought it would be ineffective, but the Drake let out a sudden scream of pain so loud that it brought me down to a knee as I covered my ears. It cut off as the flames sputtered out.

But the fight wasn't over.

The Drake had one or two scorch marks on it, but other than that, it looked perfectly healthy as steam wafted off its scales.

It was my turn.

Infusing my blade up to maximum and flushing my muscles with essence, I rushed forward. All the lessons Michael had been giving me were fresh in my mind and I was ready to show this scaly bastard who was boss. It opened its maw and flames began to form. I cast Lightning Strike right on its face, forcing its mouth shut, while activating Speed Burst. I moved faster than the Drake could follow, slashing low on its neck. My blade sunk deeper than I thought it would and I had to release it or be forced to stay too close to a dangerous opponent. Instead, I kicked off the Drake's head, doing a backflip some ten feet away. Then, with a stray thought, I summoned back my sword, ready to go again.

"My turn," Fran said, and my stomach lurched.

"Fran no!" I called out but she didn't pause. I could already see the Drake lifting its leg, ready to devastate Fran with a single blow.

Fred had begun to build flames around himself again, but he wouldn't be able to attack until she was clear. Biting my lip and flushing essence into my mind to help me think, it came to me. I reached out my hand and cast Mana Shell on Fran, infusing it with the last bit of my free essence.

It had to be enough to stop at least a single attack, it had to be!

The Drake moved like lightning, but Fran suddenly blurred as my Mana Shell formed around her. She was using a speed boost skill and it looked like she'd dodged the attack after all. She slashed it across the face, doing no damage, then slid right underneath it, her blade cutting a line on its softer belly scales, but not quite making it all the way through. She came out the other side and before she could make it back to her feet, she was hit hard by the Drake's tail. My Mana Shell shattered and a moment later she was flying through the air, barely missing several trees as she rolled to a stop.

Fred didn't stop to check on his sister, so I ran over as he unleashed his flames again and I used Mending Touch on her. She went from raspy breathes to a calm and collected rhythm. Coughing some blood out of her mouth she looked up to me and spoke.

"I might need to sit this one out."

I smiled, checked over my shoulder, and nodded. "Let us finish this and you stay safe."

Fred began to yell in a furious display of power like none that I'd ever seen from him. The Drake was trying to match its own flame against Fred's, and it was losing. Another moment later and Fred's flames had overtaken the Chaos Drake, cooking it once more. I readied myself for another attack, despite being wiped clean of essence already, then thinking better of it I reached in and pulled out the Cores, sucking out the essence of each. I got the full amount, luckily, and readied myself for a truly powerful attack.

My entire form vibrated from the intense power inside of me and the moment the flames dissipated; I was back on the attack. Fran had the right idea and I needed to split its guts out from below. However, it was hunched a bit lower than it had been before, likely recognizing its own weakness. Either way, I would make it work. I stopped suddenly, halfway to the Drake, it looked worse for wear after Fred's last attack, but Fred was sweating, and his pale complexion did not look good.

I began pulling in Mana for a Fireball, my eyes set for just below its head. I wasn't going for something so explosive that it would put me in danger, so I infused just enough essence with the attack to turn it a blueish green, then released the ball of fire, aiming just below it. It opened its maw to blow out more fire, but I struck it again with a well-placed Lightning Strike, forcing its head down just as my Fireball hit below it.

The explosive force of the fireball actually lifted the Drake up on its back legs. I rushed forward, activating Speed Burst once more and raising my sword. I knew if I didn't deliver the killing blow here, I'd be putting myself in a very precarious situation.

My blade sunk deep into its belly and guts poured out in a steaming mess. It mulled in pain, but the deed was done, and this Drake was dead.

I expected a bit more, but perhaps I'd been wrong about it being the mother. The longer I looked at it I noted that, while it was bigger than the first one I faced, it wasn't that much bigger. Still, it had several times the power of the first one for sure. Checking on Fran and finding her fine, I went over to Fred, who was sweating buckets but also appeared fine.

"How are you feeling?" I asked, surprised at the raw show of power he'd been able to tap into. It was enough to make me wonder if I'd be a match for him.

"I'm tired," Fred said, then as I watched, his eyes rolled into the back of his head and he fainted. I caught him and put a heal on him, even though he appeared fine physically.

CHAPTER 9
GATHERING FORCES

Two days later, I found myself in Merlin's Pub sitting across from Ismene, Fred, Fran, and Emory, discussing important matters.

"We should hit up a dungeon before going to Blackridge," Emory insisted for the hundredth time.

I sighed and shook my head. "I've a duty to get back to Blackridge as soon as possible. The troops should be arriving any day if they haven't already. Plus, you all could just go on a run without me, and I'll fly Ares over to Blackridge Keep," I said, but I saw immediately that they wouldn't have that.

Fran and Ismene folded their arms and gave me a pointed look, while Fred seemed to be distracted following a fly around the tavern with his eyes.

Fran spoke first. "We aren't leaving your side and that's that."

Then Ismene laid into me. "She's right. Especially for Emory and me, you've been off playing soldier for long enough and we won't leave you now. I wish we'd been able to be around more before, but I can't change that, so now you are stuck with us like..." She hesitated as she thought of the proper term to use, but Emory finished for her with a wide grin on his face.

"Like flies on shit," he said proudly.

"Yes," Ismene said, rolling her eyes. "Like flies on shit, an apt example."

This encouraged Emory more and his grin turned into a wide smile. "I really wish I could have bashed some heads in for you back when you were at war, but if you think about it, this was probably better. Now we are all pretty close in level and can challenge some harder dungeons. Which is what we should do on our way to your keep." He finished, his smile shifting back to his usual shit eater grin.

"Only if we can get in without waiting and it is on the way," I said, finally relenting. It wasn't my plan to do more dungeons while other responsibilities awaited, but it made sense to gather some essence along the way if we could. Hell, if it went fast enough, it would give me a much-needed influx of power.

The dungeon Emory had in mind was on the way, so I agreed and went about saying my goodbyes to my family and Michael. My mother asked several times who was going with me and if I really needed to leave already, I consoled her by letting her know that 'Yes I was taking friends with me, and no I wouldn't do anything stupid' though the latter argument didn't seem as convincing as the former. The twins excitedly announced that they are going to be visiting a

Prime Mana Shrine in two weeks. Michael gave me the location, a medium-sized city to the east of Creeshaw with a Prime Mana Shrine that would be ready in time. It was pretty close to the border, but no one was currently fighting House Variyn, borders or not, so it should be fine.

Once I'd said my goodbyes, I flew with Ares to where my friends awaited me, their own mounts ready to go. Ismene rode atop Roger her massive wolf, who looked even bigger than I remembered, while Emory had the same old war horse that I'd seen him use some time ago. It was equipped with new enchanted gear and shoes, I knew this because Emory kept bragging about the deal he got, so together we'd be able to make decent speed, despite not being able to take to the air.

I led the way, with Ismene and Emory on my left and Fred and Fran atop their hippogriffs on my right, Kora ran a small distance behind and showed her incredible speed by keeping up with us on foot. We reached the dungeon at the start of the second day of our travels. It took a bit of persuasion, by means of gold, and my name being dropped before we secured a spot for the same day. Entering the dungeon, I sighed and readied myself for a kill fest. It was a level 20 dungeon so there would be nothing that would remotely challenge me or my party members, but we needed essence and this was the place to get it.

Kora had decided to watch our camp and not participate, she seemed leery to enter another dungeon. Only saying that she didn't want to encroach on another of her siblings' territory without first asking, then she muttered something about weakened Ley Lines and difficulty talking with other dungeons. I nodded along, but there was much about dungeons that was far too strange for me to understand.

So, with relative ease, we began clearing out mobs in the demon dungeon. It was a mix between a themed and straightforward dungeon, supposedly in transition to a more themed type but recently it had all but stalled out, staying with floors and mobs. I knew this because I wasn't that dense that it must do with essence and the Ley Lines, but I couldn't do anything right now to fix it. I had a mission, and I was working my way to seeing it done. I had plans to go to Blackridge Keep, get everyone there all settled, then I'd travel to Miles Manor to set my affairs in order, followed hopefully by a reunion with Alayna, if she'd returned.

From there, I was confident that any news from Alayna would help me make the next series of choices I needed. I hoped I'd be able to count on the elves to get me to the Isle of Avalon, but unless they figured out a way to make their ships fly, it wouldn't be possible.

Everyone knew the stories of the sea and the horribly strong monsters that roamed the waters past the shore. I'd even heard tales of monstrous sized monsters coming to the shore cities every hundred years or so, destroying all they found. This was one of the reasons the human nations had no interest in securing the shoreline. It was a job that had been left to the elves for hundreds of years and would likely remain their responsibility into the far-flung future.

Focusing myself back on the dungeon, I killed off an

Imp that was trying to get a shot off on Fred while he stood around, not participating in the fight. He would have been fine, his fire very well able to keep him alive offensively and defensively, but if he used his white flame he'd suck up all the essence when it inevitable killed the weak mobs. So it had been decided that he ought to sit around and watch, only participating when necessary. I convinced the group, really only Emory argued, to allow him to roast one mob per room so he could gather more large sums of essence. So far, he'd sucked clean three imps during the room pulls, but I had a feeling we were getting close to a boss fight, and he couldn't help there, so it would be up to us.

Sure enough, when we reached the final room on the floor we were greeted by a 'Horned Devil' with a two-pronged fork-like spear and long curling horns. I'm sure if we were lower level, he'd be a challenge, but as it was, I decided I wanted to have the first crack at him.

"Mind if I take this guy on by myself?" I asked, checking with the group. They gave me a series of shrugs and nods, or in Fred's case a blank stare, so I decided I'd go for it.

Facing off against the demon, I watched as it unfurled its wings and took flight. The room we fought in was a mix of cavernous stone walls, and oddly half formed fine stone pillars. Most of the dungeon was like this, as if it were stuck between a cave system and an underground temple of sorts. There were even a few narrative characters at the start of the dungeon who spoke of having to defeat a great demon, but they didn't follow along or offer any other knowledge like most themed dungeons.

I tilted my head to the side to dodge a small firebolt that flew close enough to singe my hair. Time to pay attention to this boss mob. He currently floated some twenty feet up and I wondered what a team without a decent ranged fighter would do against a foe such as this, but I let that thought fall away when I saw him readying an even bigger ball of fire. This was a spell I recognized as Fireball. It was a favorite of mine and would explode on target, so I needed to be sure not to let it hit me. Or did I...

I activated Mana Shell as the attack approached and sunk about ten percent of my mana pool into it. The barely perceivable sheen of translucent blue sprung up around me just as the ball of fire hit. It exploded against my barrier and for a brief second or two I saw nothing but the orange of the fire as it expanded around the barrier. However, the shield remained intact, not even a crack forming. I did the mental math and determined that my barrier had a health pool of just over a thousand and for it to not have cracked, meant that this fireball wouldn't have done even half that in damage.

The fire cleared and I sneered at the weak ass demon boss. Reaching out my hand, I activated Lightning Strike, and shook my head at the effects of the powerful spell. The demon fell from the sky, hitting hard on the ground as the wing I'd struck went limp on its back. I stepped forward as red haze covered the demon, a sign that it was enraging or doing a special boss mechanic. But just as it began to stand, I kicked at it hard with my boot, sending it spinning a few feet back. I raised my sword in the air, infused it with a bit of essence, and swung down, removing the boss's head in a single stroke and ending the fight.

"Pitiful boss monster," I said, glaring down at it. I couldn't put my finger on why exactly, but I felt suddenly furious at the stupid monster and wanted to cut into it more with my sword, but I restrained myself. Taking a deep breath, I felt my heart stop racing and steady itself.

"You totally two-shot K.O.'d that demonic bitch!" Emory called out as he joined me beside the boss, reaching down to gather his loot. I almost didn't bother, not really feeling like this demon would have any loot that would benefit me, besides adding more gold in my pocket, and I had more than I knew what to do with already.

I was proved right when I got the loot, nothing but trash compared to the gear I was using. Putting it away in my dimensional storage, I determined I'd sell it off later for a bit of extra gold. There was a certain feeling about earning my gold in ways separate from the discoveries I'd come across. It was like a raw sense of appreciation that the other wealth didn't have.

The rest of the dungeon went about the same as the first floor, easy kills and no surprises. I got a few interesting trinkets, but nothing worth focusing on as I planned to sell it all away. By the time we finished, I'd gathered an impressive haul of fifty thousand essence. It wasn't much in the grand scheme of my essence gathering, but it got me enough that I might be able to check out some additional spells or skills.

CHAPTER 10
HONOR GIVEN

Our travels didn't take much longer before we'd reached Blackridge Keep. It felt strange to be arriving back to the seat of my power, however limited it was. In my mind, I'd nearly vowed to myself that I'd never return and to instead let others bear the weight of my responsibility, but that wasn't the way of an Arcane Knight, a defender of the balance or the son of Elkor Miles. I would stay true to the core of my ideals, even against what felt like impossible odds. Had the war changed me? Sure it had, but if I didn't cling to the very thing that made me who I was, then I might as well give up now. And that wasn't a part of the plan.

Justice would be served upon the heads of those who had so blatantly ignored the balance of life and taken so many in the blink of an eye. The way I saw it, my very duty and purpose was tied to delivering a blow to those responsible. I was the judge, jury, and executioner when it came to matters of the Balance. No one else alive held the title of Defender of the Balance, as far as I knew, and until I was told otherwise, I'd add this one last thing to my list of impossible tasks that needed doing.

As my eyes rested on the great keep before me, another thought wormed its way into my head that I could not ignore. The Ley Lines were failing, it could be seen in the dungeons and their odd behavior. Even the end of dungeon essence seemed to be a fraction of what it was before, giving only a few hundred essence where it would normally be thousands.

"You all make yourselves comfortable, I need to seek out Gabriel and Cron to get a report on the state of things," I said, turning to my companions. I didn't wait for a response, instead, kicking off the ground Ares took flight and we moved to land in the inner courtyard.

The air smelt of meat cooking on spitfires mixed with the general smell of sweat from hard laborers. I saw why when I made it high enough, many of the repairs had been completed and new features were being added. The entire area just beside the walls had been repaired and rebuilt, providing additional housing. While the keep within no longer had any fallen towers, instead each of them gleamed in the sunlight under a fresh coat of black paint. It truly looked as if I'd arrived at an estate worthy of the name Blackridge Keep.

Light colored tiles had been painted a gaudy golden color so that the keep looked much like Ares with her black feathers accented by gold. I'm sure it was Cron's idea, he had asked me about such changes, and I hadn't given him a firm enough no to stop him it would seem.

Landing just outside the main entrance, I was greeted by an orc child wearing livery that matched the banners I'd been fighting under for the past year. He bowed and held his hand out as I dismounted, meaning to take Ares off my hands. I checked with her first and she emphatically told me that 'yes' she would prefer to be pampered and fed. Pulling out a gold coin I tossed it to the boy, he caught it deftly in his right hand and took her reins with the left, pulling her to the side where the stables were.

I'd barely made it up two steps before the doors opened wide and a familiar face greeted me, Cron. He wore armor as if he intended to go to battle but wore the colors of Black-ridge Keep. There were several others flanking him as he held out his hands to the side in way of greeting. I caught sight of my assistant Verena, Lance, the Head of House for Miles Manor, Raphael, and Gabriel, my last remaining Elite guard, as well as a few others. It was quite the entourage, and I was instantly suspicious.

"What brings all of you together?" I asked as nonchalantly as possible. I wore no armor, having opted to switch out into plain clothes for the comfort while riding on the last leg of the journey.

Cron cleared his throat and stepped forward with several of the racial leaders, an orc, goblin, and troll. Then they surprised me by taking a knee before he spoke in a tone I was not sure I'd heard from him before, almost reverent.

"Master Miles, Lord of Blackridge Keep, and protector

of the realm. Word of your power and great deeds on the field of battle have reached our ears. You saved the lives of countless soldiers and proved yourself worthy of every title given to you. But I must relay another at your feet. I name you Caldor Miles, Stonewalker of the High Peaks, the greatest title I can bestow from Clan Grantane."

I blinked, confused at the sudden show of respect in such a peculiar place. Next, the head of Tribe Ugular declared in broken common that I had earned a title of respect in his clan, naming me Orc Born. I didn't understand his explanation, but I nodded respectfully. The troll, I recognized as a shaman I'd encountered with Creed and a newcomer as far as I knew, stepped up to me next. His name was Ahk'len, and he spoke in fairly good common, as I remembered him doing before.

"Many tribes have gathered, and I have been named mouthpiece. So, by the power that grants me, I named you Troll Friend, or in our tongue Enrehlen'awktu."

Next, came the goblin, and whatever he said was lost to me as he spoke very bad common. But I saw a gleam of respect in his eyes and one phrase stuck out to me, he called me a Great Threat, which I guess to the goblins was a sign of respect.

As each of them pronounced their oddly timed blessings on me, I realized that I'd received new titles for each of their pronouncements.

. . .

Stonewalker: *Your feet have never been so surefooted as they are on stone, granting you increased speed while traveling on stone. You are also 10% more sturdy, shrugging off blows that would bring others to their knees.*

Orc Born: *The highest honor given to one born outside the blood of an orc. Orc Born gives you a 10% increase in haste when you are angry. Let your Orc Blood boil and hear the call of the ancestors. As an Orc Born you may choose a mate within their clans and participate in ritual combat.*

Enrehlen'awktu: *You have been named Troll Friend. You received an additional 10% percent in regenerating Health and can, given time, even regrow a limb. As a Troll Friend, other trolls will see you as one of their own, allowing you to pass through their lands unharmed.*

Bagayata: You have been named Great Threat by the Goblins. As such, any goblin that sees you will instantly fear you and be ready to follow your command. You will do an additional 10% damage to any enemies with a lower level than you.

I staggered back under the sheer immensity of the bonuses the titles gave me. Being wholly unprepared for such a welcome and not knowing how best to respond, I decided to do what felt right.

First, walking up to Cron I held out a hand, he took it, and I lifted him from his knees. "I name you Cron, as a Knight and a Vassal, to be given lands of your own upon my earliest available moment. Will you do me the honor of serving Blackridge Keep and help spread the influence of what we stand for?"

Cron looked at me hard and for several seconds before answering. "Aye, I accept." He bowed his head and stepped to my right-hand side. I went to each of the leaders of the individual races and asked the same of them, each of them, in their own way, accepted. I would spread the ideals of Blackridge Keep and the togetherness of the races through all the land that I could. A sudden idea struck me, and I smiled deeply.

I would send word to Tim and see if I couldn't put my blood money to good use in acquiring lands already so close to our own as we sat only miles from the border of House Attra. I looked at Verena and Lance, one of them could be trusted to get the message out, I was sure. But first, I should figure out why Lance wasn't at Miles Manor seeing to things there.

The procession broke up as all those that needed to be there, which was basically everyone who'd met me, went into a private meeting to discuss events and get me back up to speed.

CHAPTER 11
I'VE BEEN GIVEN
WHAT NOW?

"Repairs have hastened over the last month but so have the costs to keep the supplies and foodstuff required to keep your growing estate going," Lance said. He was the first to speak up and had a natural way of taking charge in meetings, so I let him do it. "Furthermore, you have ignored all requests sent to you for the last several months and if I had the power to do so, I'd be putting a reprimand on Verena's record, but she tells me that not even the might of the Ordu could get you to take a second look at the paperwork I sent to you?"

He looked at me expectantly and I realized he wanted a response. I didn't wither beneath his gaze, nor did I hold back the power of my own as I fixed him with a stern glare. However, he didn't flinch and finally I let out a sigh and answered him.

"The lives and wellbeing of my men took precedence over paperwork that I gave you full authority to see to yourself," I shot at him, my words stern and filled with a touch of malice.

It had no effect, Lance just scoffed. He was becoming fairly confident in his role and manner of speaking with me. "I understand you are new at ruling, but paperwork is part of the role. I have dealt with all but the most sensitive matters myself, so I'd suggest you take the time after this meeting to go over them or lose several new potential income streams.

I pinched the bridge of my nose, a thought occurring to me. "Did you sign off on selling our research to House Variyn?"

"I did, upon the insistence of Regina and after weeks of you ignoring the request I sent to you. These matters and more require your eye, do not allow your path to be determined by others." Lance straightened under my gaze, and I relented.

"Fine," I sighed. "I will meet with you after we are finished here. Cron," I turned to regard the sturdy dwarf, "tell me of Blackridge Keep. I have missed her, and you've done admirably in my stead as steward, I'm sure."

"Aye," Cron said, leaning forward. "With the help of the combined races and newcomers, we've turned this keep into a small city of its own. We now stand at a population of five thousand when you count men, women, and wee ones. We've even attracted a new Clan of Dwarves, all eager to serve under the Arcane Knight whose reputation has been spreading through the lands these several months. They speak of your service as if you were a devil on the field of battle and an honorable Ordu when parlaying with the enemy. If half the accounts I've heard are true, then I am all but justified in making you a Stonewalker."

I smiled, Cron had fast become a friend and it felt nice to have his admiration and respect. As with all things lately, the names of those who'd fallen trailed through my head, and I felt a heavy weight fall over me. It was so difficult to be my old cheery self when the weight of all I'd lost refused to leave me be. Why had so many died when I'd lived? Of course, I knew part of the answer had to do with my status as an Awakened and my Paragon attributes, but surely men just as capable and strong as I was, fell in battle, yet with each impossible foe and fight I ended up surviving. I would be the one standing on the last day of battle, while all around me, friends and loved ones lay dead and dying.

"Thank you for your report, Cron," I said, breaking the awkward silence that was starting to creep up from my long pause.

Kora made a show of clearing her voice, she'd made it to the meeting just as we were about to shut the doors, and I felt a bit bad about forgetting to fly her over with me. I looked over to her and could tell she wanted to say something, and I had a good idea what.

"Go ahead, Kora," I said, nodding my head to her.

She looked around the room at each of the races gathered before finally speaking up. "My children, who you know as Runeforged, are to be given freedom and citizenship. As such, they are no longer the property of Blackridge Keep to be ordered about and will require housing in exchange for currency. They are ready and willing to work hard for their keep. It is my hope that Blackridge will be the center of a great shift as it has been with so many other races."

This got a stir out of all present, including Lance who looked the most perplexed. He knew the cost of each one of the Runeforged and likely saw it as a huge loss, but he held his tongue as did the rest of the group, each of them looking first to me to see how I'd react.

"I welcome the Runeforged as equals and am equally excited to see how they can use their skills to benefit all races." I was sure to project my voice and give it an extra measure of confidence as I spoke. Like many here, I was more than a little worried about how the future would play out with Runeforged becoming a race unto themselves, especially when so many of them were still being created and sold as golem servants and soldiers.

"If there is nothing else," I began to say, but was cut off by Raphael, her voice sounding a hint annoyed.

"What of the new keeps and lands you've been gifted? Will you assign your knights to rule over the keeps, as is proper, or will you rule over them yourself?"

I looked over to Verena, so used to her giving me the layout of things over the months of war and she didn't disappoint. She handed over a paper that had a list of ten new keeps and the lands surrounding them. Each one, based on a quick glance at my map, were within a day's travel of each other with the furthest being two days from Blackridge. I now had a total of eleven keeps under my name, they included villages, towns, and even a few mines. In the memo that Verena handed over, I saw that these were meant to be a reward for my service, a sentiment that I scoffed at.

I wondered how many vassals lost their lands to give me these but remembered that House Variyn had many empty keeps on their House Attra border, so it was likely very few. The huge influx of land from House Blalor's defeat must have renewed the need to place additional lands under simple vassals. However, that thought was lost as I finished reading. I'd been appointed to the station of baron under Lord Variyn. That meant I ruled over several keeps and lands, instead of just the one. No longer was I just Lord of Blackridge Keep, no, I was a baron of the Eastern providences. This wouldn't turn out like Lord Variyn hoped, more than ever I wanted to reach out to House Attra now.

I read the memo again, before passing it back and looking over the gathered leaders. "I will work with my administration and get the details hashed out, but rest assured we have been given land plentiful enough that all Knights under me should have a place to spread the ideals that have been founded within Blackridge Keep. It is my hope that all who wish sanctuary and a better life, regardless of their race, have a place among my many land holdings. If you can maintain this virtue, then you will be called to service."

That seemed to appease Raphael and earned several respectful head nods. After that little bit, we had a few other items that Lance brought up, but I zoned most of it out, knowing that Lance would have his way with me after this meeting.

True enough, when the meeting closed Lance held me firmly in place with a dutiful stare. I was in for it. It turned out there was a literal mountain of paperwork that needed my approval, from new patents to purchase orders for more Runeforged, apparently Regina was trying to replace the force she'd lost. I approved the purchase of more but told Lance to pen a letter to Regina explaining the Runeforged's new position as citizens within my lands.

It took us well into the night, but we made it through all that he had laid out and I felt the better for it. Lance was good at his job and took care of all that he could without my say so, but some things required my personal touch. He assured me that it would only be a dozen or so a week if I kept up with it and I promised him that I would do just that.

While going through papers with Lance I had an idea of a way to honor those who had fallen. Lance was just standing when I caught his attention.

"What is it, Master Miles," he said, seeing the look on my face.

"I want you to figure out the logistics for me for a project. I want to erect a monument in Blackridge Keep square that has all of the various races, Runeforged included, with a large stand where the names of the fallen can be carved. It will be a way to memorialize their sacrifice while also paying tribute to the many races who joined together under my banner. See that you work out the details and whatever the expense, I approve. Also, see if the Runeforged are interested in helping, they learn quickly and given a few dwarven guides I bet they'd be able to finish the project several times faster than others."

"I will see to it," Lance said, making notes on a stray piece of paper.

I watched him go and realized that Verena stood at the door, taking notes as well.

"Have you been there this entire time?" I asked, chuckling a bit at the absurdity of having a meeting with my steward while my assistant took additional notes on the very same meeting.

"Yes, Lord Miles. I have detailed all that was discussed and will condense it before sending it to you to review. Is there anything else I can do to assist you?"

"The troops have arrived and gone back to their normal lives?" I asked, knowing without a doubt that she'd have this information, if not much more.

"Yes, my lord. I have seen that each of them were given suitable jobs, many wished to become guards, so our forces there have swelled by more than double, but all have been given gainful employment. Also, they arrived well over a week ago, it is a shame you couldn't be here to greet them on their return. They speak highly of you, and I believe it was odd to them that you did not ride with them on the return. Of course, I made sure to inform them that you had many duties, but we'd hold a welcoming ceremony upon your return. Would you care if I scheduled that for the day after tomorrow?"

Seeing my face, she smiled and added, "I know you don't

care for public speaking, but I assure you any words will be enough for your men."

I nodded slightly as I thought and bit my lip before finally nodding emphatically. "See that a diagram of the planned monument is put together so that I might show the men the honor we hope to show those who have fallen. Perhaps my actions will speak clearer than my words ever could."

"Wise idea, my lord. Very well, I will see to organizing the festivities. Might I also suggest you visit Mayor Valestein. I've heard whispers that he wishes an audience with you."

"I'll visit him first thing tomorrow," I yawned the words as much as I spoke them, before pushing out my chair and standing.

CHAPTER 12
MAYOR VALESTEIN

I t was early the next morning and I'd changed into clothes more appropriate for my position as an adventurer and baron, which is to say I put my armor back on after having it polished to a shine. My black Drake cloak fluttered from a sudden breeze as I walked into town, the gates opening wide before me. The first sight that caught my attention was how many non-humans were walking about here or there. It would appear that the mayor had embraced my openness policy.

The guardsmen had run off into the village upon seeing me land with Ares outside the gate, and because of his swift thinking, Mayor Valestein was well on his way to me by the time I made it to the open square. It was a bit odd, before the mayor reached me, I had several younger lads and even a few I recognized as men who fought under me, bow their heads respectfully. The mayor was no different, he stopped some five feet from me and saluted me.

After a few seconds, I awkwardly saluted him back, not wishing to leave him standing there all day. He smiled broadly and stepped forward. "You've kept your word better than I could have imagined."

I tilted my head to the side in confusion. "In what way?" I asked, several names belonging to the dead men of the village going through my head.

"Over half the men that left to fight with you returned. I am familiar with war and am no stranger to the dangers of it. I expected very few to actually return, yet here you are, having saved so many lives that I want to throw a feast in your honor. I also have seen how much you've given to the families of those who were slain, ten times the gold those men could have truly earned. You are truly a man of great honor, and I am pleased to serve beneath you."

I shrunk under his admiration but wouldn't say anything against it. He needed to be allowed to feel as he wished, I just wish the praise did more to lessen the demons that spoke in my head, whispering that I didn't do enough and so many more could have survived. With effort, I pushed the thoughts aside and put on a mask of friendliness.

"I'd be honored to attend a feast, but I'd also like to invite you and any villagers who wish to attend to a cere-mony where we will announce a project to honor those who have fallen and have a feast of our own while remembering the mighty deeds of those who fought in the unfortunate war. Would you be willing to come?" I asked.

"I'd be honored," Valestein said, his bulky form shifting uneasily as his gaze traveled toward Blackridge Keep. "I've also a request I'd like to run by you, if you'd be open to hearing it. But first, come to my office and have a drink."

I nodded along and followed his lead. Soon we were sitting across from each other in a small closet of a room, sipping a warm ale. He was having trouble meeting my eye and I wondered what he wanted to request from me that had him so troubled.

"I'm ready to hear your request," I said, after a particularly long pull on the ale.

He sputtered for a second before regaining his composure. "Ah, right. I'm already a mayor under your command as lord, well, baron now I hear, of Blackridge Keep and I'm a formidable adventurer as well. What I mean to say is." He paused taking a deep breath and meeting my gaze. "I wish to be named a knight and vassal under your direct authority. I've seen through your actions that you are a man of honor who values lives above gain. I believe that your push for diversity and acceptance of all the races to be a noble pursuit. These honorable races have proved themselves to be a boon to my town and I believe that with my help we can turn your land into a powerful force to be reckoned with. Perhaps one day even a House Miles."

He winked at me at that suggestion, and I blanched. The idea of becoming a House Lord just sounded tiring, though I did like the idea of not being beholden to anyone else. Anyone other than the king, a voice in my head reminded me. Ah yes, the king would still be over me, perhaps I could take his place and rule over all of Newaliyn. I immediately pushed that strange and frightful thought out of my mind. I would sooner swim in a lake filled with leaches than rule all of Newaliyn.

"While I appreciate the service you and your men have rendered, I'll need to discuss this matter with my advisors. Rest assured I find you an honorable man well suited for the task, but I can't act rash in this time of expansion." I chose each of my words carefully, hoping not to upset him while also keeping him open to the idea that I very much would like another powerful adventurer as a knight. I just didn't know how the logistics of that would work with him being a mayor of a town right beside Blackridge Keep.

As if he could read my thoughts from my facial expressions, he spoke. "If you're worried about my position as mayor, I have someone willing to step into the role. He isn't as hardy an adventurer as me, being mainly focused around crafting, but he has the wits to run the place well enough."

"Seems you've thought of everything," I said, biting my lip and sure I would regret acting so rash. I stood, summoning my blade and made ready to get the deed done.

He understood my meaning in a moment and moved his great bulk over to my side of the desk, finding a place to kneel. I did as I'd done with the others, appointing him a knight and swearing him to loyalty with an oath that he gladly gave. When I was finished, I patted him on the arm, and we chatted for a bit about his strengths and weaknesses as an adventurer.

On the request of the mayor turned knight, I went to the pub and shared a drink with a few locals. I even recognized a few of the soldiers. A few teenage sons came to me, asking to hear stories of their fallen fathers and that about broke me. I told tales, making them seem as heroic as possible, about how their fathers had fought off impossible odds. I relayed to them each one by one how much it tore me apart to have lost their fathers, giving them a platinum coin each. It was a weak gesture, but I had nothing to give them otherwise.

We laughed, we shouted, and several men came to tears during the exchange of stories, so many of the locals who fought with me able to tell better tales about their unit. They spoke of the mighty Runeforged and how they'd laid waste to the enemy better than any cavalry could. Or how I'd fought commander after commander in the hopes that no blood would be spilt on those days. The way they told the tale of my fight against old Ironfist made me seem like some kind of titan of war. To me, it had been the closest fight I'd ever been a part of and one that would have meant a turning point in my life if I'd lost. But I hadn't lost and if you believed these men, I'd done it with such ease as to make Ironfist no more than a child using his father's sword.

But I let them tell their tales and tried my best to keep interacting with them. It was different being around my soldiers than just plain folks. They had seen the same things as me and you could see it deep within their eyes. In a way, we shared a bond deeper than any I could create, just by means of shared horrors. It was late afternoon by the time I got out of there, but I felt all the better for it.

CHAPTER 13
CEREMONY OF THE FALLEN

The days leading up to the ceremony where I would address the troops and announce the monument came swiftly. I woke to a pounding in my head, one I'd been hearing more and more from my dreams. It was as if an alarm was going off that couldn't be silenced. Sun poured in from an open window and I walked over to it to stare out at the vast hills and trees in the distance beyond the city gates. Because that is what Blackridge Keep and the surrounding buildings had become, a true, if not small, city.

With the amount of housing and businesses we had available we could house some twenty thousand citizens, so in regard to that, the place was basically a ghost town with our nearly five thousand population. But it had a nice homey feel to it that reminded me of Creeshaw.

"You've done well to ignite the match," a familiar voice said from behind me.

I didn't jump or summon my sword, instead, I turned

to see Mah'kus standing in my room wearing a fresh set of clothing from what I'd previously seen him in. His hair was styled to one side with the sides shaved off, black straight hair falling over a part of his forehead. His face was cleanly shaven, and he had a high collared shirt buttoned halfway up his neck with silver buttons against a black material. His slacks were made of a similar silky material, and he wore thick polished leather boots with white gloves on each hand, the tips of which were singed and blackened.

"What have I ignited?" I asked, getting ready for the day in my armor and wearing the colors of Blackridge, black and gold, on a tabard showing the griffin raised up in attack.

"The fuse that will change the face of the continent," Mah'kus smiled as he spoke.

He must be feeling extra cryptic today, but I was in no mood for such games. "Since I last spoke with you, I have changed. And still I have not found the sword which you tasked me to collect. What is it you require of me now?" I asked, exasperation clear to hear in my voice.

"I require nothing this day, I only came to see you before you address your troops. Perhaps, give you a touch of encouragement. They respect you so much that they will follow you into another war. And don't be fooled by the peace you think has come, because many more battles will be fought before the end. Warrick, for instance, is waging a battle that could use your brand of justice. Not all battles have to end the way City Blalor's did."

"You knew what would happen, didn't you?" I asked,

suddenly. He's spoken so many times about being someone that could step through time, he must have known.

"Yes, but I also know that it isn't your fault. If not with this tool of destruction, then it would have been another. However, this special device that Lord Variyn has created will serve you in the end and be the deciding factor in the great war to end all wars. As difficult as you may find it, you will call for its use in the end."

I glared at Mah'kus and suddenly I had the urge to spit in his direction. The very thought that I'd ever order such a destructive device to be used again made me sick to my stomach.

"I will never call for that weapon of war to be used against living beings. Ever." I said each word with venom, pouring my hate for the weapon into my speech.

"I know," Mah'kus said, smiling knowingly at me. "Be at peace and know that those who fought and died together with will be honored together. You are a great man Caldor, keep to the path and heal the Ley Lines. Everything else will come together in time."

With that he was gone between the space of a momentary blink. The man or god or whatever he truly was left me annoyed and slightly confused. He said he knew I'd never call for the weapon to be used, yet seconds before told me I would. Well, technically I said I'd not call it to be used on living beings, perhaps there was another use for such a terrible weapon?

I rifled through my notes and grabbed the journal I kept with all the names of those who'd fallen. It frustrated me, but I didn't have all the names memorized perfectly and I wouldn't do the disrespect of forgetting one when it mattered.

With my journal in tow and my armor on, I left to go to the Ceremony of the Fallen.

***

The sun shone brightly on the soldiers that gathered in the city square. I didn't have an exact count of who'd come to the ceremony, but there were well over five hundred. Straight backed and chins held high, I stood before them on a raised platform beside my knights. Several who'd been called as squires stood before the troops, sitting atop horses dressed down in Blackridge colors.

My chest swelled with pride as I looked out among my men. Each one of them ready to follow me into hell again if I but asked. I could feel their devotion like rays of sunlight. I raised my hand in salute and held it, as one they saluted back. All eyes on me, I turned to Verena, and she gave me a quick head nod. I stood just in front of a six-foot-tall replica statue covered by a thick tarp, ready to be shown to the troops.

Clearing my throat, I said a few simple incantations to work some simple magic Warrick had tried to teach me during our short time together. If done properly, it should magnify my voice several times. I finished the incantation and touched my throat as the book instructed. I felt a small measure of my Mana melt into it and when I spoke it was with the force several times greater than I naturally could project my voice.

"Welcome to the Ceremony of the Fallen. Today we honor those that fell in battle and remember their great deeds."

The crowd remained still, the military aspects of standing at attention working well.

"But I would be remiss not to also speak on the honor and strength of those that stand before me. But first, let me say a few words to the fallen."

"There is not a single human, dwarf, orc, troll, goblin, or Runeforged that gave their life for this cause that I don't think highly of. Each and every one of them fought to the last with honor in their hearts and fire of duty burning inside their bellies."

Something Mah'kus had said reminded me of the line we'd decided to engrave upon the statue above the names. So, as I reached out to pull the tarp down, I said the words.

"Fought Together, Died Together, Honored Together."

The tarp came down to show the six-foot monument.

The audience, the non-military ones, gasped in surprise and I looked to see the majesty of the statue myself. It showed each of the races who'd fought under me, including the Runeforged, all standing at the same height and looking out in a direction all around with their back against each other as if ready to fight off foes from any direction. The words I'd spoken wrapped all the way around the base where their feet stood, while some of the shorter races stood on mounds of higher ground to give the impression everyone stood at the same height, despite racial differences.

In their right hands each of them had simple spears. In all, it was a majestic sight that I couldn't wait to see be made into the full fifty foot statue I had planned. We'd decided that it ought to be made of stone and Verena was looking at methods to preserve it against time. I suggested she take a look at the canal structure in what used to be House Blalor lands, a suggestion that she took to heart, saying she was planning a trip.

A feast had been prepared and I didn't want to keep these hungry soldiers from their meals, so I cleared my throat and determined to say my final words as swiftly as possible.

"I am not one for great speeches. But I want each of you to know that what we fought, and they died for, wasn't for the whims of some House Lord sitting high in his tower away from the battle. No. We fought for the opportunity for independence and the love of our brothers beside us. I will call on you to serve again someday, but rest assured it will only be for the most dire of need. Though we've lost so many, this is not the end. It's time to eat, fill your bellies, and tell tales of your fallen brothers."

What followed was a powerful salute from all the ground forces, including several hundred Runeforged arrayed in the back of the formation. It seemed ironic to me that they'd choose to stand in the back when they were our front line for all of the war. You'd be hard-pressed to find a single soldier that didn't admire and owe their life to a Runeforged. Just from the stories told in the pub in Valestein, I knew these men would give anything to help a Runeforged if the opportunity arose. It was part of this general sentiment that made giving them citizenship such an easy task.

Enough soldiers spread word of their Runeforged brethren's deeds to get them accepted by the general populous. It was something I was proud to see as the ruler of Blackridge Keep. Beyond just the Runeforged, those that stayed behind were all too happy to help a soldier by any means possible. I worried that with the scars, both emotional and physical, they'd be hard-pressed to find gainful employment, but it wasn't the case at all, quite the opposite in fact.

The crowd dispersed by the command of the squires and the tables were carried out into the open square, along with long benches for everyone to sit. Platters and platters of food, from roasted pigs to specialty prepared sides like yams, potatoes, and grilled onions mixed with various vegetables. In all, it smelt amazing, and I couldn't wait to sit at my own table with my knights and dig in.

The afternoon wore on into the evening, performers of all kinds entertained from goblin fire dancers to dwarven bards, to troll sword swallowers. The ale was cool and pleasant, the company fine, and the entertainment lively. The feast pressed on into the night, but still we kept the party going. More food was brought out as hunger set in again and the entertainers traded out. I got to hear the great songs of a bearded dwarven woman with a set of pipes on her that made my little utility magic seem almost laughable.

It was a good night filled with revelry and ended with me sharing a game of cards with a few of the remaining guards that served directly with Mick. I could feel the yearning they had to be around their fallen captain again, and seeing it only made me feel the pain of his loss more. I took several long drinks in his honor and toasted to his success in the afterlife, wherever it would take him. Suddenly, I wished I'd asked Mah'kus a favor and I found myself drunkenly calling out for Mah'kus when I finally made it to my bedroom, but he didn't come.

I'd love to know if the so-called dead god had the power to return life to those who had died. Perhaps with his power he could bring back some of those who'd given the ultimate sacrifice, or at the very least give me some peace of mind about where they went after death. But my night ended in a drunken haze with my thoughts on death and what came next.

CHAPTER 14
CALL FOR AID

Z ander arrived several days later atop a pegasus. Ismene was the happiest to see him, but I'd grown into friendly terms with him during the war as much as before. Though our interactions were limited during that time, we'd spent so much time in the same meetings or being called out to battle together, that we were much closer than I ever thought we'd be when I first met him.

Ismene ran forward to embrace him, he wore his gawdy gold-white armor, but I couldn't fault him for it, the armor worked well and I'd seen it turn aside many of soldiers' spears during our joint conflicts. I was surprised when Ismene pulled Zander into a deep kiss, suddenly finding myself a little jealous, my thoughts turned to Alayna and her where-abouts. The kiss ended and Ismene grabbed his hand, holding it tight.

"Baron Miles," Zander said, inclining his head, though he had a smirk on his face.

From what Verena had told me, Zander and four others had also been made into barons. So, I inclined my head, a shit grin on my face and said, "Baron Zander." It wasn't the proper way of addressing him, which made it all the funnier to me since he'd said my title properly.

Zander gave me a flat look and Emory stepped forward then, slapping him on the arm and saying, "Sup, pale boy. Ismene can't stop talking about you, kind of annoying honestly."

Ismene shot Emory a look and Fred laughed, standing beside Kora. Though, I realized as I watched them speak that it was because of an unrelated joke or news, and not Emory teasing Zander. It was good to see Fred and Kora talking again and Fred showing signs of his old self.

"Let's get inside and have a drink," I said, turning and not waiting for the group to follow, though I knew they would.

We made it to a private room, and I flagged down a servant girl, her name was Luna if remembered right. "Get some help and bring food and refreshments to us."

"Right away m'lord," she said, her black hair spinning around as she turned and hustled away.

I never thought I'd get used to being waited on, but it sure was convenient not having to do everything myself. I was careful to tip and treat them with respect, despite it being my coin that paid their wages, it just helped me feel better about it.

We got our drinks and somehow an entire roasted chicken, with bread and cheese delivered to us. I barely had any recognition of who the chef was that ran the kitchens, but I'd need to thank them for having a decent meal ready to eat at such short notice.

There were seven of us total and we tore into the food with the ravenous hunger that only adventurers felt. Kora of course didn't join in, instead she watched us all intently as we ate. I decided to ask her a question I'd meant to pose to her days before.

"What do you know of Fred's condition," I asked, before throwing more chicken into my mouth.

The flavors were exquisite, and each bite contained more bursts of flavor that I missed on the last tasting. The bread was common enough, but the richness of the cheese mixed with the sour bread could have been a meal all by itself and still left me satisfied.

"It isn't something that I've encountered before," Kora said simply. Then inclining her head toward Fred and looked back at me pointedly. "I believe it was equally my fault and yours. I tried to fix him in a way that isn't meant to be, inscribing rune work into his very flesh, as I would a Rune-forged. I strengthened his body and core, but it wasn't enough. When you infused him with so much essence that he literally was dragged back to the land of the living, it was the final key. He is still very much Fred, but I fear we've changed him in ways that cannot be healed."

"I'm sitting right here," Fred said, as if to remind us he wasn't there merely for decoration. I smiled at him, this being the most socially aware I'd ever seen him, but just nodded to Kora before going headlong back into eating.

"Don't take this the wrong way, Zander, but why are you here?" I asked, as we finished eating and settled into a quiet roar of meaningless conversation.

"I've been sent by Lord Variyn to deliver a message I'm afraid," Zander said, and he looked a bit annoyed by being made a messenger. "He says that you are to come to Variyn City and meet with him at your earliest convenience. Then he added that you 'will not avoid responsibility forever', whatever that means. I've honestly not seen my uncle so bent out of shape by something so simple as a meeting. What did you say to him before you left?"

I merely grunted and shook my head. Thinking better of it, I decided I'd share the truth with my friends. "I requested I be released from my position as Knight and Vassal, but that I wanted to buy the lands of Blackridge Keep. I don't feel the same now, but if I could get released, I think it would make life easier in the end. This isn't to leave this room though." I added the last bit, but even if it did leave this room, my actions in setting up new knights and vassals would speak louder than the rumors of my words. I didn't fear losing my people's faith just yet.

Everyone present looked at me with odd expressions on their face and I couldn't blame them. I thought Emory would speak first, his mouth opening and closing several times before snapping shut and his head going sideways. But it was Ismene who spoke out after a momentary pause.

"You'd have left all this behind, just like that?" She asked. There was a genuine confusion in her voice, and I guess I understood why. Before I could answer, Zander laughed.

"You told my uncle you wanted out and now he's terrified you might release yourself from your oaths. That's rich."

It was my turn to look perplexed. "I can release myself from my oaths, I don't need his permission?"

Zander cocked his neck at me. "Well, the Oath to serve and protect the realm is so general that the system probably won't even enforce it, you know how much infighting and maneuvering there is going on, even at a House level? I guess not. Well, just don't be surprised when you have assassins knocking down your door for a chance at your title that you so freely want to give away."

"But what of my vassalship, can it so easily be tossed away or is there a way to retain my lands if I choose to leave?" I asked, now fully engrossed in the conversation.

"House lands are House lands, but just because you are a vassal doesn't mean you have to kiss Lord Variyn's boots. Between the two of us, we have enough land to be a serious threat to my uncle if we wanted to be. Which, mind you, I don't want any part of, especially if he has more of those weapons."

I cringed at the thought and saw most of the group flinch in response to the mentioning of the weapon as well. It was well known between my friends at this point that I still held a portion of the blame, despite what I might say to myself, and it was a sore subject in general for me.

"I pray to the Ordu that a day never comes when one of those weapons needs to be deployed again. Especially when the first person to use it has yet to face judgement for his crimes," I spat out the last few words like bile on my tongue.

Shifting in my seat, I glared over at Zander, suddenly suspicious of him. He was the nephew of the man I wanted to kill after all, perhaps I was being too free with my words.

Zander must have missed my not-so-subtle threat toward his uncle, as he just nodded and said, "I don't think the king is going to pass any judgment on my uncle. In fact, he was given nearly all of House Blalor lands as a way of commendation for his swift victory. But with all the civilian deaths caused by the weapons use, I'm sure someone wants Lord Variyn's head on a pike."

With that Zander looked at me, a single eyebrow raised, and I caught his meaning. He knew all too well my mind on the matter, but was this little act a way of telling me he would assist me or a warning that his Uncle already knows of my actions? Once again, I found myself unsuited and unprepared for the rigors of politics and the subtle nuances they required.

Just then, a loud knock sounded at the door and our conversation halted abruptly. Emory was closest to the door, so he stood and pulled it open. The servant girl, Luna, was there and she stepped into view before announcing why she'd interrupted us.

"Sorry m'lord," she said, bowing her head slightly. "Someone has arrived who seeks audience with you, a one, Creed Nefrah. He bids me to tell you that you would know him by a different name, Creed Volkroy."

"Creed is here?" I asked, standing along with the rest of the group. We were all fond of Creed in a little brother sort of way. He wasn't much older than my siblings, but he'd gone off to war answering the call his father sent out. I had no idea how well the war was going for them, but he was using his family's name again so that was something. "Have him come here, and also bring another round of drinks."

"Yes, m'lord."

And with that she slipped out. A few minutes later she reappeared and stepped aside for an armored knight with icy spikes protruding off large pauldron shoulders to enter the room. He had a helmet on that made it seem like his face was that of a skeleton with frozen bits hanging off him. In a word, he looked scary. The helmet seemed to melt back into the armor below and a familiar face smiled back at us.

He looked over the group until his eyes met mine. Then, bowing his head slightly, he finally spoke. "I seek your aid in the war for the southlands," he raised his eyes, almost gray in how light blue there were, "will you come to the aid of House Nefrah?"

Creed's voice had deepened ever so slightly, a sign of the growth he'd experienced during our time away. He'd been at war for the same amount of time as I had. As I looked into his eyes, I could see that much of the young and innocent boy we'd come to know had changed, he seemed harder in gaze and had an air of confidence about him that he always lacked before.

"I do not wish to go to war once more," I said honestly, but quickly amended my response as I saw Creed's cool and calm visage diminish under my words. "However, for you Creed, I will do what I can. Sit and tell me what has happened in these many months apart. I know a bit more about the Southern war than you might realize." I added the last bit as I thought about Warrick and his work to push back the Easterners.

"I've been through hell," Creed said, sounding a lot more like the Creed I knew as his armor seemed to dissolve around him, leaving him wearing an outfit of dark blues and orange trim. I didn't know House colors well enough, but I imagined this was some kind of noble outfit. It looked comfy with a padded vest, sturdy looking pants, and black riding boots that stopped just below the knee.

"Start at the beginning and tell me everything." I shifted in my seat and got comfortable.

What followed was a tale nearly an hour long in the telling. Creed had been through a lot, but most of it rang a similar tune to the battles we'd been a part of, so lots of death and loss. He spoke of them fighting a war on two fronts against Southlanders and Easterners. This bit surprised me as I'd have thought that Warrick would have rallied the forces of Newaliyn with the Southerners by now. He went on to say that he'd lost his father in battle and his brother was now head of the house.

What was more, he didn't seem very torn up about it, not like the Creed we'd known at all. Ismene, regardless, offered condolences first, reaching out and hugging him. He'd put on a fair bit of muscle, really growing into his icy armor, but still, he didn't look like he could pass as someone more than seventeen years of age. Which in a way was an accomplishment for him, seeing as that was the age most become *Awakened*. He finally fit into the norm, age and look wise, well maybe not look wise as he still looked more Chaos Fighter than he did *Awakened* Hero.

He told us of the back and forth between the Southlanders and how they'd struggled to contain certain Easterner fighters who seemed able to wield powerful magics. My thoughts turned to the wild-sparked or Venshti as they called themselves. Warrick had no trouble against them, but I wondered how powerful they could truly grow. Eventually his tale came to why he decided to come here and seek reinforcements.

According to Creed, the Southlanders had organized into a massive army and hadn't attacked yet, but when they did, his brother seemed convinced they'd be overwhelmed. They were already fighting with the combined forces of Houses Abrye and Adron, but it isn't enough. They sent a request to the king and every other House, but so far no one has responded to requests for aid. Creed's brother thought because of my position and relationship we had, that I might be able to marshal troops from House Variyn.

When I asked if they realized we had just ended a war only weeks ago, Creed said he'd heard the news and felt like that was all the more reason to come to their aid. He figured we had forces ready to go, but I saw it differently. The men had their fill of bloodshed and wouldn't take kindly to being sent across the kingdom to fight someone else's battles. I relayed these very thoughts to Creed, and he took on a crestfallen look, but I assured him that I had no plans of abandoning him.

In the end, I promised to fly out personally and to see

Warrick, telling Creed that our best chances lay with allying ourselves with the forces of the Southlanders, not fighting a war on two fronts. Creed seemed wary of this but agreed that it would be a wise first step.

As soon as we finished our discussion, everyone, except for Zander, offered to go with us to the Southlands, but I turned them down. Instead, I told them that if I made contact with Warrick and it was prudent, that I'd have him open a portal that our troops could march through, along with any *Awakened* that wanted to be of assistance. This pacified all of them but Kora, who insisted that I take a Runeforged with me or allow her to go for my own protection. I relented and told her she could come. Apparently, Creed could now summon a flying hell steed, so he'd be able to keep up with Ares if we didn't push ourselves too hard.

Determined to return as soon as possible, Creed insisted we leave that very night. So, after a round of goodbyes and minor food preparation, we took to the skies.

CHAPTER 15
LORD NEFRAH

The trip took several days even atop flying mounts, but by the third day the vast sand filled lands of the Southlands and the mighty Paugmook River came into view. Creed had insisted that we go visit his brother first, but I'd declined, saying I needed to find Warrick and that I would be in contact afterward. But after several attempts to convince me, I folded. We traveled through wet darkened clouds as we approached the front lines.

They had set up several mighty barges that ferried troops back and forth over the Paugmook River, even going so far as having several smaller sail boats filled with archers to defend them on the passing. We flew over all that and the small fort that had been set up on the South side of the Paugmook River, instead going deeper to where Creed's House had taken a medium sized fortress from the Southlanders and maintained it as their front line, defending the supply routes coming and going.

The outpost, if you could even call it that, was barely more than a town set atop a crater inset into a plateau with natural barriers all around and a single winding road to the top, where a gate had been built into the natural walls, I saw several man sized holes cut into the side of the natural walls, most likely a way to get rid of waste but also a potential entry point for determined assassins. Creed made a wide berth around the settlement so that we could approach via the road.

I knew we did this for a reason, as Creed had earlier informed me that the ranged sentries were trained to fire on any flying beast regardless of who it appeared to be after an incident with a flying monster that could do illusion magic had infiltrated the inner walls and killed a dozen soldiers before escaping.

We landed on the hard packed ground of the road leading up to the keep and both of us dismissed our mounts. Ares didn't mind, as she wasn't a fan of the dry hot air of the Southlands.

"I don't have time to waste," I said, marching forward with Creed at my side. "Let's meet with your brother and then I am off to find Warrick."

"My brother is a," Creed searched for the right words before finishing with, "straightforward man. I'm sure he won't keep you."

We reached the top of the road where the mighty gate stood barring our path. Creed stepped forward, summoning his armor and helmet, and the gate slowly swung open. He looked back at me, like a deathly specter in massive armor, and I marveled at the contrast between the growing young adult I knew and the fierce warrior's visage he took on with his icy armor.

The outpost within was a bustle of activity, soldiers moving goods here to there and repairs being made to internal structures. We followed a street up to where his brother had set up his commander's tent, a massive circular tent made of animal hides, set over the ruins of what must have been the conquered chief's hut or something similar. Guards crossed halberds to keep us from entering.

"Lord Nefrah is in council with his commanders," one of them said, staring out at us through the slit in his full faced helmet. He wore House Nefrah colors, dark blue and orange, over sturdy looking plate armor.

The helmet around Creed's face dissolved and he spoke, "Not all his commanders, as I'm out here. Inform him immediately that I have arrived with Lord Caldor Miles."

The guard recognized Creed and snapped to attention, one turned and stepped into the tent only to come out a moment later ushering us to enter by way of hand signals. Creed went in first and I followed after.

The interior of the tent was brightly lit by several balls of white magical light, a spell I was intimately familiar with as it was one of the very first I'd learned. Looking around, I saw a large circular table and nine men standing around a massive map with troop placement markers showing troop formations. I recognized Creed's brother right away; they had the same eyes but his complexion was a dark tan, whereas Creed had the sickly white of a Death Knight's. Furthermore, they might as well have been twins when it came to facial structure, from his nose to his cheeks, to his lips, they looked eerily similar.

The biggest difference was the man's size. He stood a staggering half a foot taller than me and was built slightly thicker than Emory, and Emory was a thick man. He wore plate armor, but no spikes like his brother, and he had a stern gaze that spoke of a demeanor of no nonsense.

"Brother," Lord Nefrah said, his voice deep and rumbling.

"Lord Nefrah," Creed said in response, saluting his brother.

He made no move to salute him back, instead switching his gaze to me. For a solid three seconds he said nothing, but I didn't squirm under his gaze, instead I stared right on back.

Eventually Lord Nefrah spoke. "I've heard no reports of troops marching to our aid yet, have you come to give me military advice and to aid in my war?"

I repressed a smirk, this guy liked to play it direct, that was for sure, so I would do the same.

"The Southerners don't have to be your enemy. I have a contact among them, both sides want the Easterners out. If we work together, they won't stand a chance." My words might as well have been a futile wave hitting against an unmovable cliff side with how little anyone in the room reacted. Not so much as an eye twitch from Lord Nefrah and his commanders.

In time, he answered—he may be a straightforward person, but he took his time to respond to anything said to him. "Have you met with this contact recently? Are they still in place and what news do you bring from them?"

I held back my own reaction, but I wanted to cringe. This was part of the reason why I insisted to Creed I contact Warrick first, I had nothing to report but what I'd already said.

"I have not, but I have full faith that they are still in place. Creed, well, we thought it would be prudent that we meet with you first so that I could pass on the news that you ought not press the attack against the Southerners and focus on the Chaos riddled ranks of the Easterners."

Lord Nefrah swung his gaze over to his brother and shook his head. "I have heard your advice and I will take it into account, Lord Miles. I do not take such direction lightly as I have heard of your victories in battle and the tactics used to gain such victories. Furthermore, I've heard tales of your character from my brother, and I greatly appreciate the aid you gave him in his time of need. But I must request that you depart immediately and make contact with your agent. There is a force of Southerners greater than anything we could hope to muster, and I fear our time has come to an end if something drastic is not done. So please, go and act swiftly that we might live to see the next week."

I shared a look with Creed, and he shrugged, which looked odd when wearing such large armor. Oh well, so I guess I'm off to find Warrick now. "I will leave right away. It was an honor meeting you, Lord Nefrah."

Turning, I left the tent only a minute after entering. Creed followed behind me.

"Sorry, I told you he could be a bit straightforward. Did you want me to come with you?" Creed asked, jogging to catch up with me as I was beelining it for the gate so I could fly out of here and try to find Warrick, wherever he might be.

"I'll move faster if I go alone," I said over my shoulder. "Give me a few days and I will find Warrick. Do not let your brother go up against the gathering Southlanders in the meantime. It will likely just be a death sentence until I've spoken to them. We can work together in this, just watch."

With that, I pushed my way through the crowd until I reached the gate. It opened for me without so much as a wave and I was out and down the road a bit before I summoned Ares back. She sent me a few mental nudges, annoyed that I'd pulled her out so soon after she'd entered. I relayed our mission and pressed into her the importance that we act swiftly. That was enough to get her back into focus and I rewarded her with a wolf steak I'd collected. A few loving screeches later and we shot off the ground, the sky our road.

CHAPTER 16
UNSAFE SKIES

Hot air blew against my face, and I squinted against the rush of wind as we flew. Normally it wasn't so bad, but the hot air was mixed with sand that stung me, making it hard to keep an eye on where we were going. Ares had no such issues, so I focused my mind on becoming one with hers. After several long moments of concentration, I saw and felt through her perspective.

The weight of my body pressing lightly against hers, the currents of air pressing against her wings to give us lift, even a slight annoyance at the heat, though she was far less bothered by it than I was. It was a mesmerizing feeling that I could easily get lost in if I let myself. We flew for some time, I let her go in the general direction of the city we'd last seen Warrick, but it would take time to get there so I wasn't worried yet. Instead, we enjoyed each other's company, her mind so closely pressed against my own.

I felt the loving embrace of her mind like a warm hug

and in that moment, I forgot the pain and anguish that followed me around like an unwanted shadow. It was peace and tranquility. Unfortunately, it lasted less than an hour as Ares's keen eyes spotted a threat on the horizon.

At first, I thought it was just a bird, maybe a hawk or something, but with Ares's eyes I soon got a close enough look to activate my Inspect skill. It had great expansive wings that seemed to trail dark specks of dust behind them as it beat furiously in our direction. The closer it got, the bigger I realized it must be.

Shadow Sand Vulture, Level 48, 2,180/2,180

It certainly had a fairly decent health pool, that was for sure. I broke my connection with Ares just enough that I could function as an individual again, my hand going out to the side and my sword appearing. I flooded it with enough essence to bolster my attributes significantly and waited for it to come into range. There was no doubt in either of our minds, it had targeted us for a midday snack, but it would get more than it bargained for when fighting Ares and myself.

We sped through the air, Ares wanting to get close enough to dig her claws into the bird. Meanwhile, I waited for it to come clearly enough into view that I could unleash a spell on it. With each of us speeding straight at each other, the time to attack came sooner than I expected.

I unleashed a Lightning Strike, the focus required only a moment's time before the sky cracked and a bolt of lightning crashed into the bird. It must have been a critical hit, because it faltered and dove for several seconds before it could right itself. I didn't wait for it to recover thowugh, instead focusing my mind as sand and hot air stung at my face, casting Arcane Missile. Three sparking balls of arcane energy flew out of my hand and crashed into the flying beast.

By this time Ares had closed in and after checking with me, she dove in for an attack. I gave her the go ahead with a simple thought and readied my sword to stab at the menacing looking bird. At level 48 this would be a good chunk of essence I could earn for only a bit of effort. Long gone were the days where I was worried about even a level 48 monster being my equal. Not only had I bested a level 50 *Awakened,* but adventurers were naturally a bit tougher than monsters of the same level. This had to do with the extra attributes we could apply per level.

Though I'd read plenty of books on monsters, most assumed that if you only ever assigned your base attributes you got, each level you'd find yourself a nearly equal match to most monsters of the same level, with the only major difference being the resource pools of monsters, specifically health. For whatever reason, monsters seemed to benefit twice or in some cases three times as much from their own Constitution attribute. This was all speculation of course, as even the smartest monsters you encountered would not share any details about their internal workings, such as attributes and so forth.

I snapped out of my stray thoughts as we smashed into the Shadow Sand Vulture. Stabbing with as precise strikes as I could manage, I marveled at the design of this monster. It had a long neck with a fleshy colored beak that dripped with a red substance. It had black eyes that seemed to swirl with dots of sparkling sand. The feathers let off a trail of dust that sparkled in the same way, so dark that it looked like a night sky filled with sparkling stars. Its huge taloned feet tried to gain purchase on Ares's underbelly, but she moved expertly, using her own feet to keep it away as she bit and clawed at its skinny neck.

My sword bit deep into its chest and it screeched in pain, sounding almost like an injured chicken crossed with a goat's scream. Suddenly we were shrouded in a black mist all around and I couldn't see anything. I dropped my sword as sharp talons ripped down my armor, thankfully not doing more than knocking my sword loose. Ares panicked a bit and kicked off the vulture.

Our downward dive got us free of the black cloud of mist that had formed around the vulture and Ares caught the air, swooping back up with incredible speed. I summoned my sword back to my hand and tried something new. Rearing back, I flung my sword forward as hard as I could, tip first. The force that I was able to put behind it sent it streaking forward in a perfect line. It hit the ball of black mist in the centermost point, and I heard a screech fill the air.

Summoning my sword back, it returned to my hand with black blood dripping off it. I had no idea how weak we'd already brought this bird, but it wouldn't be in this world much longer. Ares dove fearlessly into the black mist, claws out, and I held on tight to the reins as we slammed hard into the bird hiding within. Suddenly, a flash of black light filled my peripheral vision as we left the circle of mist with the vulture folded within Ares's grasp. It had its beak open wide and was barely missing Ares's head as it spewed forth a column of black energy out of its open beak.

I reached out my hand and cast Lightning Strike, aiming right for its open maw. My spell formed and a crack split the air. The lightning hit it right in the head and, as I'd hoped, cancelled its ability, stopping the stream of energy coming from its mouth. Ares took that opportunity to bite into its neck, delivering another devastating blow to its health. But the fight wasn't over yet.

Another ball of mist appeared, and Ares released her attack, diving low as we had before. However, this time it was immediately followed up by a shadow beam attack that struck her on the left wing. I felt her pain through our bond, and I cursed the wretched monster for its attack. Placing my hands around her neck, I began to chant the words of healing for my Mending Touch spell. Two seconds into our freefall and the healing took effect, repairing the damage done to her wing.

She spread them wide, and we glided into a stable position, but I was too focused on Ares and didn't see where the vulture had gone. Claws tore into Ares first, then one grabbed a hold of my right shoulder, ripping me from my saddle. It carried me for only a second before releasing me to fall to my death. I sensed Ares was hurt again but was still able to fly. Closing my eyes I focused on our bond, urging her to get to me in time.

She moved with a fierce, almost unnatural speed, as she struggled to get to me in time. I could feel panic running through her, but also a confidence that she could do it. The ground was swiftly coming into view, and I worried that it would be too late for her to pull up. I tried to tell her to back off and let me fall, lest she injure herself, but she ignored my complaints like a mother ignoring the commands of a petulant child. It was her own mind I got the comparison and if I weren't about to slam into the desert below I'd find it amusing.

A streak of black from the corner of my eyes had me turning midair. The vulture was firing on Ares again as she came up swiftly to dive underneath me. She ignored the attacks, swirling and pivoting through the air like only a griffin could. Just a second more and...

She sent a mental command for me to grab hold as she passed under me, I obeyed immediately and nearly jerked my arm out of place. I strained to get the leg ties back into place, I had grown careless lately as I had been keeping them off most of the time. Finally, I got one, then another as Ares moved to get us back into a decent attack position. She flapped her wings mightily to give us the altitude needed to properly fight this battle.

Several times during our climb, black beams of energy shot out at us, but she dodged them all. The vulture also climbed to match altitude with us, but it had a much longer ranged attack than what I could manage. I urged Ares to get just a tad bit closer and she did so. Unleashing spell after spell I whittled down on its health until it lost some ground and we finally got into position above it.

Ares was ready to finish the fight and I agreed. The plan was simple, she would go for the throat, and I would try to injure a wing. We dove in, our minds melding into one as we did so. I felt the beat of her wings and the rush of her breath, while she experienced the tightness of my muscles as I gripped my sword and readied my strike.

Three breaths away and I was assured of our victory. The vulture had other ideas, opening its maw and letting loose the thickest black beam of energy yet, right for us. Together we reacted, Ares tilted our path just a touch, keeping us going forward but out of the direct path of the attack. I activated Mana Shell, throwing half my available mana pool into it, an impressive six hundred mana total.

The vulture moved its beam and it smashed into my barrier, but for the time being it held and all we needed was a single moment. We smashed headlong into the vulture and Ares thrashed its neck. I chopped down, activating Speed Burst to sharpen my perception of the small window of time I had, then Power Strike mixed with Swift Strike to deliver a devastatingly accurate blow to its left wing.

I didn't quite know what I expected, but chopping straight through its wing was not it. The left wing fell free and I felt a rush of essence fill me as Ares ripped her neck to the side one last time, finishing it off. She released our prey, but followed it down in a gentle glide, likely wanting to feast on its corpse.

"Let me check for an intact core first," I whispered to her, laying myself across her back as we descended.

She gave me a gentle reminder that she was hungry, but relented a moment later after I told her I'd give her a few extra wolf steaks if she let me find the core first. Her emotional impression was the equivalent of saying, 'You have until I am done eating the steaks to find what you want, then I am eating my prey.' I understood her message loud and clear, so the moment we landed I threw her two wolf steaks and dug into the bloody corpse. Unfortunately, the fall or the battle had been too much and all I found was a cracked and useless core. I still took it, the dust a reagent that sold fairly well and stepped back to let Ares eat.

CHAPTER 17
SEEKING A FRIEND

What I really needed to do was find a Mana Shrine and see if there were any abilities or spells that would give me more of an advantage fighting atop Ares. We'd done fairly well against the first and even the second vulture we fought, but the third posed an issue with its extra sharp talons. We'd been smart and whittled it down from afar, but Ares was itching to be a part of the battle and I kind of wished I could trade my sword in for a lance for the first time since getting it.

Now we soared over empty skies, no new monsters wanting to challenge our might. I fiddled with my map until finding a shrine I could check out. Directing Ares to a spot below us, we soared ever lower, keeping our guard up as we did so. I had already upgraded all my spells and skills to their tier 2 variant, but I wanted to try and find a skill that would help me get a bit more length on my melee attacks if I could.

Upon reaching the ground, we made an interesting

discovery, there was a little oasis of greenery and a small pool of water bubbling from some unseen source below and around the Mana Shrine. Leaning down low, I stuck the tip of my finger into the water and found it was the perfect warmth for a bath or just a relaxing soak. That would all be well and good if the heat of the surrounding desert weren't an oppressive force hell bent on making me sweat away all my stored liquids.

There was a space directly around the shrine that one could stand if you were careful, so I took the leap and easily crossed the six-foot gap. My increased attributes were high enough now that I could easily deal with distances twice as long. My footing held and I reached out to touch the Mana Shrine. Immediately I felt a rush and a litany of options appeared after pushing my mind toward what I wanted to see, spell and skill options for distance attacks.

Filtering through some I'd already seen before, I began the slow process of identifying ones that might be useful, focusing on the Blade Master aspects of my class. There were a few I found interesting but didn't fit my current need. For example, Whirlwind Slash allowed me to hit all targets around me for moderate damage with only an 8 second cooldown, or Executioner's Blade, which worked like a more devastating version of Power Strike to enemies with less than half their health left. Both could be useful, but neither helped me with what I needed at this moment.

Then I saw something that held some promise, a skill called Phantom Thrust. At a cost of 25 Stamina, it would send out an ethereal spear-like projection from the tip of my weapon for 2 seconds after thrusting and activating the skill. It wasn't exactly what I wanted but it offered a way of extending my strike and with only a 6 second cooldown it offered some pretty consistent reach every 4 seconds. I kept looking, surely there would be a better option.

I found none, but I did uncover a few spells that offered alternatives. One such spell was called, Arcane Weapon, and I could pick a type of weapon per day to summon and act as my main weapon. So, in theory I could summon forth a lance or even a pike to hit from a farther distance, but I had so many damage buffs and such tied to my main bonded weapon that I couldn't convince myself to do it. Instead, I decided the two I'd learn, a spell and a skill because I needed to stay in balance, where going to be Phantom Thrust and Blink.

Blink was a spell that had just shown up as an available pick from my recent attribute increases. With an Intellect over 50 I was just barely able to learn it. What Blink did was allow me to move from my current location to someplace within sight every minute. The cooldown was harsh, but the spell was an instant cast and had huge potential outside its basic ability to move me from here to there. This was a spell Warrick had talked about before. Basically, it was needed if you ever wanted to learn how to make portals from one location to another.

The principles that allowed the portals lay within the same basic principles of the Blink spell. Portal magic was so rare as to be thought of as impossible to learn, but I'd just taken the first step down the path to learning portals. And I had access to Warrick, or I soon would, so he could help me along the way in learning how to operate portals. I confirmed my choices and knowledge, raw and powerful, filled my mind as I learned my two new abilities.

The advanced rune and spell casting involved in using Blink was astonishing, but all the knowledge I needed had been deposited in its raw form directly into my mind, I just needed to sort through it well enough to make true sense of it. It was like getting a puzzle solved for you, but the message on the puzzle being written in a language you only knew a few words to. I could read it sure, but that didn't mean it made perfect sense, especially when I tried to apply that knowledge to anything outside the operation of blink.

Instead of jumping the gap, I decided to try out my new spell, Blink. I visualized the place I wanted to be, then felt myself get pulled through space and time. A moment later, I stood where I'd imagined, and the spell was on cooldown. I'd need to practice for a bit so I could overcome the touch of nausea that came with using the spell, but other than that, everything had worked as expected.

Next, I squared off against a green plant and made ready to use my new skill, Phantom Thrust. I activated the skill and thrust forward, purposely ending my strike a solid foot and a half from my target. A blue-gray spectral blade appeared thrusting outward from the tip of my blade. It struck the plant in half and after a mere 2 seconds, shifted back into my sword. Two seconds went by far too quickly for my liking. I'd spent a total of thirty thousand essence to learn the new abilities, twenty of it coming from Blink, and used several expensive reagents from my inventory, so I wouldn't be able to take them to tier 2 just yet, but I'd need to for the thrust ability if I wanted it to be useful.

Skills and Spells became increasingly expensive the higher my level got and the more advanced the spells became. Some, like Blink, required a massive amount of essence, reagents, attribute levels, and so many prior spells to already be learned before you could get your hands on it. Luckily I had the required 10 spells, if just barely, to learn the Blink spell.

Ruelock City was less than a day's flight away and I was now more eager than ever to see Warrick. Mounting back atop Ares, we took to the skies and soon the city appeared in the distance. On our way, we'd crossed over the top of a massive army gathering forces to the East, but we increased our height to be well outside of their perceptibility. As we approached Ruelock City we decided it would be best to land a ways off and avoid startling the locals.

Much like the human cities, I imagined they'd attack flying targets on sight, prepared to be safe rather than sorry. So, doing much as we'd done before, I convinced Ares to return to her statue—an easier feat now that we were in an environment she disliked—and I walked alone up to the massive gate.

The city walls were as well-made and large as I remember, something that any House of Newaliyn might wish for their own cities. Standing a mighty twenty feet tall with guard towers built into it every hundred feet, it would be hard to ignore during a siege. One noticeable change was the lack of wagons and tents on the outside of the city any longer. Instead, several rows of spiked stone had been set into place, pointing out toward potential invaders.

The gates remained open, a stream of visitors and people departing as had been before, but there were several more guards, nearly a hundred, walking through the crowds and pulling people out at random. I'd made it all of a hundred feet toward the gate, when I was called out to stand aside and submit to a questioning and a search. The orcs who approached wore iron armor and red tabards with a wolf's head depicted in the center with two swords crossing behind it.

"I'm a friend of Chief Ruelock," I said, as nearly a dozen guards approached me with weapons drawn and leveled in my direction.

One of them perked up when he saw me and in broken common spoke to the others. "Seen this human before. He came with old man who has seat by Chief Ruelock."

This seemed to pacify the lot of them, but still I was asked several questions that I easily answered before they determined I was fit to enter their city. Simple ones like, do you have any fruit, are you here to kill us all, are you a part of the invading forces? Stuff like that.

The haphazard construction I remembered from before was still in full effect, except that several new tents filled the edges of many buildings now, refugees most likely with no place to go. The city was full to bursting, but still the orcs allowed more to enter and even made a point of questioning those who chose to leave. Walking through the packed streets I eventually made it to where I was looking to get, the red stone keep of Ruelock, the ruler of this city.

Walking right up to the two heavily armored guards I did as Warrick had done, speaking loudly and with authority. "I need audience with Chieftain Ruelock, immediately!"

"No," the guard on the right said. I even managed to get the same response as before. The guard's eyes ran over me and a flicker of recognition ignited in his eyes.

Before I could come up with a response, the guard and the one on the left shared whispered words, and the leftmost guard opened the door and entered, leaving me and righty by ourselves. We stood in awkward silence for nearly a minute before I attempted any conversation.

"So, how goes the war?" I asked. Really I should have stopped by someplace and gotten a bit more information from the locals before I went straight to Warrick, but I was tired and impatient, wanting nothing more than to catch up with my friend.

Righty didn't seem interested in conversing and merely grunted at me in response. So, I waited another two minutes in silence before lefty made his way back, with none other than Warrick at his side.

"Good memory, Gar'rignac," Warrick called out, slapping the orc lightly on the back in congratulations. "This is indeed one of the soft skins I traveled with before arriving in your fair city and it is good you didn't try to strike him down as you wanted. I fear he is your match in fighting power if not in magical knowledge."

Gar'rignac looked me over again and scoffed but said nothing else.

"Warrick!" I stepped forward and pulled my friend into a hug, however, I passed right through him, stumbling nearly to the ground. This got a round of chuckling from the guards.

"Oh sorry, my boy." Warrick shifted and turned to look down at me. "I'm here only in projection. Gar'rignac will you show you up to my quarters, and have someone bring me more tea will you?"

Gar'rignac nodded his head once at the projection of Warrick and turned into the keep, walking at a hurried pace. I followed after, watching as Warrick's visage dissipated into nothing but colored sand that collected on the ground. The orc didn't slow for me, so I hurried my pace and did my best to keep up with his near jogging pace.

The inside of the keep was much what I remembered, a labyrinth of turns and hallways, doors set into the wall here and there at random, but not much foot traffic. It was after a minute of walking that we neared a room with a sturdy looking wooden door set into it, instead of the usual cloth that hung over most of the doors we passed. Gar'rignac inclined his head to the door and turned, leaving me alone.

I understood well enough and knocked on the door. From inside came a voice I knew all too well. "Enter."

Pulling the door open I found Warrick, sitting alone in a bed with covers up to his waist and a cup of tea in his hands. At least I assumed it was tea, because it was being served in very crude looking metal cups that looked just as likely to hold some kind of ale.

"Are you not well?" I asked, standing beside his bed.

"I've more need to rest than to stand about while nothing is done," Warrick said, shaking his head.

What did he mean about nothing being done? Perhaps the time he'd spent hadn't been as fruitful as I imagined it would be. "I've come with urgent news, but first, there is so much I want to hear and need to tell you."

Warrick looked at me, his blue eyes twinkling with unknown wisdom and power. "You've changed a fair bit, my boy." His soothing baritone voice was a welcome sound to my ears. "This change is what your father feared, I believe. It is a shame I couldn't prevent it."

Suddenly it was like I'd taken several hits right into my stomach, as much of the emotional baggage I'd been dealing with rushed to the surface. There were few I felt like I could discuss literally anything with, but Warrick was one of them. So, I did just that, starting with the beginning of the war and even a few weeks before. I told him everything, even going so far as to recite the names of the dead I'd memorized. I told him of how that terrible weapon had been used and my own discoveries had aided in the use of it.

He did as he always did, offering no words of comfort during the telling, but nodding along wisely at the words poured out of me. It had been at least an hour into talking before I got him up to speed, by telling him about how I'd picked up Blink and was excited to learn about how to create portals or teleport now. This got him to raise an eyebrow and finally speak.

"It will be long in the learning of it, but I can teach you and set you on the right path. But first, I must tell you something very important."

I still had tears threatening to pour out of my eyes from the retelling of events and I braced myself for a rebuke of my idiocy for allowing such a weapon to be created.

Warrick set his cup aside and pulled me down into a warm hug. In my ear he whispered, "You have put a great weight on your shoulders, and you have stood strong. Remember that sometimes all we can be asked to do is stand. No greater task can be asked of us somedays. Know that your father would be proud of you. But if you intend to bring justice on the head of Lord Variyn, remember the path you walk is one of balance." He looked at me knowingly, releasing me from his tight hug. "If he must die to balance the scales, then have no doubt that your father, if we ever find him, would stand at your side as you mete justice."

It had taken great effort not to breakdown during the telling of my tale, but now it was too much, and I broke under the weight of Warrick's words. He hadn't rebuked me after all, even going so far as to say that my father would stand by my side when the time came to face Lord Variyn...it was all too much to believe, and I bawled like a child at the thought of it. Warrick patted my back while I cried and I knew that I didn't have to feel shame in his presence, he supported me in all I did, and I loved him for it.

After a time, I pulled myself together and despite

trusting that I could shed tears without judgement, I felt a bit silly. I cleared my throat and averted my eyes when I asked my question. "So, tell me, how has the war been here in the south?"

Warrick's telling of events took much the same amount of time but filled with more frustrations than anything else. Because of what I'd done by challenging the dungeon, they'd agreed to go to war, but they never said when they'd go. There had been some small skirmishes with both sides, but Chief Ruelock was dead set on having an army big enough to deal with all the threats before marching into battle. It was an admirable approach, but one that Warrick didn't agree with. I stopped him mid explanation to tell him of Creed's brother's forces and how they'd be willing to join with the Southlanders against the forces of the East.

He took the knowledge in stride, finishing his retelling of events and ending with how he'd interceded in the last battle, which is why he was bedridden currently. Apparently there had been a battle between some of the stronger Wild-Sparks and many thousands of troops, when their combined forces made a play to get closer to Ruelock City. Ruelock himself had marched out to battle and Warrick attended him as an advisor, however, two dozen Wild-Sparks had tried to attack the commanders and Chief, forcing Warrick's hand.

He said he'd been forced to slay all but one of them, as well as wipe out half of their combined forces, while in turn he'd expended a great deal of stored mana that would take him literal months to replenish. I still didn't understand the full damage done to Warrick from that wretched Chaos

Knight, but whatever she'd done it hadn't stopped his ability to wreak havoc upon the enemy, merely slowed him down in the recovery period.

"You see," Warrick continued, "if you truly have any forces you can bring to bear, I think that we might be at an end of this conflict. We must only convince this Chaos General who leads the Easterners that we are more of a challenge than that of the Beastkin they claim to face in their own lands. Once that is done, I think a treaty of sorts might even be able to be put in place. Perhaps the path to peace is turning our armies against the beastkin who've caused such a stir in their need for expansion."

"Should we meet with Ruelock and inform him of the plan?" I asked, Warrick nodded and a perfect copy of him appeared next to the bed.

"Let's go," his duplicate said, and I saw that Warrick had drifted off into some type of deep sleep on the bed.

I nodded and we departed, the projection of Warrick leading the way.

CHAPTER 18
SHOW OF STRENGTH

Several weeks passed and finally our plan was ready to execute. We'd gotten Ruelock to agree easily enough and now Warrick would be opening portals to allow Nefrah's troops to join forces with the mass of Southerners. And I, with great difficulty, tried to open a portal to Blackridge Keep. I'd successfully teleported only hours before, but Warrick claimed that if I could teleport then I could open a stable portal. It took an insane amount of Mana, but the gem Merlin had given me was doing just fine in giving me enough to work with, so I did as Warrick commanded.

I concentrated on the phrases and focus that I needed to teleport, then tried to imagine a doorway between the two places, that would allow for the entrance to be seen by others as well. Despite his claims that it should be easy once I'd done the initial teleportation, I found myself not up to the task after five hours of trying.

"You'll learn, just give it time," Warrick assured me,

taking the gem I'd been using and tapping into it. I described Blackridge Keep to him and he said he'd been to the village and keep before, so he'd be able to connect a portal. Then he proceeded to summon one in five seconds, which I couldn't do in five hours.

With the portal open, I stepped through and was happy to find my troops all in formation. They knew what lay ahead and despite my promise that if all went well no blood would need to be shed, I urged them to say their goodbyes all the same.

"Remember all we've learned of war, the glory, the power, and the loss." My words carried over the area, enhanced by my simple spell. "If all is done right, this battle will be won before a single sword must fall. But if a blade is needed to be drawn, I want you to know that mine will be the first to taste blood and the last to be put away!"

The men cheered at this simple notion that they'd grown to expect from me. I would never ask them to do what I wasn't willing to do myself and I'd always make sure I was the last one fighting. There was a certain feeling that came with knowing your commander was fighting beside you, that the men had tried to express, but I understood well enough. Knowing that they fought beside me gave me all the strength I needed.

"Onward into battle!" I yelled, turning atop Ares and marching for the portal. Warrick had made it big enough that we could now fit an entire column of men at a time into the portal, but even at that speed it would take some time to move the troops.

If I'd had this power during the war, the ability to make portals from here or there, I imagined I'd have been able to end the conflict much swifter and without the need of such a terrible weapon.

We joined an already massive force of orcs, goblins, trolls, and humans all in formation and ready to march on command. Our forces filtered into the open fields behind the armies, but from the raised hill we arrived on the entire battlefield could be seen before us. An army only half our size made up of Easterners stood before us, probably quaking in their boots as my legions came through to join an even bigger force. It was telling that all around the enemy forces dark clouds sat low over them, like a deep gloom that wouldn't be expelled.

My knights stood beside me, and I welcomed an unexpected sight by way of one of my knights. I'd invited him to serve as a knight if he wished but didn't actually expect him to take me up on the offer. Cam stood in full plate armor— helmet visor up—, his new hands working well beneath gauntleted armor. He held a massive two-handed sword with ease, it was long enough that it might be able to be used like a spear—which also happened to be the only weapon I knew he was fully trained on.

He refused any land ownership, wishing only to take the roll of knight so that he could serve his fellow soldiers, a condition that I accepted. He was one of two other knights that had refused land holdings and I wasn't Lord Variyn, so I wouldn't force it on them if they didn't want it. I had to stop that train of thought, it wasn't helpful, and I'd taken the lands freely and willingly when it wasn't such a burden, so I would deal with the consequences now.

"His new arms have increased strength?" I asked, looking to Kora who stood armored with two of her own second in commands by my side. The three Runeforged turned to regard me at the same time, their heads moving in an eerily synchronized fashion.

"The essence infusing his muscles will likely make his general strength increase two or three-fold, however, his grip strength will rival that of a Runeforged, so well beyond that of a normal human," Ventus said, Kora looking at him with an inclined head as he chose to speak before she got a chance.

"That is correct," Kora added, before regarding the approaching knight with a curious expression. "I believe his new weapon will be much more suited for him. He has no worry of cutting his hand flesh as it has been upgraded, so he could easily use the large weapon as a spear or a sweeping sword."

"He'll be able to cut three men in half with that sword and still not put himself in a precarious situation," I said, smiling at Cam as he drew close.

My knights all drew close, and I addressed them.

"Good to see you at my side, are your men ready?" I asked. Each of them knew what I expected of them and though they each commanded much less men—I had many more knights than previously. Plus, we had a surprisingly high number of new recruits. Our forces numbered just under three thousand, southlanders having no issues with sending their young and women into battle. I'd made sure that only those of the proper age by Newaliyn standards were given permission to come, but I know a few must have snuck by, so determined they were to fight.

I'd even managed to get several more humans than before to volunteer and it got to the point where we ran low on tabards, arms, and armor when all accounting was said and done. In theory, we looked like a pretty massive force of reinforcements, when in fact we were an untrained mass of peasants posing as true soldiers. But the enemy didn't need to know that, and I'd had them spend the last few days drilling march patterns into them and how to stand, so by first glance we looked damn impressive.

I bid my knights farewell, they left calling orders to get the soldiers into formation behind the gathered forces. I took Kora with me to join up with Creed, Lord Nefrah, Warrick, Chief Ruelock, and many more in the Commanders tent set in the middle of the gathered forces. Why they felt like they needed a tent on such a peacefully cool day, I couldn't say, but I went.

Fred, Fran, Ismene, Emory, and dozens more Awakened stood guard around the tent, and I was surprised to see Zander inside conversing with Lord Nefrah. Perhaps he'd decided to bring forces to bear as well, despite his reluctance from before.

"Welcome, Lord Miles," Lord Nefrah said, inclining his head. He looked in a much better mood than I'd last seen him at the border to the Southlands.

"Ah, Caldor," Zander said, grinning in my direction. He walked over and said in a lower tone, but still loud enough any Awakened ears would make out. "I decided to bring over a thousand troops just to spite my uncle who declared this conflict, 'none of our business'. I'm sure by knowing you so well, you've brought ,what? Several more thousand and perhaps a dragon to fight for us?"

I chuckled, I liked this new non-asshat version of Zander and anything that spited his uncle was something I approved of. "Three thousand soldiers, but alas, no dragon," I said, grinning back.

We moved back to the main table where they talked of troop movements and such. Warrick stood across the table and focusing I determined that he was actually here, which meant he'd used his visage to open the portal and that explained how he'd disappeared so fast afterward. Damn, Warrick was so powerful that I couldn't even wrap my head around his so casual use of magic.

He caught my eye and winked at me. From here, the plan was pretty simple, we'd march forward and offer the opposing side a chance to speak terms. If they chose to challenge us, we were banking on the fact they wouldn't, then we'd pound them into the ground. I pitied whoever came at us first, as we had several hundred Runeforged mixed into the front lines ready to obliterate any opposition.

Kora joined us at the table with her two Runeforged, only one I knew the name to, Ventus.

I looked across the table and inclined my head to all those gathered. "Time to see how they react." With that, we set our plan into motion.

CHAPTER 19
PARLAY

The wind whipped at the banners each side carried as we met in the middle of the arrayed armies. On our side, we'd agreed to bring myself, Chief Ruelock, Creed, Zander, Lord Nefrah, Warrick, and upon her own insistence, Kora, to meet with the opposing army's commanders. One figure out of the nine approaching from the opposing side stood out, being at least a foot or two taller than the next tallest and clad in black armor that seemed to sheath with black mist.

"Is that a Chaos..." I was about to ask, but Warrick leaned in and finished my thought.

"A Chaos Knight, yes. However, if this army is led by him, then where is the Chaos Lord?" Warrick said, his head inclining barely to one side as he pondered over this new information. "Surely a new one has been appointed since Elkor slew the last one."

"I thought Elkor Miles slew a lich?" Zander asked. He

stood next to us and clearly had no problem eavesdropping on our not so private conversation. Creed had also heard and was looking a bit perplexed as well.

"Did he really kill the previous Chaos Lord?" I asked. Scratching my head at the fact that he had never told me this before. Then it hit me that he had inadvertently told me. But because the weight of the news I was getting about my father possibly being alive it had all but slipped my mind, only now thinking back to the conversation did I recall him saying that my father had slew a Chaos Lord, not a lich as I'd first believed.

"Oh, ah yes, I told you didn't I, I could have sworn I had," Warrick said, brushing it off as if it were nothing important. "Be ready Caldor, your time is coming."

The delegation from the opposing army arrived and I stepped forward. It had been Warrick's idea to have me speak to them, but I was unsure why the responsibility should come to me. My nerves were calm and my heartbeat steady, I was ready.

Before I had a chance to speak, the large armored one summoned forth a huge sword out of nowhere and slammed it into the ground. All around, the earth blackened and died. But no one attacked, just the ground continuing to blacken. So, I did what I felt was the right move. I summoned my sword then slammed it into the ground while casting Restoring Light through my sword and into the ground. It pulsed a white light all around and ate back at the blackened ground.

Our two swords stood and the area in the ground that

they seeped into, created a sort of half circle of black and white that sat before us. The Chaos Knight laughed, his voice ethereal and echoing.

"I suspected that one of your kind were present, it seems to always be the case," his words were that of a smooth baritone, very much opposite of what I'd have thought, and his manner of speech was rather refined, like a lord trained to speak any words as if they were special.

"Where is your leader?" I asked, going off script from what we'd planned. What Warrick had said was bugging me and I needed more intel on why the Chaos Lord wouldn't be present.

"I am the leader," he growled. "My name is Lucian Vargas. General of this great Army and your downfall, Knight of the Ordu." Lucian looked at me with disdain from out of his raised helmet visor. From what I could see of the man, which was very little, he had pale, pink skin and eyes that gave off a slight reddish glow as he stared down at me. Standing roughly a foot taller than me, it would be easy to be intimidated by him, but I felt nothing but humor rising in my chest.

"I've seen many battles won, but you must have great faith in your numbers if you think to oppose us in direct battle. How many lives are you willing to give to see that you are victorious? I hope the answer is all of them, because you won't win this day," I spoke the words boldly and let a touch of arrogance slip into my tone, as we'd planned.

Warrick was our expert on all things Chaos Knight related and they had a pride that would allow them to be pulled about if you played it right. The trick, Warrick said, was to not push them so far that they felt like they'd need to prove a point. I hoped I hadn't already taken it too far.

Lucian Vargas raised his hands and lifted his helmet from his face. I stifled a gasp, but I heard Creed let one out and this made the Chaos Knight smile. He had a jagged scar across his face, along with a mess of smaller ones that turned his face into a mess of white lines. This was a man who'd either been tortured his entire life or enjoyed torturing himself. I couldn't see any other parts of his skin, but I imagined they were in a similar condition.

"You're right, the forces you've gathered are great and I think my only hope in winning this day lies in a bit of chaos," he smiled, and all those around him pulled swords. "What happens when I kill all of you, will your forces be driven to the wind perhaps? Confused at how to act when the head of the snake has been cut free? Shall we find out?"

This time, I heard a laugh from none other than Warrick, so boisterous was it that it had me laughing a bit as well. I turned to see him almost belly over in his laughter.

"This old codger ought to think what his last words will be, because I will end him first," Lucian said as he pulled out the sword from the ground. The laughter suddenly ceased, and energy crackled thickly all around us. A barrier formed and Warrick leaned on his staff before speaking, all humor gone from his voice.

"Break through this barrier and I'll stop laughing at your pitiful weakness. Don't play me for a fool, Lucian," Warrick practically spit his name, "You can feel well enough the power our combined delegation holds. I could all but disintegrate your entire envoys with a thought, only leaving you for young Miles here so he might learn the joy of killing Chaos Knights."

This caused Lucian Vargas to visibly shudder and take a step back. Perhaps he wasn't so good at bluffing as he first thought. I smiled at the sheer show of force, and it wasn't missed by Lucian.

"You think you can take me, young Knight?" Lucian said, a grin appearing on his grim looking face. "Then perhaps you'd be willing to stake your armies success on a duel to the death? I'm willing to die for my cause, are you?"

I don't know what effect Lucian hoped this would elicit but I was all for the idea of dueling to decide a battle. However, that wasn't the plan, and I reluctantly looked to Warrick as he nodded his head, 'no'.

"I have no need to duel you when our forces so greatly outnumber yours. Surrender the field and take your forces back into the Easternlands. Do this and we might be open to an alliance against the forces that you flee from." I made sure to add the last little bit as an insult, meaning to spur him onward.

It worked.

Lucian's face went from angry to considerate within a flash of a moment and a smile crossed his face as he looked on our combined forces with new eyes. "Perhaps you are right. Our homeland is where we ought to be, if you are truly willing to join forces against one such as I?" His eyes went to Warrick as if he knew who truly had the most power here now.

Warrick gave him a curt nod and Lucian inclined his head ever so slightly, something mischievous played behind that mask of scars he wore but I couldn't put my finger on it.

The air crackled from a sudden energy, as Lucian's blade came down and struck the barrier. All nine of his companions fell backward from the blowback, but the barrier held, and we felt no effect of it. Again, and again the Chaos Knight smashed into the barrier, but it didn't crack and finally while panting heavily, he spoke.

"It would appear I am outmatched. Promise me this wizard will be at the battles with us and you have a truce," Lucian said, the frenzy that had been there just a moment ago, now gone as quick as it had come.

I recognized one of the people in his retinue as they stood, and I called out to him.

"Jared Nullspar, since we have a truce perhaps, you'd be willing to join me in my tent for drinks and words," I said the words and only remembered after, that Warrick had cleared their mind of our meeting.

Lucian looked hard at Jared, his gaze speaking volumes. Before Jared had the opportunity to speak, Lucian was weaving words together on his behalf. "Jared of the Nullspar clan gladly welcomes the invitation to exchange information. But only if you take young Elana as well." The shortest and smallest of the nine, a girl that looked no older than fourteen, and that was stretching it, stepped forward with a blank look on her face.

I shared a look with Warrick, who shrugged and spoke, "That is agreeable." I had hoped to ask Jared more about the Chaos Lord and his possible whereabouts, but with this newcomer and the fact his mind had been wiped of our first meeting, I wondered how successful my ploy would be after all.

The group split then, the small girl, Elana, with her over-sized black robes and dead looking eyes stood back while Jared looked on in awkward silence. The barrier finally faded, and I could see by the way he sagged on his staff how much of a toll the spell and the teleporting had taken on Warrick, despite him keeping a strong face.

"How do you know me, Knight of the Ordu?" Jared asked, coming up to stand beside me.

"We met months before, around the time you lost a team member I believe," I said, not sure how much I should give up or how angry it might make him if I told him the truth.

"Allow me to help," Warrick said, waving his hand.

Jared's eyes went wide and suddenly he looked on with fear toward Warrick, then to me. He stuttered out a few words before finally finding his tongue. "You." Were the only words he managed as we walked back to camp, the small girl quiet all the while.

The day, despite the dark clouds that circled over the Easterners' camp, was rather sunny everywhere else. It felt good to feel the cool air mixed with the warm sun on my face and I savored the feeling while I could.

I caught a look from Warrick, which I took to mean he was going to be watching over me, despite not following me.

I found my tent newly risen toward the back of my forces and entered to find Emory and Fred drinking alone, an odd sight to be sure.

"So, it's like I was saying," Emory said, his hand over Fred's shoulder while Fred looked absolutely terrified, "It's all about how you approach the matter and not really what you say anyway."

I cleared my throat and Emory, clearly half-drunk already, stood swiftly squinting his eyes at me. "Did we win?" He asked, smiling stupidly.

"Emory and Fred," I said by way of introductions. Jared raised a hand in polite greetings, but the little girl Elana just scrunched her forehead while staring at Fred's fair complexion and white hair.

CHAPTER 20
CHAOS LORD

F red helped Emory from the tent and gave me his best apologetic look, which from Fred wasn't much more than a constipated glance. I'd never seen the pair hanging out exclusively and it made me wonder what odd circumstance had led to their gathering. Turning to Jared, he wore plate armor over loose dark blue cloth that also made up his hood and cloak around his shoulders. Once more, I was surprised by his elven features and wondered what circumstances brought an elf to the Easternlands.

Handing him over a drink, he sniffed at it apprehensively but gave it a sip after a moment or two. I offered a drink to the dead-eyed girl, but she looked at the cup like she'd rather eat it whole than drink whatever liquid resided inside.

"So, how common are elves in your lands?" I asked, gesturing to my ears. His hair was pulled up into a tight bun and his ears were clearly visible. It seemed an innocent enough question, as all other easterners I'd encountered had been humans, but Jared cast his eyes down at the mention of it.

We drank in silence for several long seconds before he responded. With a sigh he said, "My tribe is one of the last elven settlements, but soon even they will be gone, leaving by great ships to the old lands as many others have done. It is only the humans and their quick breeding that keep our lands filled with life. I am sort of an outsider among my people because of the circumstances of my birth."

I connected the dots before he said it and blurted out what he must be. "You're a half elf then." I didn't mean to blurt it out and sound so insensitive, but it occurred to me that I'd read about how rare half breeds were and they normally weren't accepted easily into the elven courts after birth. It had been a stray mentioning in a book directed at monsters found within the elven realms.

"Indeed, I am," Jared said, he seemed to swell with pride and met my eyes in challenge.

I nodded sagely at him, knowing his path must have been one of great difficulty in a place where elves were already so rare. "I can imagine your path must have been a challenging one, but you seem to have risen to the top well enough."

"Indeed, I have," Jared said, then relaxing a bit he glanced over at the girl—she currently walked around the tent and poked at the exterior several times. "How long are you to interrogate us before we can return to our people?"

I sighed; this wasn't going as I'd planned at all. "This isn't an interrogation," I assured him, meeting his eyes with my own and hoping that he could see the genuine look there. "Although, I do have some questions that I'd like you to answer."

"Let's get on with it," Jared said, a smirk rising on his face. He wasn't so annoyed about it as he was putting on. He drank deeply of the ale I'd provided him before placing the mug gently on the table we sat at, and fixed me with his best stare.

"Let's start with the Wild-Sparks," I said, not remembering the name they'd given themselves but sure he'd correct me.

"Venshti," Jared corrected. "What would you know of us?"

"You mentioned in our last encounter that you challenged dungeons, how could that be? Dungeons are creations of the Ordu and as such, only *Awakened* can enter their halls."

Jared's smirk deepened. "Dungeons are more natural than you've been told. It is true that we cannot enter dungeons in this part of the Wyrd, not yet at least. I believe, as do many in my clan and other Venshti clans, that if we turn enough waystones, the dungeons will open to all as they have in the past. But now we must return to our lands and reclaim lost territory from the bestial forces that have washed over our lands and slain our people."

This flew in the face of what I knew to be true, and I suddenly wished I had Kora at my side to question her regarding it. I half stood, ready to go find Kora and bring her in on the conversation but thought better of it. "Assuming what you are saying is true, can anyone challenge a dungeon in the East?"

"Only Venshti have the power to survive a dungeon and, even so, it is with great care, as dungeons are dangerous places to even the most well trained Venshti. In fact, I know some even in my own clan that have never set foot into a dungeon, preferring to hunt out the dens of monsters and slay the queens that lay in wait. I have answered a question for you, now you will return the favor. Tell me, is it true that you have tens of thousands who have been, what did you call it, *Awakened*?"

I rubbed at the back of my neck, I had no idea if what Warrick had said was true, but I remember the claim he gave, and it surprised me as well. To think that there were so many *Awakened* seemed a bit off. "I think Warrick listed off how many we had before the last great war with Chaos, the Chaos Lord brought against us demons, and other creatures that slew our *Awakened* by the thousands. I'd probably guess that in the human nations alone, we have several thousand adventurers, but I can't speak of the elven nations. I know that in Newaliyn, every week we add several dozen if not hundreds of new adventurers to the fold."

Jared shook his head, clearly still in shock. "I wonder how we might get access to an *Awakening* and if it could save the hundreds of lives lost each year to the spark."

It was my turn to appear confused. "By the sound of it, you go through a similar process as us, you just never *Awaken* so instead you learn to harness your spark's wild powers. I don't know enough about it to really say, but I'd be interested for sure to see what would happen if you interacted with a Prime Mana Shrine. It's like the waystones you speak of, but a bit bigger than normal and every month or so it glows bright with gathered power. You have any of those?"

"All waystones I've encountered have looked the same, I don't recall ever seeing one as you describe," Jared said, his brow scrunched in concentration.

The young girl had been silent up until now and she scoffed, rolling her eyes when I looked over at her. "Prime Mana Shrines are under the control of the Dark Mountain and the Council of Chaos. No Venshti would ever be given permission to view their majesty."

"Who are you?" Jared asked, turning on her suddenly and power crackling around him. This was a surprising turn of events and I watched with more than passing curiosity.

"As if you don't suspect," she said, her voice like oil dripping out of a rusty pot, not at all young like she appeared.

"A spy for the general no doubt. Here to report what secrets I divulge, but you've heard my words. I say nothing that is not general knowledge to any common citizen. They will have heard it all from those they've captured. Slink off and tell your master as much."

I had a sudden idea, and turned on the small, cloaked figure pretending to be a small innocent girl. "Is your master the Chaos Lord? What can you tell me about his plans and intentions?"

She whirled to face me, her eyes now deep pools of red and flickering black, much like the two other Chaos Knights I'd encountered. "The fool that sits as the Chaos Lord knows not our ways and does nothing but spread dissension among our ranks." She was practically spitting the words. "That is why the Council of Chaos has been so successful these last ten years." She cackled a laugh, her mouth held open and a hunger burning in her eyes. "If not for that rebellious little stain of a Chaos Knight, Vikari, and her small retinue of followers, we might have even been able to take over the Dark Mountain's seat of power back from the pretender, but the might of a Chaos Lord is a bonfire compared to the flickering candle flame of a Chaos Knight."

This was all very useful information, but I immediately wondered why she'd be sharing it so freely. Jared seemed to be having the same thought as he stood and drew his sword.

"You mean to dispatch us, but you will find me no easy target and this Knight of the Ordu can likely turn you aside without much effort," Jared spoke in a terse manner as he regarded the diminutive girl.

I could feel power pulsing off her now and I stood as well, my sword coming to my hand in an instant. An atmospheric tear began to form behind her and in it I saw Chaos Beasts lurking in a void of red and black. But just as it opened, a moment later it snapped shut and the girl fell right on her ass. Warrick walked in, leaning on his staff and looking around the tent with a hint of annoyance.

"Who's working such shoddy portal magic in here? Caldor, I thought I told you to only try portals when I could supervise! Oh, excuse me little lady are you alright?" Warrick asked, offering a hand to the fallen Chaos Knight.

She grimaced and stood, ignoring his hand. Her forehead scrunched in concentration, but nothing happened. What Warrick did next nearly made me laugh out loud. He tapped her on the forehead with his staff and said, "You should be careful trying to wield such dangerous magics, you might get hurt."

She wobbled on her feet and fell back to her bottom with a soft thump. Her face shifted from perplexed to angry to just plain confused.

It was clear she meant to kill me and possibly Jared, so her telling us any secrets hadn't mattered, but now that she'd failed so miserably, I was sure she regretted giving up the nuggets of information she'd divulged.

"So, the Chaos Lord doesn't rule this army, but rather a council of Chaos Knights?" I asked, letting my sword disappear and crouching down beside her.

She nodded, looking defeated, then spoke. "We are not so different, you and I."

"Oh? And how is that?" I asked, Warrick took a seat, keeping an eye on the offending Chaos summoner.

"We may be prone to Chaos and the unpredictability that comes with it, but in the end, our mission is to maintain the balance. We brought the armies of our greatest nations upon your land to ensure the balance was kept. If we don't claim this land or reclaim our lost land, a greater evil than anything this world has ever known will descend upon us."

My dreams, terrible and filled with images of dark beings traveling between the stars flashed in my mind. I knew suddenly who she meant, but how did they know this information when I'd only heard of it in dreams.

Warrick spoke up, surprising me. "You speak of the Final Vielkrea when the sky will turn black and the very ground beneath our feet will burn as if molten. This is a myth and will not come to pass."

I knew of the Vielkrea, or the last great war between Chaos and Order when the Ordu themselves fought by our sides, but the final Vielkrea was new to me. As far as I knew there was only a single Vielkrea and it happened so long ago to be nothing more than myth and fable.

The small female Chaos Knight scoffed at Warrick, doing an odd sign with her right hand that I didn't recognize. "You are a fool. A powerful fool, but a fool, nonetheless. Our mystics have known for years that the time was coming, the last Chaos Lord believed the only way to stop it was to unite the lands. However, his brand of uniting the Wyrd wasn't up to your liking, and you slew him. This new Chaos Lord has the vast power of Chaos at his fingertips but chooses to sit on it, forcing our hand. But it is enough that he doesn't rise against us, for if he wished, he has the power to sweep us aside like chaff in the wind."

"You have a loose tongue for someone who tried to kill me just moments ago," I said, trying to see beyond the young-faced girl and into the Chaos Knight beneath. It was hard to see her as much more than a lost child, an angry lost child, but a child all the same.

"I tell you now, so that you might see our paths are aligned. I do not guess at your motivations or how true your word is regarding the aid you promised in the East, but if you are sincere, we will accept your assistance. I give you my word, as the true General and leader of this conquest. My name is Lilith Cragborn, leader of the Council of Chaos and would-be ally to the Knight of the Ordu."

She stood again, this time her form shifting as she stood, her hood fell back, revealing a woman in her early twenties with crystal white hair. Her bosom filled out considerably and I looked away as the top part of her loose attire stretched to contain them.

"Shall we make a formal agreement?" She asked, her voice had not changed at all but now more fitting to her appearance.

"I can see to it," I said, nodding to Warrick as I left the tent to gather up the proper folk to draw up a formal alliance or some document stating we'd offer aid in exchange for something, though I knew not what to ask for, personally. I was sure Lord Nefrah would come up with something advantageous for each party.

I made myself busy with other things, not even bothering to go to the signing of the new alliance or accord, as they were calling it. It was simple enough, for the sum cost of whatever troops were deployed, meaning wages, gear, food, etc. the nation of House Nefrah and Ruelock's combined forces would march into the Easternlands, plus a small mark up on cost for the benefits of the House Nefrah and Ruelock treasury. As promised, the next day the forces of the East began to retreat, but several of Lord Nefrah's and Ruelock's troops left with them, part of the first wave of support.

I met with Creed and learned that he would be returning

to adventuring for the foreseeable future, and he asked if I wanted to run a dungeon with him. Asking his level, I learned he too had grown significantly during this time of conflict, however at 25 he was still several levels below me. I told him my plans, an idea I had that I hoped would pan out, to bring news of the easterners' retreat to the king himself in hopes that he might order more aid to push back the beastkin armies. I didn't know if it was a foolhardy mission, but I told Creed and all of my friends to meet me in Variyn City, because I had big plans when I got back. I impressed upon them that I'd need all their help if I was to manage my plans, and they all agreed wholeheartedly.

So, as it were, I found myself on the road so to speak, since I was technically flying high above it, and on my way to visit the King of Newaliyn. I only hoped that words of my deeds were enough to grant me an audience with someone so powerful as the King.

CHAPTER 21
KING'S GUARD

I couldn't teleport to the capital city of Newaliyn as I'd never been there, but I had managed to teleport to Cree-shaw and fly south from there. It cut at least a day or two off my trip, but as I flew into the borders of the capital, I marveled at how many large cities and towns dotted the landscape. I passed over at least a dozen cities half the size of Variyn city, before I neared the grand capital.

Most of the northern bit of Newaliyn territory was laden with thick forest, but cities were still easy enough to spot, like little pock marks on the face of the land. What I didn't expect, was on the final day when entering closer to the capital, a squad of soldiers appeared around me, each of them riding black pegasus, except the lead rider who flew atop a griffin nearly twice the size of Ares and with white and brown feathers.

They signaled for me to land, and just looking at the lances they carried with their barbed ends was enough to get me to comply. It would only take a strike or two from one of those to render Ares unable to fly until I healed her. The skies were blue and clear, yet I hadn't seen them approach and neither had Ares. It was like one moment the sky around us was empty and the next they appeared on our flanks.

The terrain below was all open meadows and grassy fields, with farmlands cut into the distant horizon. Past those farmlands, and now out of sight as we descended to the ground below, lay the city of Newaliyn and the seat of power for King Newaliyn. He has ruled for over a hundred years and his father before him ruled a hundred years, but from what little I knew about the King, he had no offspring of his own, so his rule might end with him. But that was the thing about *Awakened* individuals, they could live hundreds of years if they didn't fall in battle and there had been no major threat to the king in the last one hundred years.

I knew very little about how his father had died, but it had been in battle. Once again I wished I had someone who was a student of history with me to fill in the gaps of my ignorance. Alayna would be nice to have around right now.

Alayna.

How I ached to know how she was doing, that she was safe and not in the clutches of her father, yet I found myself pulled this way or that not able to go to Variyn City just yet. But soon, after I convinced the king to help in the Easternlands, I'd go seek her out.

"Submit under the authority of the King's Guard," a

heavily armored man said, his voice like iron and his lance pointed right for my face.

I lifted my helmet off my head and clipped it to my belt. "I am Caldor Miles. Baron Lord of House Variyn and slayer of Chaos Beasts. I seek an audience with King Newaliyn." I infused my words with as much confidence as I could muster, despite the precarious situation I found myself in.

The rider atop the griffin pulled his helmet off as well and a blonde mane of hair fell to his shoulders. He had a face cut of marble, all rigid edges and solid smooth skin. His gaze burned into me with power similar to what I'd felt from Warrick when he cut loose. Immediately I knew that this man was an Awakened and extremely powerful.

"Are you truly Caldor Miles?" He asked, he had a manly voice, deep and resonating.

"I am."

"Well met." He saluted me, then went even further to incline his head a fraction of a hair in my direction. "My name is Gavin Melantis and I am captain of the King's Guard. I've heard much of your exploits from Lord Marco Busard and Gadwell, both hold you up in high regard. Tell me, why do you wish audience with the king?"

"It is urgent business that concerns the balance of Order and Chaos," I said, not sure how much I should divulge. When my response got nothing but a raised eyebrow from the captain of the King's Guard, I hesitantly continued. "The conflict at the southern border has been resolved. The Easterners have been pushed out of the southlands, which will stop the southlanders from pushing further into

Newaliyn. Furthermore, a truce unlike any before has been formed with the Easterners but it is reliant on our aid in their conflict against the invading forces of the beastkin nations."

By the look on the guard captain's face, I'd said too much, but he nodded slowly looking to some of his other guardsmen before smiling. "Surely you jest?"

"I am utterly serious," I said, not liking the humorous look the man had on his face.

"Well, Lord Miles, you have a right to request an audience with the king, but I'd work on your story first. Think of something far more believable than what I just heard. But before I send you on your way, I must ask something of you." The guard captain's smile disappeared, and he looked at me with a very serious expression. "Will you consider joining the King's Guard? I could use someone as raw and powerful as you. You'd lose claim to your lands, but the title of King's Guard holds more weight than even a baron of one of the lesser Houses."

He cleared his throat before continuing, "Furthermore, I could train you to your full potential. You might not know this, but the King's Guard are considered to be the most elite force in all of the Wyrd. You will not find any among the ranks of nobility or adventurers that can match our strength or cunning in battle. What say you?"

I say I was surprised is what I wanted to say, but I held my tongue. Instead, I looked at the man and those he had around him. Each and every one of them radiated power in such a way that I did not doubt their claims. I wouldn't be surprised to learn that each of them was close to level one hundred even, if not lower with higher attributes. Their armor was plain, but I suspected that their weapons and armor had grand enchantments on them as well, ways to increase their strength and speed beyond their natural limits.

"Just like that and you'd take me on as a King's Guard?" I asked, shaking my head ever so slightly at the perplexing nature of such a request.

"I tried to recruit your father many times, so once I'd learned that he had a son, I've been looking for an opportunity to meet you. When our scryers detected an object blocked by them moving into the capital at great speed, we assumed a powerful assassin was here to try their hand against our king, but to find you is even more of a welcome sight. As much as I'd loved to have wet my blade against a powerful assassin this afternoon, recruiting the son of the most powerful adventurer in a hundred years would be all the sweeter."

There was an eagerness to his request that I couldn't help but notice. In truth, he was offering me a way out, whether or not he realized it, but why did I feel like it wasn't the path for me? "What kind of time commitment does being a King's Guard have?" I asked, wondering how much time I'd have for all my other endeavors and responsibilities as defender of the balance.

Gavin looked at me knowingly and confirmed my fear. "It is pretty strict for the first decade or so. We have to train you up and get you to our standards before we can allow you to go out and about. Would do us no good to lose a King's

Guard recruit from something like bandits or a simple dungeon. But I can promise you half of each year you are free as a bird, to go where you please, but most choose to bank their time and take several years off at once, which you are free to do."

"But the initial commitment requires all my time?" I asked, confirming that this wouldn't be what I was looking for after all. I just had too much right now that needed to be done, stepping aside wouldn't help progress any of my goals and quests. Plus, I doubted that I'd be free to exact vengeance on Lord Variyn as a King's Guard.

"That's correct," Gavin said, then added, "But what is a decade to someone who could live a hundred or more years? You will find no swifter way to the top than joining our ranks."

I decided that sidestepping the question altogether was the best option. Maybe one day I could take him up on the offer and receive specialty training from them, if nothing else it would be a novel way to get my titles stripped from me. Taking a deep breath, I delivered my answer. "Must I decide now? I admit your offer is appealing, but there is much that I need to tend to before I make such an all-consuming commitment."

It was impossible to read his reaction, his face stayed as still as stone. Only when he looked to his left at one of his fellow King's Guard, did I see a hint of a grimace play across his face. This was a man that didn't take nicely to being told no. I'm sure I was giving him an answer far different than my father, who no doubt would have just said no. But I was in need of something he offered, just not right at this moment, so I had to cling to the possible path without burning it away.

"That is fair," Gavin said, shaking his head as if convincing himself of his own words. "Such a commitment shouldn't be jumped into so swiftly. Come seek me out if you change your mind and wish to begin your training. My offer won't last forever, but for the son of Elkor Miles, it can linger for now."

I shifted uneasily under his gaze, he was not happy, and I could sense it from the tone of his voice to the way his power shifted around him. "Thank you," I finally managed to say, before it occurred to me I didn't know what to do next. Was I due to get my audience with the king or would they be leaving me now to work that out myself.

"It is rare for such a noble creature to seek out a rider," Gavin said, gesturing to Ares. She'd been mostly still since we landed, but now that I focused on our bond I could tell she was curious about the other griffin.

"Ares has been with me since the start of my adventure as an Awakened, in fact, without her I'd surely have died many times over," I said, petting her neck proudly.

Our bond deepened as I focused my admiration on her, and I felt something besides just curiosity from her. She had an attraction toward the male griffin and his obvious power. I didn't know anything about griffin mating patterns, but I surely didn't like the idea of her fawning over his griffin, especially if I ever decided to work under him. I let my mind distance itself a bit as the feelings she was having weren't ones I wanted a part of.

"What of my visit with the king?" I asked, my mind snapping back into complete focus.

Gavin, the Captain of the King's Guard, smirked at me. "You are free to travel to his majesty, but I must warn you. If you arrive without a gift, then you will be turned away by his steward before you make it two steps into the palace."

I scrunched my forehead at that. "What kind of gift?" I asked. Surely the king wasn't concerned with gifts and such protocol with so much at stake.

"Many things could do, but I would offer a suggestion if you are open to it," Gavin said, nodding sagely.

"Yes, tell me what I can get that will appease the king and get me before his royal throne that I might deliver my message." I was growing annoyed at all the different doors I had to go through just to get to where I needed to be.

"In these very woods lives a creature known as a Fae Mistress. A monster that takes the form of a woman to lure young men to their deaths. Seek it out and secure a vial of its blood. A single vial is worth its weight in gold several times over and will be a fitting gift for King Newaliyn."

That sounded easy enough. "Thank you kind sir. If that is all, I will take my leave to accomplish my quest and speak with the king."

Collect a Vial of Fae Blood

You've been charged by Gavin Melantis to gather a vial of

Fae Mistress Blood to give to King Newaliyn as a gift
showing your good faith.
Objective: Collect a Vial of Fae Blood
Rewards: Audience with the King, 5,000 Essence

I took the arrival of a quest as assurance that I was on the right track. Gavin and his team of riders took to the sky, and I checked my map to see if a location blip came with the quest. Not far from here in some of the deeper forest back where I'd come from was a single dot on my map indicating an area where I might collect the Fae blood. Petting Ares and sensing the hold the larger male griffin had on her wanning, I mounted up and prepared to take flight.

CHAPTER 22
FAE MISTRESS

The forest became too dense to make anything out from above, so I was forced to have Ares land on the outskirts. The day was turning to night, but the early evening sun still burned with enough light to see by. Ares wanted to stay by my side, but I could sense her hunger and released her to hunt while I ventured deeper into the forest. Branches low and scraping made movement forward difficult, but possible.

My mind wandered as I walked ever deeper into the darkening forest. This felt much like the last time I'd hunted Fae, but then I had company, back up ready to put their lives on the line for me. But I wasn't the same man I'd been then, with my single spell and ability. No. I was a force to be reckoned with and I wouldn't go quietly into the night if attacked. It would take an immensely overwhelming force to put me down.

But I was getting ahead of myself and letting my nerves direct my thoughts. The most I'd seen so far had been a bunnicorn and it moved with a swiftness that even my eyes had trouble following. Brush and undergrowth tried its best to impede my way forward, but I found that if I just walked through it my armor protected me well enough from the thorns that would scratch me while ripping free even the most stubborn of bushes. Basically, I powerwalked my way through the forest not letting anything stop me.

It was while going onward at a steady, if not a bit slow, pace that I saw a light from ahead and a moment after, the most beautiful of songs filled the air. I was immediately entranced by the song and felt my pace slow even more. My first fall happened without me so much as noticing until I was lifting myself off the forest floor, thorns cutting into the palms of my hands. The next fall I realized I was tripping over a bush before I went all the way down and caught myself on a tree trunk. But the bark seemed to turn to razors and cut into my flesh. I jerked my hand back only to see it healing several small red lines.

My mind reeling at whatever was happening to me, I forced my feet forward, but suddenly my thoughts were a blur, and I could only think about Alayna. How sweet her lips felt pressed against my own, how wonderful the warmth of her body was. I recalled the first time I met her, so afraid and screaming out because of the injury she'd received by that wretched Chaos Drake. Something about the thoughts of violence and pain she'd suffered pulled me out of the daze that overcame me.

I looked around only to notice that the faint pulsing red light had turned soft and white. It was closer now or I'd moved closer, I really couldn't say so fuddled my thoughts were, but I was moving towards it again. Try as I might not to listen to the call or song that came from the light, I couldn't. It was like being drunk but also concussed at the same time. I barely held on to any sense of myself as I was pulled deeper into the forest toward the light.

It moved suddenly, pushing further away as I grew near, and I felt a sudden urging to chase it. My slow steady footsteps turned to a jog, then to a steady run. Branches slapped into me, making me stagger and almost fall three times before I finally ran headlong into a branch that wouldn't snap out of the way. That is what saved me.

The daze of hitting my head so hard, sort of snapped me out of it as a ringing filled my ears. I looked around and saw the light first, then right under it, a drop off. Moving slowly forward I saw that the ground dropped off about fifty feet into a stoney cavern below. It might not have killed me with my increased attributes, but I'd have been out of the fight for several long minutes if not an hour depending on how I fell.

Looking up, the lights danced, and I watched them dart to the left. The calling had stopped, and my mind seemed my own again, so I stood and followed after the light. It skirted around the big hole in the ground, leading me deeper into the dense forest. Wary from the ease at which I'd been snared into its web, but eager to do what needed to be done to meet with the king, I followed.

Whatever magical effects had been present before, they

were no longer in effect. My mind was clear, and I began to wonder if I should follow this thing after all, but again, the need to see my quests through pushed me forward. The trees began to thin until the light reached a grove with a pool of water, in the middle of that pool sat a naked, green-skinned elf.

She was taking her time, scooping up water and pouring it down her chest and didn't even look up when I approached. My sword came to my hand, I would be ready for anything.

"You broke my spell by sheer chance, many mortals have fallen to their deaths following my call." Her voice was sweet and slow, each word carefully said as if she had to concentrate to speak in a language that I would understand.

"Are you the Fae Mistress?" I asked. I tried to inspect her a moment after asking, but something blocked my attempt, I could feel it repelling my ability.

"I am a Fae Mistress," she said, finally turning her gaze in my direction. I was surprised by the golden irises of her eyes and recoiled a bit from the raw power that pulsed off her in waves. If this came down to a fight, I would need to be careful, she was much more dangerous than she seemed.

"I-I've come for your blood," I said, the words coming out unsure, now that I was meeting this so-called monster. A monster that could speak common, block my ability to inspect her, and seemed very much like an elf right down to the ears, if not unnatural coloring.

"And if I don't want to give you my blood, will you kill

me for it?" She asked, her tone neither accusing or afraid, merely curious.

I thought her question over. Was I willing to kill a clearly sapient being just to get an audience with the king? Yes, I decided, the lives of so many could be saved if I could convince the combined armies of Newalyin to join the battle in the East. But perhaps it wouldn't come to that, perhaps there was another way.

"I am willing to do what I must," I answered. "Will you give me a vial of your blood and allow me to leave unharmed?"

"I might," she said, teasingly. "But I also might kill you for making such a bold request."

My grip tightened on the hilt of my sword, and I made ready to attack if she so much as twitched in my direction. I was dealing with a deadly beast, and I couldn't let the fact that she could speak get in the way of that. My litany of spells that I could call down at any moment flashed through my head and I decided a nicely placed Lightning Strike would be in order. Focusing my mind, I prepared to let one loose and get the battle started.

"Last chance to give me a small bit of your blood before I am forced to take it myself," I said, sounding more confident than I felt. The moment I finished speaking I pushed essence into my blade and felt my attributes rise as a result. I'd need to start off with everything I could dish out and just make sure I left enough of her to collect some blood.

"Wait," she said, her words coming quickly and not as

smooth and seductive as they'd been just a moment ago. "I do not wish to die, nor do I truly want to kill you. However, I am not in the business of giving away my blood without a cost. Fight my champion and if you defeat him, I will willingly give you a vial of my blood. Do we have a deal?"

I had no way to gauge her power or threat level, so this seemed as good a bargain as I'd be likely to get. I nodded my head, then thought better of it and spoke aloud. "Yes, I will face your champion."

"Good, give me a moment to summon him," she said, her seductive voice returning.

She stood, her full nakedness on show in front of me as she began to weave her arms and sway her hips in a very seductive manner. I could feel the buildup of energy around her as she moved and realized it must be some sort of spell casting. The Fae were weird beings.

As I waited and watched, something in front of me moved. I looked to see vines coming together in the space between us and I deduced that this must be the champion forming. Vines layered upon vines as first a leg, then two formed in front of me, all withered and slithering vines. The light that had led me here appeared again, but all the alluring magics were not to be found. Instead, it swirled around the champion, until finally, as a head was being formed, it dove into the chest.

I used Inspect on the creature standing before me and sighed. Now this was something I could deal with.

· · ·

Nature Elemental Level 38, 900/900

But as I watched it, the vines kept moving into it and it grew several sizes bigger than before, until finally letting out a cry that sounded like a wounded animal screaming for help. It shook my chest, and I took a step back involuntarily. Sensing something was up, I Inspected it again.

Nature Elemental Brute Level 52, 1,650/1,650

Okay this was a going to be a bit more of a challenge. My sword came up to block a blow from the already moving behemoth. The edge of my sword sliced easily through, and I almost re-thought my earlier worry.

The air went out of my lungs as I took a hit to the chest and suddenly, I was thrown backward into a tree. This monster had purposely let me take a swipe at his left arm so his right could get in a hit. Rolling out of the way as another strike followed, I swiped low, my sword cutting clean through its leg. But, as before, the damage it did damage was not enough for it to even remotely bother the monster. It hit me with a kick to the face and my vision filled with a flash of black before returning to normal.

Getting to my feet, I spit out a mouthful of blood and laughed.

The monster paused, seemingly confused by this, and I heard the Fae female speak.

"Is my champion really that amusing?" She asked, I caught her eye and saw a look of perplexed irritation on it.

I savored the moment for my minor wounds to heal and wiped blood from my lip before answering. "Very much so," I finally said. "I've not had a challenge this close since fighting with old Ironfist. But it's funny because I've not even begun to warm up yet. I hope he can keep up." I enunciated my point by unleashing a Lightning Strike right into his mass of vines that made up the head. It blew apart in a spray of charred green vines, then moments later reformed.

But I'd been holding back my most effective way of dealing with vegetation, and I decided to keep doing so while I tested the limits of this monster. With a flash of speed from activating Speed Burst, I was within feet of the brute and thrust my sword forward. Using Phantom Thrust I ended my attack with a slash downward, cutting a line into the vines. Then using Swift Strike, I spun and parried one of its blows only to come back with a Power Strike down its middle, splitting it again.

It was barely noticeable, but the speed at which it put itself back together was a hair slower than before, so I was weakening it, just not by much. Throwing myself backward I activated Light Blade then slashed downward and released it while activating Force Wave at the same time. The arc of energy glowed and crackled as it slammed into the still recovering monster.

It recovered a second later, but I was ready with an Arcane Missile. Each one hit with a satisfying thump, but it barely slowed the monster and for my trouble I got a sharp painful whip across my exposed neck. The attack came much quicker than I expected; it would appear this monster had also been holding back.

As I flew backward, I reached out and grabbed a branch, it snapped almost instantly from the force, but it slowed me enough to land on my feet. Dust billowed around me as my feet dug into the forest ground, but the brute hadn't been idle. It appeared in front of me and as I went to raise my sword to block its attack, I found myself bound around my wrist. Vines had burst forth from the ground around me and now entangled me fully.

I took the hit right in the face and would have gone flying backward if not for the vines holding me fast. Blow after blow rained down on me and I sensed my health dip below seventy percent. With a roar of rage, I channeled essence into my muscles and burst the bonds holding me fast just as it went for another meaty punch.

The swipe of my blade took its entire arm off, but I didn't stop there. Instead, I thrust my hand into its chest, all withering vines and sharp burning light, and activated my Firebolt spell. A flash of pain and yellow orange light followed as the beast screamed that otherworldly noise once more.

I knew one thing for sure, it had felt that one.

It staggered back and all the vines trying to hold me in place withered from his lack of focus. Now was my time to end this silly fight before I took too much more damage. I began channeling my Fireball spell, even sinking some essence into it, just enough to ensure I wouldn't have to cast the spell twice. It grew to the size of a kelt fruit, and I released it just as the thing recovered.

I aimed low, so that the resulting blast would take it out without spreading the flames too far. The last thing I wanted to deal with was a forest fire.

My moment to attack came and immediately a cloud of dust was kicked up, blocking my view of the destruction that came next. Fire orange, red and blue, flared next, coloring the thick layer of dust.

I gripped the hilt of my sword and waited. If it hadn't been enough, I'd need to be ready to finish it off. Slowly but surely the dust began to settle, and I cast a Light spell to see more clearly in the gloom of the forest. A smoldering pile of blackened vines was all that remained of the monster and a smirk formed on my face. I looked to where the Fae woman stood and saw that she too was smirking, that wasn't a good sign.

The pile of vines shuddered and moved. This fight wasn't over yet.

Casting a quick Firebolt into the pile, I shot backward and raised my sword. The attack did seemingly nothing to the already charred vines as they began to form the creature, one limb at a time. What kind of regenerative powers must this monster have for it to still be kicking. I Inspected it and got a surprise.

. . .

Blackened Nature Elemental Level 38, 554/900

Its level and aspects had changed again!

I could see now that this Fae wasn't playing fair, so I guess neither would I. The Firebolt spell hadn't been very effective, most likely because of its new Blackened nature, so I would prepare this overgrown salad the old fashion way, slicing and dicing. Essence infused my muscles as I shot forward and went to work. Each cut slowed its regeneration process by a noticeable degree as I refused to let it completely form up again. My sword, with the essence it still held, thrummed with power and cut the vines with ease.

So intent on my attack and desire to finish it off, I missed its next attack. Vines wild and thorny wrapped around my legs and dragged me back. The small respite from my attack was enough to allow it to fully form again and the battle was on. Just as I freed my legs with a slash of my sword, the monster was on me. A thorny fist slammed against my armor but did little damage. This was a weakened form of the brute and one I was well equipped to deal with.

This fight was over, the monster just didn't know it yet.

I came forward, slashing it in half at the midsection then twirled midair, slashing its head off for good measure. Then I hit it with spell after spell, throwing everything I had at it save for Fireball, which tended to be far too destructive.

It fell in pieces at my feet and suddenly the smirk on the Fae Mistress's face had gone. I saw her concentrate, her forehead pinching, but nothing happened. She let out a sigh and set her gaze on me.

"You've beaten my champion," she declared, obviously not happy about it. "Take my blood and leave. I hope the effects are everything you hoped for."

I didn't know what she meant but came forward to collect my prize anyway.

CHAPTER 23
TO MEET A KING

It was a simple matter of finding my way out of the forest after collecting the blood. I felt a sense of disdain or wrongness about how things had turned out. On the one hand, I was glad to have not taken a life, but on the other the taking of blood from such a being seemed to diminish her somehow. It was odd to put a finger on the emotions that accompanied it, but one thing was for certain, I didn't want to do that again, so the king better enjoy his gift.

We took to the skies and soon we were soaring over the treetops. Whatever wards and senses the kingdom employed, they worked wonderfully, because as I neared the capital I got a pegasus escort from the sky to a landing area just inside the city walls. It was clear they'd been expecting me, or perhaps flights into the city were more common than I realized, because they had personnel spread out and ready to work.

One such gentleman took Ares's reins and bowed to her.

Ares, confused by the stranger's proper etiquette, sent me a mental questioning thought. I just smiled and called out to the man.

"You'd be well to ask her before taking hold or you might lose a hand." However, my warning didn't dissuade him, he held tight to the reins and spoke in a hushed tone directly to Ares.

"I can see you to the royal groomers where they have much experience tending to proud and powerful griffins such as yourself. Would you do me the honor of allowing me to escort you?"

A touch of humor spread through our emotional bond, but I could tell she was enjoying the pampered words and what would follow. She bowed her head, giving her assent and I let her go, sending her a feeling of comfort to ease the slight anxiety she felt going someplace new. What I didn't send through the bond was the fact that I felt the same anxiousness pounding in my chest as I imagined what lay ahead.

To meet a king, the King of all Newaliyn. I'd always been more of a nose in a book about magic or monsters kind of kid, but that doesn't mean I never fantasized about the honors of being a king or played out fantasies in my mind about what it would be like to take on such a role. It all ended with me messing one thing up or another in my mind, so I tended to keep my thoughts focused on the topics I excelled at.

While I sorted through my thoughts and expectations of what I was soon to experience, a man I recognized approached through the small sea of people walking here and there. It was the King's Guard Captain Gavin Melantis.

"Have you given up your pursuit of a present so quick?" He asked, assuming that my hasty arrival meant I had failed.

Little did he know that wasn't the case at all. "I've acquired the suggested gift and need only to see the king to present it to him," I said, my words more confident than I felt.

He nodded and, though seeming skeptical, turned and bid me to follow him.

The place we'd landed was a large circular platform with tables and such set into the edges where people went to and fro. I now saw a pegasus landing and was immediately bombarded by people holding clipboards and such. This was some sort of arrival entry point into the city, and I guessed they were having to declare goods or basic intentions. That I wasn't mobbed immediately spoke more to Gavin expecting me than it did any importance I held as a land-owning baron.

The sky had just reached that point where the sun was cresting the horizon and casting an array of dark purples and reds across the skyline. It was breathtaking in a word, but I didn't get much time to enjoy it as I would if I were up in the sky. Gavin took us into a long hallway that bent slightly downward to the lower city. Where I'd landed had been set several stories up and I realized as I looked around that this city had very distinct layers to it.

Landing at one of the topmost layers meant if we wanted to get to the ground, we had to travel a good distance, which we did, walking through a hallway of stone and wood lit by torches that burned but gave no smoke. I wondered why they didn't use the similar light globes I'd seen in city Variyn and must have been staring at them for too long because Gavin noticed. He commented with a grin on his face.

"The Mage's Guild say they are a sensible lot." Gavin gestured at the fire and chuckled. "But I swear they are just cheap bastards. The entire town is lit by their smokeless fire instead of the superior white light of mage light, you know the spherical balls every other city's Mage Guild uses."

"In Variyn we had globes of white light that do not produce heat or smoke," I said, stepping to the side and feeling an even heat coming from the smokeless fire.

"As I said, our Mage's guild claims they are being sensible, but I have it on good authority that they are money grubbing old farts who've lived far too long to want to change. I think the king recognizes this and isn't a big fan of change himself, so here we are with flames instead of what every other city uses. But it isn't all bad."

"No?" I asked, falling back into step with him as we made our way slowly downward.

"In the winter these same smokeless flames can be used to heat entire streets, something I know globes of light can't accomplish." Gavin chuckled at his words, and I just gave him the side eye.

"I guess the old ways can be the best way sometimes. But I prefer my light globes," I said, thinking about what the guilds must have to deal with lighting an entire city and maintaining the enchantments. I'd done a bit of book studying on the topic of light globes and they weren't a walk in the park to create.

I knew very little about the various guilds that helped the cities run and function, but I had been getting a few requests for formal guild formation in Blackridge that I'd all but ignored. It wasn't like I didn't want to cede power to other factions or groups, but I felt like we were still too small to warrant such actions. Sooner than later, I'd need to deal with the formation of guilds and perhaps interact with the officials in Variyn city at some level.

I thought back to one of the encounters I'd had with a member of the Guardsmen's guild. It hadn't been pleasant and to this day I wondered if that old man suffered some injustice from Alayna and my actions. However, I didn't have time to dwell on it much as we neared a door at the end of the ever-descending hallway that let out into a busy street. Here, two more guards awaited us with weapons—both had halberds—standing at a rigid attention with backs straight and weapons risen to the sky. With a look they joined his side, with one stepping forward to part the crowd before us.

The crowd thinned as we got deeper into the city, but our walk didn't last too terribly long before we stood outside a grand keep that put Keep Variyn to shame. Literal dozens of towers rose up from the several story high stone and metal keep. It had been painted a light white color, some of the grey stone color coming through, with the colors of the King's crest painted on the towers, black and gold.

I knew it was an old custom, mostly because of depictions of keeps I'd occasionally saw in books, to paint the stone, but it had fallen out of fashion years before, with Keep Variyn and Blackridge Keep both being unpainted. But it was like Gavin had said, the king was likely very much like the mage's guild, preferring the old ways. Flags of the different Houses flew at the top of various towers, likely signifying the togetherness the Capital wished us to believe was normal. I noticed that House Blalor still had a flag flying, as well as two others I didn't recognize.

Seeing where my gaze was directed, Gavin interjected.

"Even fallen Houses remain a part of the Kingdom, though it seems silly that we fly colors to landless monarchs who hold no voice on any councils, as that requires land ownership."

"House Blalor is no more then?" I asked, seeing the flag but suspecting that Lord Blalor, if he survived the attack, would be landless now.

"House Blalor is no more in more ways than one," Gavin said, his tone turning serious. "Your Lord Variyn was ruthless in his execution of his plans. No living member of House Blalor has been seen since the destruction of their capital city, not so much as a second cousin."

This twisted the pit in my stomach that I'd grown accustomed to feeling most of the time. How had he managed to wipe out every member of House Blalor? It seemed almost unbelievable that not even a single heir to the blood would have survived. That brought my mind to the carnage of Blalor City and the deaths of so many innocents. Before the weight of it could crush me into depressed oblivion, I changed my thoughts and forced my focus elsewhere.

"I'm ready to meet the King," I said, wondering when the gate would open to allow us over the moat and into the keep proper.

"Very well," Gavin said, stepping forward he motioned to the soldiers on the other side of the golden colored gate, and it swung open wide.

There wasn't much fanfare once we got into the keep, but it was like a city of its own. Within the protective outer walls, a massive courtyard opened up that bustled with as much activity as the markets we'd passed through outside the keep. I kept close to Gavin, and he led me through it all, his guard attendants breaking off shortly after we entered the keep.

I didn't know what to expect when it came to meeting a King, but for some reason I imagined him sitting atop a mighty throne, powerful guards all around. Instead, I was taken to an office of sorts and Gavin ushered me inside. It had a big desk, everything atop it stacked in neat piles and a massive chair that could pass as a throne on the other side. I sat where I was directed, a plush red velvet chair across from the desk and pulled out the gift I'd gotten for the king.

"When he enters, stand and bow your head low enough that he can't see your eyes, then present him with your gift. Good luck, young Miles," Gavin said, slipping out of the room and leaving me alone.

I thought the door we'd entered was the only way in or out, so I was surprised when a bookshelf to the left slid open and a plainly dressed man entered. It took me several awkward moments before I realized who had entered, I broke off my stare and lowered my head, holding out the vial of blood to the king in offering.

Of all the reactions I expected what I got wasn't one of them. The King, a middle-aged looking man with golden curly locks and a short trimmed beard of the same color, began to laugh. It continued for a solid few seconds and I finally looked up to see what was so funny.

The vial of blood had been taken from my hand, I hadn't even felt it happen, and the king was looking at it with a huge grin on his face.

"I take it Gavin put you up to this?" He asked, his purple eyes light and friendly. "I really should have a talk with him."

Setting the vial of blood aside he sat in his chair and bid me to do the same.

"Do you know the alchemical use for this Fae blood?" The king asked, his voice was plain and not at all kingly as I might have imagined. Just your everyday male baritone voice, not even all that deep.

"I don't," I admitted and then added, "your majesty." At the end, as I wasn't sure the proper way of addressing him.

"Call me, Edwin. At least here in private," the king said, then looking about the room he shrugged and raised the vial of blood. "This a sexual stimulant, used to aid in the excitement level of intercourse. Hardly a gift for a king who has no such issues."

CHAPTER 24
PARAGON TO PARAGON

I gasped at what I'd just heard, but he continued unphased by reaction.

"You see, Caldor Miles, I wanted to meet with you in a way I never got to with your father. Informal and between two Paragons."

He paused, looking at me with a raised eyebrow. I chose not to confirm or deny his assumption, but it didn't matter either way as if anyone knew how to feel out a paragon, I'm sure it was the King, one of the oldest Paragons I'd heard of.

"Though I have to say, I didn't expect to receive Fae blood from you, Gavin should have told you that no gift is required of Elkor's kin. I'd have given that man his own House to rule if he'd let me, but your father was a stubborn one. It was a miracle that I got him to take on the role of Protector of the Realm. I don't wish to make that mistake twice."

When he said nothing further, I was left to my own

imaginations as to what exactly he meant. So far, he'd taken hold of the conversation and I'd not even had chance to mention the reason I wished to meet with him. I would change that right now.

"I'm here to request assistance in the Easternlands. I have committed some of my own forces and rallied a legion of Southerners to do the same. House Nefrah marches to war on a peace accord with the Easterners to push out the Beastkin invaders. The balance of Order and Chaos must be maintained. Will you help?" I asked, the sentence flowing out without pause as I released the practiced words to the King, or Edwin as he requested I call him.

"I've been made aware of your activities recently and I must say," Edwin paused, running his hands across his short cut beard, "you are much more brazen in your actions than your father ever was and maybe a fair bit brighter as well. The discoveries that you've been releasing to the highest bidder have gotten many of my own scholars riled up. But we can speak of those matters another time. Explain to me why I should send my armies to a conflict that has no direct barring or threat to my kingdom?"

I'd practiced this conversation many times in my head, and this was a response I expected. "As the Southlands fell under the Easterners' armies, surely, you've heard the reports of Southlanders spreading across your kingdom. This will only get worse if the problem is left to fester. What happens when the entire Eastern nation seeks new lands and finds them within our borders? Will Houses Attra, Thouca, Neshium, and Abrye be able to defend our Eastern borders against the Easterners, or worse, what if the Beastkin are not satisfied and decide to take their conquest over the High Peak Mountains?"

The King's purple eyes met mine and I thought maybe I was convincing him. He pinched the bridge of his nose and shook his head. "And what if the great Ordu and their ancient foes return to our lands? I cannot make decisions based off of what ifs. I need facts and I need proof of the threats before I can take any action."

I sighed, my defeat coming swiftly. "What can I say to convince you?" I asked, feeling desperation setting in.

King Edwin Newaliyn perked up at that and a smile crossed his face. "Perhaps you'd be open to a bargain?"

It was my turn to look suspicious and I didn't try to hide my reaction. "What kind of bargain?"

"You are now a baron under Lord Variyn, is that right?" Edwin asked, leaning back in his throne like chair.

"Yes."

"What would you say to becoming a baron under the king? You'd be given landholdings and not quite be to the level of a House Lord, but very few could claim a title higher than yours. Being in my service also comes with great benefits, but many responsibilities as well. I'd want you trained properly; it does our nation no good to waste a Paragon. Given time and the right focus you could rival me in power."

Then as if to show off that very power I felt something stir around him. It was like a veil being lifted and the truth of his immense power being shown to me in stark clarity. His aura lashed out and I felt myself take actual damage just being in his presence. I focused my mind and as best as I could, hardened my power to resist the immense pull of his own. Looking at Edwin, no, looking at the king now I could feel and see the true power of a Paragon.

It was like looking into a blazing sun, so immense was his power and so great and terrible the aura surrounding it. Then just as fast as it had come, something fell over it and it was like sitting across from the most normal powerless person I'd ever encountered.

"What level are you?" I blurted out the question before I had the good sense to think better of it.

"That's a very private question for one such as us. You should continue to protect yourself from such inquiries as you are now with those earrings. You have already caused quite a stir among the court with your defeat of old Ironfist, one of the more adept fighters in the kingdom. From that fight alone, people guess you've reached level 55 or higher, but now that you are in front of me, I can sense you can't be above," he paused to really squint his eyes at me before continuing, "level 35? No, I'd guess you are level 32 or 33 by the way your power flares around you. But Paragons like us don't have to rely on mere levels, do we?"

He really wasn't letting go of the Paragon assumption and I found myself wanting to confirm his suspicions just for the hell of it. What really could the harm be, he'd already pegged me as much, and I doubted the king went around gossiping secrets away.

"I am a Paragon, and I welcome advice to help keep my

secrets," I finally said, and watched as the king just gave a knowing nod of his head.

Edwin suddenly went still as if listening to something only he could hear. He sighed and glanced at the floor before looking back at me. "My time with you is coming to an end. What say you to my offer, will you become a baron under me, and I will send off a sizable army to the East via portals to assess the facts? I can only promise a legion, perhaps two. I would also be willing to speak with the ambassadors the beastkin keep in the capital. Perhaps a diplomatic end to this little incursion could be had. I will also tell you I am encouraged by the idea of talks opening up with the Eastlanders. If nothing else, you've proven yourself a capable leader and diplomat in that accomplishment."

Edwin spoke fast, obviously he was in a hurry to be someplace else and my importance, despite what he said, wasn't as important as whatever he had to do next.

"Is this an offer I can consider? I have lands and people I care for in Variyn, but I will say, your offer is tempting," I said, choosing my words as carefully as I could considering the rush.

The king smiled. "This is already farther than I got with your father. How about a compromise. I will send off the troops I mentioned, I will have my ambassadors speak with theirs, but you will give me your word as a Paragon that you will become my baron when the time is right. And who knows, perhaps you will find yourself in a position to rule over a section of House Variyn, but under the banner of my capital. Borders are shifting and I am owed substantial payment for the aid I sent."

My mind reeled at the possibilities. Becoming a baron under the king would be a life changing event, so much more so than my current titles and authority. But I wasn't the same eager to please young boy that I was when I accepted a seemingly generous offer from Lord Variyn. No, I was a man now and I understood why my father chose to stay out of politics and the responsibilities that came with it.

"Do what you've said, and I will consider it. But I will not make any oath to solidify such an offer until I've had much time to think about it. You see, I may be a Paragon, but I am not one that wishes to be entrenched in the politics of being a baron. I wish to help maintain the balance, grow stronger, and help all those that I can. There are souls meant to rule, but I don't know that I am one of them." My words came out slow and careful, and I hoped I was getting my point across.

The King, however, answered swiftly and without hesitation. "We have an accord then. I must be off, but please consider my offer seriously as it will come with benefits you can't afford to pass up if you truly want to help your fellow men." And with that, the king turned and placed a hand on the bookshelf. It swung open and he left, disappearing behind it.

With the king gone, I sat in the room, unsure if I should leave now or if I'd done what needed to be done. I felt like there was so much more to be said and details to be relayed. With that thought in mind, I pulled free paper and pen. The time I'd spent undercover, as short as it had been, had fostered a small love for writing or at least copy work. It had been some time since I'd been able to write much, mostly I tried to account my experiences in a journal-like fashion, but during the tail end of the war I'd ceased even that.

Taking several long minutes, I penned out as many details as I felt was necessary to give the king all the information that I felt he needed. By the end, I'd even given some of my thoughts toward being a baron and made small promises to serve in a capacity of Protector of the Realm if he'd send the troops as promised. I was sure that would be enough to at least get some action going, but I had plans for House mobilization as well, which I outlined to the king in hopes he'd agree. If all the Houses combined their might with the Easterners and Southerners we'd be an easy match for the Beastkin armies, no matter their famed might and powers in battle. I even left mention that the captain of his guard wished to recruit me as well, thinking he might already know but I wanted to be completely transparent.

When I finished, I opened the door to find Gavin standing at attention outside. He inclined his head and spoke. "You're in one piece, that bodes well. I felt him unleash a small part of his aura and almost came in to see if he'd taken offense to the lovely gift you'd given him."

The king had made it a point to leave the blood behind and I'd scooped it up, unwilling to waste something that was so hard to earn. I let the vial slip into my inventory and gave Gavin a flat look.

"He mentioned wanting to speak to you after seeing the

gift, I'm not sure he found it as funny as you did," I said, raising an eyebrow.

Gavin just laughed and slapped me hard on the shoulder, nearly bowling me over. "He loved it, don't lie." Then, still chuckling heartily at his joke, he motioned that I should follow him, and he led me away from the secret meeting chamber of the king.

CHAPTER 25
RETURNING TO VARIYN

Gavin and I exchanged a bit of chitchat, he tried to recruit me again, but I refused again, telling him the time wasn't right. A part of me wanted to tell him that the king had offered a far better deal, so to speak, but I knew better than to start spreading information around freely. Besides, I wondered if joining the King's Guard and getting training that didn't require land ownership wasn't actually the better option. He offered to show me the best place to get a drink, but I was in a hurry and instead settled for a raincheck.

He left after delivering me to the top of the platform, where a preening and happy Ares awaited me. She sent vague images of the care she'd received, and I felt like she wanted to come back here at our earliest convenience.

It made me smile to think of how much she enjoyed the pampering. Perhaps I wasn't giving her all the care she required, so I made a mental note to see about purchasing better care equipment for her. In her exchange of emotions and images, our bond had grown strong enough to pass some memories back and forth, I saw an instrument used to clean her talons that she yearned for. I would do better in caring for her, I told myself.

Despite her being saddled up and ready to fly, I had other plans. I told her I needed her to return to her stone form, and she was all but ready to fly off to go hunting. Basically, saying to me that she wanted to test the sharpness of her talons now that she'd been cared for so nicely.

"You will get a chance to hunt when we return to Variyn, but I plan on teleporting and I'm not good enough to open a portal for the both of us yet. Please, Ares," I said, rubbing the sides of her face while matching her intense gaze.

She reluctantly relented and pushed images of hunting to my mind, as if to tell me not to forget my promise. I smiled, happy to have such a lively companion in my life, before speaking the words and having her return to the stone figurine. She'd be in the astral plane or wherever it took her in-between, a place I know she enjoyed, so it wasn't all bad.

Next, I had to use the great gift Warrick had given me by teaching me the basics of teleportation. I'd very rarely used Blink, but the knowledge it implanted in my mind was priceless. Truly it was an ability that any caster should take if they could, however, the attribute requirements for it were extremely high, so much so that Fred had no hope of getting it until he'd reach level 40 or higher.

I'd even asked him if his mother had learned the spell, as she was the spellcaster of the family like Fred, but he'd told me she didn't have it, preferring to stand her ground with Fire.

It made sense, they both had a class that benefited from a more stationary form of fighting, allowing their flames to act as a defensive shield and an offensive weapon. But that was different than how most casters worked, preferring to be as mobile as possible due to their often-weaker Constitution attribute score.

Channeling power around my form, similar to how Blink worked, I instead focused on a place far greater than the distance required for Blink. Pulling out a gem filled with mana, I drew on it until enough had been pulled together to warp the surrounding air around me. I noticed a few people looking in my direction, but I re-focused and pictured a spot just outside the gate of Variyn City. It was a simple tree just off the road, but one I'd teleported to before and I knew that I could do it again.

Part of making it happen was the confidence that I could do it and that I'd done it already. With this confidence, I was able to carefully press both points together, feeding it the mana I'd collected as an energy source until I felt the two points were so close that I could just step through to the other.

I stepped forward, not a necessary step but something I'd begun to do as it felt natural, and a moment later Variyn City loomed over me as I stood next to a tree that I knew all too well now.

True to my word, I summoned Ares and let her know she was free to go hunt. She came back with an appreciative screech, lifting into the air and going on her way happily. She was ready to test her new sharpened talons and I wouldn't stand in her way.

Walking up to the gate, I gained entry easily enough and caught a carriage to Miles Manor. I used Blink to avoid having to speak with anyone but the gate guard. However, my Blinking around caught the attention of a very eager little lady who informed me that Regina was requesting a meeting with me. I was quick to tell her I was busy, but after more insistence, I agreed to a dinner that night. It worked out, because I did need to have a word with her, I just wasn't prepared at this very moment.

Finding my way to my suite, I undressed and began going over what I'd say.

First and foremost, I no longer wanted to spread what I'd learned to all corners of the Wyrd. It was clear to me now that there would always be an element that was ready and willing to take advantage of any good discovery I made, so it would be better to not spread anything at all. I couldn't stop her from doing so, she had an equal stake in the discoveries and honestly, short of the initial ones, it all relied heavily on her. So, would it do any good at all for me to start disconnecting myself from the business or would I just be making life harder for myself?

Two parts of my mind battled out on what the proper way of dealing with this situation were, on the one hand, something I'd had a hand in creating was used for mass murdering, but on the other, just because I sold secrets that helped it along it would be foolish to think someone else wouldn't have eventually discovered the same knowledge. Surely the Ordu knew how to manipulate essence and mana like I'd learned to. I doubted very much that they'd scorn themselves because of the potential that such a discovery in doing harm.

No, it seemed more likely to me and my musings that they'd seek more control and not less. So, as I saw it, I had two paths forward. I could assert more control in the day to day or I could sell my stake and focus on the ever-growing list of tasks I needed to see to. Either way, I refused to do as I'd done before and let so much to be decided without me. But which path was the right one now? Could I leave behind the academic advantages given to me? Working with Regina had allowed me to progress leaps and bounds in my profession, which in turn, yielded benefits to my combat potency as I unlocked the ability to make more and more potent gems.

But I'd learned enough from her that going off on my own was a very real possibility as well. I didn't need someone looking over my shoulder to make the newest discoveries I might come upon. Plus, I had access to several libraries worth of books and a personal collection I'd inherited from my father that I'd barely broken the surface of. I didn't know for sure what path I'd take forward, but the time for the dinner came and I decided to follow my gut feelings on the matter when I spoke to Regina.

CHAPTER 26
DINNER FEAST & IMPORTANT DECISIONS

I wanted to dress in my armor, but resisted the urge despite how comfortable it was due to the Finer Things enchantment. Instead, I took out a practical outfit and dressed, slicking back my hair with water from a nearby bowl. Splashing more water on my face, I prepared myself for a potentially difficult conversation.

Light streamed in from the window, making the black silk of the shirt I'd chosen dance with iridescent colors. I wore black slacks as well, but a thick pair that fell loose around my muscular legs and tucked into a pair of dark brown stained boots that ended just below my knee. Looking at my reflection in the window, I marveled at the physical changes I'd gone through, as well as my general clothing.

No longer would I be mistaken for anything but nobility or perhaps a well-to-do merchant or guildsman. I noticed I had a scowl on my face, my natural resting face having changed during my time fighting against House Blalor. I tried to shift it to one with a quiet smile, but it wouldn't stick. I sighed and turned away from my reflection.

It was hard to come to terms with what I was now. I wanted so very much to be the honor-filled hero that I saw myself as before the war. Unfortunately, the best I could manage was to see myself as someone who would do what needed to be done, and in many of the cases I was coming up against, that meant the honorable path forward. My mind drifted toward my father and how he had managed to stay aloof from so much of the world that dragged me down.

I felt a small unfamiliar emotion creep into my chest as I thought of him. It took only a moment before I placed it, and I was surprised to find it there.

Jealousy.

Somehow I'd grown jealous of my father's ability to stay out of the politics and wars that weren't monster or Chaos related. I found myself filled with disdain as I realized how easily I'd fallen from everything my father hadn't. He is truly my hero, or was, but now if I found out that he truly was still alive and hiding out all these years, what was he then? A coward? It hurt to think those thoughts about my father, the man that I idolized above all others, but what else could have happened?

Much like with my thoughts on City Blalor and those who died there, I found myself having to focus on something else and repress the feelings I got when thinking about my father. It sickened me to think he was still alive, but at the same time I battled with the supreme joy that I would feel if I found him alive. I couldn't help but think my mother deserved to be able to see him one last time, or at least was owed an explanation.

I took a deep breath and spoke to myself. "Focus on the here and now. Get through the dinner with Regina and decide your path forward, then you can let all the other things weighing down on you do their damage. But for now, put away the emotions, and focus."

The words helped and soon I found myself thinking only of Regina and the dinner as I walked through the hallways to her private lab. However, before I made it there I was intercepted by a servant and told to meet her in her quarters, as a table was set and ready there.

I thanked the woman and turned around to head in the direction of her quarters. She'd taken up residence on the other side of the compound, so I got to see all the improvements as I walked through Miles Manor. All available buildings had people working, doing one thing or another. We even had a section where carriages were being loaded and goods shipped off. This place that had started as an experiment of what I could do with Regina's help, had turned into its own manufacturing, researching, and shipping monster.

It bugged me that I didn't know what exactly it was we were selling, but I imagined the Essence Bands were among the items being shipped out. Those had started as a dream that would allow everyone low-cost entry to higher rates of essence capturing, but now all I could think was it would allow potentially evil weak people who'd not have a chance to grow strong enough to be a threat, the capability to turn into a great threat. My mindset had shifted and not for the first time I realized it wasn't for the better.

Gone were the days of trusting someone just for the asking of it. Even the offers from Gavin and Edwin stunk to me as a way to use me. It was very exciting in the moment, but what did they really want from me and why did they think to so easily capture me in this role or that?

No, I wouldn't let Regina do the same to me. Sure, she'd been nothing but good to me, but it was always tied to her profit and that is what she cared about over all else. Yes, that was it. I'd made up my mind by the time I reached her quarters, I wanted nothing to do with this industry any longer and I would tell her as much.

Just inside her rather sizable quarters, a table had been set up, filling up a good area of the sitting room. Regina sat at the head of the table, another gnome I didn't recognize sat to her right, and Lance Terook on her left.

"Lance, you aren't at Blackridge Keep any longer?" I asked, wondering if he'd finished the project I'd assigned him before leaving.

"I go where I am needed, but rest assured I've not left any stone unturned. The memorial project is near completion already and has been left in very capable hands," he said, smiling warmly in my direction. I was immediately suspicious as he rarely smiled and was almost always all business.

"Sit and stay a while," Regina said, giving me a knowing look.

I felt so transparent before her, like she already knew what I was going to say or do. But I decided the business could wait until after the meal. I smiled politely, thanked her and sat down.

It was a pulled pork meal with a mess of vegetables and cubed potatoes. The seasoning was divine and soon I forgot all my worries as the food melted in my mouth. Hardly the best meal I'd ever eaten, but it did the necessary work of filling my belly. I'd not eaten all day, as I was so distracted with the tasks that I needed to address that I'd all but forgotten.

After washing down my meal with a cold glass of ale, I turned my attention to the rest of the table. After a few minutes, we'd all finished, and servants came clearing off the table. Regina produced paperwork from seemingly nowhere, likely a storage device of some kind, and began to hand out packets of paper to each of us.

"I know it has been some time since we've been able to talk, Caldor, but I'm afraid I've had to make some hard business decisions due to your inability to pull your weight in this partnership," Regina said, each word sharp and crisp as ever. She had likely rehearsed this speech of hers and I thought I knew what was coming.

"Before you continue," I said, raising a hand to forestall her. "I have something I need to say."

She seemed put off by my interruption, but she nodded, giving me the respect she always afforded me during our conversations. At least she hadn't written me off completely yet.

"Much has changed for me during the last few months," I said, searching for the right words. She nodded as if she knew as much. "Our research, the precious secrets we've uncovered have been used in the construction of weapons capable of mass destruction. The fact that I didn't have the foresight to anticipate such an evil use of knowledge is on me. I do not blame anyone else, but I can't continue to be a part of an institution who sells its knowledge to be used for evil means. And because of that I wish to announce that I am willing to share all my stake in the company, along with having my name removed from any patents. I want no part of it."

I searched her reaction for any sign that what I said stung or meant anything to her and I was surprised to find hurt flicker across her face, before a stoney expression solidified there.

She looked at me for a long couple of seconds before speaking. "Hand me back the paperwork I pushed over." I did so, not even looking to see what it was she'd given me to read. After collecting them all she looked down at the papers and shook her head.

"Inside these papers I had an offer to buy you out, thinking that perhaps the use of our research had left a sour taste in your mouth. But I need to have it amended to include removing and buying out your patents. I wish you'd never went to war or taken a position in the House of Variyn. You have a bright mind and together we could have made a fortune. But as it is, I will work with Lance to transfer all your assets within this compound and your payout will be delivered within the week. Stay in town until it is over, and I bid you farewell, young friend."

I nodded but said nothing, choosing to stand and excuse myself. Something about this entire process stung at my heart, but what else was I to do. It seemed like whether or not I wanted to distance myself it was going to happen. Regina had guessed at my mind on the matter, and I couldn't blame her. Even if I were to receive no more coin, I had enough platinum stashed away that I'd be able to buy up my own keep several times over.

Walking back to my quarters I marveled at how quickly my life and the events around me where changing. I'd met with a king, my business endeavors had all changed, I'd worked to stop an invasion, learned teleportation magic, all within a small window of time. What would be next on the horizon, I wondered.

A week passed by in what felt like a flash. I worked on raising my profession and working out the details of a new gem cut recipe. Lance struck a deal with Regina, ending his service to me and taking up a position with her. I still had Serene, she'd arrived two days ago and agreed to additional responsibilities and pay to take over Lance's work. I didn't know if she was up to it, but she'd rarely disappointed me and someone needed to do the work.

I signed lots of paperwork at the end of the week and packed away my belongings into the Arcane Asylum, emptying my suite for the last time. Regina said I was welcome, as well as all of my adventurer friends, to stay on the site when we passed through town, but she assigned me a smaller room to be used, similar to the ones my friends had taken to sleeping in when they were around. I thanked her for her kindness, and we parted amicably.

I barely looked at the ridiculous sum that I got for giving up my portion, but it was enough that it made me wonder if I couldn't just pay to start my own little kingdom. Surely Lord Variyn couldn't say no if I offered enough platinum? But I knew him enough that the accumulation of gold wasn't his primary concern, he wanted power and control. Which he currently wielded both over me, despite my wish to get out from under his thumb.

It was late on the last night of my time at Miles Manor when a messenger dropped off a note for me. It wasn't sealed and I recognized the handwriting immediately.

It read simply, "Meet me where we first kissed and don't be late."

Alayna was back and I'd finally find out what happened to her to make her miss the entire war. I could barely contain my enthusiasm as I donned my armor and slipped out of my Arcane Asylum. The door disappeared behind me and eager as a schoolboy with a crush, I went to find Alayna. Perhaps my feelings for her hadn't dwindled as low as I'd first thought. Each step brought me closer to her and with it my excitement grew.

CHAPTER 27
FORGOTTEN ENEMIES

The note didn't have a date on it, but I assumed she meant tomorrow, as it arrived after sunset. But I wanted to go check it out anyway, maybe even stop by the keep and see if I could catch her in the library. It was dark out, only the light orbs that lit the city providing any amount of illumination. My gauntlets hung on the right side of my belt and my helmet on the left. Seemingly out of nowhere, a drunk knocked into me, and I apologized for not seeing him.

I felt a prick on my hand as the average height, brown-haired man stumbled drunkenly away, his hair messy and his stride erratic. When I looked at my finger I saw I had a bead of blood forming there and looked back toward the drunken man confused at how he'd pricked my finger. The man was gone and suddenly I became very aware at how alone I was on this dark alley street. I looked about, then began walking fast for the main road, cursing my stupidity for taking a short cut through the alleys.

Some random bum had collected a bit of my blood, I was sure of it, but now I was on guard and ready for anything. My thoughts went to the skull coin Sneal had given me, perhaps I should summon him as blood magic was nothing to joke about, but no. I would deal with this problem by myself, plus he'd insisted I only call him for the most dire of situations and we weren't there yet.

Sneal. I often wondered during random times what had happened to him, but I just assumed he was off adventuring or doing whatever it was a high-level rogue did during their free time. Did he even know that Warrick was free? Should I have summoned him months ago to tell him perhaps?

My thoughts did little to distract me as I reached a less deserted street, however, before I could step out something deep within me began to burn. I fell backward into the alley, yelling out as I did so. But, no one, not even the guard only twenty feet or so away, came to my rescue. Something was pulling me back to a specific location and my vision was beginning to blur.

I might as well be a drunk at this point, each thought I tried to keep wandered away before it would form. My feet moved on instinct alone. I tried to force myself to focus, but nothing would work. I needed essence inside of me, to flush essence, but how to do that? It was all too much, with my blood burning, my vision all but gone, I reached out with my hands desperate to find something to hold on to. In my confusion, I somehow summoned my blade and began to swing it about wildly, not thinking or caring who I hit.

Then everything went still. My sword fell from my grasp and my body just gave up. I fell over and could no longer take anything in. I wasn't knocked out or anything, but my internal thoughts and abilities seemed cut off from my sense of self. Whatever magic was being worked against me was strong and terribly effective.

An undetermined amount of time passed, and I was vaguely aware of my senses coming back to me. Feeling came first. I was tied up by heavy strands of rope against a hard chair. Next came smell. Wherever I'd been taken, it stunk like rot. Then came my hearing. Voices spoke and as I focused, I made out what they were saying.

"She guarantees that he will be out of commission for an entire day if not more," a voice that sounded vaguely familiar said.

"I don't like it, we should just kill him and be done with it," another voice said, this one too had a hint of familiarity around it that I couldn't place with my mind as muddled as it was.

I kept myself still as I heard footsteps approach and suddenly a hand smacked across my face. It took very little to pretend I couldn't feel it as my face was still extremely numb.

"See he is out for the count," the first voice said. "We've got him where we want him. Once we finish these binding circles he won't be going anywhere."

"And you are sure that stuffy Lord Variyn will pay a

ransom for him. I want revenge and all, but I'm here for the coin you promised," the second voice said.

"I'm positive," the first voice said, his tone dripping with malice. "And we will get a few days of torture on him, maybe he'll crack and give us access to his inventory items. If not, I know a guy who might be able to get around the soul bind, or at least he claims."

"Good," said the second voice. "Teach him to take out our crews and mess with the likes of us again."

"Finished," said the first voice and suddenly my mind was muddled again. Everything around me seemed to be sucked away, but before my mind gave out to the darkness from the strain of it all, I felt a presence touch my mind and a fierce retribution was transferred between our bond. Ares had felt what was being done to me and she was on her way. My last thought before going under was that these fools didn't know who they'd pissed off.

"Wake up already," the first voice said, and I groggily swung my head up from where it had been resting and opened my eyes.

For a moment, I worried I'd gone blind, but the room we were in was dark and after a moment for them to adjust, my eyes saw the first of my captors. The roaring sound of water could be heard just outside of the building we were in and suddenly I had a vague idea of where we were as well. The City Variyn Lowers, or lower city.

The man standing over me was completely and utterly ordinary looking. He had brown hair, light eyes, and a face that I swear I'd seen before but it was so forgettable that I couldn't be sure. He wore a long trench coat and a conical hat. It was while looking at him and noticing how wet he looked that it clicked into place where I'd seen him before.

"You're the thug that tried to steal my gold months back, Cline Brown or something," I said, nodding my head enthusiastically despite the odd circumstances I found myself in.

"It's Clyde Black, the one and only," Clyde said, bowing dramatically and causing drips of water to hit the floor from atop his hat.

"Thanks for the positive identification," I said casually, then turning my tone dark I met his eyes and finished. "Now I know what to put on your headstone after I kill you." I spoke slow and deliberate, my words causing the man to take a step back as I flexed my muscles against the bonds that held me.

Clyde smirked when he saw I wasn't getting free so easily and gestured at the floor. "I'm not a one trick pony you know," he said, waggling his head. "I've been working on my profession with a mad fury since your friend off 'ed my crew. I figure I can't get old Sneal back, but I can kill you, that's for sure. That's after we get our ransom though, our little secret." He held his finger up over his lips as if to shush me.

My body still felt very little, but I was done listening to this idiot. Reaching out for my power I tried to grasp hold of my mana to Lightning Strike him in the face. But as it had when Tim and his cronies had taken me, the power remained just out of reach. How had this low-level thug gotten access to such powerful magic? I struggled to look at the ground and saw the answer.

Delicate and precise runescript had been carved into the floor. Just studying the outer rings, I could tell it was more advanced than anything I'd worked with, but what were the chances this was the work of that fool Clyde Black. And better yet, how had they worked blood magic against me?

Memories of the conversation I'd overheard locked that little fact into place, they'd been working with a blood sorcerer or something similar. If there was one type of magic above all others that was looked down upon as much as Chaos magic, it was blood magic. In Newaliyn it was outlawed to practice blood magic all together, but people could hide their magic well enough by purchasing a spell or two outside their normal class.

It gave me a small amount of pleasure to imagine the cost of such magic and the sorcerer's services. That, and the fact that these two numbskulls thought Lord Variyn would pay a ransom for me brought me to the point of hysterical laughter. However, I contained myself and instead reached out through our mental bond until I felt Ares brush against my mind.

She flew above the city, feeling generally where I was but unable to get a lock when I was unconscious. I sent her all my memories about my last visit to the area, then closed my eyes and focused on sending her the smells and sounds that I could hear. She had much keener senses and would be able to find me without knowing my exact location. Sure enough, as soon as I sent her the information she began to dive for the opening to the lowers.

She sent me her version of comforting thoughts, her

own imagination of ripping whoever did this to me into several pieces. All I had to do now was wait and see about freeing myself if the opportunity arose.

"You listening to me?" Clyde yelled suddenly. I must have missed something while focusing on Ares. A sudden flash of pain across my face brought my furious attention back to Clyde.

He held the knife that had just cut a bloody line across my face and brought it up to his nose. Giving it a mighty sniff, he made a gagging noise.

"I don't know how that bitch could stand it, she drank up the blood I gave her and then siphoned off a pitcher full more from you, drinking it all. Makes me sick just thinking about it." He wiped the blood off his blade and onto his cloak, shaking his head all the while.

A clutter and falling noise from another room made my heart leap. Was Ares here already? But no, another figure, brushing water off himself as he entered, stepped into the room.

Wearing black leather armor that had been damaged and repaired in the chest from a clawed like slash and a hood up over his face, the man sauntered into the room with a dangerous swagger.

Both of these men were killers, and I would be wise to end them at my first opportunity. Of course, I didn't want to kill anymore, so many men had fallen beneath my blade that it made me sick to think about, but for these two bastards, I would make an exception. Who the second man was finally hit me, though I'd never really gotten a clear look at his face.

"Ted the bandit leader," I said, shaking my head in surprise. "How in the seven hells did you two get together?"

"Funny story," Clyde began to say, but Ted shot him a look and he halted his explanation.

Ted had been the second voice I recognized now, so despite their little show, it would be Clyde who was stronger. Of course, levels changed but the last time I'd seen each of them, Clyde had been level 39 and Ted had only been level 31. That was months ago for Ted, and even longer for Clyde. Despite their levels, I knew I could take them, if only I could activate a spell or summon my sword.

Focusing on my sword I felt the barest tingle and knew that with a bit more focus I might be able to do it. My blade bond was different than a normal spell, I was bonded to it in a way that surpassed mere use of mana. It was a part of me, like an arm or a leg, and access couldn't be completely shut off while my conscious mind was active.

I strained against my bonds once more to test how strong they were. My hands had been tied separately to my body, but all the bonds were strong enough that without an influx of essence I'd be unlikely to break them. There was something left to try, I took the tiniest bit of essence and flushed it into my arms. I was a bit surprised with how easily it worked, completely ignoring whatever was blocking my use of Mana.

This was going to be easier than I thought.

"Let's start the torture already," Ted said, pulling out a

pair of hand pliers with a pointed edge. They didn't look like tools I wanted pressed or gripped against my flesh, so I did the only thing I could think of in the circumstance, I growled at him.

The sound came out as a guttural and visceral roar that would make Ares proud and stopped him in his tracks. While I growled, I infused my body with essence and strained against my bonds.

"It's fine," Clyde said, as my muscles bulged. "He can't use any Mana or Stamina abilities while he's in the circle, let him growl and strain, because he ain't getting out."

Contrary to Clyde's words, I felt the bonds begin to strain and fray, but I focused most of my effort on my hands, while focusing on summoning my blade. It wouldn't be long before I'd be free.

Suddenly, Ted rushed forward and pulled free a dagger. He planted it firmly into my neck and twisted. All my concentration ended then and the essence infusion faltered. Pain, familiar and sharp, ran up my neck as he cut into me. If I hadn't been an *Awakened* and experienced much worse pain before, this would be enough to cause most men to pass out.

But I wasn't most men.

I spit blood into Ted's face as it filled my mouth. My increased attributes and the thresholds I passed made even this wound something that would heal within minutes. It wasn't even life threatening unless he kept moving his blade around to saw my head off.

"Easy," Clyde said, putting a hand on Ted's shoulder as

he dug the blade deeper into my neck, damaging my throat. "If we kill him now, we won't be able to show proof of life. Shit, he's probably going to die now, let me find a healing potion."

Clyde scrambled out of the room and Ted removed his blade, his entire arm now covered in my blood as it spurt out. I focused my breathing and let my body do what it was good at, putting me back together. It took only ten seconds before the blood stopped spurting, then the flesh began to slowly knit back together. By the time Clyde returned, five minutes later and with a new fresh layer of wetness on him, I was nearly healed, though I looked a bloody mess of red exposed flesh.

CHAPTER 28
A GRIFFIN'S RAGE

"He still alive?" Clyde asked, huffing and puffing. He'd clearly just gone a great distance to get a healing potion as it took a good deal to make an *Awakened* get out of breath.

I'd ignored Ted the entire time and he hadn't inflicted any more wounds, so I was surprised when he spoke from another room, calling out loud. "I think he passed out, but he was still breathing."

I'd focused so deeply on healing and repairing my body that I hadn't noticed him leave the room. I needed to do better, if I'd known he was gone I might have been able to infuse more essence and free myself without injury.

"He seems like he's recovering already," Clyde said. "That's not good. What if he is a higher level than we thought? You said you fought him, and he was barely a match for you."

Ted came back into the main room, all dark wood and

shuttered windows that barely let any light in. He approached and took a closer look at my neck, sticking his finger in the mostly closed wound.

"Well shit," he said, looking back to Clyde. "Will your circle hold him if he is closer to level 50?"

Clyde's relaxed look and nature seemed to crack at the edges as he looked down at his work, but after a moment, he stiffened his spine and looked back confidently. "It's airtight. No one inside the circle will be using Mana or Stamina abilities. Based on his healing though, we ought to start cutting into him if we want to keep him weak. He's passed at least his first threshold in constitution, probably his second as well."

What they couldn't know is that I'd passed my second threshold for all my attributes and my Paragon affinity in Constitution made me a hard person to kill. I felt a familiar presence press into my mind and I knew she was close. It was now or never. Because if they began to cut into me, I would be hard-pressed to help Ares when she arrived. These little rogues were likely to be an issue for her as she didn't have the massive increase in attributes that I did, having a more normal layout for someone level 30.

I ignored them as they readied their daggers and cutting instruments. Instead, I focused on pushing essence deep into my bones and muscles, just giving myself a general increase in my strength and hardiness. I must have worked too much too fast because my body began to spark blue lightning and they immediately knew something was going on.

No time to waste now!

I burst the bonds on my hands and stood, the chair crumbling beneath the strain of my powerful legs. With the chair falling apart, also went the tight bonds that had used the back of the chair to keep me in place. I was still in a tangle of ropes, but I would have the time to unwrap myself.

A loud crash was followed by a powerful screech of rage and the room fell into chaos.

Light of the early morning poured into the room from a griffin sized hole. Ares didn't pause to take in her surroundings, her senses already connected with my own and was ready to strike out. She slashed first at Ted, as he was the closest, scoring a hit on his chest and ripping his armor open once more.

I fell over while trying to get my feet free, barely dodging a dagger headed for my face from Clyde. His higher level showed as he appeared above me in a blur of movement. He seemed confused though, as he went to stab down at my face, almost like he expected something to happen and it didn't. I slashed wide with my sword, rolling to the side.

We were both still firmly within the circle of cancellation and unable to use any abilities, which likely explained Clyde's confusion. I felt pain run through our bond as Ares took a dagger across the face, but she wasn't even close to being out of this fight. She slashed back at the rogue and took him across the face with a wound that looked doubly as painful as her own.

I had to trust she could take care of herself, as Clyde was no pushover and needed my full attention.

"Damnit!" He yelled, cutting a jagged line across his

rune work. It seemed to buzz the air around it as he did, and I felt a release then.

Raising my blade I activated Lightning Strike, but Clyde blurred and appeared in front of me, dagger glowing with a purple light. I used Blink, only barely avoiding a strike to the face. I appeared just behind him and raised my sword above my head, activating Speed Burst and Power Strike. But as before, he seemed to blur and suddenly he was in a position to deliver a critical strike against me, dagger near my throat.

Activating Swift Strike, I stepped back and slapped his blade away with my own. I hadn't fought Clyde before, but he was obviously stronger than level 39 now and I needed to be careful.

Thinking to put some space between us so I could level a spell at him, I used Force Wave. He dodged backward and to the side, giving me the opening I needed.

First, I activated Mana Shell, then as he closed the distance, I let loose Arcane Missile. I'd just enough time to create a weak shell, but my Arcane Missile was much more effective. Clyde blurred and dodged, but my three buzzing balls of energy turned mid-strike to intercept him, catching him in the back with three strikes.

It wasn't enough to take him out of the fight, but it gave me a chance to attack again without him being able to block. I struck out with a Lightning Strike and the air cracked as my spell smashed into his exposed back. He cried out in pain, but his form shimmered, and he disappeared a moment later.

But invisible or not, there were other ways to feel for

your opponents. I closed my eyes and focused on sensing his aura. The barest of tingles went off right behind me and I heard the air swish around an incoming blow. Activating Speed Burst again to give me the time to turn, I swirled and used Swift Strike at the sound of the air.

My eyes shot open just as I caught Clyde's blade and he shimmered back into the visible spectrum. He had a grin on his face, but I didn't know why until I saw where his other hand had gone. He had two daggers, not one, and he'd found an opening where my armor connected to my leg plates.

How had he beat my Reinforcement enchantment? I didn't have time to consider it as I felt a white-hot heat begin to spread from the blade wound as he twisted it before pulling it free. Through clenched teeth I decided it must be a rogue ability that allowed him to find weak spots where there shouldn't be any.

The poison on his blade was doing little damage to my health, but it made me feel sluggish and slow. I swung out, my slash going wide and he easily dodged it. He came in for another strike, his daggers turning a sickly green color. One slash caught me across my face while the other clanked harmlessly off my chest plate armor.

I was done playing around. Flushing essence into my very blood, I felt the effects of the poison lessen. Next, I filled my blades with essence, increasing my already substantial attribute scores. I feigned a slow swing of my sword, then activated Power Strike midway through and slashed hard at his left arm.

He moved it to block the strike that had come too quickly for him, but it was too late. My cut took him across his arm and straight through it. Clyde screamed in pain as his arm fell at his feet. Blood spurt out, covering the floor as he tried to process what had happened.

I didn't give him such a luxury, activating Swift Strike once more I cut a line across his neck, removing his head from his body.

Blood covered my front, but I ignored it as I turned to face off against Ted. He wasn't looking good, and I decided to watch Ares instead as she obviously had everything under control.

Ted bled from several large gashes on his chest, face, and arm while Ares had several cuts into her hide. Feeling like I could at least alleviate her pain a touch, I cast Restoring Light on her.

She preened as she readied another attack. Ted, to his credit, caught her talons with his dagger and cut low with another. The blade lengthened with purple energy and cut her across the chest. Ares screeched loud enough to cause Ted to stumble backward, holding his ears.

That was all the opening she needed as her dagger-like talons, newly sharpened and tested, raked across his throat. The attack nearly took his head off, but it held on by several large chunks of flesh. His body went stiff, no longer able to keep him alive under so many devastating injuries.

Ted fell to the floor, dead.

CHAPTER 29
MEETING WITH ALAYNA

I took their weapons, armor, and searched their hideout for any loot as well. Whatever wasn't nailed down or broken, I took with me, storing it away in my inventory to sell later. It wasn't that I needed the gold or the loot, but I was feeling very spiteful about the injuries Ares and I took and the trouble these two idiots caused me. I wondered as I left the ruined building in the deep Lowers if they were working with anyone else but pushed the thought aside in favor of seeking out a bath.

Yes, a bath would do me some real good right now. My armor was already cleaning itself off, but my skin and hair remained stained with blood and gore. Gone were any plans to seek out Alayna before tonight, replaced with a desire to bathe, rest, and read. I was close to making a few discoveries with my profession and I had several thick tomes that weren't going to read themselves on the topic of enchanting, rune scribing, and general theory.

I found a decent place that welcomed stabling a griffin, and I tipped the stableboy with what was likely the equivalent of several month's wages to feed Ares. I gave him specific instructions to not brush her down, I'd be out after a meal to do it myself. I owed her that much at the very least.

First, I found my way into the bathing room, one of the few Inns that had such a room as an extra amenity and bathed thoroughly. There were two others in the water when I got there, the tub was more of a large soaking pool than an individual affair, but they soon exited when they saw the filth I was about to introduce into the water.

One hard scrub at a time I cleared my hair of gore and washed myself clean. The water was a welcome warmth against my cold skin and attendants took my armor to be cleaned. I let them go, despite the enchantment that kept it clean there could be a few places where gunk would build up and with it a terrible stink. For the most part the magic did its job wonderfully.

I tried not to linger but the warmth of the water called to me like a warm blanket on a cold night. So, as it was, it took me nearly an hour before I got out, my hands and feet spongy from the soak. Inside the main eating hall of the Inn, I scarfed down a hot bowl of stew, barely tasting it as I hurried to get to Ares and tend to her.

I pulled out what equipment I had gathered for such a grooming session and soon went to work, brushing her out and cleaning her talons, even going so far as to sharpen one that had been nicked during the battle. It was a pleasant experience as we shared our feelings through our bond. The pleasure of it being akin to a warm bath for Ares. I went a step further as I finished and shared with her the experience I had while bathing and she preened her feathers from the thought of it.

"Sleep well, my friend," I said, petting her one final time before I retired for the night.

The evening came swiftly, and I woke up from a dead slumber just in time. Dressing back in my armor, you never could be too careful, I headed for the door and to Kissing Point to meet with Alayna.

The streets bustled with evening activity, adventurers, merchants, peasants, and the like, all moving about their business. The sun was beginning to set just as I reached the uphill climb. But my body was something else entirely now and I easily climbed the hill without so much as a labored breath.

Sitting on the same bench where we'd shared our first kiss was an angelic beauty with rosy, red cheeks, wavy blonde hair, and a kind smile that captured my heart as she turned toward me.

"Alayna!" I exclaimed, rushing forward and pulling her into an embrace.

"Caldor!"

The embrace turned to a kiss and all the time lost between us seemed to melt away in the moment of our embrace. All my doubts and fears about her were gone in an instant when put against the pure joy I experienced at our reunion. Long months had gone by, and I thought myself free of any strong emotional ties, thinking that perhaps that part of me had died out on the battlefield, but no. Here it was, burning fiercely in my chest the desire to never let her out of my sight again, lest I lose her for good.

I held back tears, not wanting to embarrass myself, but the emotions were hard to deal with and soon I felt the cold run of tears on my cheeks. Covertly I wiped them away before she looked up at me, our embrace turning into a passionate kiss where we both moved together as if we were seeking water after a long dry journey. Each of us kissing stronger and harder than the other until finally with a soft gentle touch, we ended the kiss and gazed into each other's eyes.

Purple orbs accented against her purple eye makeup that she wore, making her appear all the more stunning for it. I'd hardly noticed what she wore until we finally parted. Instead of a dress or even simple but elegant clothing, she wore armor, new armor I'd never seen before. It had the look of flowing water, wind, and nature all wrapped into one.

"Elven armor?" I asked, running my hand down her shoulder and following one of the many swirling lines built into it.

"I've got so much to tell you," she whispered, but then buried her head into my chest. "Not here. Can we go to your Manor for privacy?"

I embraced her firmly, before pushing her off my chest to look into her eyes once more. "About that," I said, giving her my best awkward smile. I launched into a short explanation to why I no longer had Miles Manor and she listened quietly, seeming to understand there was more to it than my simple explanation.

"I'm so sorry," she said, caressing my face. I could tell she could sense the pain that lingered below the surface. "I should have been there, I'm so sorry."

I shook my head, tears running freely down my face at this point. "No. For all the fortune of this world and the next, I am glad that you didn't have to live through that hell. I have changed, I even thought that perhaps I'd no longer be able to love you with how deep the wounds were that have run through me. But now I know that was foolhardy. Seeing you now after so long just makes me think of happier times. I've missed you dearly, Alayna."

"And I you," she said, giving me a soft gentle kiss on the lips. "Let's get dinner and speak of light matters. Then if you have any place where we can set up wards, we will talk more."

"We can eat and speak of heavy matters, and I know just the place to do so," I said, already thinking of where we could go that would guarantee privacy. My Arcane Asylum.

We returned to my room at the Inn, nothing at all unusual about two armored adventurers sharing such a room and we barely turned any heads. Alayna's armor, elven in make for sure, had a hood that must have had an additional enchantment on it because once she raised it, the front of her face was obscured with shadow. It helped her go undetected by any common folk that would know of her and none, despite my station, seemed to know my face well enough to recognize me.

I summoned forth the door and we entered together. The area had been cleared out and organized, however my recent quick move left the immediate entrance more than a bit cluttered. Apologizing as I led her in, I guided her through the mess and to an armchair next to the fireplace. It burned brightly, lighting up the room with its orange light and soon the door disappeared, leaving us to our own devices and in perfect privacy.

"So, tell me, did you get in contact with the elves?" I asked. It was hard sitting across from her, all I wanted to do was hold her close and pretend like the last few months hadn't happened after all.

"I did and they sort of held me prisoner," Alayna said, rubbing at the back of her neck. She appeared a bit embarrassed by the notion, her cheeks going a darker shade of red.

"They what?" I asked, moving to the edge of my seat.

"It wasn't like they put me in a dungeon or anything, I just couldn't leave my suite or venture out anywhere without elven guard. They claimed it was simple precautions for diplomatic reasons, but I know what it feels like to be held prisoner without chains."

That comment took me back a bit, was she referring to her father? I didn't have time to ask as she launched back into it.

"After I showed them the designs that would allow flight, they treated me like that, but it wasn't all bad. I got to train with some of their best healers, read from their extensive libraries, and I was gifted this armor by the queen herself as a show of good faith."

She waved her hand down her armor as if to show how glorious it truly was and I agreed, without even looking at the attributes, the armor looked pretty awesome and unique when put against other armor I'd seen among adventurers. The metal had a white color to it but a sheen of blue when the light hit it. What metal it could be I didn't know, but I would be sure to ask her when she gave me a chance to speak.

"I worked on them a little with the design and before they let me go I saw one of their naval ships rise from the ground. But best of all is, they've agreed to grant us passage to Avalon. We have three months before they plan on leaving, but I suggest we gather together the strongest friends you have, and we begin our journey to the elven lands."

"I'm finally going to get to Avalon," I said the words a measure above a whisper as I processed what that meant. Then a thought occurred to me, and I couldn't help but ask if she knew yet.

"What is it?" She asked as I stared at her trying to figure out how to ask.

"What do you know about the fall of House Blalor?" I asked, a lump forming in my throat as I did.

"I've just got back, and I've heard rumors that my father's campaign went well, but I'm afraid I don't know the details yet. I'm actually meeting with him tomorrow to officially request leave to go to Avalon with you."

"Don't," I said, shaking my head. "It will be best if you don't tell your father my plans. I can no longer trust him and all that you've said about him has proved to be right. And much more."

"What do you mean?" She asked.

I took a deep breath and launched into it. First I told her how the war went, how I'd struggled with the loss from war, and she came to sit beside me as I spoke, my words somber. She was very interested in the barges and asked more questions than I had answers to, but eventually I couldn't hold off any longer and I told her about the weapon that wiped House Blalor from the map. Then I told her that I discovered part of the information that led to the construction of the weapon, and she stopped me.

"So did I," she said looking horrified. "But how could he use such a weapon on innocent people? No, no, not even my father could be so callous with innocent lives."

"But he did, and well, the blame isn't to be laid at our feet, but at his. Someone has to avenge those who died. There has to be a balance to all things, and I think it has to be me," I said, swallowing hard and awaiting her reaction.

"You mean," she began to say, and put her hand over her face. "You can't, I mean you actually can't, he is too strong for you and I can't lose you too."

"You will never lose me." I hugged her tightly and hoped she understood what I needed to do.

"But I've lost him," she whispered. Her voice turned harsh as she continued to speak. "He has done the unthinkable and I can't stand by him any longer. Oh, my poor mother, what must she think? I doubt she'll be able to look at him. I always knew my father was determined to keep the peace and I wanted to believe he had good reason to invade House Blalor, but to kill so many innocent lives..."

"I'm sorry," I said. I was finally letting myself see it from her perspective and it was too terrible a thing to consider. That your father was truly a monster and needed to be put down before he took more lives.

"How many more of these weapons does he have? What are we going to do to prevent them from being used again? Why is the king okay with such a terrible weapon being used against his own people?" Alayna rattled off question after question while shaking her head.

They were good questions, ones I should have posed to the king when I had my chance, but as I did sometimes while in the moment, I'd forgotten or not even considered such things.

I said all I knew to say in response. "I don't know. But what I do know is that I was being praised alongside your father as a hero because of his actions. I want none of that praise and it makes me sick to consider it."

Alayna appeared torn suddenly, as she looked at me. "You can't tell me how or when you plan on doing it. He is a monster and needs to pay, but I can't help you kill him. He's been distant most of my life, but he's still my father."

I looked her in the eyes, wishing I hadn't needed to tell her any of this, but in my heart, I knew I was right. "I don't really have a plan yet, but while I'm a baron under him, I don't know how strict the oath is that I took when it comes to harming the lord I am sworn under."

"Your oath holds you to protect the people of the realm,

not my father specifically. No, I would say you are free to attack him I just don't know that you will succeed, and I can't lose you as well."

I could see in her eyes she wanted to say more, but instead, we just sat next to each other while I went over ways I might kill her father and she worried about losing me and what was left of who her father had been.

"I can't do anything until I've dealt with the Ley Lines and stopped this Chaos Knight from further infecting them," I said, deciding on the matter around the same moment I let the words spill from my lips.

Alayna nodded, tears in her eyes. She pressed herself close to me and I held her while I thought about the Chaos Knight. She was still a great threat and one that needed to be dealt with before I could be free to live my life. Chaos, pure and powerful, was never meant to interact directly with the deep rivers of essence that traveled through the Wyrd like veins in the arm, giving life blood and power to the magic of our world.

The more I thought about the Wild-Sparked and there claims of dungeons that they could enter, the more everything I thought I knew was brought into an unclear focus. If dungeons weren't only beings created and employed by the Ordu, then what were they really? A natural byproduct of the essence and the Ley Lines? And if that were true, why had the Chaos Knight tried to turn and corrupt a dungeon, what would be the point?

It all came back down to the Ley Lines and the damage that was being done to the fabric of magic as Chaos corruption spread within them. Only the Ordu and their powerful weapons could deal with such a threat, so I would travel to Avalon and return with the Blade of the Ordu, the last blade of Order. I had faith that either Mah'kus or the blade itself would somehow guide me to what to do next, perhaps I could confer with an Arbiter on the matter? Either way, I would see to it that Order was restored, and Chaos would be pushed back so that the balance reigned.

Hopefully I could do this and end the threat of the Chaos Knight in time to gather the forces of the Wyrd together to face whatever else was coming our way. Because I knew now from my dreams that more than Chaos was at work here and one day, a day sooner than I could imagine, whatever darkness that lurks out beyond the space between planets would come as it did in my nightmares. And when that great black dragon arrives, it will take the full force of the Wyrd, both Order and Chaos, to beat back the threat.

CHAPTER 30
ALTERNATIVE ALLIANCES

W e talked late into the night, but avoided the subject of her father and eventually discussed my fears of what was to come. I told her I needed to find a way to get more Houses involved in the Eastern conflict so that we can end it before it was too late. We had to be united, I told her, and she agreed, giving me a suggestion that I hadn't really considered. She asked me if I had tried to reach out individually to some of the Houses, saying that my reputation and titles might get my foot in the door.

We left the Arcane Asylum and enjoyed a quiet night laying together on the bed. There was nothing sexual about the night, though it had been a while, both our minds were focused on heavier matters. So instead, I held her close and enjoyed the warmth of her body and the sweet scents of her hair. While lying there, thinking of what to do next, I decided that I would reach out to my assistant and have her come to Variyn, there was work to do here and I needed to see things through.

One of those unfortunate tasks was meeting with Lord Variyn. I didn't know if I'd be able to look him in the eyes or not, but I wanted a few days to get my bearings, so I stayed in the Inn, but used my Arcane Asylum exclusively. The room I rented worked more as a place where I could summon the door in privacy.

Several days went by before Verena joined me in Variyn, she took up her own room, but spent much time with me so that we could work out details. She was going to send messages to all the Houses with requests to meet an ambassador of Blackridge Keep to discuss 'urgent' matters. I hoped that being vague would help us get a first meeting and sending Cron—Verena's idea—as the ambassador would remind them of the conflict with Chaos not so many years ago.

Dwarves were rare to be seen since the fall of their kingdom and having one with a silver togue like Cron would be an asset to our cause.

Alayna found me several days later with an urgent look on her face and flanked by two elite guards. She wore the armor that disguised her appearance, but with two guardsmen at her side, it was hard to not notice she was nobility.

"You will wait outside while I speak with Caldor," she instructed them. They shared a look and seemed about to protest, but Alayna grabbed my hand and pulled me into the Inn and up to my room. "Summon the door." She instructed with the same harsh and cold words used on the guards.

When I finally did and we were safely inside, her demeanor broke and she began to cry.

"What's happened?" I asked, pulling her against my chest to comfort her. She'd seemed so strong only moments ago, now her sudden change of emotion had my head spinning.

"My mother is going into exile," she said, looking up with tear-stained cheeks. "She called me in to tell me she'd be leaving and told me a secret that she'd been keeping since my birth. I'm not Lord Variyn's daughter."

I pulled her from my chest, the shocking and confusing news totally startling me. "What do you mean, are you saying you were switched at birth or something?"

"What? No, my mother says she was unfaithful to my father, and she told me who my real father is..."

"Well, who is it?" I asked, several faces flashed through my mind but one in particular lingered.

"Galt," she said, whispering the words. "He's always been so protective and kind to me, like a father might be to his daughter."

"Does Lord Variyn know?" I asked, now worried about the retribution that might follow. "Are you and Galt safe at the keep now?"

"I don't think so," Alayna said, her sobs subsiding finally. "My mother claimed to have never spoken the words aloud until this morning and her chamber is warded against scrying like most nobles' bedrooms."

"What are you going to do?" I asked, my head still shaking back and forth from the shock of it all.

"I need to escape and convince Galt to come with me," Alayna said, her gaze hardening. "I think Galt knows she told me, because he insisted that Elijah and Elias, his two strongest Elite guards, be with me at all times now. He even considered escorting me himself, but I told him they'd be enough to ward off any trouble. So much is changing so fast."

"How strong is Galt?" I asked, a devious seed of a plan forming in my head. I tried to push it away, but I couldn't help but think how convenient it would be if Galt killed Lord Variyn in a fit of fatherly rage. How I would get him to that point of anger I didn't know, but I couldn't let anything happen to Alayna.

"I don't know," Alayna said honestly. "I've never seen him lose a fight, but he's mentioned in passing that he used to be a King's Guard, so at least as strong as one of them. He told me several times that he'd left the King's Guard for love, but I'd never gotten him to say who his sweetheart was or how long ago it had been. I was so dense. He'd spent almost all his time doting over me and making sure I was safe, but I just thought it was his job."

"The most important job," I said, our eyes met, and I saw the swirling emotions inside of her. She was truly unsure how to deal with the powerful news she'd gotten, and I didn't have the right words to comfort her.

But words didn't matter right now, she needed to work out how she felt, and I could be a listening ear. She went on and on sharing stories about Galt. Going into detail about how he'd trained her in swordplay even when her father forbade it. Saying that he was instrumental in getting herself trained enough to even *Awaken*. She shared how proud Galt had been when she'd finally ascended and chosen her class.

Then she lamented the way she'd treated him through the years, exerting her authority over him whenever it suited her. She cried about the simple things like forcing him to cover for her when she would escape from the keep to explore the city. It really wasn't so bad, but each new remembrance brought more tears, and I held her all the tighter for it.

"Do you think Galt would come to Avalon with us?" I asked after several minutes of silence. She'd worn herself out and we now sat together on a sofa, staring into the magical fire burning across the room.

"I don't know," Alayna said, her eyes alit with the reflection of the flames. "If I asked he probably would, but is that fair of me? His career will be at risk, he can't just up and leave, can he?"

"For you I bet he would," I said. "Think about what he said, that he left the King's Guard for love. I'm sure that love started with your mother, but it's all but transferred to you now. I can't say that I can understand the love of a father for his daughter personally, but if its anything like what I feel for you then he'd face a hundred, no, a thousand angry Lord Variyn's for you and be all the happier for it. No amount of danger will hold back a true father from protecting his daughter."

"Will you ask him for me?" Alayna asked, turning her gaze upon me. "It is too risky for me to speak to him about it, lest I get overheard, but you could, and your anti-scrying earrings will keep anyone from overhearing."

"An unlikely alliance, but I will try," I said, already thinking over how best to speak to him when most of our interactions had been shoddy at best.

***

I wasn't keen to go to the keep, but I knew that was the only way I'd encounter Galt. Surely no one knew of my intentions against Lord Variyn, so I was just as welcome in the keep as I'd always been. I would have to be careful not to bump into Lord Variyn as he wished to have a meeting with me that I wasn't quite ready for. The guards at the entrance let me in without so much of a look in my direction.

It was much the same as I remember, servants walking here and there, occasionally a more noble looking person, but no one approached me or tried to bar my path. I stopped a pair of guards after several minutes of roaming the hallways and making no progress.

"Direct me to Galt, will you?" I asked, thinking I recognized one of them, but I couldn't recall his name.

"He's out in the training grounds with some new recruits," the one on the left said, inclining his head toward me.

I turned and headed back for the entrance. The training grounds were on the opposite side of the garden that used to hold the Prime Mana Shrine, but I could get there faster by going another way I knew, which meant going back to the entrance and circling around.

Galt had a dozen or so young-faced men doing drills while he yelled orders at them in his usual tone of gruff anger. He noticed me and turned to a grizzled man beside him, giving him orders to keep the training going while he approached me.

"What?" He asked, seeming more gruff than usual. When I didn't immediately answer him he continued, "Well out with it, can't you see I'm busy."

"Is there someplace we can speak in private?" I asked, doing my best to signal with my eyes the importance of the upcoming conversation.

Sharp as a newly cared for blade, Galt understood my meaning and gave additional orders to his second before leading me out of the courtyard. There was always a purpose behind Galt as he moved, like a predator always on the hunt. He was a powerful man and one I didn't want on my bad side, so I thought as best I could how I could tell him that I knew his secret and that he should join my little anti Lord Variyn faction.

It wasn't like I'd come straight out and tell him I wanted Lord Variyn dead, no, that would be foolish. Initially I'd planned on telling no one, but I couldn't keep secrets from Alayna, as much as I might want to at times.

He led me to a guard room set into the side of the keep. It didn't look super private, but I didn't hear the rumble of activity from any of the adjacent rooms, so I assumed it must be empty. Turning back to Galt I readied my explanation.

"Are you certain no one will overhear our words here?" I asked, looking about the neatly cared for room. It had a table, four chairs, and three doors set into the walls that led deeper into the keep or adjacent rooms.

Galt sighed, shaking his head before leading me deeper through one of the doors and into what looked like a private office. He gestured to some runes cut into the stone and sat across from me on the other side of a large desk. This must be an office of his or something.

"Not even Non could penetrate these runes, or at least I paid enough to have them put in, so if we are overheard, I've got to have words with an extrinsic wizard," Galt said, grumbling through the sentence.

Satisfied that they would do after looking over a few of the formations and recognizing them, I turned my attention back to Galt. "I don't really know where to start, so I guess I will just say it."

"Usually a good tactic," Galt said, clearly annoyed by me taking him from his work.

"Alayna knows that you are her father, Lady Variyn has fled the capital, and Alayna and I plan to leave soon as well. We are going on a dangerous quest to recover a lost Ordu artifact before the damage caused by the Prime Mana Shrine becomes permanent. Will you come with us and help me protect Alayna?"

I never thought to see Galt with a completely and utterly shocked expression, but here it was, plain to see. His eyes had gone wide and stayed that way, his mouth ajar as his gaze drifted off me and to the wall. He looked like someone just told him the world was about to end or that up was down and down was up. Giving him the time he needed to process the information, I looked around his office.

He had books, not many but a few, on a bookshelf behind the desk and lots of paperwork neatly stacked and organized on his desk. All in all, the office was pretty well organized and I wouldn't have guessed Galt to be such an organized and neat person. He made a grunting noise, then licked his lips as he tried to say something, but the words were lost as he just shook his head, still too stunned to speak.

Finally, after what felt like several long minutes, but probably only a dozen seconds or so, he spoke. "Who else knows?" His gruff voice was back in full swing, and it almost sounded as if he were admonishing me with his words.

I flinched from the sudden words, but quickly recovered. "Lady Variyn told Alayna and Alayna told me. No one else."

He matched my gaze, his one of intensity and mine as disarming as I could make it. "I'm due a leave of absence. I will take it and be at Alayna's side, but no one must speak of our situation. She is heir to the throne of House Variyn, and I won't take that from her because of my own desires to be close to my daughter."

I nodded. "We will be in touch about when we will be leaving, but Alayna tells me they gave her three months when she left the elven nation. Oh, I didn't mention, the elves are going to fly us to an island named Avalon using advanced Ordu technology that Alayna helped to discover.

It's the same rune powers that allowed us to use floating barges during the war."

Mention of the war darkened my mood immediately and Galt must have noticed because he nodded in my direction before saying, "War is a dark hell, I'm not happy you had to experience it boy. I can see the light in your eyes has diminished since our last meeting, a damn shame to see it go. Hold tight to who you were before the war and be forgiving to the person you've become after. Don't let the darkness define you."

"Thank you," I said, holding his gaze. I felt a sudden wave of appreciation for Galt, and I was glad in that moment that he was Alayna's father and not Lord Variyn. This was the fatherly type of person that I could respect and understand, not the scheming and aloof Lord Variyn.

With that, I departed, but before I could make it to the gate I was intercepted by Non.

"Follow me at once and say nothing."

I looked toward the gate, too far to make a run for it and the guards would likely catch me if I tried. What did Non want, and did he somehow know what I'd been talking about with Galt? No that couldn't be it, surely something else was going on.

"Okay," I said, turning and following Non into the keep.

CHAPTER 31
WHISPERS SPEAK VOLUMES

I followed Non through the various hallways as he weaved through them expertly. Eventually coming to a secret door set into a wall that led to his hid away office. Despite the fact that I was certain we weren't in the right place inside the keep, his office awaited us down the narrow hallway. Like before, the door swung open and shut behind me without any need to touch it. Some sort of magical automation that Non had likely put into place when creating his little home away from home.

I was beginning to suspect that perhaps his office worked similar to Warrick's tower, in that it was magical and did odd things like moving around. It made sense for someone in Non's position to have a place that never could be found in the same place. My eyes ran over the many stacks of notebooks and loose papers, but nothing written on any of them made any sense, his own personal language at work.

"Do you know what my job is?" Non asked, breaking

the silence growing between us. He had a stern way of talking, like I was being lectured or something.

I took his hard look and gave it right back to him. "To protect House Variyn I imagine," I said, not hiding the confusion in my words at being asked such a leading question.

"I am a close and personal friend and servant directly to Lord Variyn. While it is my job to protect House Variyn and its interest, I am also careful to keep an eye on threats to him. Now, tell me Caldor, is there a threat to Lord Variyn that I should be made aware of?"

What was happening, how could he know my intentions when I'd only told a single person, someone I knew I could trust with my life. No, this had to be something else and I just wasn't understanding his meaning.

"No more than usual I suspect," I said, my words as calm as I could keep them, given the circumstances. I didn't trust Non, not sure that I ever did, but since my time at war I definitely didn't trust the man.

"Then why are you reaching out to several other houses, including a man you know to be a traitor and a spy, Tim?" Non asked, his voice completely free of emotions.

"Oh that," I said, shaking my head at the ridiculousness of it. Of course, Non had some way of finding out who I sent messages to. If he'd gotten into the actual contents of the letter he'd have known it was nothing, so he must have just received word that I'd sent out the messages.

"Yes, that," Non said, a touch of sass entering his tone.

I looked at Non, surprised at how little I feared him

now. He worked in shadows and did as he was told, just another cog in the machine of House Variyn. "I'm on duty by the king to reach out to all Houses to help address a looming threat in the East." I couldn't help but let a small smile come over my face when I saw the hint of confusion on Non's. He'd either not heard I'd visited the king or my 'duty to the king' statement that was mostly false, caught him off guard.

"I see," Non said, clearing his throat. "If it is business of the king then it is no business of mine. However, we must speak on your lack of decorum and failure to live up to your oaths."

This caught me off guard and I gave him my best, 'what the hell do you mean' look. This caused him to smile, a fake wicked thing, but a smile, nonetheless. "You have missed every ball and meeting that has been put forth since you became a vassal. As a baron, you are no longer exempt from missing these occasions. There is a ball in two days, and you will be there or you will risk punishment."

I wanted to ask him what sort of punishment it was, thinking it might be preferable to going to a ball, but I held my tongue. Instead, I nodded politely and stood. "I'll be there," I said, turning to leave.

"Be careful, Young Miles. The more responsibility you take on, the bigger the target on your back. I'd hate to see you fall before your time. You'd be much like your father in that respect."

My blood seethed suddenly, and I turned, staring red hot coals into Non's nonplused face. "Don't speak of my father." My words came out hard and threatening, but Non just smiled.

"Of course, excuse my brashness." Non didn't look apologetic, but I took a deep breath and got myself under control.

Why had that affected me so much? Just the thought that this weasel of a man would compare my father's sacrifice and death to save the kingdom as a simple miscalculation or misstep, just churned a deep anger inside of me. I respected my father, I loved my father, and I wanted most of my life to be just like my father.

The darkness inside of me settled over my mood as I left the room and headed out into the hallways. I was let out in a different section of the keep and once again, I was sure this stupid office of his had magical qualities to it. Non was perhaps a bigger threat than I truly realized, but his power didn't lie in strength of arm or force, but in secrets. I would do well to keep mine safe.

CHAPTER 32
THE BALL

Two days went by far too quickly, but I had one saving grace. When I'd told Alayna about the ball, she offered to go with me, saying she normally didn't attend them if she could help it, but for me she'd love to go.

"I've missed several meals with him already, but I just can't imagine how hard it is going to be seeing him after everything I've learned," Alayna said, as we bounced along inside a private carriage heading towards the keep.

I nodded, completely agreeing with her. "Just wear a smile like a mask," I said. It was something I'd been getting better and better at myself, as I went about my daily tasks. Everyone expected you to be content and happy, but of course I was neither of those things.

It was a cool evening, the moonlight out in force illuminating the street, as well as any lamp. I let the curtain fall and focused my attention on Alayna. She wore a magnificently beautiful purple gown that matched the black and purple outfit she'd picked out for me.

She shared what was likely to be the only true smile of the night as the carriage bumped to a halt and our doors were opened.

"Announcing Lady Variyn and Lord Miles," came a stuffy voice as we stepped out onto the cobbled path leading up to the stairs.

There was quite a gathering outside the keep, people chatting and standing around. It was different than I remembered from the one other event I'd attended like this, where all the festivities were contained to the actual ballroom.

"We should just go straight in," Alayna said, leaning toward me to whisper into my ear.

I nodded and we passed several expectant looking faces without interacting.

The ballroom we went to was closer to the entrance than the previous one and a good measure smaller. There was still a raised area with a throne, currently empty, but other than that the room was rather plain when put up against the grand ballroom.

Sure, there were tapestries depicting battles long past and the few pillars that connected with the vaulted ceiling had carvings of the Ordu, but something about it just didn't reach the grandeur of the other ballroom.

We found a table easy enough and my mouth watered at the thought of food. However, I knew that only appetizers would be served, per Alayna's warning, and I'd eaten plenty accordingly. As we sat, several people approached our table and interacted with Alayna. She was a professional when it came to court interactions though and never missed a beat. Meanwhile, I faltered in the two conversations where I was included, saying nothing particularly exciting or worthwhile.

"You probably know my son from the war," a noblewoman said, directing her inquiry toward me and catching me off guard as I was staring off toward the other side of the room.

"What's that?" I asked, turning my attention to her then to the man standing beside her. He looked vaguely familiar with blonde hair, a stiff build, and a look in his eyes that I could relate to. He couldn't have been any older than Zander, and as I watched him I did finally place his name.

"Good day to you, Commander Gortain," I said, inclining my head and giving him my mask of a smile.

He did the same, and I recognized him as a man I might be able to get along with after all. Too easily so many of these commanders had let the horrors of war wash off them like water from the back of a duct, but this man had obviously internalized some of the horrors. "To you as well, Commander Miles" he said, inclining his head.

"Shall we let them catch up on events while we go find a drink," the woman, whose name I hadn't gotten, suggested to Alayna. Alayna gave me a look that was one part apologetic and one part frustration, before leaving with the slightly older looking lady.

"Word is that you are building forces to make an assault east," Gortain said matter-of-factly. "I've been given a sizable estate and could rally men to your cause if you have need of me."

There was a haunting look in his eyes that said he didn't want to be needed, but also something else. A glimmer of true respect and honor that shone through the mark that the horrors of war had left. He didn't want to fight, but he would if it were the right thing to do. It was easy to pick out the look, because it was one I'd seen every time I'd looked in the mirror as of late.

"There might soon come a day that I do, and I would welcome one such as you at my side," I said, holding his gaze as I measured the man up. "If, when the time comes, I can marshal enough troops together we might be able to prevent any actual combat from occurring. A show of force as it were."

"Perhaps you can call out whatever force we face and have their general fight you in single combat," Gortain said, a hint of a true smile on his lips. "I still remember the time we were deployed together, and you got their commander to agree to single combat. I thought you were a fool, but then you brought him to his knees in a matter of seconds. I toasted your name to my troops that night and we celebrated the lives that were saved."

I fought so many battles that I was surprised when I couldn't recall the exact one he meant. But it was all the same to me, the battles I won by duel were the least memorable for me, my mind instead put to task to remember the dead each time dueling failed.

"On the rare occasions that a duel was accepted and

honored, I too toasted victory with my troops. I'm honored to have fought beside you," I said, and I meant it. This man seemed much more in tune with his troops than most commanders I'd come across and I found myself wishing I knew him better.

"Are we interrupting," came a familiar voice, and I turned to find Zander wearing a black suit with white highlights throughout. He looked good outside his armor and on his arm was none other than Ismene dressed in a simple, but elegant black gown.

"Not at all, my Lord," Gortain said, bowing his head and turning to leave.

I didn't stop him but did make a note to remember the man and his offer of help. In the end, every bit of troops I could muster would be useful, so I couldn't afford to turn anyone down.

"Was Joran bothering you?" Zander said, a smirk on his mouth. "I grew up with the boy and he honestly reminds me of you. So stuck on the concepts of honor and doing the right thing that he often ruined our fun."

"Not at all," I said, directing my fake smile at Zander then faltering as I looked upon Ismene. "I didn't know you came to these?" I asked, directing my question back to Zander after smiling at Ismene.

"My father always forced me to go," Zander said, his smirk disappearing. "After he, well you know, I've made it a point to go to as many as I could. My mother's health permitting, I will get her to one soon too."

"How is she doing?" I asked, remembering Zander's

reluctance to go to war had hinged on his mother's health and not wanting to leave her alone to die. But all those months had passed, and no word ever came of her death.

"Surprisingly well," Zander said, his entire mood brightening as he talked about his mother. "According to the healers she came close several times while I was gone, but she fought just as hard as we did and pulled through. They are saying that with the right tonics she might have some time left now."

Now was as good a time as any to ask Zander about the voyage and having him and Ismene by our side, so I went for it. "I know we only just got back from the war, but I have an expedition in mind." I lowered my voice and motioned for him to come closer with my hand. "It would be to an Island called Avalon and might take several months, but I want you and Ismene at my side."

Zander reeled back a bit, looking at me like I was mad. But before he spoke, Ismene did. "You want me to go back to Avalon, without Merlin?"

She seemed completely aghast by the thought, and I couldn't blame her. She'd gone there at her weakest and seen the awful power of Merlin at work killing the strong monsters that lurked in the jungles there.

"Merlin is gone, somewhere, and I don't know how to contact him," I said by way of explanation. Zander finally found his voice and what he said surprised me.

"I'm in." He said simply, the smirk that loomed on his face most of the time was gone and in its place was a genuine smile. "As long as Ismene is going, that is." He added, looking to her for her response.

"Of course, I'm in," Ismene said, shaking her head. "I wasn't keen about the war you two went and got lost in the last few months, but this is adventuring at its finest. I just hope you have a good plan on how to deal with the crazy strong monsters that we will find on Avalon."

I had a few ideas but nothing concrete yet, so I just nodded appreciatively to them both and lifted my drink, taking a sip. Alayna returned shortly afterward, new drinks in tow, and niceties were exchanged between everyone.

It turns out we worried in vain about Lord Variyn. He didn't show the entire night. We stayed as late as was expected, mostly speaking with Zander and Ismene before excusing ourselves and making our way out of the main ballroom.

We'd made it all of two feet, when a voice called out to me.

"Lord Miles," the voice said, and I turned to find a servant in fine clothing. "Lord Variyn wishes a word before you depart. Excuse me Lady Variyn, but he requested to speak with Lord Miles alone."

I turned to Alayna, and she gave me a look that I took to say, tonight isn't the night to do it, but I already knew that, so I just smiled at her and nodded to the attendant.

"Can you find your way back to the carriage and I will meet you shortly?" I asked, she nodded and was off. "Lead the way."

The servant was well dressed in dark colors and the

emblem of the house on his breast. He led me through the halls with practiced ease and grace until we stopped in front of a door I hadn't been to yet. It was unmarked and might as well have been a closet for how simple it looked. The attendant nodded his head at me, indicating the door, and I reached forward, pushing it open.

Inside was Lord Variyn's office. It looked much the same as before, however this room was slightly larger than his last, which just added to the oddity of it all. Sitting across the desk and looking dressed for the ball was Lord Variyn.

"Come in and sit," he commanded without looking up from a report he was going over.

I did so, taking a seat in a red velvet chair across from him and sitting tall.

"You've been busy, meeting with kings, stopping wars, and reaching out to my enemies," Lord Variyn said, finally looking up to regard me. He had a cruel smile on his lips that I couldn't help but imagine smacking off his face.

I could no longer see the kindhearted ruler I pretended him to be all those months ago. Now, as I looked across the table from me, I saw only the monster I knew lurked beneath the disguise of flesh. In Lord Variyn there was evil, pure and simple. I almost wished he would take the side of Chaos and it would be easier for me to extinguish the flame of his life, as it was my very duty but seeing him here sitting across from me and pretending to be anything but the monster he was made me tremble with anger.

"I've done my part in keeping the peace," I said, restraining myself as best I could but unable to keep all the malice from my words. If he only knew how far my hatred for him went now. I tried to keep from imagining my blade plunging into his gut, but it was difficult.

"I'm sure the king offered you land holdings, why wouldn't he? But you've not made any public announcement, so I take it you've not taken him up on his offer yet. I can't match the prestige that would come from a king appointed title, but I can offer you additional lands if it will appease you. Perhaps you'd even like the fertile lands of the House Blalor capital?"

My anger hit a new level hearing him speak about the capital as if it were anything but a husk of desolate land now. I clenched hard on the wood of the chair, and it creaked under the pressure of my grip.

"Not enough?" Lord Variyn asked, mistaking my anger for him as anger toward his offer. "The capital lands are worthy of your consideration, I assure you. Ever since we cleansed-"

"Since *you* cleansed them," I corrected, cutting him off.

Lord Variyn looked confused by my interruption and must have decided to just ignore it as he continued a moment later.

"Ever since they were cleansed by the essence device, monsters have flocked to the area, powerful ones too. The entire area is off limits to all but the strongest adventurers now. I've even had word that the dungeon there has grown in strength several fold. Here I was thinking they'd lost their dungeon years ago, a pity we lost ours during my predecessor's reign. It is handy to have a dungeon at the heart of your city."

It was like Lord Variyn had no clue what I really cared for and only now was I beginning to realize how one-track his mind must be. Thinking that everyone thought similar to him, progress, power, and authority being the things he craved.

There was a certain allure to his words that I couldn't push out of my mind. Had the area really turned into a monster paradise where even the dungeon flourished in the wake of the destructive power of his device? It could be a useful training ground for power leveling my allies before we leave on an even more dangerous adventure.

"I'll take the lands, but I want your word on something," I said, finding my tongue.

"I'm listening," he said, scratching at his thick, clean-cut beard.

"I want you to consider selling me the lands you've gifted that I might be considered a free state in the future. I want what you have, to rule over a land of my own," I said, only partially lying. I truly did want to be free of him, which would require my breaking from him, but I wasn't so sure I actually wanted to rule over any bit of land as badly as he did. In fact, I'd be happy to be a free agent able to go about my business as a normal adventurer, something I'd never really got the chance to experience as I always had some responsibility or another hanging over my head.

"I take it the king offered you something similar?" Lord Variyn asked, his expression searching. Was he truly considering such an offer? He must really be worried about what the king offered me by way of lands.

"Perhaps," I said, not outright lying, but willing to let him make his own assumptions if he wished.

"I will consider it, but not until we can stabilize the realm. I need strong barons such as you by my side, not splintering off or creating new Houses by the order of the king. Now tell me, why have you petitioned the other Houses?"

"Surely Non told you?" I asked, not wanting to waste anymore words with him.

"Yes, he told me that you have your eyes set on the East, but surely you don't mean to waste manpower in an untamed land with a wild people? They can't be held to oaths or be trusted to keep to their honor."

"I have seen honorable acts from them, but I agree that it isn't a perfect solution," I said, sighing. "However, the threat, as I told the king, must be dealt with otherwise it will spill into our lands much like it did during the time of my father and his battle at Lynsteen Pass. I won't allow such an incursion into our lands to happen again."

"You've changed much since the bright-eyed boy I met healing in a bed so many months ago. You are a man I could see standing beside Alayna while she rules my House. Perhaps that would be reason enough for you to stay attached to my lands, a chance to rule over a House?"

"Perhaps," I said, not able to keep my face emotionless, but succeeding enough that I didn't smirk, just smiled. It was a difficult thing speaking to Lord Variyn when I wanted him dead. What was worse was having the secret of his daughter and knowing she wanted nothing to do with his House any longer.

It was a shame in part, really. Alayna might be the best thing for this House if her father were taken care of. She was honorable, caring, and devoted to her responsibilities. If given the opportunity she'd be the perfect House Lady, ruling with a fair hand and a kind heart. Perhaps I should encourage her to take up the position when the threat of war, Chaos, and an unending darkness that couldn't be escaped had all resolved itself.

I smiled then, a genuine smile, thinking of the sheer amount of insane tasks that lay ahead. I would meet them head on, I would be the cliff they break against, and I would not falter or fall. Because of the pain and horrors I'd endured, I am stronger now than ever before. My honor tested and tried in the fires of war. My trusting nature hardened to the point of a blade, ready to cut through any obstacles, and my heart hardened against the losses that would surely come. I wasn't perfect, but I had been crafted in the fires of war to be a tool wielded in a glorious purpose. I would set right the injustices of this world and right the balance. For I am an Arcane Knight, defender of the weak and champion of the just.

"There is one more thing we should address," Lord Variyn said, passing a piece of paper over to me. It depicted armor for a griffin and looked rather epic with its well-made saddle and armored plates. "Part of the gift I meant to give you during the ceremony that you refused to attend. I had it constructed from Chaos hides and rune-infused steel, so your mount will be as durable as you have proven to be."

I took the paper and imagined Ares in the armor. "Thank you," I said, the most genuine thank you I'd likely ever give the mass murder.

"See the quartermaster about having it fitted, but it has been completed for several weeks now."

The meeting ended shortly after, Lord Variyn giving me access to the 'Essence Grounds' as he named them, the place where House Blalor capital had once been. It was infested with monsters and the Guild was defending the border, holding back the spread. I had my sight set on venturing into the lands and growing stronger in the coming months, nothing would stand in my way.

CHAPTER 33
ESSENCE GROUNDS

A week went by before everyone had gathered together so I could share my plans in full. Fred, Fran, Ismene, Emory, Alayna, Zander, Kora, and Creed all agreed to join the expedition without reservation, but Warrick on the other hand had words to say on the matter. Part of what I'd proposed was we all go into the 'Essence Grounds' first to get stronger, then meet in the elven lands to depart. Warrick didn't like that idea.

"How about you get to the island then portal me over like I showed you," Warrick said, only half paying attention as he rifled through a book in a language I didn't understand. "I've got myself into too much trouble as of late and need time to recharge the old batteries. I would warn you about going into those essence rich areas though, be ready for anything. Essence rich lands tend to be ones of high mutations and many queens fighting for dominance, and I'd wager this will be no different."

"We'll be smart about it," I assured him, but Fran cut in with a laugh.

"We don't have to bring Fred, do we? He sort of sucks all the essence out of essence gathering," Fran elbowed her brother who stood beside a reserved Kora. Fred didn't smile, merely rubbed at the affected area as if it hurt. It had been a while since he'd been out to gather essence and he looked worse off than when he first changed. Something about his new condition required a constant stream of essence and he would do well to remember as much.

"Yes, your brother has the most curious of ailments," Warrick said, turning his wise gaze upon the white-haired young man. "I have essence enough collected in stones purchased, thanks to your ingenious discoveries Caldor, perhaps he ought to stay with me so I can study him for a time, at least until you finish in the essence lands."

"Fred?" I asked, as it wasn't my place to dictate where he ought to be. I wasn't a tyrant after all.

"I can stay," Fred said, sounding a bit defeated. Perhaps he'd been looking forward to going after all. This seemed to surprise Fran and I saw her about to open her mouth, but Kora beat her to it.

"I will also stay if he is," Kora said, putting a gentle hand on his shoulder. "I believe my knowledge on the matter could be just as insightful."

"Wonderful, it's a party," Warrick said, clasping his hands together and laughing.

"Should I?" Fran said, looking toward me. I shook my head.

"He has plenty of support and is already stronger than he has any right being for his level. We need to get you up to a higher level along with the rest of us if we are going to have a decent chance."

"What about gear," Zander said, looking around the room. "We will get plenty of monster parts, but without a dungeon we won't be getting any higher level gear to go with our gains. Are we meant to purchase that ourselves?"

"There is a dungeon," Alayna said, her words coming before my own. I smiled in her direction and took over.

"Once we've cleared the monsters out a bit, I want to try our hands at the dungeon. I figure we have enough to do a dungeon run while a couple of us stay behind to watch the camp and kill roaming monsters. Then we can switch, it up, keeping the lowest and highest out of the mix until we can even off the levels a bit."

"Intriguing," Zander said, scratching his chin much like his uncle did when he was considering something. "Perhaps I can find someone willing, and we formed up two full groups? One killing roaming monsters and one doing the dungeon dive, then we can alternate. We already have two healers and Emory is tanking enough for one group."

This made Emory frown as he was still wanting to be considered more of a damage dealer despite his status as purely Tank type class. "Hey now, I can tank but we all know I'm better as a damage dealer," Emory said, unconvincingly. Everyone smiled at him, but we all knew he would cave when the time came.

"See what you can do about finding a few people but

keep them honest. I don't want any ruffians in the party if I can help it. I think if they are around level 25 to 35 it should be enough," I said, and Zander nodded.

With that, we broke up our little meeting and went our separate ways. Warrick opened up a portal right at the end of the table, luckily we had a private room rented out otherwise I'm sure it would have turned a good number of heads. Fred, Kora, and Warrick disappeared into the portal, and it winked out. Despite knowing how it worked it always took my breath away a little bit seeing the magic performed. Truly we lived in a time of magic and discovery, perhaps closer to the age of the Ordu than I previously thought.

***

The groups had been decided. Myself, Creed, Alayna, Emory, and Fran made up the first group. We were a bit melee heavy, but Ismene really wanted to be in a group with Zander, so I let it slide. Meanwhile, Zander recruited a few adventurers from a group called the Silver Hawk Clan, Nabi, a tank, and Tom, a damage dealer and tank. Both adventurers that we'd worked with before, so I guess they were trustworthy enough. The third was a caster by the name of Samuel and his brother James. Technically that made six for his group, but the James fellow said he'd wait outside the dungeon, but he and his brother were a package deal.

I purchased Essence Bands for everyone, the newest models that held the most essence before having to be emptied, well for all the people besides those that Zander brought, figuring if they wanted one then they could purchase some themselves. I wasn't so worried about us outpacing them that it would be necessary to give them one. After all, they were each of them around level thirty-five, so on the higher end versus everyone else.

We decided that it would be best to split up right away, that way we didn't dilute the essence gathering too far too fast. So, we determined we'd head in first, going straight for the dungeon entrance, while the second group would circle around and search out queens to farm for experience. It was strange, the area around the capital city of what used to be House Blalor was a mostly rocky area, but so many trees had grown up in the area that it had become a vast forest in an almost perfect circle starting where the device was detonated at the heart of the city.

"Feels weird doing this without Fred," Fran said, shooting me a look that was one part distress and one part smile.

"He'll be fine, if anyone can help him it's Warrick and Kora," I said, doing my best to reassure her.

I understood, in theory, where she was coming from. She'd spent her entire time as an adventurer with her brother, both of them watching each other's back and fighting by each other's side. She joked about wanting to be rid of him, but in her heart, she obviously didn't mean it. Their bond made me wonder what could be possible in the future with my own siblings, or perhaps just between them.

They had a whole new world of adventure waiting for them and I hoped against hope that they'd choose to do what Fred and Fran had, sticking together to watch each other's backs. I had a sudden bout of inspiration while standing at the edge of the forest, getting ready to dive into its deep depths.

"Hey Fran," I said, walking a few steps closer to her. "You should talk to my twin siblings and tell them how great it's been having your brother watch your back. I'd really love it if they did like you and Fred do, sticking together through it all."

"Except right now when he needs me," Fran said, looking longingly back the way we came. "Perhaps I should go back, I'm sure I'll find a way to level up before we leave on your little trip."

"It's up to you Fran, but I'd prefer it if you stayed. He is in good hands, and you know Kora won't let anything happen to him," I said, putting a comforting hand on her shoulder. A part of me wished Ismene was here to give her some better advice or comfort her in the way only she could, but my words would have to do for now, because we had work to do.

"You're right," Fran said, then laughing added. "They are a strange couple aren't they. Figures Fred would fall for a metal girl that someone else made. Plus, I always said Fred was an old soul, now he's coupled up with an even older soul."

I laughed, mostly for Fran's benefit, but she did have an amusing point. Fred and Kora were a strange coupling, but I wasn't about to stand in the way of love, no matter how strange.

With that settled, we took up position. Emory was in front, shield and sword ready. I followed behind him, planning on focusing on mid to long range attacks with my spells as we were lacking in that area. Creed took up the back, with Alayna and Fran behind me walking side by side.

The guild members maintaining the perimeter had been pretty reserved about what monsters they'd faced out on the edge, only saying that most had been what you'd expect out of a forest: bears, wolves, and the like. But one loose-lipped man had made a joke about mutated green squirrels that caught my attention. Apparently, they spit acid and moved like lightning, several having gotten past their line, and they were a pain to hunt down.

"Keep your eyes and ears open, we could get hit on any side," I said, speaking barely above a whisper but sure that everyone's enhanced ears had heard.

The first attack came from directly ahead and we heard it coming for at least a minute before it appeared, crashing down trees as it went.

Giant Badger, Level 22

It looked familiar enough that I knew what we were facing before my Inspect even went off. This Giant Badger was larger than the first I'd faced with Fran and Fred, and its coloring was different as well. It was all black with a red stripe down the center from its snout to its tail. Massive claws with a tint of red coloring slashed through the air and were caught by Emory, who grunted from the force of it. He was pushed back several feet, before he dug his feet deep and halted the advance.

The moment the push stopped, fire exploded all around Emory and I could suddenly hear the sizzle of his flesh as the fire ate away at him. Chanting from Alayna began as Fran skirted the edge looking for an opening, Creed however, didn't need to wait for such an opening. His entire armor glowed blue and took on its icy look as an aura of ice swirled around him. He stepped right into the blaze, and it flared around him, not touching him.

He slashed down on the Giant Badger, and it screamed out in pain as it took a deep gash into its arm. That must have been his Runic Strike ability, I absently thought as I stepped forward to put a hand on Emory and let off my own heal, Mending Touch. Emory stopped screaming and began to push back on the giant fireball as the flames slowed and dissipated all together. Fran, not to be left out of the mix, blurred suddenly as she darted forward, several slashes of energy arcing through the air at the badger in front of her.

It screamed and slashed wildly as each hit cut open a new wound and a moment later, she arrived in front of it, delivering a one-two into its face, before kicking off to avoid a strike from its clawed paw. I lashed out with a Lightning Strike, keeping my essence inside of me as this was meant to be an exercise in gaining essence not spending it all on attacks. The end was already in sight with this Giant Badger, its swings slowing as Emory stabbed into its gut and deftly avoided several bloody strikes with his shield held out in front.

All the while, Alayna stood at the ready to either heal or shield us as needed. Fran for instance, got a nice bubble around her just as one of her abilities ran out and her speed diminished greatly. I was sure she'd have gotten her blade up in time if not for the shield, but she sent a thankful look to Alayna all the same. Meanwhile, I whittled down its health with Arcane Missile and Firebolt, the latter being less successful because of the fire nature of the monster. Just when I thought the beast was close to being dead, I decided to show off a little.

First, I activated Speed Burst to put myself within ten feet of the monster. Alayna threw up a barrier between Emory and the badger just as it unleashed a fiery hell on him. I closed the distance in a flash, activating Blink to bring myself just above the back of the badger and a good eight feet up in the air as I'd planned. Only then summoning my blade, I aimed it at the monster's spine and activated Phantom Thrust. My strike dove down deep and split its stomach wide open, spilling forth blood as I activated Swift Strike to twist the blade.

It screamed in such agony that I almost felt bad for it, but the noises cut off a moment later as the last of its strength gave out and it fell forward, slowly at first, then faster as it gained momentum. Emory cursed and dove out of the way, and I saw Fran just step a quick two feet to the side and watch the badger fall right in front of her. Meanwhile, I rode the monster all the way down, sword still firmly planted into its spine and working well as a handhold.

"Not a bad first fight. A bit rough and rusty, but we'll get there," I said, smiling at the lot of them. There had been a satisfying rush of essence as it fell, so I checked my status screen to see how much I'd earned. Several thousand, but I captured almost the same amount in my Essence Band, so that was something. What was more, we found an intact Monster Core that had close to twenty thousand essence inside. That got stored away, we decided we'd give them to whoever had the least amount of essence gains by the end of the adventure.

Upon Fran's insistence, we cut into the Giant Badger and stored away several useful parts that either, sold well or were used for one thing or another. I was knee deep in Giant Badger guts when the next one came upon us, throwing a plume of fire right at me. I managed to get a Mana Shell up in time, but it had so little mana infused into it that it shattered only seconds into the attack, leaving my body steaming from the fiery attack.

What was odd about this last encounter and the one I just found myself in, was the trees here. I just saw several smaller trees, most were tall but thin, take a blast of fire and it didn't do much other than blacken them. No fires were starting, and I took a moment to focus on the feeling of essence around us to figure out why.

My team engaged while I slowly worked my way out of the guts. This new badger was weaker than the last and only about half the size, so I knew they'd be able to take care of it no problem. I reached out with my senses and got a surprise. The essence in this forest was as thick and potent as a dungeon's. I could almost feel the heavy trickle of essence being pulled into my Essence Band as I stood doing nothing. Just being in this forest was going to pay off immensely and we were in for a wild ride when it came to leveling up.

Absently, I wondered if the Prime Mana Shrine had survived the explosion and whether or not we'd be able to access it to solidify our gains from monster hunting. I finished my musings just in time for essence to pour into me from another kill. This time I only got less than four hundred total, but that was already a gain of over three thousand for very little work. It wasn't dungeon essence, but it was nice.

"Any idea where a Giant Badger Queen might be?" I asked Fran as I readied my knife to go looking for the monster core inside the base of the skull or spine, you never could be certain where you'd find it.

"If they are anything like the normal sized badgers, then it'll be a burrow somewhere, but they don't usually like dense tree areas, so I'm not sure if it applies here," Fran said, surprising me with her knowledge about badgers. She grinned and added, "Looked up a bit about them since they were our very first kill. Figure I should know enough to embellish the story for my kids and sound legit about it."

I laughed, then plunged my dagger deep into the dead giant badger's neck, getting myself covered in blood and guts. It took a solid twenty minutes, but I recovered a cracked core, a fire sack, and several other useful items for reagents and whatnot.

"Time to hunt and grind out badgers while we look for the queen's nest," I announced, flicking blood and viscera off my hands before summoning water to help clean myself off.

CHAPTER 34
MONSTER HUNTING

We were meant to go straight for the dungeon some few miles deep into the blast zone, but I wanted to know where the queen lairs were so we could share the information, and it never hurt to grind up a little essence before getting to the dungeon. So, as it happened, we killed another fourteen fire badgers, as I was beginning to refer to them since they had the unique fire mutation, whose levels ranged from sixteen to thirty-one. The Essence Bands were sucking in the latent essence so swiftly that I made sure everyone was emptying them periodically so they wouldn't get filled.

We all had enough to level up, so abundant was the essence in the area and from the monsters. But obviously that was just a drop in the bucket as I needed much more than that if I were to add the several extra attributes as I planned to. At this rate, though, I could level up a fair bit in just a matter of weeks. I could only imagine how effective the dungeon dive was going to be. What kind of dungeon lay waiting for us I couldn't say, not even my map had information about it, only listing it as a known dungeon.

House Blalor had restricted access and did not let much information about what kind of dungeon it was get out, guarding it like a state secret or something.

Fran was taking her turn to clean out the dead badger after I found out she'd purchased the self-cleaning enchantment for her armor, and she had her father's tonics that allowed for the cleanest-clean one could ever imagine getting. I watched her, a bit of disdain on my face at having done nearly a dozen before finding out this little tidbit of information.

Despite the unfortunate news that I'd been overworked, I was really having fun. We'd only killed about four hours and the sun was still high in the sky, with several more hours left before we needed to think about setting up camp. I was just about ready to call it quits on the queen hunt and begin heading for the dungeon when the biggest and strongest Giant Badger we'd encountered yet, appeared. And by appeared, I mean we heard it coming from nearly a mile off and made ready.

We were in a fairly big opening, a large rock preventing trees from growing up in this opening and giving us a bit of height, which made seeing oncoming monsters easy enough. This particular Giant Badger was different, and I used Inspect to learn why.

Elite Inferno Giant Badger, Level 48

. . .

"Get ready for a big one," I yelled. I looked over my shoulder at Alayna and saw a bit of fear flash across her face. She must have Inspected it as well. "Don't be worried, we got this! Just play it smart and let's go for the early kill if we can get it. Alayna, I will assist with heals as needed, but Emory be ready to use your defensive abilities because this guy is an elite and close to double your level."

I was worried, but only about my teammates and not myself. I wasn't lying when I said I'd help with heals, but I also didn't plan on playing with this monster. He would get the full fury of my powers, just not with any essence boosting if I could help it. I did need to get gains after all. But that didn't mean I couldn't fill my blade to bursting with essence that I could retrieve afterward. My attributes swelled and my muscles bulged as the effects of my sword took hold, boosting my attributes. Then I recast Arcane Armor, letting the blue translucent armor form around my own like a second skin. Next, I activated Light Blade for the extra bit of damage and made ready.

Trees came crashing down in front of us as a ten-foot-tall badger, nearly as wide as it was tall, came slashing into the clearing. It saw its fallen giant badger friend and screamed at us, fire forming just outside its mouth.

"Incoming!" I screamed, erecting a Mana Shell in front of the party and pushing hard to fill it with enough mana. The beam of red and white fire hit the barrier, reflecting off. The powerful beam of heat cut trees in two, fire resistance not enough to stop the intense damage. The two parts of the trees began to burn and suddenly I had a new worry on my mind as I struggled to maintain the barrier.

Just as half my mana was sunk into the barrier and it was riddled with cracks, the attack stopped, only for it to come on fast with a massive slash of its claws, shattering the remaining barrier.

Fran was there a moment later, catching its massive claw on her blade. Normally I'd say this was not a good idea, but she was using an ability that caused her to glow in a reddish haze and she threw off its attack as if it were a quarter of its level. Then, slashing down she actually cut right through its left clawed fingers, blunting them. As fast as she came, she retreated back, the red haze fading and sweat beading on her forehead. Whatever the ability was, she'd just worn herself out for that small victory.

Time to show her what I could do.

Emory was catching blow after blow; massive ethereal shields circled him as he burned through his abilities to keep himself in place in front of the giant monster. Lances of light smashed into the monster, doing almost nothing, while Creed slashed icy waves of power through the air at it, drawing blood with each attack. Creed joined Emory's side and a massive icy shield appeared between them, stopping the next attack and giving Emory a moment to breathe.

I unleashed a Lightning Strike, followed by an Arcane Missile, and avoided using any fire-based attacks due to the mutated nature of the monster. Throwing a Mending Touch on Emory, I activated Blink and appeared behind the monster, this time on the ground, as showing off wasn't what I needed this time.

First, I cut at its back leg with a devastating Power Strike, Swift Strike combo, my sword going so deep that it stopped when it hit bone and I was forced to summon it back to my hand to free it. Next, I slashed out with a combined arc of Light from Light Blade's secondary effect and combo'd that with Force Wave, my Slashing Proficiency upping the damage significantly.

Just as my slashing attack hit the leg I'd stabbed, the Giant Elite Badger tried in vain to turn and face me, but Creed and Emory slashed away at it, forcing it back. It was already favoring the leg so my job at slowing it down had worked, and Creed and Emory could backpedal to gain a breather now. The fight was under control and now it was time to deal some real damage.

Casting Lightning Strike and Arcane Missile right after each other, I began filling up a Fireball, figuring the raw damage of it would be enough to deal with any fire-based resistances.

"Get clear!" I yelled as the fireball reached the size of a man's torso, burning away at my hands and face. I hurled the fireball at the target and with my remaining twenty percent of my mana, I threw up a Mana Shell while the rest of the team got behind a barrier that Alayna erected.

In the moments before the fireball hit, I pulled out a mana potion and downed its contents, bringing my mana swiftly up to half full once more. My stamina was flagging from the overuse of my Rank 2 abilities, so I activated

Stamina Surge as well, bringing me back to full within 5 seconds and effectively putting me back to peak operation.

The blast instantly shattered my Mana Shell, and I took several hundred points of damage as I was thrown backward. From what little I could see as the fire spread outward, blackening trees, the golden barrier that Alayna erected held where mine had not. And good thing too, because the Elite Badger used the moment of blindness that came with the blast to advance on the rest of the team, a beam of power forming in its mouth again.

If I didn't do something fast, they would be decimated, and I wasn't sure they had any cooldowns left to use against such an attack. I activated Speed Burst and pushed essence into my legs for additional speed, essence or not it was time to just end this fight. It only took a few hundred to infuse my entire body with enough essence to essentially slow down the entire battle in my own eyes and speed level.

I watched it as I moved, the elite monster slowly charging an attack that would shatter the remaining barrier, and it barely appeared hurt from my fireball attack. Lifting my sword up into an attack position I set my sights on its neck and activated Blink. I appeared right behind it in the air, and I hung there, so keen was my perception that I felt like I had several seconds to react instead of the single moment that I had.

Infusing my next abilities with essence, I let loose. Slashing out I managed to activate Force Wave, Light Arc, Power Strike, and Swift Strike. Some of them hadn't even come off cooldown, but with how much essence I forced into it I felt my mind bend and though it hurt, I somehow was able to get them to activate anyways. Sharp green and blue energy with a white core sparked all around me as I slashed with everything I had for its thick neck.

My blade cut through smoothly, taking the elite's head off and ending the fight.

Before I hit the ground my head ignited in pain as if I were being seared alive. I screamed and hit the ground at an off angle, hurting my leg but not breaking it. I kept screaming as something in my head burned and ripped at me. Instinctually I knew this was the result of ignoring cooldowns and I was lucky not to be dead, but I didn't care as the pain was more intense than anything I'd ever experienced. I just kept kicking and screaming until finally at long last the pain began to subside. Heal after heal was thrown on me, but it wasn't that kind of pain. I managed to signal to Alayna to stop and I rolled up into a ball, tears running down my face as I waited for the rest of the pain to subside.

***

Cleaning up and gathering reagents took a bit longer than normal, as this giant elite was easily five feet wider and taller than the previous ones. The battle had been quick but revealing, there were monsters in this pop-up forest that could kill us, and we needed to be careful.

After some exploring, we found several more elites outside a massive burrow that I marked on my map. It had to be the queen's lair, there just wasn't anything else that made any sense.

"I don't think we are ready to take it on just yet," I said, we stood at the edge of a clearing of trees, far enough away that the other badgers didn't appear to notice us. These were only level 35 elites, but still, I didn't want to fight them all at once and we had another path forward, finding the dungeon.

"I still can't believe you killed a level 48 elite," Alayna said, looking at me as if I weren't quite human.

I just smiled, she hadn't seen my power firsthand in some time and I'd grown by leaps and bounds since our last dungeon run. I lost a solid thousand essence to the kill, but it had provided me with an additional forty thousand essence when I took in account my essence band, so it wasn't a total loss. However, I needed to be wary using so much essence to enhance myself, I could still feel the ache of the headache that burned into me from ignoring cooldowns.

It wasn't an experience I wanted to repeat.

"I bent the rules to do it, but if I were alone, I'm sure I could have taken care of it without essence infusing," I said, more to myself than to Alayna. Fran scoffed as if something I said offended her and I looked over realizing how my words must have sounded. "I didn't mean it like that."

"Yeah, sure you didn't," Emory said, slapping me on the back. "We are just little lost puppies who can't fend for ourselves, and we need the mighty Caldor, the too strong for his own good, to save us." He began to laugh uproariously after that, and I couldn't help but laugh too.

After getting control of myself I looked at each of them with a serious expression. "We are here to get you all stronger so that we can face even more monstrous foes than that dead badger. I'm hoping we can spam run the dungeon and we can all get to at least level 40 or 50. I know it sounds a bit much, but I think we can do it, so let's go find that dungeon and get you all power leveled!"

CHAPTER 35
CITY DUNGEON FOUND

Traveling through the forest and eventually into rock terrain that opened up into a vast valley filled with yellow grass as tall as a man, we encountered several monsters. We fought Dire Wolves, Owlbears, a few Harpies, and even a Gargoyle, so varied were the monsters roaming the wilds. The sun was finally beginning to set on our first day, but I wanted to catch sight of the dungeon before we camped for the night, so we pushed onward. It seemed like the deeper we got, the more powerful the monsters, but not necessarily by level so much as abilities.

For instance, the last gargoyle we fought was shooting out rays of moonlight from his hands, not an ability I'd ever have imagined a gargoyle would mutate into having. Then there was the water Dire Wolves, spitting power jets of water that moved so fast they cut the skin. Or the Harpies that threw out arcs of air so fast it split open my skin. Needless to say, it had been an exciting few hours.

What monster we faced next was something out of a nightmare and came at us in a pack of three. We walked through the tall grass, Fran having the bright idea of attaching rope to each other to prevent us from getting lost, while I took lead and cut down the grass in huge swaths. It wouldn't do any good to fight a monster in such conditions, but it couldn't be helped.

The first one appeared in a blur and hit me with two large, clawed feet, scraping harmlessly against my armor but bringing me to the ground. My sword slashed at its side just as its mighty jaw came down aiming for my neck. I managed to drop my sword and put my gauntlet in the way, catching the blow when I heard Alayna and Fran scream.

Focusing hard and pushing the massive beast off myself I Inspected the new monsters.

Grassland Giant Raptors, Level 20

For their level they sure packed a punch, also the description of 'giant' was overstated as these feathered lizard looking guys couldn't have been taller than seven feet at most.

The one that attacked me had an array of yellow and white feathers up its spine, on its arms like wings, and at the tip of its tail, everywhere else covered in a thick lizard hide. It had a large head with razor sharp teeth, small arms that didn't look like much other than unusable wings, and massive clawed feet. Honestly it looked like a giant chicken but moved like a bird of prey.

If it weren't for how bright the sun still shone just over the horizon, we'd have a hard time dealing with just swift predators, no matter the level. But as it was, I recovered just in time for a second attack, and I was ready this time. The giant yellow bird lizard made a sort of squawking clicking noise at me, stopping a few feet away.

It wasn't until a moment too late that I realized it was baiting me and I was tackled once more to the ground by a second raptor. I was still more ready than I had been before, casting Lightning Strike, a bolt of power traveled down from above and struck the raptor atop me. It squawked in my face, but I was stronger and pushed it aside. Summoning my sword back, I raised up my blade to cleave this little asshole lizard in two but then the rope went taut, and I was pulled off balance again.

I caught myself at the last moment and squared off my feet, slicing down to sever the rope and sparing a quick glance toward my teammates. Emory had already rallied together with Fran, Alayna, and Creed, and they faced off against a pack of four of the creatures, but they were doing good, so I turned my attention back to my two opponents.

Both had somehow disappeared into the yellow grass and if it weren't for my keen hearing, I'd have likely took a blow to my chest. As it were, I heard a crackling of energy and saw the beam of yellow light before it hit me. I dodged and as the beam passed me, I heard Creed shout something.

I cursed when I realized the raptor had shot an energy beam at me, but also lined it up to hit my team if it missed.

So, they were big yellow chicken lizards that could shoot out yellow hot light energy, what else could they do? I shouldn't have asked because I found out when the next one attacked. It came in fast from the side and as I went to step out of the way the grass all around my legs wrapped firmly around my boots. It wasn't enough to stop me from moving altogether but it slowed me enough to give the raptor the time it needed to attack.

It jumped at the last second, its clawed feet ready to cut against my armor. I extended my sword and activated Phantom Thrust, thrusting forward at its chest. The blow took it straight on and did devastating damage but didn't kill it. It did, however, put it off course enough that it fell to the side and its grass-holding ability stopped working. I turned and cut its head clean off, activating Power Strike for good measure. However, the time I took to deal with the wounded raptor gave the other one enough time to get into position.

From six feet in the air, it released a cone of searing bright light that hit me full in the face. I felt several health points slip away as my body was seared and burned under my armor, not even my Arcane Armor being enough to diminish the magical attack very much. I slashed blindly with my sword and caught against something meaty a moment before the full weight of the seven-hundred-pound chicken landed atop me, this time a wild kicking mess of injured limbs.

It knocked the air right out of me and brought me off my feet to fall into a heap. I really needed to figure out how to bond two weapons, I thought during the moment of annoyance. My sword was only so effective when I was basically holding the enemy in my arms. Then a thought occurred to me, and I decided I could solve this problem with a little page out of Emory's playbook. I let my sword drop free and pulled the raptor into a bear hug.

Its face was away from my own, so I didn't have to worry about the massive jaws, but it squirmed and kicked so viciously that it took me a moment to lock my hands around its bulk. But once I did it was game over for the raptor. With my thresholds passed, my Strength attribute sitting over a hundred with my gear, and my sheer will of wanting this fucker dead, it was too much for it. I squeezed until I heard bones give way and cracked then broke altogether.

It took longer than I would have expected to squeeze the life out of it, but I did it. By the time I was done, Emory stood over me admiring my tactics with a look of appreciation.

He helped me roll the dead thing off me before saying, "I bet I could squeeze two of them at the same time." He made a show of opening his arms wide and I just laughed at the sight of him. He had a bloody cut on his face, and he looked like he'd just wrestled with a bear, which funnily enough he could probably do that now with how strong he'd gotten. Emory had focused on purely strength and constitution, bringing his Strength over the second threshold already by forgoing a balanced build. It worked for him, but as an agent of literal balance I couldn't see myself favoring one attribute too strongly over another.

That might have to change, I realized as I went to work searching for Monster Cores in the raptors. The king had so freely mentioned that he was a Paragon and I'm sure the reduced cost of buying whatever specific attribute he was a Paragon for is what made him so remarkable. What was to happen, I wonder, if I focused on just my three Paragon attributes?

Constitution, Core, and Intellect.

Constitution and Intellect were easy enough to predict. I'd be a very hearty and hard to kill caster whose spells hit like an avalanche. But my class was twofold and I couldn't just ignore my physical side for my caster side, that would cause an unbalanced state that hurt my head to even consider. Eventually though it would be extremely cheaper to purchase from my Paragon attributes.

Then an idea hit me that might work if I were careful in the future with what gear I found, purchased, or had crafted. I could focus on Strength, Endurance, and Concentration through gear attributes, while flooding my Paragon attributes to raise their base values. That could be a good stop gap method to dealing with the issue, but what would happen if I ever approached the third threshold? Was such a high threshold subject to the same imbalance laws of the lower thresholds? There was too much I didn't know and too few places to learn it among those I adventured with.

It was far too rare to find adventurers over level 50, not

to mention someone strong enough to have passed their third threshold. It just wasn't practical to keep leveling after 50, as everything I'd read said the essence cost to level more than tripled. But Warrick was above level 50, he had to be. And even as diminished as his powers were from the events with the Chaos Knight, he still wielded impossibly immense power. Suddenly I wished people were freer about telling me what level they actually were so I could make more informed decisions.

We faced a total of twenty raptors before we made it out of the grasslands and into a thick forest once more. It wasn't long before the forest gave way into an open rocky area that I recognized, a second before the rest, was the ruins of City Blalor.

The city circle that at first, I assumed was a rocky area was a several mile wide ruins of buildings that looked no bigger than a foot high off the ground, basically, just the stone foundations remained and only barely. In the middle of the city was a hill and atop it, even from this distance, I could see the entrance to a dungeon. It glowed with an ethereal blue light; several times stronger than any dungeon I'd even seen before.

As we watched, something moved from the small stone door opening, and a pack of some sort of creatures appeared from within its walls, running fast toward the east. I got an Inspect off and gasped.

. . .

Gnoll Bandits, Level 31

"The Dungeon is releasing monsters into the wild somehow," I said, my mouth hanging ajar as I turned to see similar reactions on the faces of my companions. "We need to be very careful."

CHAPTER 36
BLALOR RUINS

We set up camp just inside the dense forest and I took first watch. I needed to keep an eye on the dungeon as much as I needed to watch over my group and decided that rest could wait. I equipped my Charm of the Sleepless One to make sure I was fresh the next morning, though it probably wasn't needed as I could go days without sleep at this point in my life without feeling any ill effects. Either way, I added a third Charge to my little trinket and was all the happier to do so as an idea occurred to me as a target came to mind for the enchantment, Lord Variyn.

I didn't know how easy the hex would be to dispel, but I figured it wouldn't be easy to detect as it was basically harmless and only caused nightmares without doing any real damage to the target. The next chance I got, I would test it out on him and hope he didn't notice. I was sure it was within my power and not blockable by any oath to do so.

The night went on in mostly silence, with only a few

distance roars breaking the stillness of the night. They were far enough off that I didn't even turn my head in their direction, instead focusing on the dungeon and any additional monsters that might spill out. The dungeon itself was like a beacon of light in the darkness, the glowing runes bright enough that I could see a good area around it, but I had difficultly looking right at it. It was because of this that I nearly missed the next batch of monsters to come out of the dungeon nearly six hours after the first ones we'd seen.

A flash of movement, dark shadows against the bright dungeon, had me scanning the horizon. Whatever had been released was flying up into the sky and not running out like the Gnolls had. Unfortunately, with the limited light, I wasn't able to get an Inspect off so whatever new threat had been released was lost to me.

What would cause a dungeon to release monsters like this? Was it related to the device used to destroy this area or was it just the nature of this dungeon? I wished Kora was with us right now so I could ask her questions about monsters escaping dungeons. If anyone would know about it, she would, but she wasn't with us now and I had only my stray thoughts to work with. What if it had to do with the amount of extra essence released into the area?

This area was unique in all of the Wyrd currently, as most dungeons were having to deal with reduced essence since the Ley Lines struggled against the contamination below, yet this dungeon would have received literally millions of essence all at once. Or at least I guessed as much considering the destructive release the essence had caused. It still hurt to think of something like essence, pure and powerful energy that spurred life forward, being used as a weapon to wipe life from off the map.

How many souls were extinguished at once and how much essence had been released just by the deaths of so many? There was so much I didn't know about this place, and I began to wonder why the hell I'd agreed to go here. Sure, it made sense the need to grow stronger and I was going to suggest dungeon diving until we needed to leave, but to come here to the very place where it happened.

I felt a sick tightness in my gut, and I knew why I'd done it. A part of me wanted to see that it was real. A part of me wanted to have a sense for the place where so many had died, an immense loss that I struggled not to attribute to myself. I was done feeling sorry for myself, that much was damn true, but fuck me if I couldn't drag myself through the emotional mud a little bit during our adventure. I wasn't weak because I wanted to feel, I wasn't an emotional mess just because I wondered what the final moments of so many had been like.

No...I was going to be strong and use the place of my greatest regret as the place I grew the strongest from.

Weakness to strength, strength to vengeance, vengeance to justice, justice to balance.

Try as I might, I couldn't pull a phrase or saying from my father to help me through such a time, so instead I just remembered the great deeds he accomplished. Not only as an adventurer—the more I interacted with those that knew him the more I learned how little I truly knew about his adventures—but his role at home. He was the best father any boy could ask for and I cherished the memories we had together.

He was the perfect listening ear, ready to listen to any complaint and offer a sage word of advice or guidance. More than that he knew when I just wanted to complain about one thing or another, he had the ability to know when words weren't needed and when they were. Right now, there were no words to bring me comfort, only the grim silence of the night.

Something stirred behind me, and I decided it was either Emory or Alayna based on where the sound came from, but a moment later I knew. "I'm really under leveled for this place," Alayna said, slowly moving through the darkness toward me.

I turned to give her a comforting look in the moonlight, but her face was veiled in shadows until she was right in front of me. We exchanged a smile and she sat beside me. "That's why we're here, to get you stronger," I said, putting my arm around her and pulling her warmth into me.

"You aren't tired yet?" She asked, but I just shook my head.

"I've got a trinket and my second threshold keeping me fresh. I wanted to keep an eye on the state of the dungeon, have you ever heard of dungeons releasing monsters like that?"

"No, but I'm not a dungeon expert, so who knows what they are capable of," she laughed lightly before continuing, "If you'd told me before meeting Kora that you could put a dungeon inside a golem and it could summon monsters, talk to you, and walk around, I'd have called you crazy. There is so much I don't know about the world, so much to discover."

"And an entire *Awakened* extended lifetime to discover it." I looked down at her, kissing the top of her golden hair.

"I don't know what to do," Alayna said suddenly sounding somber.

"In what regard?" I asked, not sure which direction she was taking the conversation, but wanting to be supportive, nonetheless.

She took a deep breath and let it out slowly before responding. "Galt is my father, I'm not a full heir to the House Variyn throne, but the more I think about how free that makes me, the more I wonder who will rule after my fath-I mean Lord Variyn dies. Between your vendetta against him and his advancing years, someone will have to take over the house eventually, but can I trust anyone to do right by the House and lead it with the care and mercy it deserves?"

"If you want to rule, I'm sure Galt will take your secret to his grave. I doubt anyone, not even the king, could get Galt to admit something that would put you in potential harm. That man has always cared for you and been overly protective. It makes sense now, but at first, I thought he just really took his job seriously. Perhaps a bit of both." I scratched at the back of my head, my helmet hanging on my belt with my gauntlets.

"I just want to make a difference," Alayna said with a heavy sigh in her tone. Her voice trailed off at the end and I saw she was staring into the light of the dungeon, probably as transfixed as I was with it all.

"You will, we both will. And the mark we leave on history won't be defined by our mistakes," I looked out at the desolation caused by my discovery and took a steadying breath. "We will do great things, but first we have to survive this place, grow stronger, and I need to help right the imbalances in this world. If I'm known for nothing else, I hope to be known for that."

We sat in silence as the sun began to rise, slow and steady, over the horizon. Warm orange-red light filtered through the trees' edge as we cuddled close against the night chill. The trees here had a brown bark that had veins of green glowing in them that only became visible in the orange light of the morning. It was odd, but I felt the essence surge in the trees as the morning came as if they were waking up along with the rest of my team.

We broke camp and put away our gear, I'd put out a bedroll despite knowing I wasn't likely to use it. Through morning chit chat, I shared what I'd learned and told them that soon, within the hour, another set of monsters would be released. Sure enough, a new monster did appear, but this was unlike anything I expected to see. A single monster, huge and intimidating, stepped out of the dungeon doorway. It seemed small at first, but glowed with a green-blue light, morphing and changing until it stood an easy three times my height and twice as long.

I used Inspect and my jaw dropped further as I considered the best way to defeat such a foe.

. . .

Elite Razorback Tyrannosaurus Rex, Level 36

Level 36 or not I didn't see an easy way to take down such a behemoth of a monster. This wasn't like the Pirate dungeon we'd done where the dungeon gave us specialty weapons to deal increased damage to a massive monster, no, this was real life and we only had what we brought to deal with the threat. It was a hard thing to swallow but I decided against engaging the monstrous Tyrannosaurus Rex. Perhaps after we'd grown even stronger.

"I want to kill that thing and make a cloak from its hide," Emory said, practically drooling as he watched the massive monster walk in our direction.

"We need to move, I don't think we are ready to engage it yet," I said, shaking my head. Everyone but Emory agreed, but after some hard looks we got him to admit defeat and follow after us before the behemoth headed our way. Once more, I wished Kora was with us, but this time for a different reason. I'd love to have her add this monstrous Rex into her summons, maybe if I got the monster core, she'd still be able to add it.

We made it out of the way with minutes to spare, but the ground shook from this new threat and I knew we wouldn't be able to ignore it for long. If we didn't take care of it, then the other team would have to take care of it, but it would be much harder to get the Core off them if they did. Not that it much mattered to me, I had so much gold that I was sure I'd be able to pay whatever price was needed if the Core survived.

We walked inward toward the dungeon, over small mounds that must have been the wall at some point, but now was nothing more than a half a foot of rock. It was like a thousand or more years had gone by and time itself was against the ruins of this once thriving city. I couldn't help but picture the streets and buildings as they must have been, and the people that filled this once vast thriving city. It hurt, but pain of every kind was becoming my trademark as of late, so I took it in stride.

I didn't know the exact area, but I'd heard rumors during the war about the layout of the city and where its Prime Mana Shrine had been, so we did a wide circle looking for any sign of it in the eastern inner city. We actually found it, half buried in rubble and dirt, but oddly enough the lights on it barely flickered, as if it were being deprived of essence or something. A strange occurrence indeed, considering the abundance of essence in the area and how the dungeon was reacting.

Regardless, we all took turns pressing our hands on it and leveling up or assigning essence. For my part, I leveled up to 31 and assigned the 3 attribute points I got into Strength, bringing it from 52 to 55. I'd focus on using my free points on non-Paragon attributes, that way, purchasing new attributes could cost a fair bit less since the cost of raising each one depended on the affinity of each attribute individually.

Next, I used the crazy amount of essence I'd collected,

nearly double as much as I'd normally have had thanks to the super-efficient essence band, and purchased 3 attributes for intellect, bringing it from 53 to 56. That left me with enough essence to go to level 32, so I did so, spending 100,800 essence. I assigned the free 3 attribute points to Endurance, then purchased 3 points at the cost of 144,113 essence to increase my Constitution by 3 as well. That brought my Endurance and Constitution to 53 attribute points each.

After finding the stone we made our way to the dungeon entrance, the light gave off a steady warmth, but it wasn't painful. While my health pool stayed full, I just hoped that it wasn't damaging us in ways we didn't understand. There was much we didn't know about this dungeon, but we'd only learn more by going inside.

Name: Caldor Miles | Classification: Arcane Knight | Species: Human

Level: 32, 103,950 Essence to Lvl. 33 | Essence: 530,520 | Reputation: Rank 4, 32%

Health: 1,530/1,530 | Mana: 1,610/1,610 | Stamina: 1,150/1,150

Health Regen: 133 Per Minute | Mana Regen: 55 Per Minute | Stamina Regen: 95 Per Minute

Constitution: 133 (53 Base) | Intellect: 151 (56 Base) | Endurance: 95 (53 Base)

Core: 60 (50 Base) | Concentration: 50 (50 Base) | Strength: 144 (55 Base)

CHAPTER 37
DUNGEON STAGING ROOM

From close up, several things became apparent to me about this dungeon. It was the same design as all other dungeons I'd seen before, a rock formation that hid a door covered in runes that opened into a room with a pedestal filled with mana-rich water. However, it was in the few ways that made the dungeon different that caught my attention. We approached carefully, the light of the runes making it hard to focus on the surface of the stone, but I managed.

What I found all around the surface of the stone was cracks, and through the cracks a reflected white metal that must have been adding to the glow of the dungeon, so harsh was the light that shone from the metallic surface. I thought it might be some form of Mythril, but it was hard to tell with the largest of the cracks reflecting the most light.

Why the stone surface was cracked, I did not know, but I couldn't imagine it was a good sign.

"This stone or whatever material it really is, I've never seen so much as a scratch on it before," Alayna said, running her hand across it. "This dungeon might not be safe to enter if the internal structure is dead to the outer frame. Are we sure we want to risk it?"

I knew I wanted to risk it, but I wasn't about to force everyone else along if they didn't. Looking at each of the team, I got shrugs and nods until I made it to Creed.

He spoke up and I marveled at how his voice was slowly changing, growing slightly deeper with every passing month. It was now the voice of a young man and not a boy. "I think we should assume this is an event dungeon, given how old it must be if it was established around the same time as City Blalor. And theme dungeons are notoriously hard to exit once the events begin, not impossible, but harder to find what passes as an exit. I am willing to put my life on the line to grow stronger, but I want all the facts on the table."

I nodded, seeing Fran looking less than enthusiastic about the process, I gestured to her to speak next, and she did so.

"I mean I want to be strong too, but what happens if we get stuck inside with monsters far stronger than us? I know you can kill stuff way higher level than you Caldor, and you are skilled with the blade, possibly as skilled as I am now with your increased speed and strength, but you won't be able to protect us if we get inside and the dungeon throws level fifty or higher monsters at us. I think if we do go in, that the first thing we do is find an exit to test that we can leave if we want to."

I nodded and seeing that no one else had any objections, spoke my peace. "I think that would be prudent," I nodded to Fran, "but I would also say that I don't think we are likely to encounter monsters higher than level 30."

"What makes you say that?" Emory asked, breaking his silence. "I mean we just saw it spit out a monster you thought we wouldn't have a chance against, what if the dungeon is filled with those rex guys? Oh, wouldn't that be fucking awesome!" He seemed genuinely excited by the prospect, and I sighed at his oddly placed enthusiasm.

"I think you are right in part. I bet that each monster being released is a monster that we could possibly find inside the dungeon. But it is because of the rex and the other monster that it let out that I think it will be around the level 20 to 30 mark, as each of the monsters it released was within that range. I think that the dungeon has been over charged with essence and is releasing monsters from within as a way to burn off the excess essence."

Alayna smiled appreciatively. "That's a nice theory, but what evidence do you have?" She was enjoying getting me to think analytically, she'd likely came up with the same theory and wanted to hear my logic before correcting me with her superior logic.

I smiled back at her, happy to play along. "Kora is what makes me think so. The fact that her Core is a gem and, though it is different than any monster core or gem I've worked with, it has a certain amount of essence it can hold. It works similar to our Core attribute, the higher our attribute the more we can hold. I believe that she has a similar functionality and if I am right, then the Dungeon Core here is overcharged and needs to badly dispel enough essence to normalize but can't because so much essence has been soaked into the ground that it likely is having a hard time keeping up."

"If you're right, then us running the dungeon and soaking up the essence inside will actually help the problem, giving the Dungeon Core relief. I bet it will even release more essence than normal, especially at the end when it normally releases a large chunk." Alayna was talking faster and faster, excited by the prospect for sure.

I wouldn't lie, I was getting excited too. If my theory held, then we might face more monsters than normal and deal with a higher threat than would be normal, but the payoff ought to be huge for the first few runs at least. And even after it balances out, the area is so rich with essence that here it doesn't matter that the Ley Lines are only providing a trickle of essence to the dungeon. Instead of the reduced pay offs like all other dungeons, this dungeon was likely paying out more essence than ever before.

With our theories presented, Fran looked a little more excited to check the dungeon out, even taking a step forward to peak down toward the dungeon door.

"Let's get in there and kill some monsters!" I declared, stepping forward and pushing at the dungeon door. It opened as smoothly as ever and we went down a small bit of stairs into what was expected, a small room with a pedestal and inside mana-rich water that we all took a drink from, topping all our resource pools off.

"Be sure to clear your Essence Bands often," Fran said, tapping her arm to remind us all. It was good she did, because already a steady stream filled mine, whereas it was only a trickle outside above ground.

I looked over the team, checking that they were all ready and taking a good look at their gear. Helmets were clicked and belted into place, gauntlets taken off belts and faceted in place, we were all ready.

I examined Emory first. He wore an actual matching set of armor, new, since he'd made a great series of advances while I was at war. It was metallic grey, no paint or coloring like most adventurers liked to do. He had a massive leather belt on that when I'd asked about it days earlier, he'd just said it was a 'fashion statement' but I knew him well enough that it must provide a decent increase to strength or constitution. His pauldrons were bigger than I would have thought they needed to be, bordering on the absurd, but he was a big guy and used to having to go into doorways sideways and the like, so it didn't bother him, I'm sure.

His helmet had a crest to it to better send head blows to either the left or the right and attached to the back was a black feather plume. When asked about that, he shrugged and admitted that he thought it looked cool. I'd provided him with some gems to socket the armor, it had a total of nine sockets, but they were all well-hidden on the interior of the armor, providing the best safety for the somewhat fragile gems. Lastly, I looked at his new shield and weapon. He had a black kite shield that he lifted and moved around as if it weighed nothing, it even had several spikes at the bottom for planting it into the ground or hitting an opponent in the face.

He had two weapons, a one-handed mace and the massive 'Hungry Blade of the Minotaur' that I'd given him from our dungeon run some time ago. Mostly he used his new mace, a black iron affair with sharp edges and a dangerous black glow to it.

I wore the same old armor I'd used during the war, 'Lord Black's Enchanted Armor', only upgrading the gem sockets to slightly better ones over the last few weeks. My sword, Fulgar'vi'lectus, with its essence pathways remained my go-to weapon and I wasn't likely to change it anytime soon as it was uniquely suited for my use. Plus, the fact it increased a percentage of my attributes instead of a set amount made it a weapon I'd likely use for a lifetime, despite the silly name it had.

Alayna wore the elven armor she'd been given, wielding a small buckle and a mace that stayed hanging at her side most of the time, so she could focus on casting heals and barriers. With the helmet on that closed over her face completely and elf ears carved into the face-like design, she looked rather elegant, like an elven noble.

Meanwhile, Creed sported plain chestplate armor, nothing fancy, painted in his family's colors. However, rarely did we see it as his class had many builtin skills that surpassed any traditional armor he could wear. When he activated his Icy Armor, which he did each time he went into battle, he looked like a titan of ice, skulls, and spikes. The same happened to his weapon now, he was using a plain knight's long sword, but ice would cover it and make it look like an icy spike plucked straight from a frozen hell. He was proving to be the next strongest fighter behind me, doing far more damage than either Fran or Emory.

Fran wore simple chain armor with a small plate chest piece, preferring fluidity of movement over traditional protection. I knew by experience that the armor's look could be deceiving as she'd taken several big hits and shrugged them off without much damage. That or she was good at ignoring pain, honestly it could be either and I doubted she'd tell me which if I asked. Her helmet had the entire face open so as to not impede her sight and her gauntlets were fingerless and thin to better grip her weapon. Her sword was the same elegant blade that she'd gotten from her father and used from day one of being an adventurer. She did have a new cloak however, it was red and looked more like a thin scarf than a cloak, but she said it had good attributes to help her with her biggest weakness, her speed.

There was something to be said about skill, but when your opponent was just faster than you, it was hard to employ that skill, no matter your mastery of the blade. That was what she'd meant when she said I was likely a match for her in the blade. She was obviously still the better swordswoman, but it didn't matter if she couldn't counter a strike before it arrived. Even if I telegraphed my attack, I was fast enough to alter it without a skill and strike her open defenses. But that was why we were doing this dungeon and in this hellscape of death.

Having given everyone a once over and liking what I found, we stepped through the portal and into the dungeon.

CHAPTER 38
AN ORDU CITY

"Welcome to the city of Olim," a voice said, smooth and steady. My eyes were all white and the adjustment was taking longer than I was used to, so I listened instead, rubbing at my eyes. "You must be the five monster hunters who've had their Cores unlocked and prepped to aid us in my task. Please state your names for the record and I will give you the brief so we can begin."

Finally, my eyes adjusted and what I saw took my breath away in a way nothing else ever had. First, I noticed the area around us, not even seeing the person who'd spoken to us yet. All the buildings, and we were surrounded by dozens of them, reached into the sky and shone with a gentle white light, traces of blue could be seen from intricate blue runic script. Carriages without horses or any visible way to give them movement soared through the air like silver and white oval pills. If not for the translucent bottoms and sides, I'd not even known they were carriages.

Then it hit me, and I saw the beings talking to us. Soft features, bald head, large forehead, standing taller than Emory or me by a third of our height and wearing flowing silks that glowed with the smallest bits of rune work I'd ever seen. Surely that couldn't be what I was thinking it was, were we standing before an Ordu.

Alayna spoke next, confirming the rest of my quickly growing realization. "We are in an Ordu city," her words were barely a whisper and she fell dramatically to her knees before the Ordu. I wasn't about to start worshiping them, but I couldn't help but pull my helmet off for a better view of the being. It had greyish white skin and it was textured with tiny wrinkles, nothing in the text had said that about the Ordu. And their eyes! They had eyes that were all black with many dozens of tiny orange spots that must have allowed sight of some kind.

"Please, we have told your kind before, we do not wish you to worship us, please rise and attend to your duty. Much work needs to be done, introduce yourselves and we will begin. I can go first if that helps. My name is Inspector Zel'hu and I oversee this sector of the city, policing crime, suppressing outbreaks of the dangerous experiments, and today, hunting monsters that have escaped from the before mentioned dangerous experiments."

Alayna stood, taking her helmet off as well, I could see she was blushing a bit, but she looked at me wide-eyed and I totally understood. House Blalor was sitting on a gold mine's worth of history and potential knowledge with this dungeon. For a dungeon to actually be themed around the

Ordu civilization, with enough runs and the right questions...

"House Blalor's successful enterprises make more sense now," I said, focusing on Alayna I smiled wide. "This is an incredible discovery, and your father gave me this land. He must not have known or even guessed what lay at the heart of the city. We have to keep this a secret until we can best figure out how to deal with the knowledge locked inside the dungeon. This could be world shattering."

"We can't keep it a secret, this has to be open to everyone so that we can grow as a society. Imagine the effect on religion this is going to have, you can talk to an Ordu in here. Sure, not a real one, but dungeons make convincing copies of things they know. This dungeon must be much older than we previously thought, it could be so powerful. We should find an exit."

"Introduce yourselves," Zel'hu said, this time with fire in his voice. "You shall not shirk your responsibilities and leave before you finish the task you've been sent for."

This caught both Alayna and I off guard and I shared a look with her. I'd just give it a straightforward go and see if I could get an idea where the exit could be. "My name is Caldor Miles. We are in a dungeon, and I want to find the exit, can you show it to me."

"I am aware this is a dungeon simulation. However, as the Dungeon Core is in dire need, an exit cannot be provided. I can assure you that this simulation will bend to your specific strengths and potential. You needn't worry that it is outside your power to complete. Please finish introductions and we will begin."

What the hell was a simulation? The word sounded so foreign and yet he used it like it meant something simple. A dungeon simulation he'd called it. From the context, I obviously understood that this Ordu knew that the dungeon was, well, a dungeon and he wasn't real, however he refused to show us an exit. Instead, he is assuring us that we are up to the challenge. I thought back to all my previous dungeon experiences. The best we could hope for was to push forward to see where it takes us.

"Give him your names and get your gear back on, we are going to clear this dungeon. Keep your eyes out for anything strange," I added, though as I looked around the majestic city with its tall, thin Ordu in silk-like runic cloth, and buildings that touched the sky, I couldn't say what didn't look strange to me.

Everyone introduced themselves and the Ordu opened his palm showing us a little grey round rock with runic script on it. He passed it to me and said, "This device will help you track your target. You have three escaped monsters, identities unknown at present, but their tracker scripts are intact, so you'll be able to find them. You are to locate and destroy, anything recovered after their destruction is yours to keep. But I will remind you that while you are in the Olim you will not try to take any of our technology or magic with you outside the objects the monsters provide. Is that clear?" Zel'hu tilted his head and looked right at Alayna as he said this. She was squinting her eyes and staring at his runic inscribed clothing, making gestures with her finger as if working out which runes were used.

She finally noticed the attention and reddened again. "Oh sorry, but I, could I see your shirt?"

"For your own protection you are only given the basic Runic formations. When your people have proved themselves in our service, we will consider expanding your knowledge base," Zel'hu said, he had a parental way of talking as if he spoke to children, soft and gentle.

"Helmets on," I said, catching her eye. She frowned at me but did as I asked. We were hunting monsters after all, we needed to be prepared.

I held out the rock, unsure of what to do with it. Zel'hu made a sound that almost resembled a sigh and reached out with a long finger to touch the stone. "Simply tap the surface to activate the tracker. It should interface with your global positioning system that was programmed into you at your Awakening. You do know how to use a map don't you?"

I was starting to detect a good measure of snark from this Ordu, and my mind didn't know how to process a snarky Ordu, so I just nodded. Tapping on the rock I saw several points appear in a translucent multilayered map. Checking my own personal map, I saw three moving points had been added in a dark red color, each one blipping outward with a ring that grew bigger until it repeated, and the dot moved. This was much easier to read than whatever that rock was showing me, but I palmed the rock anyways and slipped it into my inventory for safekeeping.

"Is there anything else you can tell us, you said you don't

know what type of monsters, but perhaps you can tell us something about where they escaped or how?" I asked, pressing our Ordu guide for information. You could never be too careful or have too much information when it came to a themed dungeon. Hell, I might even be able to convince the Ordu to come with us so we can ask unrelated questions.

"Those are questions I will be leaving to find out myself. Once you've isolated or illuminated the threats to the city, meet me back here and I might have use for you if I've narrowed down what events transpired and who is responsible. Be swift, hunters, and do not give these monsters your mercy, for they shall offer you none."

***

"Are we going to talk about how amazing this is?" Alayna asked, her mask helmet still on and her voice slightly muffled.

I looked at the Ordu walking in groups all around the wide platforms that connected huge discs where shops and other businesses that I couldn't begin to fathom were set up, each of them so tall and giving off a powerful presence. "Sear everything you can about this place into your mind. This world is simply insane."

"I don't think they have any of those Rex guys here," Emory said, his own helmet pulled up on his head to make it easy for him to talk. "I mean if they did it would be making a bigger mess of the place, don't you think?"

I laughed. "We are literally walking among the Ordu

right now and you are concerned about that giant lizard?" I asked, rolling my eyes from behind my closed visor.

"Did you see that shop back there, they had swords with so many runes that I couldn't even begin to understand what kind of benefits it must give," Fran said, looking back to where she'd seen the weapons. I looked as well and noticed something different.

Standing outside the shop was a Runeforged that very much looked like Kora, white metal and sleek design with many thousands of runic formations running across the surface. It picked up a sword and examined it before putting it back. None of the Ordu seemed bothered by it or giving it any commands, it was like it was a free entity similar to what Kora had become.

I turned to go approach it, but suddenly a darker clothed Ordu barred my path, his eyes weren't orange like Zel'hu's but purple instead. "Stay on task, human." His words were sharp and not at all as caring or gentle as Zel'hu's. Several more Ordu put themselves in our way, keeping us from moving toward the shop. It would appear the dungeon wanted us to stay on task, so on task we would remain. I held up my hands in mock surrender and turned back towards the closest dot.

The weird map made a little sense after we got near the dot. My map failed to show the multilevel nature of the city, with its many walkways and platforms. There were some that tilted downward and some that would bring you up, but according to the strange rock, we needed to go down.

I peeked over the edge and saw that the deeper I looked,

the more foggy and dark it appeared. The surface must be nearly pitch black and that was where the monster awaited us.

"We need to find a way down to the surface. Our prey is hiding in the dark."

CHAPTER 39
THE HUNT IS ON

For every path we found downward, we encountered a dozen more that led up. It was like the very design of the city wanted you to ascend and not descend. It was odd, I never saw any of the paths change, but after taking a particularly steep downward path, we turned around thinking to double back to find new ways forward only to be met with straight paths. But as with most things, it just took time until we finally reached the bottom level of the city.

Thin mist hung in the air and made seeing more than a foot or so in front of us nearly impossible. For the last five levels of downward travel, we hadn't witnessed any Ordu, but oddly enough we began encountering all manner of other races. From elves to orcs to humans, they all walked around in the lower levels wearing simple garb and had looks of sad contentment on their faces. I'd tried to interact with a few but they just hurried on their way, ignoring us with averted eyes. This was not the life I imagined when I pictured the time of the Ordu, something was definitely off here.

"A bit weird, isn't it?" Alayna asked, touching a nearby wall. It was the base of one of the many cloud touching buildings. "Down here all the rune work is obscured, but I can feel it just below the surface. The Ordu seem a bit stingy with their magical knowledge."

"And what's with all these sad looking people, they act like they aren't living in the greatest time in history," Fran said, gesturing to a goblin walking by in nothing but rags and looking like it had been beaten up recently.

I nodded my head. "Doesn't seem like paradise for everyone," I said. "We should focus on finishing the dungeon. If each run takes this long and doesn't have that many mobs I don't know if it is going to be the wellspring of essence I'd hoped."

"I bet they know something," Emory said, pointing at a group rushing through the misty streets, shirts ripped and faces bloody.

"I'll heal them," Alayna offered, and I didn't move to stop her. Instead, I ran forward and grabbed a human male about my height with a crazed look in his eyes.

"What did this to you?" I asked, a heal from Alayna washed over him and he calmed just a measure.

"Monsters lurk in the shadows," he spoke the words with a wavering voice filled with fear. "Chaos in the streets, the darkness comes." His last few words came out as a mumble and his eyes glazed over.

I tried questioning him further, but he wouldn't

respond and the others had already gotten away, disappearing into the mist. I let him go and he too disappeared seconds later.

"Whatever attacked them left shallow cuts, nothing life threatening, especially for us. Let's just move the way they came from and see what we find."

So, we did, trudging through the mist with weapons drawn and ready. I paid special mind to any shadows, which meant I was constantly distracted as they were literally everywhere. The only light down here came from the bright glow of runes from above, creating a perpetual dusk, just enough light to see by but not enough to see anything clearly. I could only imagine how bad it was for someone without *Awakened* senses.

"When he said Chaos in the streets, you don't think he meant?" Alayna didn't even have to finish the question before I knew where her mind was, as I'd been thinking the same moment before.

"In the heart of an Ordu city?" I asked, the very idea seemed absurd.

"Down here doesn't feel like an Ordu city," Alayna said, shaking her head. "I wish I'd been able to take a look at the runes on those horseless carriages. I bet they use similar formations to what I discovered. The elves would be greatly aided by new rune sets to balance the weight and lift ratios."

"I sense something ahead," I said, bringing my sword in front of me. "Let's stay quiet and be ready for anything." A round of nods followed and we turned the bend to an alleyway between two massive buildings. Down here the white of whatever material was being used had been stained by a layer of dust and dirt, so it looked more grey than anything. Which made it fit in all the more in this mist filled wasteland of the lower city.

A flash of movement through the mist below eye level caught my attention and I heard the distinct flap of wings but couldn't pinpoint where it was coming from. The darkness seemed to deepen the harder I strained my eyes to see what lay ahead, until frustration got the better of me and I cast Light. Directing the globe about twice my height into the air and out of the way, our path forward was illuminated.

Several figures, not just one, flicked and flittered about each one as big as a large Tom cat. The mist obscured them to a certain extend but I recognized the draconian features from my many encounters with Chaos beasts. But before I let my assumptions and fears take over, I tried to Inspect one. I felt a resisting pull as I tried to activate the skill, but eventually it did work and I got information.

Baby Wyvern, Level 25

Well, that was different. Never before had I been able to get a specific read on a Chaos monster, perhaps because it was a dungeon monster? "Be careful everyone," I shouted through the stillness of the night. "I think we are dealing with Chaos Monsters or at least the dungeon equivalent."

A thought came to mind then and I reached out with

my hand, casting Restoring Light on the closest one. Perhaps if it was a Chaos monster this spell could do damage to it or unravel the Chaos that gave it its terrible strength. The one I'd targeted squealed and fell to the ground, a bit of the darkened shadow that blackened its scaly flesh disappeared, showing a vibrant blue color.

They seemed fixated on something on the ground and only the one I targeted had stopped long enough to notice we were close. I soon realized that despite removing a measure of the Chaos from the wyvern, it was still a monster and it screeched at us before flying straight for me with incredible speed.

With my weapon already raised and in position I thought it would be an easy kill, but the draconic flying monster had unreal speed. It swooped around the cut of my blade, sharp thin talons scratching lines in my neck as it passed. However, Fran, and she could say what she wanted about speed verse technique, was ready and caught the flying monster square in the face, killing it in a single blow.

These were fragile baby versions of the mighty beast we'd faced in the past. It was worrisome seeing them here in what was meant to be an Ordu city, dungeon or not. Our quick fight with the first baby wyvern went unnoticed by the dozen or so others as they scurried and ripped at something in the dark shadows ahead.

"Keep guard," I said, Creed, Emory, and Fran stepped forward ready for anything.

I stepped over to the fallen wyvern and inspected the bisected corpse. The scales were a deep blue, like the sky turned when a storm was beginning to blow in, dark and broody. I touched the corpse and used my Restoring Light spell again, this time the scales lost all pretext of darkness and glittered a vibrant blue. I heard movement and turned away from the kill, looting could wait.

A few of the wyverns had lost interest in whatever had been holding their attention thus far and now they screeched at us, just noticing the large group of onlookers. My team parted to let me through, and I stood next to Emory, sword raised.

"They are fast but easy to kill, don't hold back and this should be easy enough," I said, then added under my breath, "Assuming they don't swarm us."

"Fuck man! You went there, really man, you know better," Emory moaned. He was right, I should have known better. Whatever had been holding the attention of the rest of the little flying wyverns ceased to be enticing enough not to notice us and suddenly we were facing down a small horde of baby wyverns.

I had a moment of hesitation and it cost me several hits, though they didn't penetrate my armor. I couldn't decide between using Restoring Light on them or just flat out killing them. It was a dungeon after all, and we were in this for the essence. Deciding my most offensive spells were the way to go, I lashed out with Lightning Strike, my free hand clenching into a fist as I called the spell down, with how they swarmed and flew at us it would be impossible to miss.

Sure enough, the air split and the buzz of the night was interrupted by the crack of lightning as one of the wyverns took the hit, cascading into a nearby wall before falling still. They were numerous but not extremely strong, nor did they seem to have developed the intense sound attack or fire breath of the larger wyvern I'd faced. It took time, but one by one we whittled down their numbers until the battle was won.

"That," Alayna said, panting, "was not fun." She'd taken the worst of it, if only by how hard she'd had to exert herself to keep Emory and Fran up and fighting.

Creed and my armor had provided near perfect defense against the needle like claws of the baby wyverns, so we literally spent the entire time casting and swinging our swords about, killing with reckless abandon. Fran had her face cut up several times over and even now, after being healed, I could see several light red lines where cuts were still healing.

"I agree, that sucked," Fran said, she'd put her sword away and wouldn't meet my eyes, instead she seemed transfixed at the place the wyverns had been before they attacked us. "Is that an Ordu?"

I turned to see where she was looking and realized that a mostly eaten body lay some mere feet from us, the wyverns had been eating away at the flesh of someone when we'd arrived. Leaning down, I picked up a piece of the cloth covering the remains, before seeing the faint rune script words, I'd already guessed that Fran was correct.

This had been an Ordu, and it had died from the wyvern attack.

"I thought the Ordu were masters of magic and extremely powerful," Emory said, not looking impressed as he picked at his teeth, freeing some piece of a prior meal from between them.

"That is what the legends say," I said, knowing enough about the Ordu to at least confirm their supposed amazing power. Yet these weak baby wyverns had been too much for this Ordu. Not for the first time I found myself wondering how accurate this dungeon was to the reality of the time of the Ordu. Perhaps this was a fiction created by the dungeon and had no basis in reality.

I held to the idea, as it made the most sense. Thinking back to my very first dungeon helped solidify the notion in my mind. There had been boats in that dungeon that fought each other with explosive cannons and traveled on the waters, something that just wasn't done in open sea because of the incredibly strong monsters guaranteed to sink boats of any size. I'd accepted then that the dungeon was telling a story and it hadn't been based in any truth that I knew of, although...I had heard of a time when ships sailed the open seas hundreds of years ago. In fact, it was likely during the time of the Ordu when such feats would have been possible.

Though, why would they bother with sea travel when they clearly appeared to be masters of the sky, if not masters of life. I stood, handing over the bit of cloth to Alayna. It had visible runes that I was sure she'd want to commit to memory before we left.

We looted the corpses, and I got nothing but low-level trash loot. Well, it wasn't trash per se as it might have been useful were I still level 15 or 20, but at 31 and with gear that granted so many wonderful benefits it just wasn't up to my standards. Fran, however, got a nice wyvern's cloak made of vibrant blue scales and Emory got a trinket called 'Draconic Vial of Blood'. It allowed him to take on draconic features for a minute once a day, he didn't try it, but we were all eager to see what exactly that meant. The essence we got was decent, but nothing out of the ordinary. So far, our trip to the dungeon had been the most profitable essence wise.

CHAPTER 40
ORDU GARDENS

The warm glow of runic formations on the side of the buildings seemed to wash away the gloom from the lower floors the higher we got, and we were going pretty high. The map indicated an area about halfway up toward the clouds, so, high up but not as high as you could get. We made it a point to walk close to vendors and buildings so Alayna could get a glimpse of any and all runic formations. Surprisingly we encountered only minimal push back from our attempts, not anywhere like the first encounter.

"Are you going to be able to remember it all?" I asked in a hushed whisper as we passed a pair of Ordu.

They were dressed in the usual garb that almost all the Ordu seemed to be wearing, but at their sides they had thin blades sheathed. I turned to watch them go, only to find one of them looking over at us as well. Tilting my head in their direction I looked to Alayna, she'd said something, and I'd missed it.

"Sorry, say that again," I said, and she raised her visor likely thinking it had been the reason I'd missed her words.

"I doubt I'll remember it all and I'm not sure I would get away with writing them down, but just seeing how they pattern the runes is helpful. I've identified at least two I've never even seen before and can't wait to work out the meaning. I'm focusing on formation and new ones, but who knows the implications this dungeon will have."

I met her eyes and she sighed. She knew my mind on the matter already, this wasn't knowledge that ought to be spread out far and wide. Already I'd had my discoveries perverted to do mass destruction, I wouldn't allow it again if I could help it.

"I look forward to seeing what *you* can do with it," I said, emphasizing the 'you' to further push my point home. She let out another long, exaggerated sigh before flipping her faceplate down.

We neared the point on the map, and I was surprised to see a team of six Ordu with thin swords at their hips standing guard over an ornate set of doors, as clear as crystal and twice as tall as them. The doors were attached to a pathway that led to a clear dome, as if the entire structure was made of pure glass or perhaps transparent crystal. Where each hexagonal edge met another, you could see the slightly blue-green glow of runes at work. Through the transparent walls I could see a vast forest or garden filled with all manner of vegetation.

"Halt, return to the lower levels," the Ordu speaking

paused to eye us more critically before continuing, "Humans."

I didn't skip a beat, stepping forward I said, "We are hunters called to deal with monsters by Zel'hu."

This prompted a round of grumbles from the half dozen guards, or at least I assumed that is what they were meant to be. The one who'd spoken first stepped forward, hand on his sword now.

"You think because we tempered your wild magic that you are better than us now, don't you. I bet I could still take you in a fair fight."

I couldn't believe what I was hearing, this Ordu sounded threatened by us. And what did he mean they tempered our wild magic? Sure, I knew the Ordu and the *Awakening* was all about putting a layer of order over the chaos of the magics that burned within those who sparked, but he made it sound like a burden and less like a gift.

The Ordu were meant to represent Order and balance, but all those I'd met so far didn't give me that impression at all. They just seemed like ordinary people with grudges and prejudices like any other I'd encountered. I looked the angsty guard in the face and inclined my head, trying to be respectful to avoid a conflict like I would any other man or woman.

"We have a duty to attend, please allow us to pass."

I noticed a measure of his bravado falter and he shook his head but stepped aside. "Allow them to pass. Be quick about it, this area is meant to be off limits to your kind."

"Thank you," I said, further inclining my head before

standing tall and walking past him with my head held high. It paid off not to be a dick sometimes, a lesson Emory and Zander hadn't learned very well.

As if to punctuate my point I heard a grunt and a curse, looking back I deduced what had happened when I saw one of the Ordu helping another stand. Emory had just checked one of them with his shoulder as he walked by, and they'd fallen right over. Despite this, they didn't draw their weapons. Perhaps they were all talk after all. If I didn't know better, I would even say they feared us.

A wave of humid warmth washed over us as we pushed through the doors and into the entryway. Benches, a bit bigger than would be comfortable for humans, had been arranged around a circular area just inside and several winding paths led into the dimly lit garden. From what I'd seen outside the domed room, this area was easily half a mile across, and was ginormous. Finding anything inside here, especially if it were as small as the baby wyverns, would be next to impossible. The map stone was no help, simply blipping at the very center of the room and erratically moving from one edge to the other a moment later.

"Should we split up and see what we can find?" Fran suggested, looking at the dozens of paths leading out into the gardens.

The vegetation grew nearly as tall as us, but the trees reached ten times that height, so seeing anything by just looking over the area wasn't possible. Whatever we were hunting couldn't be too terribly big though, because the doors were only so big and they seemed intact, unless there was another entrance someplace. I did some quick calculations in my head and decided, much to Emory's dismay I was sure, that the doors weren't tall enough or wide enough for a Rex to fit through.

"I'm not a fan of splitting the party," I said, looking into the ominous low lighting between the trees and brush. Sure, the tops of the trees were lit enough, as well as the trails cut into it, but if we needed to go off the path then we'd be at a severe disadvantage.

"I'm actually with Fran, this dungeon has so far been pretty easy. If we stick a healer with both halves, we will be able to cover twice as much ground and listen. It is so quiet in here that I bet just calling out would be enough to alert the other group if anything is found. Why don't Creed, Fran, and I go down this way," Alayna gestured to the left, "and you and Emory can check out the right."

Creed nodded but remained quiet. Emory just laughed before giving his own opinion on the matter. "And what if we come across a Rex and you miss out on all that sweet essence because Caldor and I whoop its ass?"

"I don't want to miss out on any essence, but the chances that one of those Rexes got into this room are very slim. I'd even go so far as to say improbable," Creed said, suddenly chiming in and sounding very academic. His helmet's visor was up and the ice effect off right now, so despite how much he'd grown into his role as a scary death knight, he looked pretty tame at the moment and sounded like the boy we'd first met for a second there.

"Let's vote on it," I said, deciding that as much as I

didn't want to split the party no one had elected me party dictator, so I should probably let everyone have a chance to speak their minds.

I lost, four to one, and we split the party.

Watching Alayna go with Creed and Fran, I tried to tell myself it was going to be alright, but I honestly didn't know. There was no telling how powerful the monster might turn out to be or if we'd get the jump on it. Alayna was a talented healer though, and Creed might as well be a tank, between that, and Fran's skill at the blade I finally convinced myself to turn back to Emory.

"Emory Fadel, you walking pile of horse shit, you ready to go kill a dungeon boss by ourselves?" I laughed out loud, breaking the silence and Emory grinned so wide it looked like it would break his face in two.

He did as he had done all those months ago and grabbed his weapon, then leaning forward menacingly, he lowered his voice and said, "You are an awfully slimy son of a bitch you know that." Then with his voice back to normal he added. "Just the boys hanging out and killing Rexes. You think there will be enough hide left after I make a suit of armor to make a more formal suit?"

A sudden picture of Emory wearing formal clothing made of a giant lizard had me cracking up. I shook my head and slapped him intentionally hard on the arm, "Let's get moving before they have all the fun without us." I hadn't really had a chance to cut loose with Emory in some time and felt that this could be fun.

He rubbed at his arm, glaring mockingly in my direction. "You hit like a...well I don't even know what to compare you to, but I took like fifty health damage from that slap, can't imagine going at it for real against you. I'm pissed at you, by the way."

We began our walk down the lane, keeping our eyes open for any signs of monsters or movement of any kind. "Why's that?" I asked, my smile fading as I suddenly thought of Mick. I missed him, despite how much money he'd won from me during our occasional nights spent gambling and drinking. I hadn't gambled since he'd died, but I might pull out the old deck of cards I had tucked away and play a few hands with Emory tonight, in honor of Mick I might even let Emory win a few. He was a terrible gambler, worse than me by far.

"I'm pissed," Emory said, "because I had a year head start on you and you've left me in the dust. If it weren't for this gift, I'd be stuck at only the Ordu knows what level." He tapped at his arm where the Essence Band would have been tucked under his armor.

I made a show of breathing hot air on my fingernails, despite having metal gauntlets on, and rubbed it against my armor as if to polish them. "I've always been faster than you," I said, trying to capture the jovial banter we shared, but it came off as vain and I immediately felt bad. "But seriously, you can't measure yourself against me. You know my circumstances are different and you've done well for yourself in the last year, growing far more than I bet you ever imagined."

"Because of you," Emory said, his tone going serious for

once. "Thank you, I'm not sure I've ever said, but thank you."

"Don't," I said, shaking my head. "You earned every drop of essence you've used to level up. It wasn't like I carried you through powerful dungeons. We bled, sweated, and bruised for every single bit of the essence we got, remember that. My Essence Band helps you get essence that is already being released from killing the monster. It's only fair you get a decent share of it."

"This essence band collects about three times as much essence as I do when I kill monsters," Emory said, shaking his head in disbelief. "Without it, I'd be far, far behind. Now I just need another one to make attributes less expensive. At two per level for free and two purchased, I'm leveling slower than I'd like."

I looked around, making sure we were actually alone before speaking. "I get three per level and purchase three. It is the secret to how I'm so strong. I get a normal person's level worth of attributes extra per level even if you take into account them purchasing two extra, which is the normal spread as you well know."

Emory didn't even have the decency to act surprised. "No shit," he said, elbowing me in the chest, his armor clinking against my own. "Did you think we didn't know you'd figured out a way to get way more attributes? We know you well enough to have worked it out."

"Ismene told you, didn't she?"

"Yeah, Ismene told me."

I laughed, he was all ready to claim he'd worked it out

himself when he knew damn well Ismene had just spilled the beans, classic Emory.

Something moved ahead and for a moment I thought I saw a face, but it happened too quickly to be sure. I held up a hand to silence Emory and I just waited, listening for any sign that something had been just ahead in the dense brush.

"Let's go off the path," I said after several seconds of waiting. "I think I saw something."

Emory nodded and I pulled out my sword, ready to cut down the brush ahead when Mick stepped out of from behind a thick tree trunk.

"Howdy boys, you need a hand?" He asked, raising his massive, short sword of a dagger up, then faster than I'd ever seen him move he slashed at the space between my helmet and breastplate. If not for my armor's properties to distribute the damage over the weak points he might have scored a critical hit.

I didn't know what to do, so stunned by his appearance, so I looked to Emory, but his gaze was to the left and he appeared to be reaching out to hug someone, but there was nothing there. Pain lanced across my neck, and I looked back to Mick, his dagger was wet with red blood.

"This is a knife," he assured me, licking the blood off by running his tongue down the length of the blade.

CHAPTER 41
TRICKS OF THE MIND

The pain doubled as I stepped back away from Mick, so fully out of my mind in trying to understand what was happening. He smirked at me in the way he had so many times before, but I couldn't believe this phantasm was him. There was no way for my logical mind to connect it. So think, what else could be going on? I pushed away the pain in my neck, ignoring it as I had so many other injuries before. If this wasn't Mick, and it was trying to harm me, then this must be the monster.

I ignored the taunting this fake Mick gave me and readied my sword. Slashing outward, I hit nothing and suddenly the Mick that had been in front of me was gone. Emory looked at me, then his eyes widened, and his hands went up to his own throat as if he were choking.

"It's not real!" I yelled, but it was like he couldn't hear me.

What could I do? How could I reach him? Something

moved just beyond him, and I caught sight of a black form one moment and gone the next. There was something out there and it was messing with our heads. Emory fell to his knees gasping for air.

"Just breathe! You are fine!" I yelled, but it was making no difference and I didn't know what else to do. Reaching out I unlatched his helmet, ripped it off his head and struck him with the pommel of my sword. His eyes rolled into the back of his head, and he slumped down, knocked out. But as I thought, he was breathing again, if not a bit ragged. But he was breathing and that was what was important.

I was going to have some explaining to do, and I hoped my blow hadn't caused too much damage to his head, but I needed to hit him hard enough that it would put him unconscious, and I had. With Emory taken care of, for now, I turned my sight onto the edge of the garden path, looking for any sight of a monster that I could sink my blade into.

A distant scream and a mighty roar drew my attention away from my hunt. I turned back to Emory, not willing to leave him behind. Scooping him up and carrying him rather awkwardly over one shoulder, I cut through the thick vegetation toward the sound of the scream. It wasn't a sense of honor or responsibility that drew me forward now, but a fear for the safety of my friends. When we got out of this in one piece, I was going to tell them 'I told you so' so hard. You never split the party!

It was hard work and twice I dropped Emory during our flight to reach the other group, but eventually the vegetation opened up and we stumbled into an open clearing. A terrifying scene was laid out before me, bodies of Ordu strewn about and blood everywhere. Alayna chanted words to a healing spell over a still form of Fran, while Creed faced off alone against the largest Drake I'd ever seen. It had orange and red scales, with terribly sharp looking talons and a maw able to close over your entire midsection with ease.

Creed was slowly giving ground, but he didn't appear as outmatched as I'd first assumed. This was the first Drake I'd ever seen that wasn't a pure black color, so I used Inspect and once again was surprised at what I found.

Fire Drake, Level 37

As if to punctuate the fact that it was indeed a *Fire* Drake, it opened its maw and let flames spill out, engulfing Creed. An aura of icy blue power swirled around Creed, and I heard echoing deep laughter coming from within the flames.

"You'll need to do better than that!" He yelled and I was surprised to hear a hint of humor in his voice. Creed was having a good time it would appear. Setting Emory down at the edge of the forest garden, I stepped onto the path and walked into the wide opening.

Blood, sticky and hot, clung to my feet as I walked and both Creed and the drake seemed to sense my approach. Creed snapped his gaze over to me and gestured with his sword, while the drake looked over and spit fire in my direction by way of welcoming me.

I took his welcome and blocked it with a quick Mana Shell, the barrier lasted only a moment before shattering but it gave me enough time to get out of the way and unleash my own attack. Lightning, quick and deadly, shot down from the sky above as I used Lightning Strike, but I didn't stop there. Blips of magical energy shot forth from my hands—one, two, three—from my Arcane Missile attack. Each one smashed into the drake with impressive force, leaving scorch marks.

Whatever this drake was, it wasn't a Chaos beast and not nearly as sturdy as the ones I'd faced before. Creed moved in, scoring a strike on the front leg and drawing blood. Just then, as I prepared to Blink forward, I saw bodies appear and my head began to swim in dizziness. One by one the bodies of those fallen soldiers I'd failed to save fell from the sky and landed in squelching horror all around me.

"It's not real, this is not real," I told myself, my sword clattering noisily to the ground. I knew that I was being attacked by some mental illusion meant to mess with my head, there was no other explanation, but I didn't know how to dispel the images. What had I done just moments before? The act of attacking Mick and realizing he wasn't real had done it, but I already knew these bodies weren't real and I couldn't bring myself to cut down at the mutilated dead corpses of my allies.

Instead, I did something that was most likely stupid, but I was keen on following almost any instinct at this point. I flushed essence into myself, using my Essence Infusion ability, only I targeted just my eyes, ears, and any other sense that

I could hone in on. I wanted to force my body to see, hear, and feel what was truly real. I blinked, my ears burning, everything I saw had a haze of blue to it and I could see motes of a white energy perfusing everything all around me. It was too intense, I needed to cut off the power, but I dared not, because the bodies were gone now.

I saw the hot white outlines of Creed facing off against the drake, but there was something odd about the drake. It had a blackened swirl deep inside itself fighting against the white light all around, like some sort of infection taking hold deep inside. The more I focused on the deep blackness, the more sick I felt inside. This was Chaos corruption, I realized in a stroke of inspiration. I could deal with that. Reaching out, I cast Restoring Light.

There was a point while casting where I nearly lost hold of it, so bright was the light as I did the spell. It was like motes of light from all around gathered and swirled around me, forming a spear that struck the drake and ate away at the darkness inside. By this point, I was sick to my stomach and my eyes hurt to the point that plucking them out seemed like a viable option.

I released the essence from my senses, but not before I heard a voice distant but somehow directed toward me.

It was dark and sinister, very inhuman in the way it spoke. "I will spread the darkness for my master, this rot will take hold and you can't stop it."

My vision flickered back to reality, and I was pleased to see that the nightmares hadn't returned. What was more, Emory had gotten to his feet and joined the battle against the drake beside Creed along with a newly healed Fran. Alayna moved toward me with hands moving, likely working a spell to heal me, even though I was in decent condition, all things considered.

A moment later, I felt the warmth of her heal wash over me and I gave her a thumbs up, before summoning my blade back into my grasp and running back into battle. I cured the beginnings of the Chaos corruption in this drake, but it was still a fierce foe that needed slaying.

Fran, moving as graceful and purposeful as possible, slashed the drake across the face, drawing blood. Meanwhile, Creed used an ability that spread his aura wide to encompass all three of the fighters, just as a blast of fire came from the monster. It dissipated before it could do any harm against the powerful icy aura. Emory slammed his shield into the hard ground and a wave of energy traveled out, hitting the drake. What it did exactly, I didn't know, but it seemed like it was moving a fair bit slower than it had before. Whether that was due to the damage it was taking or an ability from Emory, I couldn't say.

It slashed out, long powerful claws ready to sunder anyone it hit. Emory ripped the shield from the ground and threw himself in front of the strike, the air ringing from the blow. Shaking myself out of my stupor and gathering my wits back, I fulfilled my role of midrange attacker. I began the cast for Firebolt. Flaming energy gathered in my hands, sparking as the mana ignited into a flaming ball of fire. When the cast completed, it was like the back portion of the ball opened up and in doing so, launched it forward with deadly purpose. At 60 mana, the Rank 2 version of this spell did a fair bit more damage at an impressive 150-foot radius.

Whereas before, and with lower levels, my Firebolt spell would do anywhere between 30 and a 100 damage, I could now expect a range of 300 to 500 even without essence infusion. There was of course the base resistances and armor of the target to consider, so when my firebolt spell hit the drake, I only did 150 or so points of damage, which was over half of its potential. The drake had impressive fire and magical resistances.

While waiting out the 2.5 second cooldown I switched to Arcane Missile, spending 150 points of mana to send three missiles of arcane energy at the drake. Mana surged down my pathways, and I felt the three distinct balls of energy begin to form during the 3 seconds it took to cast the spell. My hands moved and I chanted the required words. Just as I felt the energy couldn't possibly build up anymore, it released, honing in on the target I'd selected.

This spell was unique in that it did not miss and would follow the target unless actively intercepted in flight or blocked by a shield of some kind. With a mana pool of 1,610 and a regen of only 55 per minute or roughly a point of mana per second, I'd blown through over 500 mana in a matter of a dozen seconds. My spells packed a dangerous punch, but evoking so many powerful spells close together drained me considerably. I had ten minutes before I could restore the mana, I'd spent in only ten seconds.

Perhaps I should invest more into my Concentration attribute or find some armor to increase it so that I had more longevity in battle without the aid of mana potions. Those were thoughts for another time, as my Firebolt spell came off cooldown and it was my most economic spell when taken into account the balance of damage to cost. It simply amazed me that I had the power in my spells to end most foes with my same health pool in three to four hits, but that was what being an evoker was all about.

Luckily, I was also a Blade Master and the skills, abilities, and heavy armor I could wear because of it made me a force to be reckoned with on the battlefield. My Blade Master and Evoker classes of course combined to the pseudo class I'd named Arcane Knight after my father's example, but it was that only in name, as truly I was a master of the blade who could summon forth powerful evocation to aid me in battle.

Although mixing the classes did have drawbacks, I didn't have the massive Mana pool that a true evoker would have or some of the damage bonuses they got in their class abilities or buffs. The same was true for the Blade Master class. Fran, who had the same class, had certain abilities that I didn't have access to that allowed her to perform amazing feats of skill and finesse. Luckily, I passed my second threshold and was fast enough to match what she could do using her class skills, that and I was almost ten levels higher than her.

The battle ended as I waited for my mana to rise and cooldowns to run out. The drake, all red and orange scales, fell to the ground from the sheer number of wounds it had taken, not from one decisive strike like I'd accomplished with the Elite outside the dungeon.

"What in the actual fuck," Emory said, walking over to

me and taking his helmet off. "You knocked the shit out of me, look at this lump."

He did indeed have a sizable lump and a line where the skin had been broken. I smiled sheepishly at him and shrugged my shoulders. "You were choking or something. I didn't know what else to do."

"You knocked my ass out because I was choking? Remind me to never have you help if I get steak stuck in my throat," Emory said, his demeanor shifting and a smile spreading across his lips.

"I wouldn't help you if you were choking on steak, you'd probably just re-choke yourself after I dislodged it," I said, laughing all the while. I missed the times we got to shit talk to each other, but now wasn't the right time and there was loot to be collected.

CHAPTER 42
FULL CIRCLE

Sometimes I wonder if dungeons can read my mind or at the very least, my layout of attributes. It was something I'd never asked Kora about, but I really should. For what felt like far too often I ended up with dungeon drops that specifically helped me or filled an attribute layout I wanted to try, even if sometimes the gear was just too low level. This cloak I'd just gotten from the Fire Drake was no exception, and it was eerily similar to my precious Cloak of Negation.

Cloak of Fiery Concentration
+20 Constitution
+20 Concentration
+10% Fire Resistance
Drake Hardiness: This Cloak came from the Hide of a

Fire Drake and as such will provide additional resistance against Physical and Magical attacks when placed in the path of such attacks.

Durability: 500/500

Rarity: Rare

Weight: 1 pound

Item Level: 50, Level Required to use: 32, Dropped by: Fire Drake

It wouldn't provide the negation of Chaos attacks, but it was too good of a find not to equip immediately. For the first time in ages, I took off my Cloak of Negation and stored it away. Then, with Emory's help I got my new cloak into place, marveling at the red and orange coloring. It went from deep red on the edges to a cool white orange in the very center of the cloak, creating a cool, flame-like effect.

The scales were just as supple and soft as my previous cloak, though I knew by reading the information that came with the cloak that while it was incredibly durable, it wasn't a match when put against my previous cloak. But that had to do with the masterwork quality more than anything else. Five hundred was already about as durable as my armor, which meant the cloak could likely withstand many attacks before visible damage would happen.

I checked with everyone else to see what they'd gotten, not a single one of them was as lucky as me with my amazing cloak, but Fran got a pretty cool item. It was a ring that allowed her to light her weapon on fire to give it a small bit of extra damage as fire damage as well as raising her Strength Attribute by an impressive 30 points. Rings were something I needed a better option for. I decided now would be a good time to look over the gear I had equipped and decide what I wanted to replace. If my theory about dungeons was right, then maybe speaking aloud what I needed might help in getting what I wanted.

I wore my 'Lord Black's Enchanted Armor' of course. It came with a set bonus of 30 Endurance, 50 Constitution, as well as the 'Reinforcement' enchantment that had saved my bacon many times over. It distributed the damage along my entire armor, making hitting weak points like the neck, armpits, and other places incredibly hard to damage. It also had twelve gem slots that I'd recently had upgraded to stronger gems that provided an additional plus 10 Strength and Intellect instead of the normal plus 5 that I used before. That gave me an additional 120 Strength and Intellect, an amazing bonus to my attributes.

And of course, there was my 'Masterwork Refined Mythril Ear Clasps' that shielded me from scrying and supposedly to block out mental intrusions and psychic attacks, however, today's illusions made me wonder how well that worked. Whatever had attacked my mind must have been strong indeed. They also gave me a flat 10% increase in my mana regeneration, can't even imagine how bad it would be without it.

Then of course, I had my 'Cloak of Fiery Concentration' and around my waist 'Marley's Belt' a decent item that provided an additional 21 constitution. Next were my trinkets, I had two of them currently, 'Elemental Strike Claw' and 'Charm of the Sleepless One'. I kept the charm put away most times, but during a dungeon or combat it was best I keep it out as it gave me an additional 9 Constitution. As for the Strike Claw, it gave a small bonus to strength at plus 5 but added elemental damage to my sword strikes every now and again. I'd witnessed it happen hundreds of times, but the effects were so minimal that it was hardly ever worth mentioning.

Lastly, I had my rings, all four of them, now that I'd passed my final threshold, I could wear four rings. My 'Horse Head Signet Ring' gave me an impressive plus 20 Endurance, while my 'Ring of Anubis', my legendary ring, provided plus 1 Core attribute per 2 levels I have. That put the additional Core attribute to 16 currently, but it would only rise with time which is what made it so legendary. That, and the fact that Core items were so hard to find. My last two rings were the storage ring I'd gotten from the Lich and my 'Ring of Ram's Might' that gave a measly plus 4 to Strength and Endurance.

"I sure could use a better ring," I said to no one in particular. Emory looked at me sideways and smirked.

Fran spoke up, looking me up and down. "With how much coin you have you'd think you'd just have outfitted yourself with the best crafted gear possible."

"I get so carried away with everything I need to do that I don't spend as much time on myself as I should," I said, shrugging. It really was a shame I hadn't used my gems and found a ring that took a socket at the very least, that would have yielded me a decent ring or two. I made a silent pact with myself that as soon as time permitted, I'd be going to Gilfoy's Emporium to make sure I had the very best gear possible for our trip to Avalon.

As dungeon monsters had a tendency to do, once we'd all looted the Fire Drake, it disappeared in a fizzle and twinkle of lights. We had one final monster to track down, assuming it wasn't another swarm of monsters like the Wyverns. But my gut told me that there was a bit of a theme going on here and what we could expect for the last monster I didn't know. I did know that it would have something to do with Chaos or possibly a draconic monster of some kind.

"That Drake was infected with Chaos," I said to the group as we walked together toward the exit. "I always thought that Draconic monsters were Chaos beings from the start. Is this dungeon making any sense to anyone else?"

"So few monsters and the reduced essence you get from killing dungeon monsters still being in effect is what I'm bothered by," Emory said, his eyes glazing over as he addressed his menus. "At this rate, the pay off at the end better be enormous or we might as well have just stayed killing wild monsters. No decent loot but amazing essence gains."

We all checked our essence bands then, emptying them of the trace essence we'd been collecting and the small bit we'd gotten from the monster, equaling a measly five thousand and some change. At least the baby wyverns had given a fair bit more by virtue of how many we'd been forced to kill. After only a bit of walking, we reached the gates to the gardens, but I was surprised to find the six guards had left. In fact, as we got out into the walkway, I realized I didn't see any Ordu.

The sun was getting close to setting above, though that hardly mattered with the near constant glow of the runes providing a steady stream of light, shadows or no shadows.

Shrugging the change off for now, I consulted the magical map rock to see where the final blip could be found. To my surprise it had moved significantly, now looking like it was where we'd started. If I remembered right that area had one of the biggest platforms with shops and much else, so if the monster was there, then people would be getting hurt. Dungeon or not, I couldn't abide unnecessary suffering.

"Let's hurry, the monster is back where we entered the dungeon," I said, falling into a steady jog, holding myself back enough that the others could keep pace without exhausting their stamina before the fight. Mine barely moved, the regeneration a match for my current output.

We were still a way's away when I heard what it was we would be facing. A mighty roar, no, several roars overlapping each other, cried out from a great distance and the power of it shook my chest. We kept moving, winding through the too tall buildings and empty walkways. It was like the entire city had been evacuated and only we'd been left to deal with whatever awaited us.

Just as we turned the final corner before a long stretch of platform that would take us within view of where we started, an Ordu came running toward us, covered in red blood and cuts. Although all of the Ordu looked similar and it was hard to tell, this particular Ordu was one we'd just seen, the same moody one that had tried to challenge us outside the garden.

He made it two more steps around the corner, his saber out and glowing with magical light, before he collapsed in front of us. I immediately went down to my knee to check on him, but as far as I could tell he was already dead. His chest didn't move, and I found no signs of a heartbeat, assuming Ordu had to breathe or had heartbeats as we did.

"He's dead," I declared, grabbing his weapon as I rose. Using Inspect on it gave no information but it looked dangerous, so I held on to it, careful not to touch the gentle white glow that thrummed as I moved it through the air. "Be ready for anything."

I recast my Arcane Armor, and my other buffs, then infused essence into my blade all the way up to 1,600, giving me 125% more base attributes. I checked where I stood status wise and saw that my Health pool had reached 2,300, my Mana Pool, 2,810, and my Stamina 1,720. It would last ten minutes and the bulging of my muscles and increased focus told me my other attributes had increased as well. It wasn't just the increased resource pools that made this sword so amazing, it was the increased regenerations that came with the change and the overall lift I felt while under the effects. Essence was truly a game changer.

We stepped out to face our foe and I used Inspect on the multiheaded dragon that stood before us. Dozens of Ordu lay dead or dying and only a handful were up and fighting the monster. Several Ordu wearing white robes stood a way's back, powerful magic barriers surrounding them as they launched white bolts of energy at the monster. We were outmatched for sure, and it took more effort than I wanted to admit to keep my feet moving forward.

Elite Hydra, Level 75

CHAPTER 43
AN IMPOSSIBLE TASK

"I want to make armor out of that," Emory yelled over the shouting of the dying Ordu. He pointed his mace at the hydra and yelled out in challenge. One of the nine heads turned to regard us, opening its maw as if to spit something at us. An energy gathered there and a moment before the attack came, I knew what it was.

"Hit the dirt!" I yelled, throwing myself to the side just as a giant arc of lightning ripped the ground apart where we'd been standing only seconds before.

The stench of acid smoke filled my nose, and I rolled over, then jumped to my feet. The ground, whatever odd material was used for the walkways and platforms, had melted instead of cracking like stone. It bubbled and smoked from the attack, and I knew without a doubt that if that had hit us, someone would have died. Doing a quick head count I determined that we were all in fact alive.

"We need a plan," I said, as we gathered up, weapons

ready but wholly unprepared for a threat so impossible. I looked around, there had to be a catch or something that the dungeon would provide to aid us. Several of the heads locked onto the Ordu casters and spit fire, green acid, and icy beams of power at them. When the attacks finished, only smears of bloody Ordu were left standing. In a single attack from four of the heads, all but four of the dozen casters had died.

Where was the impressive might of the Ordu? This dungeon had gotten all this wrong, the Ordu were powerful beyond measure, fighting back Chaos itself ages ago. So, what was the plan, what were we going to do? As long as we didn't shout at the hydra it seemed content to leave us alone while it finished the remaining Ordu, so I took advantage of the moment we had. Channeling Essence into my eyes I beheld the Hydra.

It had a large section inside its singular massive draconian body that swirled with black Chaos corruption, some even spreading up a single head, the only one with black scales, I realized. The others had colors as varied as the powers they wielded, all coming together into a black scaled massive body. But what I saw next gave me the start of a plan.

Above the swirling black, was a figure that pulsed a red and black light. With my vision as it was, I could only see that it was humanoid and could make out no other detail about it. Though it stood behind the hydra its blackened aura shone through, almost as if it were the source of the corruption. If we could get rid of the corruption, perhaps that would give us a way to figuring out how to slay this hydra.

Now we just had to figure out how to get close enough to do something about it. There was no way I wanted to let my team get anywhere near the hydra, so it would have to be me, and I would have to be fast. Perhaps...

"I'm going in," I said, cracking my neck to the side.

Immediately they all began to argue with me, but I turned to them and held up a hand.

"I've got a plan, just do me a favor and stay alive long enough to get the sweet essence we'll pull when we defeat this monstrous beast. If the time comes that you get targeted, dodge and block, but don't ever be directly in the path of those breath attacks. It will kill you, barrier or not."

Alayna nodded, understanding the raw and terrible power that we were up against. But I was beginning to think that perhaps we didn't have to kill the hydra ourselves, if I could just deal with the corruption, then perhaps Zel'hu would step in with a dungeon enhanced weapon or something, similar to how we'd killed the Kraken all those months ago.

I infused Essence directly into my body, focusing on my muscles and my mind, as I'd need to be able to be sharp if I were to move as fast as I planned. Next, I began running as fast as possible toward the hydra. It wasn't fast enough, not even close, but I moved with terrible speed. Two heads turned to target me, and my death was certain, as fire and light began to build in their maw. I activated Speed Burst, infusing it with essence as I did, and more than doubled my speed for several seconds. I was unclear how many seconds it would last as the enhancements of essence did unpredictable things to strengthen the abilities used.

I'd been going fast before, but now I entered an entirely new realm of speed. My own perception enhanced by the ability and essence, made it seem like I was slowly jogging through a room as still as a winter night. The four seconds that it would normally last, felt like an eternity with how slow time was passing for me. I reached the base of the hydra, sword in hand and I cut into it as I passed, not wanting to lose a chance to do a little damage.

My sword, as strong as infused as it was, struggled to cut through the thick hide of the hydra. If not for my speed I doubted that I'd have made it through at all. Pulling my blade out of its hide, I rushed past it and got a glimpse of what was hidden by the hind quarters of the monster.

A creature straight from a nightmare, wreathed in black and red energy, and a face twisted and wrong, stared at me. Despite my speed still being active, its head followed me as if I were merely walking. It wore a flowing robe of black and red with a silver crest of some kind on its chest. It depicted a roaring dragon breaking out of a hexagonal shape. Something about the dragon in the symbol made me quake in fear and feel sick to my stomach. I had to purposely stop looking at it to block the feelings.

My speed ran out and the world came crashing back in all its noise and terrible smells. The hydra had such an acrid assaulting smell that being this close to it made me want to throw up. Several Ordu stood behind the black robed monstrosity of a figure, each of them wearing black armor and eyes that glowed red. I could sense what they were the moment my eyes laid on them as if my appointment as a defender of the balance, an agent of Order, put me in direct opposition to them.

Another Ordu, one that I recognized as Zel'hu, kneeled between the half dozen black armored Ordu. Beaten, bloody, and in black chains he was obviously their prisoner. I was outnumbered, outmatched, and really not liking the position I'd just put myself in.

The dark sinister voice I'd heard before in the gardens filled my mind again and by the way the black clad Ordu flinched, they'd heard it to, but the twisted figure with no visible mouth or lips didn't speak verbally, instead his words cut into my mind like a jagged knife in need of sharpening. It was painful and I hated every word of it.

"Defeat this interloper and allow me to finish my task. Once we've corrupted enough of this world, my people will hear my call and come searching. This world, like so many, will fall to the power of the endless dragon, praise to his unknowable power." The voice seemed to suck any will to fight from me and when it withdrew, I found myself coughing as if to expel bile from my stomach.

The Ordu, the Chaos Knights all, stepped forward ready to deliver their brand of Chaotic justice. However, this left Zel'hu chained but by himself. I waited for them to reach me, none of them in a hurry and each of them holding wicked looking weapons. Gnarled black stone swords, daggers, and in one instance a weapon that looked more like a butcher's blade than anything else. When they were all but upon me, I activated Blink and appeared at Zel'hu's side.

Raising my blade, I activated Power Strike infusing it with Essence and swung downward with all my strength. His chains didn't have a chance as they were cleaved apart by the immense power of my blow. Zel'hu looked up at me shocked, and quite frankly I didn't know what to do next, so I was glad when he stood and began to work some magic of his own.

"You caught me off guard, creature of shadow, but I am free now and you will pay for your crimes." As he spoke, flashes of light appeared around him and an entire host of Runeforged looking creatures began to be summoned, first a dozen, then two dozen, then three.

Armor appeared around him, white and translucent. "The balance will be maintained!" He yelled as a sword that I recognized appeared out of thin air and into his hands. The moment he grasped the sword the battle was on, each of the Runeforged looking knights in white armor and metal bodies rushed forward runic light swords in hand. I readied the two blades I held, one taken from the guard, and rushed forward with them to deliver Ordu justice.

The show of power that Zel'hu was demonstrating now was what I expected from a true Ordu. He raised his blade up and light struck out all around, throwing all the dark armored Ordu to the ground and searing a painful looking line across the disfigured dark being. The light, cascading and hitting everything, touched me as well, but instead of pain or anguish I was filled with power and energy.

I met the dark figure, swinging my swords to cleave it in two. Draconic clawed hands reached out from under the cloak and grabbed hold of my blades, ripping them from my grasp. Then, throwing my blades aside, it pushed me down and raised a clawed foot to crush my chest. Zel'hu was there in an instant, standing over me in a protective stance and kicking back the shadow creature.

"Allow me to handle this one, you deal with the hydra." And with that he reached out a hand and hot white energy shot out, hitting the hydra and warping it from the massive dragon-like monster it was, to a twenty-foot-tall version of it.

Somehow, he'd literally warped reality and made the hydra something we actually had a chance against. I stood and summoned my blade back to my hand.

"I'll see what I can do," I said, and activated Speed Burst, cutting down a Chaos Knight Ordu as it tried to stand, just to see if I got any essence for it. I did, and I almost turned back to try and finish off the rest of them, but I had my team to worry about.

I could see them already engaging the hydra along with three surviving Ordu guards and two sorcerers, but none of them had the power that Zel'hu was displaying, not even a fraction of it.

The battle was on, and this was finally a fight that I was certain we at least had a chance to win.

CHAPTER 44
ORDER & CHAOS

I dove and slid low beneath one of the many heads snapping out at my teammates as they closed in, my blade at the ready. It sliced deep and easily into the hide now that our prey had been shrunk to a reasonable size. There was no telling how long the magic that did this would last, so I wanted to finish this fight as quick as possible. A head got around and in front of my slide, maw open and ready to hit me with a blast of lightning.

Blinking out of the way, I felt the heat of the powerful blast that just barely missed me. One thing was for sure, their attacks still held a good punch, so we'd need to avoid them as much as possible.

"Let's take this hydra down!" I shouted, falling into position with my team, Creed and Emory at the head as our most armored fighters. Fran and I took the mid ground, ready to strike out when an opportunity arose, and Alayna behind, casting buffs and heals as we went.

Emory started it off with a taunting call at the hydra, getting its attention as it finished off yet another Ordu guard. Fire filled its maw and poured down at us, but Emory expected it, and he slammed his shield down and a barrier of red sparking energy enclosed us just as the flames hit. It seemed to suck up the power of the fire until his shield glowed a hot red, then surprising me as I'd never seen such an ability from him, the attack rebounded and fired from out of his shield back to the hydra.

It struck the head with the yellow scales and left a bloody black scorch mark. We were doing some damage finally! Creed stepped up next as I let out a Lightning Strike into the same place Emory had injured. Just as my attack hit, so did Creed's icy slash. It cut so deep that it severed most of the head leaving a flailing, blood spurting neck writhing about.

"One down," I cried out, just as all of the heads narrowed in on us, no longer paying attention to the remaining Ordu forces. I spared a glance past the hydra to see how the battle was going for Zel'hu.

He fought with his sword, fending off all of the remaining Chaos infused Ordu, and on the ground laid the darkened husk of the creature that's voice had turned my insides into fire. I noticed that he was mostly defending and not trying to strike down his fellow Ordu, hopefully that wouldn't lead to his downfall. One of the Chaos Knights held out a hand and dark fire poured out, all-consuming and deadly. It was at that moment that I was forced to pay attention to our own problem as the hydra was knocking at the door, so to speak.

Dodging to the left, I narrowly avoided a snapping jaw. Rolling back to my feet, I activated Speed Burst and decided it was time to take care of this beast. I ran up on the hydra, my speed fast but not a match for the reduced power of the hydra. Dodging another strike, I slashed out mid-air and activated Swift Strike and Power Strike, nearly cleaving the head in two. For good measure, I thrusted forward at the gaping wound and activated Phantom Thrust, then slashed downward, finishing off the fire-breath head. Blood covered me and it burned like I was set ablaze.

I screamed but kept moving to put myself out of range of the hydra's remaining heads. A cold wash of healing came over me and stemmed the stinging pain, even washing some of the blood off me as it hit. The battle raged on, and the hydra fought fiercely, but it was no longer a match for us with its reduced size. Toward the end, only four heads remaining, it began to grow red and its size increased a small amount, but we struck hard and fast, finishing it off within a few minutes of intense combat.

Moving to where Zel'hu had been only minutes before, I found a disturbing scene. Half of the Chaos Knights, or at least the Chaos infused Ordu, had been slain and lay bleeding out on the ground. However, the dark figure, the remaining Chaos Ordu, and Zel'hu had all gone missing.

The dungeon wasn't over I realized suddenly. There had been no rush of essence or anything to indicate that we were finished yet. Turning back to my team, I met Alayna's eyes, she nodded and pulled her mace from her belt, likely thinking the same as me. Before I'd made it back to my team, a voice filled my mind and once more, I was reminded that my Mythril ear clasps were not a hundred percent effective at blocking out mental intrusions.

"Be at peace young warrior, the deed is done, and you have won. I will take a form and speak with you, please separate yourself from your group so that we may talk."

The voice had a very powerful presence, but it lacked the disgusting vileness that the shadow man had, so I felt inclined to heed its words. It had to be the dungeon reaching out, something that was becoming a fairly common occurrence for me, however strange that may be.

"I'm going to go speak with the dungeon," I said, my words unsure but what other option did I have really?

"You what?" Emory said, looking as confused as I felt.

"Is that even possible?" Alayna asked.

"There is Kora, she proves a certain amount of higher intelligence that dungeons must have," Creed added, intellectual as always.

"Have fun, weirdo," Fran said, waving at me while smirking.

"I'll be alright," I assured them and picked a building behind the hydra, one that had been destroyed a good bit, but thought of something first and reached out to the hydra to collect my loot. Nothing happened.

"You will be rewarded, in time, come to me so that we may speak properly. It is difficult to pierce your mental barrier, even for me."

The voice weakened at the end, and I smiled. Well at

least it wasn't easy for the all-powerful dungeon to pierce my mind. That offered me some reassurance, if only a little.

Entering the ruined building I was amazed at the construction. Strong pillars of white stone shone from runic light and stood strong while the walls around it crumbled. Just inside the room I found Zel'hu sitting on a bench with his leg up and arms folded.

"How did you enjoy my story?" Zel'hu said, smiling kindly in my direction.

I approached cautiously, wary of a trap. But nothing came as I approached, and eventually I took a seat across from him, but not so close that I couldn't try to make an escape.

"Story?" I asked. "Are you saying this was all a made-up narrative?"

"Embellished perhaps, but these events happened many years ago. I've held this image inside the dungeon and held conference with four others like you, beholden to maintain the balance. Only when one of you arrive do I show the last act of the story, where the minion of the Black Dragon seeks to call his master to our planet."

I opened my mouth to speak but he held up a hand to silence me.

"There will be opportunities for questions but let me finish and ask a few of my own first."

"Alright," I said, making a show of shutting my mouth tight.

"Each time one of you comes here, I do as I was commanded so many years ago and I try to give you tools that will help you succeed in your mission. But never have I been in the situation I am in now."

"What situation is that?" I asked, then caught myself when Zel'hu gave me a look with raised brows, clearly wanting me to shut up and listen.

"I've more raw essence than ever before and yet the Ley Lines beneath me are infected with the rot of Chaos. I have done what I can to stem the flow, but even I, one of the oldest of my kind, can only do so much. You, champion of the balance, must find a way to cleanse the Ley Lines. Seek an instrument of the Ordu, one of their sacred artifacts and key to their immense power."

"A Sword of the Ordu, like you used earlier. I am on a quest to obtain such a weapon, but I am not strong enough yet, which is why I came here to grow stronger."

"Ah and here lies where I can help you, but you must make a choice. First, let me finish my tale and fill in some gaps for you. What you witnessed was the start of the events that led to the need for Balance. You see, naturally every being has a certain amount of Chaos and Order inside of them, but this shadowy fiend created a living manifestation of that power and infected his followers with it. Great power comes from the infection, giving one, known to you as a Chaos Lord, immense power and the ability to spread the infection to others, Chaos Knights. These Chaos Knights have the same ability in a limited capacity to spread the sickness."

"So, Chaos is a sickness then, but you just said it was a living manifestation."

"It is both, the force you know as Chaos is a small, imperceptible living force but so is the power of Order from the day the Ordu decided to forever cut our planet off from the natural order of the Titan System. We exist in a bubble, separate from other planets and the influences of the Titans. But that isn't what is important. What you must know is that the balance we speak of, and you defend with your life, is what saves us. If the balance is tipped either way for too long, he will sense it and his minions will come to investigate. The Black Dragon must not come, for if he does, I fear, as did the Ordu before their untimely end, that it will be the end of all life on this planet."

"You speak so casually of planets and other worlds. Are we so common as to be just one world in a sea of hundreds?"

"Worry not for that which is outside your reach. I've questions for you. What events led to the destruction and loss of life above and around my dungeon? How was so much essence released in such a destructive manner?"

I explained, in ugly detail, the events that led to it and my own part in the making of such a device. Zel'hu, or the Dungeon Core controlling him, listened without showing any sign of judgement or sorrow.

"Death is a natural part of life, even one such as I will pass beyond when the time comes. Think not of your part in this tragedy but marvel in the steps your people have taken to overtake even the Ordu, in magical and technological knowledge. For the Ordu could never have imagined creating such a destructive device, nor did they see the potential of many inventions. But the wandering people, your people, have always had a keen understanding of destruction. There was even a time when you had technology to match that of the Black Dragon and his minions. But in the unending wisdom of the Ordu, it was taken from you and put to different uses."

I hung on to his every word as he spoke so casually about things I'd never even imagined. In my mind, the Ordu were always the force of Order and were powerful beyond measure. But this dungeon and what I was hearing made them sound as fallible and prone to mistakes as anyone.

"If you have any questions, now is the time to ask them before we move on," Zel'hu said, his friendly warm smile putting me at ease.

I had so many questions but after he addressed me, they all seemed to flee my mind. Struggling, I tried to think of the right question to ask a dungeon that seemed to have intimate knowledge of the Ordu and their time.

"What can you tell me about this Black Dragon and his minions? I've always known of the Black Dragons to be the cause and nature of the Chaos, as the legends say, but you make it sound like we have yet to truly see the Black Dragon," I asked, my own nightmares and the whispers of Mah'kus telling me that perhaps an encounter with them was inevitable and despite all that I had on my plate I would need to be prepared for them as well.

"You speak of the legends surrounding Vielkrea, that terrible battle between Chaos and Order. Several hundred years after the events I depicted today, the seed of Chaos takes root and war spreads across the continent. But that information will not help you, I can only tell you that the Black Dragon is yet to have shown his true face and if he does, if they arrive, there is no weapon created by the Ordu that can match their strength."

The way he said the last bit gave me pause. Mah'kus had implied that I might one day call for the terrible essence weapon to be used again, was this what he meant? Did he foresee the terrible end where weapons that mankind made would need to be employed. That only one of the lesser races in their infinite need for destruction could create such a weapon boggled my mind and set me uneasy.

"I sense others approaching my dungeon from above. If I am to use the essence and not expel it as monsters outside the dungeon, we must hasten our conversation. You have several choices, Defender of the Balance, servant of the Ordu. I can create for you magnificent armor, weapons, rings with essence enhancing abilities like the sword you currently wield, or I can condense much of the extra essence I have into crystalline form so that you may absorb it. Furthermore, if you wish, I could give you a tome of knowledge containing spells and skills, I see that you are a Blade Master and an Evoker, but you are limited by only learning abilities through the system set up by the Ordu. Knowledge is free to those who know how to harness it. Tell me, what would you have me do, but be wise in your decision as I can do only one. However, I will tell you that by the laws that govern me I will be releasing a good measure of essence to you and your party upon finishing here, then my dungeon will be closed for several days while I make changes."

What did I need to be successful in my many tasks, that was the question I really had to consider. It would be helpful to have a new set of armor, my own armor was relatively new and with the gem slots granting amazing attribute benefits, but to have a percentage increase by using essence alone would be even better. But that brought up my real issue, my main reason for coming here and what I needed more than any armor or weapons.

I needed essence.

But what of the tome, surely that might contain knowledge that will set me apart from others as much as my increased attributes did. As a tool for the Ordu, I was only effective as my abilities allowed me to be. Surely the potential host of new spells and skills inside such a tome would be worth its weight several times in platinum. Then it hit me like a mountain falling on my head.

There were books containing spells and skills, and I even owned one or two. It wasn't that I couldn't learn what lay inside, as Evoker and weapon-based classes were common enough that finding abilities was easy enough, I just hadn't had the time to invest into learning them. As exciting as the tome was, I kept coming back to my main problem. I needed to be stronger, much, much stronger and to do that, I needed essence.

"How much essence are we talking about?" I asked, my decision made.

"I've released 149,918 essence so far from my creations, however, even with your clever essence capturing device I sense you only gathered a small portion of it. I'm prepared to release a burst of 999,450 shortly and it'll be split as per normal measures, so you'd get maybe a tenth of that and your companions even less. But I have an excess, and can crystallize 9,381,023 essence across ten gems, each holding just under a million essence."

That was incredible! With that much essence I might be able to reach level 40, but I would have to check the exact numbers later. Then a thought occurred to me.

"Will you be okay if you release that much essence? The Ley Lines are weakening, as you said."

"The amount I offer to give you is one tenth of what flows through me. I am able to withstand much pressure and what I offer is just enough to keep me from having to release more monsters into the wild, something I prefer not to do if it can be helped. Give me time to reconstruct myself and I will provide you with even more essence through the killing of my monsters inside my halls. I am strong and if essence is all you desire then I can provide you with enough to swell your level and attributes."

"What of loot from the hydra, am I still eligible to receive that?" I asked, hiding a smile as best I could.

"Very well, a golden chest awaits you back with your companions. I will not speak with you again, as it takes much essence to do so, but I will offer you this final advice. If the Black Dragon does come, you must find its weakness, or the end will come."

"Thank you," I said, holding out a hand. He took it and I shook the hand of yet another helpful dungeon. "I will stand against the darkness, no matter what form it takes."

CHAPTER 45
ESSENCE GAINS

Everyone had taken up their loot by the time I got back, each of them getting an exciting new upgrade. Emory a new weapon, Fran a suit of armor that looked heavy duty but was extremely light, Creed a new massive two-handed sword, and finally a spear-like weapon for Alayna.

"I don't normally use two-handed weapons, preferring the shield and one handed but the special ability on this is just what I was wanting," Alayna said when I questioned her about the new weapon.

"What does it do?" I asked.

"Allows me to throw it every ten seconds and it returns to my hand, basically I'll be able to be a part of the fight without losing concentration on my healing and shielding."

"That's neat," I said, going up to the chest and holding my breath as I reached in.

I pulled out the essence gems, one by one adding them to my inventory. Then, as I rooted around in the chest I found a single plain golden ring. I pulled it out and used Inspect.

Ring of Hercules

3 Gem Slots
+40 Strength
+40 Constitution
+40 Endurance
Durability: *200/200*
Rarity: *Epic*
Weight: *3 Grams*
Item Level 120, Level Required to use: Soulbound to Caldor Miles, Dropped by: Elite Hydra

I immediately took off my Ring of Ram's Might and slipped my new ring onto my finger. Immediately I felt the power surge as my attributes adjusted to their new normal. But I wasn't done yet, I had a few gems left over that I could slot in until I could craft others either more powerful or with a different attribute spread. Reaching into my inventory I pulled out three plus 10 Dual-Aligned Gemstones focused in Intellect and Strength, the same kind I was using in my armor.

It didn't take much work as the gems seemed to want to be set into place in the small openings, and soon I had a ring that granted an additional 30 Strength and Intellect as well as its other mighty attributes spread.

"Dungeon was alright," Emory said, touching his arm and releasing the essence into himself. "But I got twice as much out hunting monsters all day than we got in here. I wonder if it is going to be worth running the dungeon after all." He said all this while hefting his new weapon and admiring it.

"I think the new gear alone will be worth it, getting us all the best gear we can use for our level, but I have a surprise for everyone as well. Keep this to ourselves and don't tell the other team until I can get them alone, I don't want the mercenaries to be tempted to try and take us out."

With that, I'd gathered all their attention and they'd quieted down a fair bit.

"The dungeon gave me ten gemstones each one filled to nearly a million essence. It was by request, as I told it I needed to get stronger more than I needed anything else, but I want to share them with you so we can get stronger together."

"If the dungeon gave them to you, then perhaps it would be best for all of us that you use them," Alayna said, coming up to caress my face gently.

I nodded my head firmly and looked her deep in the eyes. "We rise together and with our combined powers we will defeat the enemies and challenges we face."

"But you are already so far ahead of us, does it even make sense to try and catch us up," this time it was Fran speaking. I was a bit flabbergasted that they weren't jumping at a chance for free essence.

"I think the right thing to do is bolster your strength

while we try and grow as much as we can over the coming weeks," Creed said, adding his opinion into the mix.

Looking at Emory I awaited what he thought. He looked around the room with eyebrows raised before saying, "Fuck that mess, give me a stone so I can catch up a little. I'm level 31 now, but we are hardly at the same power even though we're close in level."

"What is everyone's level?" I asked, wanting to get a feel for the room and still determined to help them all power level a bit.

Fran was level 27, with only Alayna being lower than her at 25. Creed on the other hand had just hit level 30, meaning our levels were as follows: Myself at 32, Creed at 30, Emory at 31, Alayna at 25, and Fran at 27. I moved those numbers through my head and figured that despite not knowing the cost for their attributes I imagined that with a million essence they could get at least four or five levels, perhaps more for those with better affinities.

Personally, if I stuck to raising Paragon attributes with essence buying and raising the others with level attributes, I would be able to get at least five levels off a million. I couldn't be certain until I went to do the leveling, but it seemed a fair enough guess based on how the numbers had been scaling. So, if I took two I might be able to make it to level forty. That wasn't even mentioning how much essence we'd get from running the dungeon again and slaying monsters out in the wild. I was confident that I could get myself and my teammates close to level fifty by the time we left, a power leveling extravaganza.

I shared my thoughts with everyone, and it seemed to pacify the 'we don't want your essence' mood that had taken over all but Emory. So, before the moods shifted again I passed out the gems, telling them to keep them safe as they weren't likely going to be able to fit that much essence in their cores and would have to do it a small bit at a time to level up. They agreed, Emory was the worst saying he'd filled up his core to bursting and was likely going to spend some points in his Core Attribute to help fix that issue.

After agreeing that this dungeon run would remain secret, and me telling them a bit about my discussion with the dungeon and its promise to change up the dungeon, we set off for the exit. We found it as a random door, marked with runes similar to the dungeon door not far from where we stood. I'd miss being able to walk among the Ordu and their city, but it had also been an eye-opening experience about their culture and strengths.

The Ordu had been strong, and several of them commanded impossible power through their artifacts, but they weren't so unknowingly powerful as is commonly believed. This all of course depends on how accurate this depiction of their society had been and really what point in their society it had been as well. For all I knew, in the coming years all Ordu might gain powers like Zel'hu displayed, which would account for the legends. But it was a mystery that I didn't expect an answer to.

We went to the Mana Shrine and began to use the gems to level. I had enough essence that leveling was going to take a while, plus I knew I should look at new abilities, spells, and skills. Something held me off from picking up any new stuff though, as I felt like what I had in my current kit would be sufficient for now and that perhaps I should try to bring them to Rank 3 if I had the essence for it. But in the end, I didn't even do that, the essence required was huge and it would mean much higher resource costs. Not that I couldn't use lower ranks, it was all a matter of focus, but I tended to throw out my stronger moves in the heat of combat, and Rank 2 spells and skills were still more than enough with the size of my current resource pools.

I took a little of their advice, giving myself 2 of the essence stones and putting my total essence after all the gains were put into place at a staggering 2,464,373 Essence. I leveled to 33, spending 103,950 essence and an additional 148,616 to gain three Core Attributes. Using the 3 attributes I had from leveling I added them to Concentration, bringing my Core and Concentration from a base 50 to a base 53.

I kept on going, leveling and raising my attributes by spending the points I earned and purchasing 3 extra. I was amazed that using the two gems gave me enough essence to go from level 32 to level 40. On average to raising my Paragon attributes through purchased essence, it was costing me about 150% of the amount of essence it took me to level. If I had kept going onward with my previous methods of raising non-Paragon attributes by way of purchasing, it would have been closer to 200% or even 225% per 3 attributes.

I looked over my status screen at all my improvements and marveled at the growth the dungeon had granted me. I sat at only 21,808 remaining essence, but I'd been able to increase every attribute by 9 points, except for Constitution and Strength, which I increased by 6 attribute points.

Name: Caldor Miles | Classification: Arcane Knight | Species: Human

Level: 40, 166,050 Essence to Lvl. 41 | Essence: 21,808 | Reputation: Rank 4, 52%

Health: 2,090/2,090 | Mana: 2,500/2,500 | Stamina: 1,500/1,500

Health Regen: 199 Per Minute | Mana Regen: 87 Per Minute | Stamina Regen: 140 Per Minute

Constitution: 199 (59 Base) | Intellect: 250 (65 Base) | Endurance: 140 (62 Base)

Core: 79 (59 Base) | Concentration: 79 (59 Base) | Strength: 276 (61 Base)

The raw increases in Strength and Intellect from my new gear and base attribute gains made me feel like I was on an entirely new level power wise. Gear truly was an important deciding factor when it came to being as strong as you could be. When I had a base attribute of 65 on Intellect and 61 on Strength, but my gear lifted me to the lofty levels of 250 and 276 in each I had to wonder if my approach to growing stronger wasn't a bit flawed. What if I focused on bringing my level as high as possible, then with higher levels I could use more powerful gear.

When considered like that, the smaller gains I'd made didn't seem as significant, but then I reminded myself that thresholds weren't to be taken lightly. Gear might bring your attributes to lofty levels, but you were limited in how your body moved and could use those attributes at lower thresholds. It was like storing volatile liquids in containers meant to hold water. It would become worn and thin the longer the liquid stayed within, until eventually it would crack. Or at least that was my understanding of it. The fact that I'd gotten all my attributes through their second thresholds meant my body was more than ready and able to use the full 200 plus attributes my gear was providing.

When I finished with my leveling, I turned to my companions to see what gains they'd gotten. Alayna had achieved the highest gains, but she'd also been the lowest level and so that was expected. She went from level 26 to level 31, showing off a decent affinity to be able to raise 2 attribute points per level and still spend roughly 450,000 essence purely on the leveling up process, then using the other half of the gems essence plus her gains in the dungeon and monster hunting to pay the remaining needed to increase attributes.

Emory had the least gains; I'd expected as much because it took so much essence to purchase additional attributes for him that I was amazed he'd even managed to make it to level 30 so swiftly. In the end, he increased his level to 33, gaining additional levels and paying a hefty sum of essence to get his two extra attributes. Meanwhile, Creed managed to increase by 3, bringing his level to 33 as well.

Fran, on the other hand, managed the biggest gain behind Alayna and me at 4 levels. Bringing her to 31 and now several levels above her brother. However, I planned on giving Fred a gem and Kora if she will accept it, as I had 10 in total and we'd only used six so far; Two to myself, one to Emory, Fran, Alayna, and Creed. I planned on giving the remaining four to Ismene, Zander, Fred, and Kora, helping each of them increase in level.

Out of the four that leveled up, all but Emory passed a threshold for one of their primary attributes. We rested up, figuring it would be best to go find the other group and share with them the news about the dungeon before moving onward. It was after resting, not far from the dungeon, when the other team found us, looking beaten and haggard, but in one piece.

CHAPTER 46
REX HUNT

The four newcomers looked the least beat up, with Ismene and Zander looking like they'd rolled around in the mud and grass while being pricked by thorns all the while.

"What happened to you two," I asked, giving the newcomers a side eye of distrust.

"Giant scorpions, raptors, you name it and we've been killing it," Ismene said, a wide smile on her face. "I've gained enough essence to level up and increase my attributes," she said, dropping her voice to a whisper while the other four began to pull out items to set up camp. It was late already, the moon providing plenty of light to see by, but past due time to pitch camp. They must have been waiting to find us before calling it quits.

"Why do you two look like you've gotten the worst of it?" I asked, trying to lower my voice but knowing that if these adventurers were anything worth their salt, they'd be past their first threshold and easily be able to hear me despite my whispered tone.

"That was my fault," Zander admitted, raising up his hands in mock defeat and speaking at a normal volume. "We were getting overly confident and asked them to sit out the last fight against a half dozen raptors. They took my words far too literal and just about watched us die when several unseen raptors appeared. But it all worked out and here we are."

I could see a bit of a wild look in his eyes and knew that he wasn't likely happy with his pick of adventurers, but they had done as he'd requested, even if the orders had been taken too literally. There was a certain amount of respect I could give them for that, but they had to know that safety always came first.

"You four," I said, calling out to them. They all paused to look over at me. "If you plan on staying with us and benefiting greatly from this horde of essence, then you need to follow one simple rule. Safety first. I don't care what orders you are given; you always step in and ensure the safety of all team members or you'll be asked to leave. Do you understand?"

They all gave sheepish nods, but one of them stepped forward and spoke for them all. He was a strongly built man and I recognized him from our previous adventure against the lich. His name was Tom.

"We have a contract that dictates our terms, these terms cannot be altered without a renegotiation of payment. It clearly states that we are to do as commanded even if great risks come to our client. As long as he orders us to stay back, we will do so until the contract is broken, by either death or dismissal. I am willing to take your command as an order if Lord Zander wishes it to be so." With that, he inclined his head apologetically to me and looked to Zander. He nodded and it was settled.

"Good," I said, breathing a bit easier now.

"Ismene, Zander, walk with me so I can fill you in," I said, speaking clearly enough that they could hear but not trying to rub anything into their faces.

I summoned the door to my Arcane Asylum and stepped in, welcoming them both into my special place. Zander nodded appreciatively as he scanned the filled bookshelves and the armor I had on display. Several items and suits beyond my level, however some were likely in my wheelhouse now that I'd progressed to level 40. Once they'd entered and the door went away for a time, I turned to them both and filled them in.

"You are telling me you have essence filled gems with close to a million each and you are going to share them with us?" Zander said, his tone one of disbelief. "Just when I think I've got you figured out you go and do something like this..."

Meanwhile, Ismene just smiled like a giddy child about to get a treat. She held her hand out and did a little happy dance before speaking. "This doesn't surprise me at all. Not only do you have the luck of the gods and Ordu combined, but you always think of helping others even when it might make more sense to horde it for yourself."

I just shrugged; it made tactical sense to raise others along with myself. Already we were becoming some of the fastest progressing group of adventurers in all of the kingdom, or so I liked to believe. Short of doing some sort of census there would be no way to know, but it seemed unlikely that anyone else could match our progress without essence bands. Essence Bands were literally a game changer when it came to leveling.

"The bit about what the dungeon used to be needs to remain a secret, as well as the gemstones with essence. This entire area ought to remain a secret, but I'm not so naive to think we can maintain it any longer than it takes for the mercenaries to get back and spread the word. So, at the very least we will stay here for a month, but after that, there are too many tasks that require my attention before we can leave with the elves. Basically, we have a limited window of time, and we need to take advantage of it."

They both agreed, taking their gemstones and disappearing them into their inventories. I got both their levels from them and gave them instructions to tell me where they reached after leveling up at the Prime Mana Shrine. Zander had reached level 30, thanks to some additional power leveling he'd done when I'd taken time off to rest with my family. Ismene was an impossible level 32, whatever adventuring they'd done while we fought at war had been several times more effective essence wise.

If Fred was still level 25, Fran had insisted as much, then he'd likely make it close to thirty with the gems' help. I only wish he'd come with us now that I knew how much essence there was to gain. New odd powers aside, he would do well to grow stronger before we arrived at Avalon.

We went back to the camp, leaving the privacy of my Arcane Asylum behind for the relative comfort of camping under the stars. The mercenaries had set up a tent, as well as Fran, but I chose to take first watch again with the intention of using my trinket to take care of any need for sleep. There was a lot to think about and consider.

Laying on my back, beside the embers of a fire, I went through all that had happened since I'd become *Awakened,* even going so far as to consider my spark and the fight with the boar. Looking back, I saw how foolish I had been for tracking what was clearly a monster and not a natural boar any longer. My desire to be what I wasn't had been too strong to keep my foolishness in check. But it had paid off, if only barely, and now I was a level 40 adventurer with the power of someone at a much higher level.

I wasn't so arrogant to think myself twice as strong as my level implied, but I was close to it. I imagined fighting old Ironfist now that I'd leveled to just under ten of his hard-won levels. He had incredible powers as well as raw strength, something I'd been lacking in as of late. Tim, so many days ago, had mentioned in passing that spells might be able to be evolved or even cast without reciting the words of power. I assumed at the time he might just be bragging about his own powers, but I wondered now.

Focusing on my simplest of spells, Light, I spoke the terse quick phrase, waving my hand in a specific way to summon it. As an instant cast spell already, it was easy to cast and required very little concentration, but I wanted to see if I could alter it or at least cast it without words or movement of my hands.

My first attempt did not go well. I focused on the words in my mind, but nothing happened. Then I tried to say the words while not doing the hand motions, still nothing. It was only when I did the hand motions while concentrating on the phrases and what I expected to happen that I felt the familiar warmth that came with the spell, but no Light appeared. I continued for about an hour before I finally summoned a Light globe without speaking the words, I had used the hand motion though, so there was still progress to be made.

By the time the sun began to peek over the horizon I was able to cast the spell with a mere thought, no hand motion or words needed. It was still difficult and no longer an instant spell as it took a good second or two to get it to activate wordlessly, but it was a start. Now I just had to take what I'd learned to my other far more complex spells. However, the night was spent, and I'd need to worry about it another day, because we had hunting to do.

Emory was the first one up and he hurried over to my side, throwing some wood on the fire. After a time and with some flint and tinder we had the fire going again, the morning chill fleeing before it.

"We should hunt that Rex today," Emory said, a wide grin on his face. "Imagine the armor I could make from its hide, a mighty lizard cloak perhaps."

"You really have it out for that Rex, don't you?" I asked, laughing a bit myself at the silliness of it all.

"You saw it didn't you?" Emory asked. "How could you not want to take that thing down? Just to say that we killed it is enough to get a bard to sing about us."

"Fine, but we need to be careful. Even with our higher levels, that monster was an elite and it had a powerful size advantage." A noise caught my attention and I turned to see the two youngest of the mercenary groups, each wearing robes, one white and the other blue.

"We saw the Rex but chose not to engage," the first one said, his name was Samuel I think which made the other one James.

James smiled, he wore the white and gold robes, likely a healer by the looks of it. "I bet with our groups combined we'd be able to take it out. Can you imagine the price we'd get if we took something that big down and broke it apart for reagents?"

"Even combined I'm not sure it is wise," Samuel said, giving his brother a look, I knew all too well. It's the look you gave a sibling when you wanted them to shut up, but it was lost on James, who just shrugged.

"I bet we can take it, just a few Magic Missiles from my brother and some healing from me and we are halfway there," James said, his tone was playful whereas his brother's was serious and a bit grim.

So, he was a wizard type, I wondered suddenly how well I'd match up against him in a pure battle of spells. I hadn't seen him the last time we'd worked with the Silver Hawk

Clan mercenaries, but he also wasn't blocking any scrying attempts and so I knew he was only level 30, well within my ability to take out even if I only used my spells.

James and Samuel shared a look and I swear they spoke words to each other somehow, because suddenly they were on the same page and supporting hunting down the Rex.

"Fine, gather up and let's go hunting for a Rex," I said, relenting against the pressure of the group. I guess it was time to hunt a giant lizard Rex.

***

It was surprisingly easy to find once they told us where they'd seen it last, in the raptor fields. It was still there, easy to see from a great distance, all red, yellow, and brown markings from snout to tail. It was eating something, likely a raptor, but otherwise stood alone.

"The tail and mouth are going to be the biggest issues. Healers, be ready to erect barriers to keep our melee line in the fight and out of its mouth. Meanwhile casters and ranged fighters should focus on burning down its health. Fighting out in the open like this I'm worried that we will attract additional foes from the raptor fields, so I'm going to start the fight off by getting its attention and bringing it where we want it."

I pointed to a rocky area where we could pin it with no way of easy escape for it, but a nice place where we could get a head start if we were forced to flee. It would allow all of the casters to post up just higher than its head and rain down damage on it as well.

We got into position and all that was left was for me to run out to get the monster. My heart pounded as I approached the elite monstrous Rex, it stood a frightening four times my height and even longer. It had jaws big enough to swallow me whole. The closer I got, the more items I noticed that gave me ease.

Firstly, this Rex was a fat lizard monster and despite having huge legs wasn't showing any particular pension for speed. Next, I noticed that its arms were tiny, like so small as to make them useless. They pressed against the bulbous bulk of the Rex and were not going to be a threat. I could definitely outrun this guy, I told myself as I neared.

Reaching out my hand, I tried something that had only worked half a dozen times so far, I cast Lightning Strike without saying or making any hand motions. The air cracked and I successfully cast the spell, hitting the confused Rex right in the head. It roared and swung its massive bulk around, its tail flattening the long grass around it.

"Over here you great bulky lizard!" I screamed the words, turning to sprint away a moment later. Checking behind my shoulder, though it wasn't needed as I could feel the ground shake as it pursued me, I made sure it was after me. Sure enough, it was running, or walking really fast, in my direction and gaining on me. I put a bit more speed into my run, still only going a fraction of how fast I could go when I cut loose. It was enough to keep a safe distance without leaving the Rex behind completely.

An awfully selfish thought entered my mind as I ran. Surely, I could take this monster on by myself. Another check over my shoulder convinced me otherwise. The sneaky monster had increased its speed and now had a reddish glow surrounding it like a dungeon boss might when it became enraged. Best to play this one safe, and Emory would never forgive me if I didn't let him test himself against this monstrosity of a monster.

I swung around and the monster followed me right into our little trap. Emory, Fran, Creed, Nabi, and Tom stood ready to intercept it, and my place was elsewhere. The second that I passed their lines I used Blink to take me halfway up the cliff and quickly scrambled up the rest with ease and skill.

Zander, Ismene, Alayna, Samuel, and James awaited me above, all of them already casting or attacking in some way. I turned and unleashed an Arcane Missile just as Samuel did the same, his own attack a slightly different color and bigger than my own. Next, I cast my Firebolt spell, infusing it with a touch of essence so as to not be left behind on the 'who has the more destructive spells' game. Samuel answered by opening his palm and spraying out green acid atop the Rex. Then he surprised me by casting another spell, a greyish brown liquid covering the top of the Rex but doing nothing more.

I turned in time to see Ismene let loose a flaming arrow at the top of the Rex's head. It hit and ignited whatever Samuel had done, suddenly we were dealing with a flaming Rex, and I worried for the melee fighters below.

However, as I regarded them, I saw they were doing just fine. Emory shield bashed the mighty maw of the Rex as it went in to swallow him whole, and as it staggered back the other fighters cut into it with deadly effectiveness. This fight was going to be over before it really had a chance to start.

That was when the raptors appeared.

All the warning I had was a screech from Ares, she'd been off hunting, and I didn't want her to be a part of the battle against such a large foe, lest she get hurt. But she was flying ahead and sent me a warning just in time.

"Raptors behind!" I yelled, turning in time to see one approaching with half a dozen at its heels. I threw mana into my Fireball spell, ready to blow apart their formation. My spell flew out, decimating the lead raptor and disorganizing their ranks just as a massive bear appeared, cutting into two wayward raptors. Next, a raptor appeared, this one colored dark blue and white, tearing into the yellow chicken raptors.

I looked to my left and right, Ismene had tamed a raptor that much I could tell with how it looked back at her for commands, but who was controlling the big bear. I saw Samuel pressing his hands against his head in intense focus and realized he must have a summoning spell of some kind. A few raptors made it through the ranks and the fight was on. A barrier leapt up in front of the healers, each one a slightly different color to match the aura of the caster, Zander and Alayna's both a golden hue but James had a white-blue color to it that I hadn't seen before in a healer.

I slashed down one raptor, but two more took its place, biting and clawing at me. I felt pain as one got hold of my arm and began to rip at it, jerking it hard against my joints. A moment later I felt a wash of healing magic settle over me, and I did what I needed to do to get the raptor off of me, I Blinked. Then activating Speed Burst, I used Power Strike and Swift Strike to one-two combo the remaining raptors in our ranks. A yell from below caught my attention and we all turned as the final raptor fell to see what had happened.

It was Emory, standing atop a fallen Rex with his weapons held high. The day was won, and we were victorious.

CHAPTER 47
GRINDING OUT ESSENCE

The rest of the month went by in a blur of essence gathering. We hunted queens, cleared out the raptor fields, and even took on the Badger infestation. Of course, we took turns going into the dungeon and it yielded a solid three hundred thousand essence for each successful run. In a single day we were able to run it twice, so we got into an every other day switching situation with the other group. By the end of the month, we'd all leveled significantly, and I felt more than ready to take on the Isle of Avalon now.

In total, the 30 days of training had added just over three million essence as well as a new ring, a new belt, and two new trinkets to replace my current ones. I went from level 40 to level 47 whereas the rest of the team had less gains, but still made progress.

Zander was now level 42, Creed level 38, Emory level 35, Alayna level 37—she was really shining through with her higher affinity—Fran at level 35, and lastly Ismene had reached level 34, her gains and Emory's being the slowest of all as they paid a literal fortune in essence to get their minimum two. But all progress was good progress and with everyone encroaching on level 40 we'd decided to make some hard decisions.

I was leaving, as well as Zander, along with the mercenaries whose contract had run out, but Fran, Creed, Alayna, Emory, and Ismene were staying behind to clean up the remaining monsters and run through the dungeon. The idea was to get everyone to level 40 or higher and I was confident that they could do it without me now. The dungeon, while difficult, was basically being farmed at this point and without the restrictions of the Adventurer's guild, we were making crazy progress.

Ares had enjoyed the hunt and feasting during our month out here as well, but she'd only just returned from an extended hunt where she'd traveled outside my range to touch her mind again. Around the same time those pesky black birds returned, and I was becoming more and more sure that someone was watching me through them. Who or why I didn't know, but they seemed unaffected by my anti-scrying ear clasps.

Soon after Ares returned, however, they disappeared. She tended to chase them off when she wasn't staring at them as if they were having a conversation. Something was up between Ares and those little sneaky birds, but I didn't have the time or patience to figure it out just yet. Instead, I trusted that in time, all would be revealed. It was just one of the many skills I was gaining when it came to patience. For instance, I really wanted to know the fate of my father, but I trusted that now wasn't the time to have answers to that question, as much as I might want it. Surely Warrick would know how to find him if he were truly still alive and hadn't fallen on that fateful day.

I looked over my new items and checked my character sheet, so much had changed in a matter of weeks.

On my body, I wore 'Lord Black's Enchanted Armor', my ears still had my 'Masterwork Refined Mythril Ear Clasps', my new cloak hung over my shoulders, 'Cloak of Fiery Concentration', and on my fingers I had my 'Ring of Hercules', 'Ring of Anubis', my storage ring, plus my newest ring called, 'Life Warded Band'. Next, I'd replaced my belt with something called, 'Enduring Leather Belt'. Lastly, I replaced my two trinkets for two new items called, 'Necklace of the Astral Planes' and 'Token of the Dire Beast'.

Life Warded Band
+75 Constitution
Durability: 25/25
Rarity: Rare
Weight: 7 Grams
Item Level: 75, Level Required to use: 40, Dropped by: Life Bound Owlbear

Enduring Leather Belt
+75 Endurance

Durability: 50/50

Rarity: Rare

Weight: 1 Pound

Item Level 75, Level Required to use: 40, Dropped by: Elite Dire Bear

Necklace of the Astral Planes

Enchanted with Astral Vision.

Astral Vision: Once per day you can see into the Astral Planes and have a small chance to summon forth an Astral Spector to fight at your side if one is near.

+50 Intellect

+50 Concentration

Rarity: Rare

Weight: 6 Grams

Item Level 100, Level Required to use: 45, Dropped by: Seer Cat

Token of the Dire Beast

Enchanted with Summon Dire Beast.

Summon Dire Beast: Once per day you can summon forth a Dire Beast to your side that matches your level and shares 75% of your attributes. Beast that is summons depends on your location and nearby beasts available.

+100 Strength

Rarity: Epic

Weight: 12 Grams

Item Level 100, Level Required to use: Soulbound, Dropped by: Dire Giant Badger Queen

Name: Caldor Miles | Classification: Arcane Knight | Species: Human

Level: 47, 216,000 Essence to Lvl. 48 | Essence: 33,303 | Reputation: Rank 4, 83%

Health: 2,630 | Mana: 3,060/3,060 | Stamina: 2,110/2,110

Health Regen: 253 Per Minute | Mana Regen: 149 Per Minute | Stamina Regen: 201 Per Minute

Constitution: 253 (68 Base) | Intellect: 306 (71 Base) | Endurance: 201 (68 Base)

Core: 88 (65 Base) | Concentration: 135 (65 Base) | Strength: 380 (70 Base)

CHAPTER 48
AWAKENING THE TWINS

I opened a portal a few miles out of Blalor lands and Zander stepped through with me just outside Variyn City. Afterward, I took flight with Ares on our way to our family farm to get word from Michael when the twins' *Awakening* would be. What I found was an empty house with a note left for me with one of the workers. Two days ago, they left to get them *Awakened* in the second largest city within Variyn, Riverwalk.

If I hurried, I would be able to get there the same time as them, so I took to the skies and after a hard day of flying we arrived in Riverwalk. It looked about half the size of Variyn City, but the walls around this city were thicker and well-manned. I got into the city easy enough and made my way to the keep, where I imagined the Prime Mana Shrine must be, however as I passed through the crowd, I saw a sight to behold.

A fully infused Prime Mana Shrine at full glow in the

middle of what looked like a marketing district. Two guards stood by it as well as a nearby table to record new Awakened. A surprising number, nearly a hundred souls, stood in a line waiting for their chance to touch it. However, I noticed something with my new enhanced senses, with each person who touched it, the ground trembled a little and the shine from the runes diminished.

At the rate of diminishing there was no way all these potentials would get *Awakened* before the power gave out and the light of the Prime Mana Shrine returned to a normalized state. Pushing forward to the registration desk I announced myself, but I didn't need to. I recognized this man from the war, a knight or something he'd been for another commander, but he was high enough in rank that I was surprised to see him doing such work.

"I am Lord Miles of Blackridge Keep," I said, momentarily forgetting my title had changed slightly, however the man I addressed had not.

"Baron Miles, how can I assist you?" He asked, his face straight and serious.

"Oh...that's right. It is in regard to the Prime Mana Shrine," I said, leaning forward a bit to get out of hearing range of those in line. "It does not have enough power to Awaken so many, surely you are aware?"

"We are," he said, lowering his voice to match my own. "However, we have been told to Awaken as many as possible, then turn away any left."

"Would you protest if I set up a screening process? I can sense who is closest to needing Awakening and those who can last another month or two. It might be we save a few lives." I didn't have much hope that this man whose name I couldn't recall would be so permitting, but he bowed his head and spoke with certainty.

"Yes, of course. Hold the line, we are going to instate an inspection before you are allowed to proceed. This by order of the Baron of Blackridge and Champion of Tenson Fields." This got the crowd quiet and suddenly I felt a bit awkward. *Awakened* and un-Awakened alike looked at me with an aura of awe that made me uncomfortable, but I went about my work, ready to save lives.

I thinned the line by at least two dozen applicants, telling them that based on their aura they could last for another event. I made sure that I only sent away those that truly could wait several months, as the Awakening ceremonies were happening less and less often with the Ley Lines disrupted. While I went to work, I came upon Grace and Gregory in the line.

"What are you doing Caldor?" Gregory asked, he looked embarrassed that I was interfering.

"Saving lives, I hope," I said, with a gentle smile. I examined his aura, then Grace's. Both weren't able to wait, in fact, they'd already probably waited too long, so I waved them to the front of the line. "Don't accept any extra responsibility unless you truly want it." I whispered to each of them as they went forward to become Awakened.

Grace went first and I watched as she touched the stone, a flash of power and the Prime Mana Shrine dimmed more than it had before. Grace fell to her knees, an awful smell surrounding her. She'd done as I had, passing several thresholds at once to start. Her aura was beginning to settle already, and she looked up at me with wide-eyed surprise.

"I'm a Monk. I could have been so much, but this just felt right," she said happily, then in a show of athletics I wouldn't have thought possible from her, she twisted and turned to her feet in a half jump movement. I took her stinking arm and shook it firmly.

"Welcome to the ranks of the Awakened, now go see Michael and mother about getting a bath," I said. Grace being Grace, she pulled me into a hug, and I was happy to have it. "Love you, sis." I whispered into her ear, proud that she'd picked a path where I felt she could excel.

Grace left and Gregory walked up ready to touch the shrine. "Did she say she was a monk?"

"Yeah, she picked a pretty rare class, I haven't come across many monks," I said, then thinking I ought to tell him as he would likely be in the same situation as her. "Don't feel you need to level up a bunch right off, you might find that you have many attributes you can purchase with your essence but be wary of going past 25 with too many at once."

He wasn't listening, instead he nodded along and looked around at the crowd gathered, obviously a bit nervous. "Here goes nothing," he said, running head long into it as he did most things.

A moment later I saw the same flash as Grace and the ground trembled enough that other less in tune people felt it as well. I ignored the murmurs in the crowd and watched as Gregory fell to a knee, his own stench as potent as Grace's had been. Of course, he didn't listen and likely leveled up as much as possible. On his hip I noticed a reagent box, I was glad they'd gotten one and that also meant they might have gotten some abilities as well.

I helped Gregory to his feet, but he didn't say anything at first, just looking up at me in awe.

"Feeling alright?" I asked, but he looked away unsure of how to answer.

"I tried to be like father, but I wasn't offered the class Arcane Knight like you were. I ended up taking the first class that did magic and fighting, I don't know what I was thinking I was just mad at that arbiter guy." He lowered his voice as he spoke of the Arbiter, though by choice or not, he wasn't able to discuss his *Awakening* with anyone who hadn't gone through the process.

"I'm sure whatever you picked is exactly what you need-ed," I said, a knot forming in my stomach. It would be Gregory that picked a class out of spite for not getting what he wanted.

"I'm a Stoneguard, basically an armored tank that has limited access to earth magic. However, I only get to pick one spell every two levels, so I leveled to six so I could pick three spells, but I only had reagents for one. So dumb. I got a spell called Stoneform, turns my body into living stone for thirty seconds. I also got a cool class ability called Earth-shatter where I stomp into the ground, and a skill called Heavy Strike, where I can hit for 1.5 damage for a little bit of stamina."

The more he spoke the more excited he seemed, and I

realized that perhaps he wasn't so upset about his choice after all. I helped him up and sent him to find Michael and mother, so I could finish my screenings.

I turned away about half of the applicants and because of that we were able to get through the rest just as the stone went out minutes after the last. The earth shook then, so much so that I worried about the buildings in the square, but everything held together.

"Shakes have been getting worse this last month," Michael said as I approached. "You have an idea why?"

I did but unless he was going to come with us to the Isle of Avalon, I didn't feel like sharing it just yet. As much as I'd like to ask him to come, his place was by my siblings' side as they did their class quests. Already they'd been cleaned off and each wore simple leather armor, but I figured we could do better than that.

"Let's go shopping and get you both proper armor for your classes," I said, leading the way toward a familiar building that I was beginning to see in every major city, Gilfoy's Emporium.

Grace did a few flips on our way to the store, my mother holding a hand out as if she might catch her if she messed up, but it wasn't needed. Her new class had given her several times more flexibility and acrobatic skill than she'd had before, and already she'd been more acrobatic than any of us combined. Even now with my attributes as they were, I didn't see how I could do some of the flips and turns she was doing while wearing stiff leather armor. Once we got her into proper monk armor she'd be ever more so.

"Welcome to Gilfoy's." An even toned Runeforged greeted us at the door. "Master Miles, you are a welcomed and valued customer, please wait here while a shopping attendant comes to tend to your every need."

Michael scoffed. "They didn't give me the royal treatment when I came in to buy the armor they're wearing right now. And it is fine armor by the way, suitable for any class."

I bit my lower lip and stole a glance at the grumpy looking Michael. He'd gotten close to the twins, and I'd just stepped on his toes regarding a gift he'd bought them.

"Perhaps we can use the store credit from returning them to purchase them suitable weapons, you strike me more as a weapon's guy anyways," I said, trying to be light and funny but just coming off wrong. Oh well, can't win them all.

Michael grumbled what I took for an agreement, and we were joined by a dark-haired attendant with bright blue eyes. She introduced herself as Jesse and led us to the upper floors.

By the time we were finished, I'd gotten them both storage bracers, one of the newest additions to mass produced storage items, heavy plated armor for Gregory and loose-fitting tunic for Grace, it seemed no more than padded cloth, but it was the recommended armor for her class, which was more common than I had first thought. Weapons wise, Gregory got a sword and shield from Michael, and Grace begrudgingly took a Bo staff but complained she didn't need weapons since she had her fists. While I wasn't looking, Michael picked out and bought her a pair of hand wraps that acted as weapons as well, adding in a damage modifier per hit, while also promising to teach her more unarmed combat.

I got them rings, ear clasps, and all manner of extra items to improve their attributes the best I could, but still, it didn't feel like enough. I'd been so eager and excited to start my journey but now I found myself worried for them and their futures. No one had talked about what they'd do when they finally unlocked their classes, but after buying each of them a map, Michael was sure he could get them what was needed with days to spare.

So, with knots in my stomach and worry on my face, I hugged them each and bid them farewell.

Mother looked at me, tears swelling in her eyes. "You look so much like your father these days. I can tell you've gotten stronger since I last saw you, I hope you've been taking extra care to be careful and safe?"

I smiled, that hadn't been the case at all of course, but she didn't need to know that. "I've been safe," I assured her. Mothers sometimes needed reassurance, despite the fact that they knew there was nothing safe about being an adventurer.

"It's a long road back, should we get moving?" She asked, looking about the busy street for something.

"Have you ever flown before?" I asked her, and her eyes brightened. Ares liked my mother and had no issue with taking on the extra weight. Soon we were off, flying among the clouds toward home.

CHAPTER 49
MEETING OVER DRINKS

We had less than a month to report to Avalon and I was still working out the logistics with my army and the aid I wanted sent to the eastern lands. Luckily, I had a fair bit of support and for once I felt like my leaving wasn't going to disrupt the ongoing affairs of Blackridge and our military plans. It was with all this in my mind that I joined my friends for a drink. They'd left after the last of them hit level 40 and joined me some weeks ago.

Fred and Kora being the exception, level wise. As I'd suspected, Kora said she did not require the essence and instead gave hers to Fred, not at all surprising me. He'd gained a few levels from Warrick's store of essence stones, but not nearly as much as we had. Warrick described his pull and Core as an unbridled storm sucking everything in and leaving none for anyone else. However, Warrick, digging deep into his library of tomes, found a process that had begun to help Fred.

His Core, as long as he concentrated and did the meditations, would act mostly normal now, but he still had the pale look that he'd gotten when he died and come back. Warrick hadn't been able to explain that, only saying that it wasn't something he could change, unless he was interested in face paint and dyes for his hair. Fred refused both, and on every occasion that I'd seen them together, Kora went out of her way to point out that he looked just fine.

It had been decided that we'd bring a small force of Runeforged with us under Kora's command, and they were currently training along with the rest of our group every day. We'd made several runs to the store to equip everyone in the best gear possible, but after my good fortune in the dungeon I didn't really need anything, so none of my gear changed.

I reached the ale hall and was flagged down by Ismene, sitting beside Zander and Emory. Marveling at her beauty, despite her just being a close dear friend, I searched the table for another beauty and found her sitting beside Fran and Fred. Alayna, as stunning as the day I'd met her, sat with her back to me as she drank from the wine glass in front of her. Everyone else had pints of ale, but of course Alayna would find the more refined tastes when they were available.

Everyone wore plain clothes, all of us tired of wearing armor all the time. Even I'd gotten out of my armor to wear a simple silk tunic and stiff slacks. I'd gotten word just that day that the twins had gotten back from unlocking their class, which meant it had happened a week or more ago as letters took some time to be delivered via horseback, especially this far out from the capital.

I was happy for them and sent a reply wishing them well for their first dungeon runs. As much as I wanted to go and be a part of their leveling experience, I just didn't have the time. We'd been leaving by the end of the week to join the elves in their capital and no more time could be wasted, no matter how alluring the prospect.

"Tell me, oh great champion, what level were those dungeons you saw on the isle of Avalon again?" Emory asked.

I'd made the mistake of telling them that the three dungeons I had listed on my map read 64-71, 82-89, and lastly 110-120. These levels were far beyond what you'd expect to find in a dungeon anywhere in the Wyrd, according to my old map as well. I imagined that my father and his team would challenge dungeons in the 64-71 range, but I honestly didn't know to be certain, and Warrick wasn't much help on the topic, probe him as I might he gave up no straightforward answers. Instead, he said things like, the levels are hardly worth mentioning, just defeat the challenge and claim your rewards.

"You know damn well the levels," I said, sliding beside Alayna and across from Emory. "But we aren't going there to run dungeons, so it doesn't really matter."

"No," Emory agreed, his face red from one too many drinks already. "But imagine with me. How much weaker or stronger do you expect the monsters to be around the dungeons?"

Everyone seemed to be nodding their heads along with Emory and it was beginning to irritate me. "I never said it wasn't going to be dangerous." Taking a deep breath, I cooled my tone and continued. "But I need you all at my side. We've already done the impossible, bringing you all past level 40 in such a short amount of time. I don't know what else to say to convince you to come."

"We don't need convincing," Ismene said, cutting into the conversation.

Zander spoke next, his voice cooler and more collected than I was used to. "However, we do wonder if perhaps more training is in order. Surely the elves will hold their ships for another year, imagine the gains from a year of training in those essence rich lands."

"I thought you guys had all but wiped out all the queen spawners, the dungeon gives good essence gains, but really it was the wild monsters that solidified your gains and made level 40 possible, or you all said as much?" I asked, looking them up and down for any signs of conversational weakness.

"He's right," Fran admitted. "Toward the end, our gains slowed because we'd killed off too many queens. But there were still a couple and given time maybe the dungeon will produce more monsters to roam about."

"That isn't likely," I said, taking a long pull on a fresh drink a bar maiden dropped by the table for me. Wiping away the foam from my mouth I continued. "In fact, I'd be willing to say the opposite is true. The more the dungeon is used, the less essence you'd be getting. It gets its essence from the Ley Lines but had a massive store from the device detonated atop it. Once that runs out, it is back to pure Ley

Lines and the longer we wait the more the infection will spread, rendering the essence unusable. Then, the dungeons will close, monsters and queens will likely suffer and die as well. The Wyrd as we know it will cease to exist. Even our ability to channel mana and cast spells might be affected. We need to go to Avalon and retrieve that sword. With it I may be able to fix the Ley Lines and stop the end of the world as we know it."

"That's deep," Emory said, belching a moment later and swaying in his seat. For someone with such a high Strength and Constitution attribute he sure knew how to get drunk still. As if to punctuate my thought, he slammed down a pint of ale and called for another. However, as he brought the wooden cup down it hit the edge of the table and shattered into a dozen pieces.

"Maybe you've had enough," Ismene said, gently taking the handle from his hand and forcing him to sit again.

"I can already feel it fading, stupid body and its stupid thresholds, can never properly get drunk," Emory said, his words slurred as he spoke.

He must have a loose definition of what it means to not be drunk, but that was no matter. They'd brought this topic up time and time again, so it was obvious that they were worried. Was I worried? Honestly, I'd be a fool not to be, but I had a certain amount of peace when I thought of the trip and the challenges that likely lay ahead. We would conquer this challenge as we had so many others.

"A toast to our victory!" I raised my glass, and my team

of amazing friends joined their glass with mine. We drank, laughed, and had a generally great time that night. During the dark nights that were sure to come, I knew this night would remain as a bright light to look back on.

CHAPTER 50
A SPARRING MATCH AMONG FRIENDS

The next morning came sooner than I would have liked and apparently, I'd agreed to a dueling session between, well basically everyone. Fran, Fred, Emory, Ismene, Zander, Creed, and Alayna all were onto this idea of dueling in a tournament style event. If you hit 50% health, you were out, but that was a good deal of damage to take, and we'd need to be careful not to cause lethal damage. You could also knock out your opponent or they could yield, but other than that, we weren't putting any restrictions. Though I did promise myself that I wouldn't do any essence infusion. Everyone was eager to test their new limits, so I agreed to the events and now, fully armored and armed, I was ready to go.

The morning had the coolness that I liked, but I could hardly feel it under my armor. A gentle breeze stirred the cool air and I felt it across my face. It kicked up a bit of dust from the fifty paces by fifty paces arena that we'd set up just outside the walls. Seating had been erected and hundreds sat, stood, leaned, or laid in places that would allow them to see well enough. What was more, Warrick had agreed to erect a barrier to keep stray spells and such from killing any onlookers. Without his agreement I wasn't going to participate, so I was glad he'd come around.

Warrick truly looked much better than he'd been before, and our lessons had been improving my ability to summon portals. I even managed to do one the other day. Despite that, he'd given me a tome of magic that had all sorts of spells that I'd been trying to learn. One of which was a spell similar to my Lightning Strike, but it built and released the lightning from my hands or at the point of a focus, like a sword, wand, or staff. The rest were useful utility spells, with only a half dozen having the combat focus that I liked to focus on.

One such spell, I hadn't mastered it yet or even been able to cast it and hold it for more than a few seconds, was 'Elemental Fury'. It allowed me to tap into elemental forces and temporarily infuse my strikes with different elements, causing additional effects and damage. Trying to learn a spell outside the system was like trying to eat food from a plate without utensils and not being allowed to use your hands or dirty your face. Can it be done? Sure, with a lot of care and finesse, but it isn't ideal.

Warrick stepped forward, he'd taken it upon himself to be the referee and announcer, another fact I was perfectly fine with as I trusted his judgement more than most. "We will have a clean, but exciting bout. If either of those terms are breached, I will help it along."

What did he mean by that? Perhaps I should speak with him before we got started.

Warrick's voice boomed over my thoughts, and I found myself listening to him once more. "The first two to fight are Caldor and Creed, please step forward and prepare yourself."

I looked over and Creed waved awkwardly at me. He'd grown considerably, his height and awkwardness balancing out nicely in his muscled frame with the several inches he'd grown. He wasn't quite as tall as me or Emory yet, but if he kept growing, he might reach our height.

Walking over, I held out a hand. "Good luck and I apologize in advance. I'll try not to hurt you too bad." I wasn't trying to be coy; I was seriously worried I'd hurt him. Despite his level being 41 now, I was a match for someone twice his power. But I didn't tell him that, instead I let my words sink in and awaited the fear I imagined would cross his face.

He surprised me by smiling and summoning his armor wordlessly. So, he was working on wordless casting as well, it would figure that Creed had a few tricks up his sleeves as well.

In his death knight ethereal voice, he spoke. "Good luck to you and may the strongest and wisest win." With that, he turned his back on me, and I began to buff myself. I cast everything from Physical Resistance to my Arcane Armor, prepping myself as best I could and taking the duel seriously. My blade appeared in my hand so I could cast Light Blade, a subtle glow traveled the length of the blade and was ready to be unleashed to buff my damage.

Then as a last second decision I didn't infuse my blade with essence, figuring I'd keep it as a backup if I truly needed the extra attributes against a foe, I was confident in defeating. I cracked my neck to the side and did one last check of my armor, all the belts and buckles I could see were tight. I let my sword fade away, trusting my buffs to remain on it when I needed it. Then, just because I wanted to mess with Creed, I pulled out my blackened magical bow and stood ready.

"This match has begun!" Warrick cried, his voice booming for all to hear.

I pulled back the string and let loose one arcane arrow after another, using the special ability of this bow to shoot out magical arrows if no physical arrows were strung. Creed didn't even try to stop the attacks, each blue buzzing arrow chunking away bits of his frozen armor. He raised his sword into the air and energy poured out of it. A moment later it formed into two frozen ghouls, hulking icy beasts of swirling darkness.

Switching to focus my weak arrows against the ghouls I let loose a barrage. The arrows did barely any damage, but I kept it going wanting to see how Creed truly planned on dealing with me. An icy wall of power surged from him and suddenly I found myself unable to see Creed, only his ghouls that had flanked him on either side. Then a series of walls sprang up, creating a loose maze and preventing me from getting a clear shot at all but one ghoul. I peppered it over and over again, putting my bow away as it stumbled into melee range.

With a powerful non-skilled slash, I took its head off and it fell into a heap in front of me. The barest sound of scratching caught my attention, and I turned as three more ghouls appeared from the other side of an ice wall that stood some eight feet tall. I slashed down the first one, but the other two weren't trying to strike me, instead they jumped atop me. I rolled and avoided one, but it got my legs entangled and the other fell atop me. I fell over, hitting hard on the ground, but I was far from being in any danger, not a single strike had penetrated my armor or Arcane Armor.

Then something weird happened, several more ghouls appeared, piling atop me, and all at once they began to vibrate and let off a harsh blue light.

Oh no he didn't...

The ghouls exploded atop me, sending bone, ice, and a wave of teeth shaking force. I was thrown from the pile along with bone and debris. Making it to my knees I coughed up blood; the force of the explosions had done significant damage to my insides, but not nearly enough to bring me to half health. Currently I sat at just over 80% or 2,204 health points. He'd need to bring me down to 1,315 if he hoped to win this fight.

I spit out blood, ridding my mouth of the metallic taste. Before I'd made it back to my feet, Creed was there. His massive runic blade covered in ice swung down at my head. It moved fast enough that I wasn't going to be able to dodge, so I didn't.

Blink went off and I was behind him, my blade appeared in my hand, and I struck down with a Power Strike, shattering ice across his back and hitting the armor beneath. Creed fell forward, yelling in surprise, but I wasn't done, and neither was he. I cast a wordless Lightning Strike, it hit him just as he got to his knees and brought him back to the ground. Planting my foot on his back I reached back to deliver a strike to the back of his helmet. Before I could complete my Phantom Thrust, his body turned to a blue icy form and cracked into a million pieces.

This wasn't something I'd seen him do before, so I was fooled at first that perhaps I'd done too much damage. Reaching down, I scooped up some of the ice and then I heard his steps behind me. I turned in time to catch a sword strike upside my head, dealing several hundred health damage and tweaking my neck badly. That had been a Runic Strike for sure, I thought as I rolled in the dirt from the force of the attack. Finally stopping the roll, I used Speed Burst, finished playing it safe with him, and made it to my feet.

Creed had kept pace, but now he looked sluggish and slow compared to just moments before. I cast a Rank 2 Firebolt at his chest, followed by a Blink to close the distance the moment after it hit. Using Phantom Thrust and Swift Strike, I plunged my blade into his chest. It cracked through the armor and sunk a few good inches through his armor beneath.

Blood spurted from his mouth and his skeleton icy helmet seemed to mirror the look of shock that was likely on his face. Before Warrick made the announcement, I knew I'd taken him below half, so I was already casting Mending Touch as Warrick called the match.

"This match goes to Caldor! Creed has sustained damage equal to more than half his health. Next up, we have Zander against Alayna."

"Sorry about the armor, we will get that patched up," I said to Creed after my heal topped him off. "You feeling alright?"

"Fine," Creed said, shaking his head and dismissing his helmet. "I really thought I might get the upper hand, but you are an impossible foe."

"I'm a bit stronger than I look, but you are getting there. That move with the ghouls was pure genius and if you'd been up against anyone else, that would have been the end of the match."

Creed smiled at my praise, clearly tired though, as he limped toward the sidelines, and I followed after him.

Emory nudged me as I sat in some chairs just outside the shield Warrick had erected. "You were just messing with him, weren't you? I bet you could have K.O.'d him in like two seconds."

I smiled innocently at Emory but said nothing.

"Yeah, fuck this mess, I hope that Fred guy whoops my ass, so I don't have to go up against you."

Fred looked over from a few chairs down, to say, "I will beat you quite easily, but I don't stand a chance against Caldor either."

Chuckling, I focused on the fight that had already begun and enjoyed watching two healers go at it. The enjoyment turned to boredom after the first twenty minutes went by, then assumingly because he was bored, Warrick began throwing out fire balls at random locations. One such fireball hit Zander just as Alayna threw him back with a powerful spear throw, and it was over. The fireball hit Zander so hard and powerfully that it blackened his armor. Luckily, we had healers aplenty and he was back on his feet, a bit confused, but ready to walk it off.

The next bout was between Fran and Ismene. Using her raptor and several ingenious traps to slow and control Fran's movements, Ismene came out ahead. Next came the fight between Emory and Fred, despite Fred's claims and his amazing powers, Emory put up a crazy good effort and it was one of the more entertaining fights of the morning. However, Fred had been right, and he won it by sheer force of power and fire.

Next, we had Warrick versus Kora, an extra match up that took much convincing on both parties to get going. Kora had already raised her level to 53, but she claimed that level didn't matter anymore as she finally had enough latent essence stored to do pretty much anything she required, including enhancing her body.

This was a fight I wanted to pay close attention to. The entire crowd quieted and watched as the two fighters took their places.

Warrick, ever the cool-headed combatant, was smiling friendly toward Kora. Meanwhile, Kora had cloaked herself in an overly large material that made it difficult to see her hand movements. I'm sure this was part of her strategy, but I was excited to see how she planned on matching the destructive might of Warrick.

Kora shouted several long words, a spell of some kind and energy swarmed around her as a monster was summoned, as far as I knew most of her power was tied into her summoning, so this was bound to be a fierce monster if she thought it had a chance. Low and behold, a massive Rex appeared, bigger and fiercer than the one I'd given her the Core of. It was also meant to be a secret and a trump card that we could pull in a time of need, but Kora had other plans I suppose.

The Rex took a single step and Warrick waved a single finger, as if telling it 'no', and it burst into a million dust like motes of light. Then, to my utter astonishment, the motes swarmed into Warrick's mouth. He made a show of wiping away something from his mouth and even went so far as to belch.

"If that is the best you've got to offer, then this match is over, and I win." Warrick called out; his voice still amplified for all to hear.

In response, Kora blurred and punched at Warrick's face. Before the blow could land, Warrick was across the arena, chanting the words of a spell. The ground around us began to shake and I was worried how far this battle might go. Kora turned and charged, but hands reached out of the ground and grabbed hold of her. She fell hard, but the hands didn't stop. They pulled themselves out of the ground and dozens upon dozens of rocky man-shaped forms beat down on Kora as she struggled to stand.

I watched and saw that she got her hand around a single one's ankle, and it flared with blue light. Runes danced across its surface, and it turned on its stoney brothers, destroying heads one punch at a time. When the other stoney figures got wise, it was too late, all but three were still functioning. Her runic stone man finished them off, clearly stronger than its brothers, and then ran with frightening speed at Warrick, Kora just behind it.

Warrick waved a hand and it turned to dust, then with his other hand lightning sprung forth, hitting Kora and laying her flat. But it wasn't just a strike like my spell, it kept coming and Kora struggled to do much more than shield her chest with her forearms.

"I yield!" Kora screamed over the din of the crackling magic. The lightning ceased instantly and then a wave of blue energy surrounded Kora as Warrick chanted. The motes of power infused Kora to the point that all her tiny runic symbols were burning a hot white.

"I've topped you off, that was fun, and you've proven yourself very clever. However, your defensive wards on your third rib need an adjustment. I could have disintegrated you with a thought, but I can teach you how to resist that as well."

"Any help would be welcome, wise sage," Kora said, inclining her head in a way I'd not seen from her when she dealt with other humans. I knew they shared a bit of comradery, but how would Warrick know more than a dungeon regarding runes. He was truly a prize to have on our side.

With the first round complete the second round commenced. Warrick took back his position and wouldn't be competing any longer, despite his win. That was part of the deal we'd struck, so I didn't complain, instead waiting eagerly to find out who I'd be fighting in the second round.

"Going first will be Fred and Alayna, followed by Ismene and Caldor. The winner of these bouts will fight each other."

I looked across the seats and found Ismene, she looked annoyed and rolled her eyes at me when I stared in her direction. It wasn't really a fair fight, but she had bested Fran by controlling her movements, maybe she had a chance. I smiled at that, of course she didn't, and I wasn't going to string it out to give a false sense of victory, she deserved better than that.

Watching the fight between Alayna and Fred was enlightening. Fred was the obvious stronger fighter, but Alayna's barriers proved effective against his fire, she even managed to get a few spear-strikes off, bringing his health nearly half before everything went sideways. He'd just been hit by a spear when his eyes flared white and the fire surrounding him lost its normal fiery look. He'd been working with Kora and Warrick to bring his power down to its normal levels as going all out all the time was burning him up, they said.

Warrick appeared suddenly before the white flames, and they smashed against his barrier as he chanted. I even saw a crack form on his hastily erected barrier before Fred's white glow diminished and he fell to his knees, breathing hard.

"This match is over; Fred is the winner." Then looking down at a confused Alayna he added in a lower voice but still loud enough for *Awakened* ears to hear. "That attack would have shattered your barrier and killed you within seconds. No shame in loss, pretty lass."

Alayna's eyes went a bit wide, and she nodded, brushing dirt off her knees before coming to sit down next to me.

"He is insanely powerful," she muttered. I looked at Warrick and nodded.

"Warrick has had a long time to learn and grow powerful, we'll get there one day," I said.

Alayna shook her head. "No, I mean Fred. Warrick said that, well he saved me from being obliterated and Fred is the lowest level of all of us now. Are you going to be okay against him?" She asked, assuming as I had, that my match would be easily won against Ismene.

"I have to beat Ismene first, but yeah, I think I'll be alright. You got him to a hair above half health, so if I hit him quick, he won't stand a chance," I said, letting my thoughts pour out my mouth as I considered how I would beat him.

"You're up," Alayna reminded me as Warrick announced our fight.

I thanked her and stood, heading out to join Ismene out in the field of battle.

CHAPTER 51
BATTLE OF THE WHITE FLAME

"It won't be as easy as you think," Ismene said, twirling an arrow in her hand and in her other hand, bow ready.

"Give it your best, but I won't hold back," I said, grinning back at her.

I'd get this over in one strike, but I had to be careful not to hurt her too badly. A Lightning Strike followed up by a Force Wave ought to be enough to finish her.

She whistled and her Raptor, she'd named it Chad, appeared all black and red feathers. Then she surprised me by whistling again and summoning a giant spider I'd never seen before, as well as Roger, her pet wolf.

"You know Roger and Chad, but meet Brett, my clingy spider friend," Ismene called out from across the way.

Great. Now I'd need to watch four targets and be careful not to kill them as well. I really ought to learn how pets work for her class, truth might be that I don't need to worry about

killing or maiming her pets, but it was too late to ask now...
or was it?

"What happens if I kill your pets?" I asked, Warrick had
already called for the fight to start as we'd both summoned
and buffed ourselves, but she hadn't attacked so I wasn't
going to just yet.

"I'd be upset," Ismene said, pouting her bottom lip. I
just looked at her with a deadpan expression until she elaborated. "I'd have to do a long summoning spell to bring them
back, but it wouldn't be the end of them if that is what you
mean."

"Shouldn't have told me that," I said, smirking. I
pointed the tip of my sword at Roger and let loose a Lightning Strike. It was enough to bring down the wolf, it yelped
and fell to the dirt. I thought I'd completely killed it, but
Ismene let loose an arrow and I had to move. To my surprise,
Roger showed up in my peripheral vision, running as fast as
ever and what was worse, he appeared uninjured.

Nope, I wasn't going to play this game, I found Ismene
and made a beeline for her. My sword was ready, and I batted
away arrow after arrow, so keen was my perception and
speed now. Then just as I got within ten paces of her, my feet
locked up. As I fell, I held out my hand and let loose another
Lightning Strike. It hit Ismene on the shoulder, charring her
armor and her body locked up, the stun effect had worked.

Reaching out with my sword I activated Phantom
Thrust, and my blade lengthened just enough to pierce her
injured shoulder, causing additional damage. Something
attempted to bite me, but between my armor's ability to

spread the protection over weak spots and my Ring of Anubis with its Elite Protection, the attacks did nothing but push me to the ground again and again. I used Blink to stand over the stunned Ismene, only seconds having passed since I hit her.

The stun wore off and I found my feet being swept as she did an acrobatic movement that would make my sister jealous. She landed on me with a foot on my chest and she loosed arrow after arrow point blank into my torso and neck. I let the missiles come, my armor protecting me as I focused on casting Arcane Missile. I wasn't able to cast it silently, but at this range she had no hope of dodging it.

Bam. Bam. Bam. She was thrown to the side, screaming in pain and I heard Warrick's announcement over the battle.

"Caldor has inflicted at least half of her total health. This battle is over! Caldor wins!"

I quickly cast a heal on Ismene, who was cursing up a storm and slamming a fist against the ground.

"How did my arrows not bring you below half?" Ismene asked when she finally made it back to her feet. I'd ruined her armor and would need to have it mended as I'd done with Creed.

I checked my health, but my fast regeneration had taken me nearly to full already. "I have good armor," I said, shrugging. "It spreads the total protection over my joints, and I've got a ring with a protection enchantment that straight up blocks a certain amount of damage each day. Good gear is just as important as being the strongest. The spider webbing on my feet was a good trick, luckily it fell off when I Blinked away."

"Now it is time for the final fight, are both combatants ready?" Warrick called, my mana still hadn't fully recovered, but I shrugged and turned around walking back to the middle.

Fred appeared, wearing white robes as he had before, but these seemed to have some padded armor around the chest and legs, leaving the sleeves flurrying around with his legs and hood. Trying to catch a look at Fred's face I realized he'd put on a mask, something I hadn't seen him wear before. It was white with eyes, and a runic symbol where the mouth should be. The runic symbol and the eyes, as well as the edges, were all done in gold paint.

I tried to remember where I'd seen that Rune before, but I couldn't recall. He looked at the crowd and gave a thumbs up. I looked to see Fran and Kora giving him a thumbs up as well. Well, I knew who they were rooting for, but I wouldn't let Fred win, white flame or not.

Warrick startled me, I was so completely focused on Fred that I hadn't noticed him approach and put an arm on my shoulder. He leaned in and spoke so softly that even I barely heard. "If he uses the white flame, be quick and don't let it touch you. It will burn away your essence and take it for itself. You can win, just be fast."

His words returning to its normal booming volume he said, "This battle has begun!"

It started off light enough of a battle, Fred's flames came quick and deadly, but not white. I struck back with a Lightning Strike, but the flames flared, protecting him and absorbing the energy of my attack. Undeterred, I struck out with a Firebolt, then an Arcane Missile a moment after casting Firebolt. Each attack was consumed by the flaring flames and with each spell it appeared his flames grew, almost like I was feeding him.

Okay, I was no one's fool, time for a melee strike. I Blinked to close the distance between us and activated Speed Burst. Fred slowed; the world churned to a halt as I moved at my normal speed. However, as I went in to cut my blade down at Fred's chest, I was met with flames that hadn't slowed at all. Armor or not, the heat was so intense that I got one strike in, and it sparked off an orange barrier just inches from Fred's cloth armor. Wizards of any kind were difficult to deal with when they were prepared, and Fred was prepared for anything I could send him.

It was almost like he'd taken a whooping from Alayna just to set me at ease, but that would denote a tactical sense that I didn't equate to Fred, however, I could see Fran suggesting as much. I heard the crowd cheering as time returned to normal and I was forced to back off or be burnt. I cast another Firebolt, just buying time to figure out my next move. It hit me in a spurt of inspiration, and I struck out with a Rank one Lighting Strike, conserving my Mana.

My attack hit the ground in front of him, therefore the fires didn't intercept it, but it did kick up a good measure of dust. I hammered the ground around him with an Arcane Missile next, and enough dust had been kicked up to obscure him from sight. Then moving as quietly as I could, I

Blinked to the left and activated Speed Burst again. This time I didn't waste my opportunity, I slashed out combining Power Strike, Swift Strike, Force Wave, and released my Light Blade arc. Then ready to go as ever, I sprinted behind my attack and cast Phantom Thrust, thrusting with all my might at where I sensed Fred inside the smoke.

I heard an audible shatter as my attacks hit almost at the same exact time, my blade sunk into his gut but before I could plunge it further to end this duel, his fire went white and exploded outward all around him. Despite how fast I was, I barely got a Mana Shell up before the flames cascaded over me. I was lifted from my feet and thrown backward so hard and far that I hit Warrick's barrier, crunching against it and taking two hundred points of blunt damage.

There was a taste of blood in my mouth, but I ignored it, landing hard on my feet and beginning to push mana into a Fireball attack, infusing it with essence despite my promise to myself that I wouldn't. Fred was too great a threat to not give him everything I had. I only let the ball grow to the size of a fist, sparking blue and green energy, before I unleashed it. It zoomed through the air and hit his white flames, he was covered in flames at this point, and I couldn't get into melee range if I wanted to without getting severely burnt.

The fireball hit his flames and they surged, but they were unable to contain the entire explosion and a boom echoed through the area as dust was kicked up and obscuring us completely. But that didn't blind me, and I knew I needed to act fast if I were to end this now. First, I activated Stamina Surge, then I Blinked back toward Fred, activated Speed

Burst and Power Strike as my skin screamed at me from the burning of it. I felt my blade hit flesh and sink deep. The flames suddenly cut out, forming into a tight ball and smashing into me. My sword was pulled from my hands, and I felt my insides burning.

"That decides it! Fred is below half health, Caldor wins!"

I heard the words, but the white flame still burnt around me as I rolled through the dirt from the force of the attack. I vaguely saw Warrick step forward and wave a hand. The flames disappeared and Fred screamed. Zander and Alayna began hitting him with heals, but Warrick yelled at them to step aside.

I sat up to see Warrick pressing his hand against Fred's chest and unleashing the white flame he'd collected from me back into Fred. His eyes flared white as the flame entered him and his wounds closed as if burnt away, leaving only a small bit of blackened char behind.

Fred sat up then, brushing himself off before standing. He looked like nothing important or scary had happened at all, instead he smiled in my direction and waved. "Good match," he said, before turning to walk toward Fran and Kora.

Fran for her part looked horrified, but Kora looked pleased. It was confusing to say the least, but I kind of got the impression that Kora and Warrick were testing Fred's limits and had used me to do so.

There was one thing that I was definitely glad about, and that was that Fred was on our side. I might have increased attributes, and the ability to infuse essence into my abilities, but Fred had raw crazy power in that white flame. It was almost like it was alive in how it moved and reacted to danger.

"I thought you two were going to kill each other," Alayna said as she finished chanting a heal spell that poured over me, soothing my burns. I couldn't even take my helmet off yet because I knew it would tear at my flesh and there was some pain I could do without.

"Me too," I admitted. "He has some intense power. I even had to infuse an attack with essence, I probably should have used my sword's ability to increase my attributes."

Alayna scoffed. "You weren't even going a 100%, were you? Of course not, I saw the way you've fought before, and you weren't even half as fast as you could have been. You really shouldn't play around with your life, a battle against someone like Fred should have taken everything you had."

"I know my limits," I assured her, then remembering how she'd faired against him I added, "I think he was holding back against you so who knows maybe he held back against me as well."

Alayna looked perplexed for a second and looked up at me laughing a little. "You're right, what if he was holding back on you as well? I think we might be better equipped to handle the Isle of Avalon than I thought. I'm sorry."

"For what?"

"For not trusting that we are strong enough. Between you two, Warrick and Kora, I think we have nothing to worry about."

"I just wish Warrick was planning on coming on the

ship. He seems fairly confident that I'll be able to summon a portal to bring him here, but I'm not so sure," I said, glancing over to the aged wizard with his incredible power. He looked like an elderly man wearing oversized grey robes, nothing special, and yet he had to be one of the strongest beings in all of the Wyrd with how much magic he'd shown.

That of course led my thoughts to a dark consideration that I'd been avoiding. If Warrick had been captured and experimented on for so long, what chance did I have to face this Chaos Knight with the power of the Ordu at his fingertips. I pushed the thought away as soon as it formed.

Soon I would have access to an Ordu artifact as well, and I'd be able to do what Zel'hu did, showing awesome power with a wave of my hand. This Chaos Knight didn't stand a chance. I would retrieve the Sword of the Ordu, fix the Ley Lines to restore Order, and kill the Chaos Knight, reclaiming the tainted artifact he wielded. Then I would unite the races and people back into Order and Chaos, hopefully before the great darkness or the black dragon as it was called, found its way to the Wyrd.

CHAPTER 52
MEETING THE QUEEN

Warrick opted to stay behind at Blackridge Keep, mentioning something about the company of elves leaving a sour taste in his mouth. He assured me that he'd be ready to portal to Avalon when the time came and all I needed to do was open a portal to Blackridge Keep. For my part, I tried one last time to convince him to go with us, but it failed, and we left. Our journey to Eldah'ren, the nation of elves, and the city bearing the same name would take only a week, but we were prepared for several months' worth of travel.

Several smaller events happened before I left, such as Cam reporting for duty with his family to Blackridge Keep. I tried to turn him away, telling him that he should be at his small farm he'd purchased with his wife and child, but he informed me that they'd sold all they had to come here. He wanted to be a part of what we were building and since proxy levels didn't transfer easily, he decided he shouldn't waste any time. So, I accepted him and helped him purchase a small farm outside of the city where he could employ his skill when not serving in the military.

Then as an extra measure, I talked with the head guard of the city and got him a shift a day or two each week, which he appreciated as it would help bridge the gap income wise. Despite the small fortune I'd given him, he wanted to be able to make ends meet without it, something I respected. I also gently reminded him that he earned that coin and ought to use it if it became necessary. He assured me that he would, and I left him to start his new life here in Blackridge.

A part of me played with the idea of bringing troops to Avalon, but in the end, I decided that if I wanted to do that it would be best done through a portal after we'd safely arrived. In fact, I was going to ask the Queen about her plans to send additional troops or personnel to the Isle of Avalon via portal. Surely the elves had great portal masters to rival even Warrick's power. It was a known fact that elves naturally lived much longer than humans, especially if they took the long-lived perk.

We'd go to Calenrah first, then move South to the city of Eldah'ren. I had hoped to speak with Elandel during my time in Variyn, however, I'd learned that she'd left Lord Variyn's service citing a family matter drawing her home, so now I looked forward to seeing her at Eldah'ren, if truly she'd been called back there. In fact, the more I thought about it I'd seen less and less elves in and around Variyn since the war, perhaps they withdrew before hostilities could spread or they had the keen sense to stay out of a war that had no point but satiating the greed of one man.

These thoughts and many more rotated through my mind as we traveled, until finally the evening came and we arrived at the outer walls of Eldah'ren, the capital city of the elves. To say the city was grand, would be to do it a disservice. Where most cities, Variyn included, had magnificent keeps that showcased the workmanship and power of a city, Eldah'ren took that same care on every building. In many ways it reminded me of the steep cloud-high buildings I'd seen in the dungeon Ordu city, however, none of these buildings reached such an impossible height.

Instead, all the buildings were built out in a natural circular fashion rising to a point so sharp you could skewer a dragon on it. Not a single building was below three stories high, but they weren't closely packed together so perhaps there were shorter buildings hiding within. Our presence hadn't gone unnoticed, and it appeared a delegation of sorts had been sent out to greet us.

At the head of the group were three people I recognized. Standing tall before them was a beautiful elf and a friend, Elandel. She wore armor, green and brown with a touch of golden edges, but had no weapon at her side. Directly to her left was Adathin Valamin, wearing similar armor as Elandel, but with a cloth aspect that draped around his waist and ended below the knee. To her right stood Bethgrok the Delvish woman I'd met all those months ago. She preferred to be called Beth and had a huge smile on her face, sneaking in a little wave as we approached.

I smiled and nodded my head back in return. All around them were armored folk, but none bore any weapons of any kind. Even Beth's signature bow was missing. These people were going out of their way not to appear hostile, and it made me suspicious of why.

"Welcome to Eldah'ren, Young Chaos Slayer," Elandel said, her pleasant smile putting me at ease once more. "I must request that all weapons, sheathed or otherwise, be stored away out of sight."

We obliged her without any question, most likely figuring that we could just take them out if we found ourselves in need. I had a dagger in my boot and attached to my lower back, I put each of them away in my inventory but left my sword to wherever it was between summoning's.

"Thank you for receiving us," I said, after seeing to my weapons. "My heart is light seeing so many friendly faces. Beth, Adathin, good to see you." I inclined my head again in their direction.

"For us as well," Adathin said, doing a half bow.

Beth on the other hand ran up and wrapped me in a hug. "Missed you!" She squealed and I couldn't help but chuckle.

Beth released me and fell back into formation. Elandel spoke next, her voice as soft and gentle as I remembered it the first time I heard it, after recovering from my battle with the Chaos Drake. "My Queen, Elsena of the Elven Nation, invites you to come and partake of her hospitality. And you, Caldor Miles, she wishes to speak with you in private, if you are open to such a meeting?" She phrased the last bit as a question, and I nodded immediately.

"Yes, of course."

With that, we fell into line with them as they turned and entered the city. Massive gates that appeared to be made of a mix of stone and wood, but all of it was textured to look like trees stacked together, a large wall of bark texture. It was as I thought after getting through the gates, the spaces between the enormous buildings were covered in tents that made the entire open areas look like sprawling markets. However, they lacked the disorganized nature of the ones I'd seen pop up in Creeshaw and Variyn, instead they followed that same circular pattern that was so prevalent.

Where no tents were pitched, instead gardens or fountains were seen. All in all, the city took my breath away as much as the beautiful people inside of it. Each of the elves we passed seemed ready for battle, wearing the simplest of armors as if they were their daily clothes. However, once more I noticed no one carried any weapons, not even daggers. The more heavily armored among us, the guards I assumed, had no weapons either. It made me wonder if they were all skilled in unarmed combat or perhaps, they were confident in their ability to pull out a weapon when needed.

Either way, I found it strange and unnecessary.

The palace, for that must be what this building was, rose up several stories above the rest, with dozens of high towers and a sizable moat around the edge where a wall as tall as the outer gates rose above our heads, obscuring our view of the inner courtyard.

"Upon your mother's request I've given her the recipe for the tonic that aids her. I believe she has begun to have it brewed locally and no longer has need of it from Lord Variyn," Elandel whispered the words to me, leaning toward me as we walked. Then added as if an afterthought. "She is cunning to cut any strings that might hold you in place to such a man."

"Thank you," I said, meeting her eyes. She was a kind woman, and I was glad to see her on my side, at least in some fashion.

The rest of the group split off and I was ushered into a grand hall beside Elandel. This was clearly a throne room of some kind, but it was empty of any people, save for a single woman sitting in a throne of green, brown, and gold. The throne looked as if it were grown straight from the ground and carved into a suitable seat.

"Presenting Champion Caldor Miles, whom you bestowed your blessing upon and whose father served the royal court. He is a Chaos Slayer, a defender of the weak, and a noble soul." Elandel spoke with conviction, and I couldn't help but feel moved by her words.

Sometimes it was hard to think of myself as what she'd said, but it was true. I am a Champion that would stand against the darkness and in that sentiment, I could solidify my resolve. Truly there was little else place I wanted to be than where I found myself now, ready to travel out into the unknown to do the impossible.

"Thank you, dear cousin. Please leave us now so that I may speak with Caldor Miles, Baron of Variyn, alone," the queen spoke with an even tone, but I sensed a touch of annoyance in her voice. She had a soothing way of speaking that mixed authority and beauty in a voice that comforted my ears.

Elandel turned and walked to the door. I watched her go, armored as if for war and wondered after the point of armor with no weapons. She was a proud woman; you could see it in her bearing. Once she'd left, I turned my gaze back on the queen and truly looked at her.

She had straight brown hair that was bone straight with braids throughout and a thin golden crown atop her head. Her eyes were the deepest of blues, like oceans swirling in the evening light with specs of white froth. And where Elandel had a proud bearing, the queen—even sitting upon her throne—emanated power equal to King Newaliyn, her aura was so great that it felt like a physical presence pushing against me.

The biggest difference that I could pinpoint between the two was the king had been able to suppress his aura to keep it from affecting me, and the queen either did not know how or couldn't, so great was her power. Either way, I was in awe of her power and eventually had to take a step back from the sheer force of it.

Then, all at once it disappeared, until she bore no aura at all. She smiled at me then, shifting in her gold and green gown as she adjusted her sitting position. She was doing as the king had done, showing his aura as a way to show the scope of their power, it seemed to be a common action among royalty and I found myself wondering how I could suppress my own aura.

"You are as bright as a sun; can you not shield your aura?" Queen Elsena asked, actually raising her hand to her face as if shielding herself from a great brightness. "The stronger we grow, the more sensitive to others we become. I thought at first you wished to show off your aura, so I did the same. But I fear that isn't the case, is it?"

Oh, I hadn't considered that I was giving off an immense amount of power myself. Before answering, I wondered why Warrick didn't have an expansive aura or seemed worried about my aura as the queen seemed. "I fear I don't know how to do that," I said honestly.

The queen brightened and stood, brushing her gown off as she did so. "I shall teach you then, and we will all be the better for it."

She walked right up to me and took my hands in hers. "Close your eyes and sense your aura. It is like a second skin, but it burns with the collected power of your ancestors. Tell me when you can feel it."

I closed my eyes, familiar enough with feeling energy and auras that it took me only a half minute of trying to do so to feel my own. It had the odd sensation of trying to roll your eyes behind your head and look into your own brain, the closest comparison I could make. At first, I saw only a bright heat coming from all around me, but as I focused, I sensed my aura as I did others, and it was truly oppressive. It lacked some of the intensity that the queen and king had shown, but there was a raw strength to it that was different from the clean edges of theirs.

The best way I could describe it was looking at the edges of a piece of paper that had been torn and one that had a crisp edge to it due to a proper tool being used to cut it. However, instead of our pieces of paper being the same thickness, mine was several times thicker than theirs, but not as brightly colored. It was confusing, but it came down to their auras being powerful and more refined, whereas mine was powerful and unrefined.

After a minute or two of paying attention to my aura, I finally could see and sense it without much trouble, so I opened my eyes and informed the queen. "I can feel it."

"Good," she said, taking a deep steadying breath, she continued. "Now, I want you to imagine taking hold of it and pressing it deep within yourself. It will be hard and perhaps a bit painful at first, but the closer you compress your aura to your core, the less others will be able to detect it."

"I'll try," I said, closing my eyes again and imagining my hands pressing down on my massive aura. But I made no progress, my hands, imaginary or not, were not big enough to press all sides down at once. The best I could do was suppress a small portion at a time, before I opened my eyes and let out an aggravated sigh. "I can't get it down, it's too big."

"You are not wrong," she said, smiling gently at me. "Think of the pressure you extend upon it as a great blanket, so large that even your massive aura isn't too big for it and try again."

This lesson in aura control was the last thing that I expected when I thought of meeting the queen, but I took her advice and imagined not my hands, but a vast blanket of pressure. Surprisingly it helped, and I began to make small strides. But as with most things to do with my magic and working around it, I exhausted quickly.

"I've done all that I can without rest," I said, lamenting my own weakness before the queen. "I'm sorry, your majesty."

She put a finger on my chin and lifted my head. "You have done well enough for a first attempt, even better than your father, I dare say. He too had an aura that could rival the intensity of the sun. I believe we still have much to discuss, so, shall we?" She gestured to a seat beside the throne, and I walked with her over to it and sat down.

"Would you like to start?" She asked when the silence grew between us while I waited for her to speak first, being the queen and all, I only thought it proper.

"I can," I said, shifting in my seat. "I guess my first question would be, why?"

The queen straightened her back and regarded me. "Why what, young Miles?"

I squirmed under her gaze but gave the best answer I could. "Why are you helping me get to Avalon? I know the importance of my mission, but I have not shared those details with you yet, so I'm surprised that you are willing to do such a great undertaking on the word of someone...well... someone like me."

"You mean the son of Elkor Miles? Or the man who has killed Chaos monster after Chaos monster? Perhaps you mean the man who thought only for the wellbeing of his mother when given a great gift of office. Or could you mean the man who discovered ancient secrets and the selling of them brought about one of the greatest destructive devices this world has ever seen? I'm able to stand behind all of them but one, care to wager which man doesn't sit well with me?"

A pit grew in my stomach as she spoke. There was nothing more that I wanted than to not be the final person she mentioned, but it was what had happened, and I needed to own up to it without letting it define me any longer.

"I'm all those men, and more. Both my successes and my unfortunate mistakes define who I am. However, I will say that my position as Baron under Lord Variyn is not a title, nor position that I sought out, nor was I able to deny it. However, I am proud of what we are doing in Blackridge and any other lands that are put under me will be just as inclusive." I wanted to say more, but she held up a finger to forestall me.

"I know you acted in ignorance and had no large part in the manufacturing of the weapon; however, it pains me deeply to know how many souls were lost in such an event. And I fear the land will be forever scarred by such a device. The balance has been upset and must be righted."

Her words spoke to me, and I couldn't agree more. I was less sure than I had been that the death of Lord Variyn would be enough to put the balance back in regard to the lives lost, but it would be a start. "There is much to be done, and I will make amends in the way that I see acceptable. Tell me, why do you support this expedition?" I wasn't comfortable being so direct with royalty, but she hadn't answered my question and I needed to know.

The queen regarded me for a solid minute, and I was about to speak again when she broke the silence. "For selfish reasons, actually. Long have we sought to return to many of our outposts in the sea, but the monster activity and the queens that have been allowed to spawn unchecked make travel by sea impossible, even for our strongest *Awakened*. The runic technology that Alayna provided has given us the means to seek out our lost kin, and perhaps bring them back into the fold or maybe even give us a place to flee should the end come to this continent as I fear it might if men like Lord Variyn are left unchecked."

"So, you don't plan on going to Avalon?" I asked, confused by the sudden turn of events.

"Oh, we do, the Isle of Avalon was once a grand nation of all races before we outgrew it. Our memories stretch much further than other races. We have records of a time when the Ordu inhabited Avalon alongside us, as well as on this continent and others. But a great end came and needing the balance to be maintained, half of the continent was given up to those who walk the path of Chaos and half given to Order."

"What are the chances that Avalon still has living Ordu?" I asked, my excitement getting the better of me.

"No, the Ordu left this land, according to our histories, several hundreds of years after our last records of Avalon. But be rest assured that we plan on going to Avalon, and we welcome you along with us."

"Thank you," I said, and meaning it.

We discussed other matters, logistics, and troop deployments when we arrived. They also planned on opening portals when we arrived to bring troops and settlers, so it answered many of my pressing questions just by listening. They also planned on depositing a few ships on each island we stopped at, there used to be outposts large enough to house thousands of elves, the queen said.

The hope was that with the combined might of her strongest *Awakened* out fighting sea monsters all through the route to Avalon, that perhaps they might defeat enough queens to enable travel once more. That was when I shared with her the threats that I faced and why getting to Avalon was so important to me. Going further, I shared with her what I'd learned about the 'black dragon' and the threat it posed to all nations if it should come. She considered my words but didn't say much on the matter. Our audience ended and I was taken to sleeping quarters so that I could rest.

I'd barely laid down when a knock at the door caught my attention. It was Alayna, and as tired as I felt, I was never too tired for her. We spent some time sharing what had happened to each of us since arriving, before snuggling up and falling asleep. She'd sneaked away from the initial tour that they were being given and instead found her way to the shipyards. She shared with me that they had three dozen ships outfitted with the devices needed for lift. Such a number boggled my mind as she said each ship could hold a crew of a hundred and fifty, as well as fifty additional passengers for a total of two hundred.

That meant, she was committing over seven thousand people to this expedition. I fell asleep worrying about the scope of such an undertaking and my dreams were filled with images of ships in flames and dead bodies sinking to a watery grave. I kept those dreams to myself, not wanting to dampen the mood.

CHAPTER 53
SHIPS AND TRAINING

I got my tour of the capital the next day and even more than before, I marveled at the scope and majesty of the place. This city, much more than any other including Newaliyn capital, was closest to what I'd seen in the dungeon regarding an Ordu city. Everywhere I went, the casual use of magic or runic systems for everything from light to plumbing to advanced lift systems caused no end to my amazement.

I walked along with Alayna, both of us wearing our armor, but no weapons. We figured that when in the Capital City of the elves we ought to do as the elves did. I'd meant to ask the queen about the no weapons policy, but I didn't have to, Alayna filled me in as we entered the pier district. Massive sea walls guarded a cove where the ships were built and launched. How they had so many seaworthy massive ships in condition to be used to fly, was another fact I needed to learn more about, but Alayna assured me I'd understand when I saw the docks.

"Ever since the war started between the houses, elves throughout Newaliyn have been returning home, but as is their custom, they have instituted a 'no arms' allowed in any populated area. It is meant to come across to others as a sign of peace, that they aren't amassing to do battle, but rather calling their people home for peaceful reasons. It's all very traditionalist if you ask me, but the elves have long lives and stick to old ways much more than humans do," Alayna said, taking my hand in hers, she added. "It does have a way of keeping our hands free, I like that at least."

We entered through a tall set of double doors, built of the same stone with an earthy bark design, and what was on the other side took my breath away. Walls four times as high as those that protected the outer edge of the city rose up into the horizon and a massive dock with hundreds of vessels stood laid out before me. Now the number of ships ready, a mere three dozen, seemed paltry compared to their fleet here.

"How do they have so many ships and do they have men," I got a look from Alayna and added, "or women to pilot such vessels? Surely the entire city's population could fit inside these ships?"

"Not by a half," a familiar voice said, and Adathin came walking up to us from somewhere inside of the long balcony overlooking the docks. "Our fair city has a population of 201,402 at last counting. These boats represent the work of our ancestors, we have but maintained their legacy by keeping the boats in fair working condition."

"Adathin," I said, raising a hand in greeting. "Have you come to see the ships as well?"

"Him and his father are overseeing the project," Alayna said, knowingly.

"And it wouldn't have been possible if not for the wonderful insights of Lady Alayna Variyn," Adathin said, bowing his head slightly in her direction.

"Shall we continue?" I asked, wanting to get a closer look at the ships below.

Adathin nodded and led the way forward. We took a series of lifting platforms until we reached the bottom, where water met stone. The boats on the left of us were normal ships, sleek in design and huge. But the ones on the right hovered just above the water and were slightly thinner than some of the biggest on the left. They had discs attached to the side that glowed with a faint blue light, I recognized the effects as what we used on the platforms during the war.

"How do you control forward thrust and side to side movements?" I asked, seeing that several additional sails had been added to the flying ships. One in particular that I found intriguing was attached to the end of the ship and spread wide like the wings of a dragon.

"See that there," Adathin pointed at the sail I'd been admiring. "It allows us to change direction and it works wonderfully. We've used monster hides and special runic formations to strengthen it to the point of armor, but still, it bends and yields enough to the wind to do its task properly. And you see those there," he pointed at several dozen smaller fins attached to the side of the hull, just down a dozen feet or so. "Those extend and will allow us to control the up and down trajectory."

"And what of thrust, have you worked out a better solution?" Alayna asked, ever the academic.

"Not yet, but we are close. The design you brought us just couldn't work at the speeds we need, but we've installed it for slower acceleration and deceleration. However, if no breakthroughs are made, it will be our wizards and their magics that push us forward. They can summon winds enough to fill our sails and direct the winds that are naturally blowing."

"And what of the air thinning dilemma you encountered when testing the height limitations, is that to be a worry?" Alayna asked.

"Not at all, we've put together some ingenious runic formations that will preserve and recycle the air, maintaining a comfortable pressure for all those aboard as long as the formation holds. On deck you should feel as if you are standing still, the only wind hitting you will be the magic from our wizards."

"You've thought of everything it would seem," I said, a thought occurring to me as I looked over the design. "What of sky monsters, are we likely to encounter anything up in the clouds that will be a threat?"

Adathin seemed to consider my words, then nodded. "We will be attended by a squad of griffin riders; they are actually eager to meet you. It is rare that a wild griffin picks a rider, and they are very curious. The Ash Flight, the ones that will be coming with us, comprise of twenty-five griffin riders all training to fight atop their mounts and powerful adventurers off them as well. I think you will like them. Oh look, here comes the Captain of the Ash Flight, Felin'dera Escline'dahn."

"But you, griffin rider, can call me Felin. For any friend of a griffin is a friend of mine," Felin said, his voice smooth and mature. "Where is your companion? I would be greatly pleased to introduce her to Ashlan, Defender of Elven kind, my griffin."

I pulled out the figurine and summoned forth Ares. "Meet Ares, a warrior of the sky and my companion," I said, wishing I had more honorifics to apply to her name.

Felin scrunched his brows in a look of confusion but reached into a bag at his side and pulled out a black figurine, summoning his griffin as well. It was black as Ares, but where she had gold trimmed on her wings, his griffin had a grey color similar to fallen ash.

"Black griffins are rare," Felin said looking over Ares with wide eyes. "And a female no less. You've a great stroke of luck, Caldor Miles, rider of Ares the golden winged beauty."

"Indeed, I was, without her I'd be dead several times over," I said, sending out encouraging thoughts to Ares as she inspected the griffin before her. She didn't seem impressed, and I was surprised to see that she was a good half foot taller in her back than the griffin Ashlan. "Is Ashlan a male?" I asked.

"He is, female griffins are rarest of them all, my entire flight in made up of males. Griffins are curious in that they seem to follow the opposite pattern of nature than birds. Females are normally the more colorful and larger of the species, whereas the males are muted colors. I used to think it was because females needed to attract a mate, but from what little of their mating rituals I've been able to observe, I can't draw that conclusion. They have such a higher intelligence than birds and other animals that color and size are more a secondary consideration I feel."

I'd never found someone else knowledgeable about griffins and I was eager to learn more. "Do you two mind if I go with Felin to see more of his flight? If that is okay," I quickly added looking to Felin, he nodded, and we went on our way with promises to meet up in an hour or so.

We only got to meet three other riders and their griffins, as the rest were out on patrol. But what followed over the next hour was interesting to say the least. Each griffin had the same proud stance and bearing, but they all seemed to yield to Ares as she asserted herself on them by stepping forward or screeching in their direction. I chatted with the other riders and each of them seemed like stand-up men and women. They invited me to a training session later in the evening and I accepted wholeheartedly.

***

I arrived at the area set up for training and found a group of elves wearing overly large cloaks over their armor and goggles on their faces. Going up to the one I recognized, I waved at Felin, he gestured me closer before speaking.

"Welcome to night training, before we get started, we will split into groups to spar. This isn't a match to see who is more powerful than the other, rather I just want your muscles warm and ready to ride, so take it easy on my second, will you?" Felin gestured to a tall elf to the left of him.

He, like all of them, had a cloak on that hid most of his bodily features other than his face, which had goggles obstructing that view. But he looked average enough from what I could tell. A strand of black hair escaped from below his helmet, and I could see through the crystal clear goggles well enough to see that he had a light orange eye color. The cloak was constructed oddly in that it had many dozens of strips of material, but no matter how he shifted I couldn't see his armor beneath. The hood of the cloak ended in a point that made everyone appear to have the silhouette of a griffin's beak and head.

"Name's Steph'en," he said, he really enunciated the 'en' part of his name and I wondered if it had some significance or if he just talked like that. "I think Felin is confused, but I will take it easy on you, I promise."

I just smiled and spread out with the rest of the twenty-five, each of them, including Felin, had paired off in ten-by-ten circles. I looked at my opponent and decided that perhaps I should go easy on him just to make sure I didn't injure his slim body.

Steph'en pulled a sword free from under his cloak and without any fanfare, lunged forward for a strike. His cloak flared around him, like undulating tentacles looking to grab hold of an enemy. I easily parried it away and struck him on the arm with the flat of my blade. The cloak with its many strips grabbed hold of my blade and wrenched it from my hands, but I recalled it into my grip a moment after releasing it.

"My cloak is made of a magically enhanced material and will turn away all but the most powerful attacks, do not worry about cutting me," Steph'en said, not even pausing to speak, instead striking a flurry of blows at my head.

Luckily, I had my armor on, as I did not have a cloak that could turn aside blows so easily. I needn't have worried though, I was far faster than Steph'en and it became clear after only seconds of the fight. I struck him again, this time letting the blade's edge run across the cloak. It folded around it and for a moment I thought it would pull my blade free, but I managed to dislodge it before another strike came.

Back and forth we went, he would get a bit faster, and I'd match his speed, until he was showing a thick sheen of sweat and moving at what I guessed was his top speed. I, however, had barely been moving at half my true speed, even less if I infused my muscles. This fight was mine for the taking, several times I saw an opening, cloak or not, that I could have used to end the fight.

"Very good, take five and we will regroup to begin sky drills," Felin called out. I looked around to see everyone but me had some amount of sweat on them. So, I decided to truly warm my body up using some of the drills Michael and Fran had pounded into my head.

First, I nodded to and thanked Steph'en for the sparring

practice, then I made room so I could go to work. Moving slow at first, I increased my speed to about half. Then as I felt the blood fill my muscles I went further, pushing my speed ever higher as I went. Until I moved, striking and swirling as I'd been taught at full speed. It took a solid five minutes before the strain on my stamina was enough to make me sweat, but after a time, I'd done it.

Panting a bit from the exertion but feeling amazing, I stopped and looked around. I'd gathered a crowd, all but Felin and two other elves stood around watching me. I gave them a weak smile and walked up to Steph'en. "Why is everyone staring?" I asked.

"You move with a speed that a diving griffin would be jealous of," he said, his mouth staying slightly ajar.

I smiled. "I could go faster if I wanted."

This made Steph'en laugh, and I followed suit, chuckling along.

"Here, take this cloak and goggles, you will need them when we take to the sky. The goggles will repel moisture and gives you a small measure of dark vision, they fit under most helmets and the cloak is mostly for temperature control, but it does provide a nice defensive shield against incoming missiles or spears."

Until I put the cloak on over my own, I didn't really see how it could provide temperature control, however, the inner strips of the cloak went to work, covering me and attaching flat pieces all over my armor. Immediately I felt the cool of the evening vanish and the warmth I'd created by working out solidified around me. Still, with the inner half of the cloak keeping me warm, there were enough outer pieces that they could do the work they needed to turn away blade strikes or random missiles.

"If you impress Felin, perhaps he'll let you get Ares fitted with armor," Steph'en said, nudging at me with his elbow. He was a friendly enough guy and there was somewhat of a bond that forms with the people you fight, so I laughed and nudged him back.

The wind pressed against my face as we hit cloud level. This was the second time I'd gone this high during our little training session and I was glad for the extra equipment I'd been given by the riders, a cloak that covered my own and goggles around my eyes. They were enchanted not to steam over, and it made my ability to see so much greater.

I'd been given a dozen javelins and asked to practice removing them from my inventory as quickly as possible. I'd awed them at the speed at which I picked it up but now that I was atop Ares and looking for a target, I wasn't as excited at my prospects. Three times I'd been hit already by these swift riders and their javelins, the cloak catching each strike before it could be deadly. I'd thrown one of my own, but they moved with such speed and purpose that it was like catching a fly between your fingertips.

A rush of wind in my ear, slightly different than the rush that pounded on it continuously, caught my attention and I turned in time to see three griffins riding in formation, each of them already throwing or in the act of throwing their javelins. I urged Ares to dive downward, and she did so a moment before I pressed my heels into her, our minds in a near perfect sync. The javelins missed, but that wasn't enough for me, I wanted to get a point by striking one of them.

We used the momentum of our dive to give us the speed necessary, and we arched with her wings wide in an upward swoop. I felt the edges of my world go shaky and my vision swam with blackness, but I remained conscious as we got above the three swift riders. Rearing back my arm, I struck out with my javelin, then summoned another from my ring storage, and not stopping until I'd released three in quick succession.

I'd learned after only a single throw that I need to aim where they would be and not where I saw them in the moment, so my strikes relied on a bit of luck that they'd stay their course. However, by releasing three in quick succession I'd at least doubled the chance I'd hit one. My first, aimed ahead of their current path, missed as they veered away from the attack, however, my next strike caught one in the shoulder as they moved right into its path, with the third one zipping by untouched.

I hooted and celebrated as we evened out and for my trouble, earned a strike to the back from another small trio of griffin riders that I'd not noticed. Pulling the javelin from my cloak and holding it fast, I took a moment to look at it. The javelin had a layer of something around it that would allow them to float, despite the weight. We'd be required to swoop low and retrieve javelins if we ran out or when we finished, if not for the bright coloring of them I'd say it would be an impossible task.

Ares swung low beneath three of the riders, just as another three engaged them in combat. This was the first part of several exercises they did as griffin riders, the next being with the royal guard. From what I'd been told before taking off, the royal guard would be in formation on the ground, and we'd swoop low acting like a cavalry to split their ranks, but for tonight we'd just be practicing diving and hitting stationary targets, likely for my benefit as the Ash Flight were all professionals and knew their job well.

By the time our night ended, I was truly exhausted and ready for the sleep that took me. What I wasn't ready for was seeing Alayna already in the bed and waiting for me with nothing but a beautiful little purple necklace hanging loose around her breasts. My body, as sore and beat up as it was, stood no chance of making it through a night with Alayna, but I gave it my best shot. When sleep came, I couldn't rightly say, but I slept well into the morning before I was able to be stirred from sleep.

"Wake up, we are going to meet the captains of the ships today," Alayna was saying, shaking me vigorously.

"I'm up," I said, pushing the covers off me and almost walking out into the hall wearing nothing because of how tired I still felt, but luckily Alayna had a better mind than I did after a bit of rest, pulling me back to safety. She pushed me in front of a wash basin, and I wiped myself down before dressing back in my armor.

Life was good, but I had no idea what lay ahead of us, and it left a knot in my stomach to imagine the challenges that we might face.

CHAPTER 54
TO THE SKIES ABOVE

I lost track of the days, but they weren't without great achievements. Though the wild monster population and the location of queens was closely monitored and culled, when necessary, I was able to get my team into a dungeon run after a week or so of learning our place on the ships. We ran it three times over the course of the week or two we waited, gaining me an impressive half million essence and my next level, bring me to level 48. I raised my Core and Concentration each by three.

We'd be guests, but everyone was required to report for the defense of the ships should such an event occur. It meant that everyone without a mount had purchased a pegasus using my funds. Storing them and feeding them wasn't going to be an issue thanks to bonding, which enabled each rider to store their companion away until a time of need should arise.

Ares had been wanting to go hunting but I was hesitant

to let her go, as I could feel how much she wanted to venture over the great waters looking for tasty fish. The water, even close to shore as we were, was dangerous. So much so that ships could not hope to venture out and survive, a fact that every elf seemed aware of and reminded us of on several occasions. I learned later, from Adathin, that there was a sect of elves who did not agree with our mission and many of their members were the ones who'd approached us about the dangers of the sea.

It was a novel approach, just wanting to discuss or convince, instead of actively sabotaging or going against the queen. I asked Adathin if we had anything to fear from these potential dissenters, and he assured me that we did not. The elves were different from humans to be sure, but one thing I had in common with them was my desire to unite the races. Delvish, gnomes, dwarves, and even a few orcs could be seen walking the city streets, and when I asked Adathin about it he said that much of the nation was mixed, with elves only accounting for half of the kingdom's population.

We were on board the ship, Phoenix's Pride, it was the lead ship and looked it. At least a dozen feet longer, it had more of the lift discs, a heavily armored exterior, and dark red sails. I'd won an argument not to split up my team on different ships and so we took up most of the 'guest' quarters, each room had nine beds, so we fit in Alayna, Creed, Ismene, Fred, Fran, Emory, Adathin, Beth, and myself; whereas Kora didn't need sleep or a bed so she planned on staying in our quarters reading while we slept.

Being Awakened and past my second threshold, I really

only needed to sleep every third night to avoid any stamina burn, so I too made sure I had books out and ready for when the time came. The rest of the group were past all of their first thresholds, so they required sleep every two days at least, but all in all it would be an interesting voyage. Today was the day we'd been leaving, and I'd already attended a speech by the queen, a meeting with our captain—an elf named Jorn— and touched bases with Felin about being made part of the weekly patrol schedule.

Ares had armor fashioned in the same smooth elven styles that I was used to seeing, mostly enchanted leather that moved and conformed to her shape without the need of shaping metals, but if it was half as effective as turning away attacks as the cloaks we wore, then it would be a wonderful addition. It had taken a few days of wearing it constantly for her to become truly comfortable in it, but now that she had, I planned on only taking it off every night to brush her out.

As with all the guests, we'd been told to go to our quarters during lift off, keeping the deck clear for the crew. So, it was while I sat looking out a small round window, that the ship lurched, and we began to depart. I knew I wouldn't have to stay down here for long, I had a patrol scheduled later in the afternoon alongside Steph'en and his squad. I longed to feel the wind in my hair and the speed against my body.

Once we'd made it out into the open sky, it barely felt like we were moving at all. If not for the low hum that the discs made, you'd think we were sitting still. None of the motions that I attributed to the sway of the ocean waves were present and yet Creed still looked green faced as he held his head over a bucket.

"I...don't...like...flying," he said, heaving every other word as if he might throw up. He'd been the worst one to convince that he needed to get a flying mount, and when it finally came time to get him one, he stopped me, informing me that he had taken a perk to upgrade his class mount, allowing it to fly. When I asked when he'd done that, he told me some time ago, but after flying once he'd decided to stay on the ground.

It was the same death steed looking horse, but now it had bat like wings that defied all logic as they had large cuts and tears ripped into them, but still, it flew as steady as any. It likely had some magic working on it that meant that the wings were more set dressing than functional wings. I wanted to test it by attacking his wings midflight, but for some reason Creed wasn't a fan of that idea.

"Oh, you poor thing. I've got a tonic that will clear that up," Beth said, she was sitting next to Creed and rubbing his back while pressing her body against his. I don't know if it was working, but I did catch Creed glancing at Beth's slightly exposed bosom and going red.

"You keep doing that for him and I think he'll soon forget we are even flying," Emory said, winking at Beth.

For her part, Beth tilted her head in confusion. Looking down she looked at her breasts, pressed hard against Creed and then to Creed before her eyes went wide and she laughed.

"You like that?" She asked, and suddenly I wasn't sure I

wanted to stay in the room, or at the very least overhear the conversation that was going on.

I turned to Alayna, but not before seeing Creed go an even brighter red.

"Does Lord Variyn know you gave this magical technology to the elves yet?" I asked, it had been on my mind every now and then, but I hadn't found the chance to ask yet.

"I suspect he does, Non has many eyes and such a huge endeavor as this can't remain secret forever. In fact, I am sure there will be consequences for the both of us when we return. I just hope that he doesn't try to take back your land while we are away."

"Could you imagine?" I asked, laughing. Alayna wasn't getting the joke, so I let her in on it. "We left Warrick at Blackridge Keep. He might not be a match for an entire army, but he is damn near close to it. Anything less than an invading force and Warrick will dust them without a second thought."

"How can he be so strong?" Alayna asked, despite what she'd seen Warrick do, she still couldn't fully comprehend his abilities.

And come to think of it, neither could I. I'd always assumed that Warrick had allowed his powers and magics to lay dormant and stagnant after my father died, but he must have been getting stronger the entire time. Pulling essence from studying and learning new spells instead of hunting monsters. It was slower but a consistent way to progress.

"I thought that whatever the Chaos Knight had done to

him was the end of his power, but he was able to work around it and now I swear he is stronger than he's ever been. I sometimes daydream what would have been different if Warrick had been as strong as he is now when my father and his group faced off against the monsters at the battle of Lynsteen Pass."

"He defies logic," Alayna said, her expression one of stubborn acceptance.

"I wish he were with us now, I can only imagine the monsters we might face in the skies above the great waters," I said, my mind going to a meeting I had with Felin and reports that they'd come across several wyverns, some black and some not, while scouting only miles from the shore.

He'd outlined for me our path and how we'd be doing the scouting by going out several miles ahead to make sure everything was clear. We had twelve islands along the way that would lead to our final destination, Avalon. The plan was to leave a ship or two, depending on the size of the outposts, until finally only a dozen or so ships, including the Phoenix's Pride, arrived to help colonize and explore Avalon. When I'd outlined the levels on the dungeons from my map, the captain had sent me to meet with the queen's men, so they too could update their maps.

Whomever had my map before me had done something impossible, as the elves data spoke of three dungeons but only half the levels that I was showing. Whoever this explorer had been, he'd had the ability to travel to distant places that not even the elves were confident at reaching.

The time came for me to go scout with Steph'en and his

squad, so I said my goodbyes and promised Alayna that I'd be safe, before leaving to the launch deck, a small platform on the port side of the ship where flying mounts could be summoned and launched.

***

The battle between the red wyvern and the four of us griffin riders had suddenly taken a turn for the worse, when Steph'en signaled for a retreat, his griffin barely able to keep up after the last attack to its wing. I signaled, 'no', using the basic hand signals they'd taught me. Instead, Ares and I turned and faced off against this monstrous flying lizard. At level 42 it shouldn't be this hard to kill, but it was an elite after all, so it made a little sense.

"Dive hard and fast, we need to get its attention," I said, my words lost to the wind but my connection with Ares getting the idea across. She dove just as I unleashed an essence infused Lightning Strike into the back of the wyvern. A great plume of fire followed after us, it had broken its chase of Steph'en and was following me like I'd planned. Unfortunately, that is as far as I'd thought, not wanting to see my new friend slain in a ball of flaming death.

I looked over my shoulder, the griffin riders had stopped, and the wyvern was closing fast. Signaling for them, 'retreat' 'retreat', I hoped that from this distance they'd seen it. We'd wounded the wyvern, but it didn't slow or seem to care, and if the battle went on as it had, one of these griffin riders would fall and I couldn't have that if I could prevent it.

A sudden and terrible idea came to my mind, and I shared it with Ares. She did not like it, but I urged her to get ready and she folded, sending me the wordless mental thought equivalent of 'you are an idiot but be careful'.

I prepared to unlatch my rider's belt, cutting me loose from Ares. The javelin I held went back into my inventory and I knew I could have my sword in my hand in an instant, so I didn't bother summoning it yet. If this plan were to work, I'd need to time everything perfectly and even then, it might not be enough. On the count of three Ares was set to do her part.

"One." The wind screamed and heat washed across my back as the fire breath of the wyvern nearly reached us.

"Two." We broke through the clouds and water, vast and terrible, could be seen in all directions.

"Three." The world lurched as Ares put her wings wide and we halted in our descent. She twisted and turned out of the grasp of the wyvern; its larger wings unable to get out fast enough to slow its descent.

As we passed by it, I unlatched my rider's belt, activated Speed Burst, then Blinked onto the back of the Red Wyvern. I landed right between its wings and marveled at the size of the monster, truly a master of the skies. My sword appeared in my hand, my legs pressed between muscles hard and moving, barely keeping me stable.

Ares moved above as the wyvern spun trying to dislodge me, but I pulled out a dagger and cut deep into its muscles, barely getting through a space between the scales. It gave me a decent way to hold on and I did, for dear life. Riding a wyvern was no easy business without a saddle or perhaps even with one. The movements of the wyvern were wild and erratic, and suddenly I felt a cold sensation and looked up to see that the wyvern had craned its neck and was preparing to bathe fire down its own body.

The energy being pulled from all around it made it go cold as all the heat was sucked away and into its maw for the attack. Praying to whatever gods were listening, I activated Mana Shell infused with essence and mana. This had to be strong enough, right? I soon got my answer as the world became orange just inches from my face, my own shell refined enough now to form around my entire body. Cracks riddled the surface almost instantly, but I flushed more mana into it until I'd brought myself to half, then as the flames kept coming, I drained my mana down to a quarter.

My core hurt, my aura flickered, and I knew I couldn't last much longer. Through our bond, I sensed Ares go into a rage, she broke from our plan, three powerful griffin riders appearing at her side as she dove for the wyvern. They refused to leave, and Ares would sooner die than see me fall to this overgrown lizard. I tried to tell her I was alright, but so weakened by the massive mana expenditure, the best I could do was share with her my senses, raw and unfiltered.

She got a taste of my fear, my resolve, and my anger at encountering such a vicious beast on our first patrol. In return, I felt her raw emotions, like a mother coming to defend her child, she screamed through the air, all rage, ferocity, and power. The very air around her seemed to part to allow her to move faster and soon she'd pulled ahead of the other three griffin riders. Through her senses I could feel each of them building up energy for attacks, but it wouldn't be fast enough.

Ares hit the wyvern just as my shell shattered and I was left with only ten percent of my mana, and a headache that made seeing anything nearly impossible. I gripped hold of the dagger while I felt through Ares's senses how her attack went. With talons, beak, and rage as her only weapons, she tore into the wyvern's face. Its skull alone was half her size, but she'd mounted it with disregard.

I felt the thrill of her victory as she slashed its eyes and it went wild with its own rage, spitting fire in a stream here and there, but hitting nothing.

It was time for me to finish my plan. Mount the wyvern and injure its wing beyond repair. I raised my hand in the air, my sword appeared, and I filled it with essence, then went even further, flushing essence into my muscles, my legs finally strong enough to keep me in place on the great monster. Using my Stamina I activated Power Strike, Swift Strike, and Phantom Thrust. I pierced through the scales of the wing's biggest muscles and deep into the bone.

If I thought the wyvern had been erratic before, it was insane with movement now. Twirling and twisting, I saw the water below coming closer and closer. But the injury wasn't enough, the wyvern was slowing itself already. Using Force Wave and Light Blade I slashed at the wing, the arcs of energy blowing apart scales and exposing flesh for me to cut deep into. The wing went limp suddenly and I knew I'd done it.

My mind connected with Ares, but she'd released the wyvern and had to slow herself. Through her eyes I saw my doom and heard the painful screech as Ares felt the same doom. The world shattered and for several painful seconds my vision went black as water closed around me and the wyvern.

It was hard to swim in full armor with a griffin cloak, but the goggles allowed me to see into the depths without water getting into my eyes. What I saw took my breath away. Several sharp toothed fish with large fins were closing in on us, some of them as big as a griffin. But what was more concerning was the hundreds of tentacles that were slowly moving up from the darkness of the great waters below, reaching out for the wyvern.

I made it to the surface, breathing in air and feeling a sense of relief to have not drowned. Ares connected with me just as I was pulled beneath the surface, I cut out, slow and sluggish because of the water, but enough that I cut the tentacle free and made it back to the surface.

At that very moment Ares swooped down and grabbed hold of me with her talons, lifting me free from the water. I grabbed hold of her saddle as she gained height and soon had myself buckled back into place.

Steph'en looked enraged and was signaling a return. I signaled back the same, confirming that this time I was ready to retreat. We'd won our essence and defeated the wyvern, but where there was one there could be two. Better to get back now so that future patrols could be prepared for such an attack.

CHAPTER 55
FIRST OUTPOST FOUND

Changes were made and the patrols strengthened by pegasus and hippogryph riders as well, a focus on casters and fighters who could rain down damage from afar while the griffin riders took care of the close up fighting. Now when patrols went out, it was at least two squads of three, plus five auxiliary fighters riding other flying mounts. Because of the new layout, we'd taken down four wyverns and several other flight bound monsters.

I jokingly suggested that perhaps we'd be better off in the sea, but Felin had assured me that wouldn't be advisable. His words and my memories of the water were enough to convince me. The size of that tentacle monster haunted my nightmares, and I wondered if the seas would ever be safe to cross without flight bound ships. Likely not, but I couldn't know what the future held, at least in this course of events. What I did know was that we were approaching a small island that wasn't even on my map and we'd have some exploring to do soon.

Horns were blown and I went with my group of ten to the upper decks to see what the matter was. All manner of whistles, loud and echoing through each deck, meant different things, and I'd only just now, two weeks into our journey, gotten to recognize the dinner whistle, so a horn was something new altogether.

The ship, Phoenix's Pride, had six decks in total. Only a single deck was used for storage, as most of the storage was done through special items on Awakened crew members. In fact, I had several huge crates of supplies, from food, to rope, to clothing, to spices even, that I'd purchased in hopes of trading and keeping my people supplied if I needed to take an army through the portal.

And of course, my own teams of Awakened would have spatial storage devices filled with all the supplies that an army would require, but it never hurt to be over prepared. I reckoned that between the two massive crates I had and the one each of my companions had, we could feed this entire expedition for a month without worrying about food and supplies. Inventory magic had to be one of the biggest utility boons of our generation. Because of the work of Gilfoy's Emporium, the rare rings and bags were a thing of the past, now anyone with enough wealth could have spatial storage devices.

The magic that encased the upper deck made it so not even the cool breeze of the evening air could be felt as we made it to the top deck. Sailors, manning the sails and scrubbing the deck, went about their business, while we tried to stay out of the way. Much of the deck had devices covered by thick wood bracings and hidden from view, but I heard them hum and new it had to do with controlling the devices that allowed flight, but not understanding much more than that.

It was because of the need for so much weight and space to be taken up by these magical machines that we'd had to have less passengers come than I originally wanted. With Kora's backing, I'd wanted to bring a hundred or more Runeforged, but I'd had to settle with only eighteen of her strongest. I didn't know what we'd face when we arrived, but the strength of arms and magic that these Runeforged had shown was a tool I'd not be caught without. All the Runeforged I'd spoken with, Ventus included, seemed happy about the deployment, especially when I told them they'd be paid for their time.

I left Verena behind to help manage Blackridge Keep and my many endeavors, but most days I wished she'd come, or I'd gotten another assistant to deal with how many people seemed to want my attention. If it wasn't an invitation to the captain's dinner, it was a meeting with Felin to be dressed down for my reckless, but effective tactics while on a griffin. There were others that wanted my time as well but sufficed to say that I wanted more time alone than I was getting.

Life on a ship was crowded so when the horns stopped and I heard what they were calling out, my heart leapt.

"Land on the horizon!" A lookout called, then blew into his horn, its call being answered by several more ships as they all made flight corrections aiming downward. It was the first time that I felt a bit of vertigo from the ship's sudden change in direction. I was due for a scouting mission in about three hours, so I wondered if the current scouts had found the island or not, if not, where were they?

The deck became even more a flurry of activity and I headed for the launch platform, deciding I'd do best to get out of the way and see what waited for us below.

"You going down without us?" Alayna asked, pulling out the white figurine of her pegasus. "We are coming."

"You are welcome to," I said, shooting a smile over my shoulder but not slowing my beeline for the launch deck.

I made it to the launch deck only to find Kora already there with her Runeforged. "I've been working on this series of upgrades for months, but please remember only to activate them when you absolutely need them as they take much essence to use properly." She was speaking to the gathered Runeforged, Ventus stepped forward first, bowing his head.

Kora put her hand on his chest and his runes flared. Suddenly, blue-green energy flared out of his back forming feathered wings with a wingspan to match a griffin. Kora nodded at him, and Ventus jumped off, going straight into a swift dive, his new translucent wings folding around him as he descended. One by one she did the same to each of the Runeforged, making no noticeable change that I could see but gifting them with a unique ability to summon temporary wings, a useful trick when flying among the clouds.

When only Kora was left, I stepped forward. "Do you need a lift?" I asked, but she just smiled and jumped off the edge. Wings of swirling and sparking energy shot out from her back as she descended to the island as well. Not wanting to be left behind or outdone, I summoned Ares and told her we needed to reach the ground in haste.

She screeched in challenge, and we were off, moving as fast as we could for the island below. It was all very exciting, passing by the Runeforged and other riders who had all transitioned into gliding. But Ares, determined to be the first, kept her wings folded in until the very last second. We skimmed so close to the water that I was worried we'd be pulled under, but being this close to land nothing disturbed the water's stillness.

The island was hardly what I'd call expansive, getting my first good look at it as we approached from just a dozen feet above the sea's level. From our vector of approach, I determined that a good ten percent of the western edge, where we were headed, was all beach. The middle of the island had a sizable mountain poking out from the infestation of trees and greenery. It wasn't just that there were a lot of trees, but there were so many that it looked like a sea of green with a tiny section of beach around the edge of the island.

I was no cartographer, nor could I judge distances so well from far off, but I'd say that it was no longer than two miles from the centermost mountain in a fairly even circle, almost as if the entire island was just a mountain sticking out of the sea, so steep was the transition from beach to forest. I saw no signs of life, no boats, nor sections of trees cleared out. However, as we approached, I did see movement on the beach and used Inspect on one of many the creatures before it disappeared, some diving into the water and the one I Inspected disappearing with several others into the forest beyond.

Naga Sorceress, Level 40

If I'd seen what I thought I'd saw, then this island had a snake infestation, and I wasn't keen on having to deal with snakes that could live in the water and the forest. At level 40 they wouldn't be the hardest monsters to kill, but they'd be a challenge for some of the elves that had come. Sure, I'd seen Felin and others show a strength potential far above even my own, but it had been small actions that gave it away. Like the time I was on patrol with Felin and he jumped off his griffin, similar to how I had, and wrapped his arms around the maw of a wyvern to keep it from shooting fire at his Ash Flight riders.

I'd joked with him over drinks that he'd done exactly what I'd been chewed out for doing, but he laughed. He claimed that he was never in any danger, but I had nearly died from falling into the sea. So as long as I don't hit the water again, I'd be praised instead of reprimanded, got it. He hadn't thought my conclusions were as humorous as I did, but I'd gotten a feel for his strength that day as an *Awakened*, and it was vast.

We hit the beach and I ordered Ares to take to the sky, reporting anything she saw from above. She did so, understanding as well as I the importance of having eyes in the sky. My sword was out as I walked on the yellow sand and made my way toward the forest's edge.

Several thump, thump, thump, sounds caught my attention and I turned to see the Runeforged landing, their wings disappearing the moment they touched the ground. Ventus approached with another Runeforged wearing red and white, similar to how Ignis used to dress. In fact, the longer I looked at it the more my jaw opened in surprise.

"Ignis? Is that you?" I asked, dumbfounded.

"I am Fotia," the Runeforged said, tilting its head to the side. Its voice was distinctly male, different from Ignis in every way. "However, I have been made aware that before my Core, this body had another. Her name was Ignis."

"He was companion to Ignis and witnessed her death," Ventus said, as if it were just a side note of information hardly worth mentioning. "We are prepared to go hunt the snake-like creatures that escaped into the forest and waters. However, I believe Nero and his team of water-based magic users should be stationed at the beach. These waters hold dangers far greater than the serpentine monsters we witnessed. I can feel the power of the water in the air, thick and prevalent."

He had changed so much since our first meeting, seeming more unique and personable than ever before. "I agree, let's wait another minute for my companions and we will make teams to scour the edges of the forest. But remember, Ventus, safety first and don't let Fotia burn the forest down." I added the last bit as an afterthought, thinking it funny, but Ventus just tilted his head to look at me.

"He will not use his powers without care, you have my word," Ventus said, perhaps still had a bit of the stiffness that seemed so prevalent in Runeforged.

When the rest landed, the boats taking their time to land slow and steady as they neared the ocean's surface, we split into groups of five and spread out to search for threats in a grid layout. I had several patrols walk the perimeter of the forest's edge. While no more than a hundred feet into the forest, another group walked alongside them, close enough that any danger would be detected and honed in on. And then a final group further out but still within earshot for a horn blast to be heard, each team on the outer edge given such a horn in case they were needed.

I was among the furthest ones out with Alayna, Creed, Fred, and Fran. Kora had taken up position on the beach, summoning a Rex to stand guard with her and the water-based Runeforged, Nero and his lot. Feeling the beach was plenty protected, I'd sent word to Ares to watch the treetops above me, and spoke with Steph'en, telling him that it would be best if the Ash Flight held the skies and reported anything they saw to the ground forces. He agreed and they swooped low over the trees, looking for threats, as well as scanning the shallow waters for threats.

It was about fifteen minutes into our outer edge search, when horns began to go off closer to the beach. "Back to the beach," I said, turning to Alayna, but as I turned, I saw a spear flying through the air toward her head. Not knowing what else to do, I cast Lightning Bolt on it and shattered it before it could reach her.

"Watch out," I yelled as we turned to face a dozen or more snake-like people slithering toward us from deeper in the forest.

A barrier of golden light kicked up in front of us as we got into position, ready to fight. Creed let loose an arc of frost followed by a wall of ice that separated two of the snake people from the rest. Fred was there with his fire a moment later, not in the white form but his soft orange fire. They screamed and Fran and I rushed in, cutting them down as they tried to deal with their burns. I got essence, a good indication that Fred hadn't taken it all after all. Whatever Warrick and Kora had done for him, they'd really helped him out. His power might even reach a semblance of normalcy now, however his hair and complexion remained strikingly white and ashy.

Honestly, he looked more corpse than human, as if someone had drained him of all his blood and left the body out in the moonlight. Although my ears could still hear his heartbeat, it was as slow as ever.

The ice wall shattered, and ten angry snake people rushed in. I got off an Inspect and found that these were the same creatures I'd seen on the beach, just lower leveled, not a one over level 30 and all of them called *Naga Fighters*. We cut, burnt, and speared them down, before turning our attention to the beach. We made it just in time to see the battle raging on all sides. Naga Fighters, Naga Champions, Naga Sorceress, and even Naga Brutes, disfigured bulbously muscled brute looking snake men, all fought. There must have been at least two hundred of them, but their numbers counted little against the forces they faced.

The Ash Flight were taking out Naga left and right with each swoop. The Runeforged at the water's edge cut down dozens at a time, using the very water the Naga appeared out of, and Kora's Rex was taking a beating by the magics of the sorceress, but giving as good as he was taking, eating up brute after brute. What was more, one of the ships must have sent reinforcements, because there was a line of some fifty elves in armor and spears, cutting and stabbing away at the Naga line.

The battle was on, and we arrived first, the rest of the forest teams slowly coming back in waves. I killed with reckless abandon, monsters were monsters after all and if I could be an effective killer, I'd rather it be against them than my own kind. I took up a place toward the middle and started giving out tactical orders, focusing our troops on the magic users, as they had the highest levels and were the biggest threats.

After only ten minutes of fighting, we'd broken their lines and they fled deeper into the forest or the water, whichever was closest. This wasn't the last we'd seen of these Naga but wouldn't be caught off guard next time. Two elves fell in battle, but my own companions were luckier, the Naga in the forest not being strong enough to defeat even a single one of our groups.

Ares played her part well, giving me a tactical view of the beach and making my job easier. In thanks, I gave her several meat steaks, raw like she liked them, before calling her back to her stone figure.

The first island was found, but if any elves still inhabited here, they were doing a poor job in keeping the local monsters in check.

CHAPTER 56
DARK CLOUDS AHEAD

By the time the rest of the ships landed, we had troops out in full force against the unending waves of Naga that were appearing from both shore and forest. The captain of the Phoenix's Pride and leader of the expedition, Jorn, came to report on how the efforts to explore were going.

"We've discovered a dungeon, but the outpost is in ruins, no survivors to be found. With the enormous population of Naga on this island, we've decided not to set up an outpost here, but if your team wants a crack at the dungeon, I'd say give it a go while we are still holding the area. I've had a team go inside and it's a puzzle dungeon, not a monster to be found."

"Can't say that I've ever done a purely puzzle based dungeon," I said, thinking back over the dungeons I'd done so far. "Could be interesting, what do you think Alayna?"

"I think that puzzles are tricky, and healers can't heal if traps are triggered that kill outright," she said.

"I love puzzles," Beth said, surprising me. I hadn't realized that she'd entered the tent alongside Adathin.

"I'd be interested in clearing it," Adathin said, brightening at the idea of clearing a dungeon.

"I'm with Alayna I think," I said, thinking it over. "I'm okay with a group being sent in but I don't think it's for me."

"Very well, Adathin, get a group together and report back to us when you've finished," Jorn said, dismissing us with a wave us his hand.

"Be careful," I said to Adathin as we left, and he nodded in my direction.

He recruited Zander, Fred, and Fran to his excursion, figuring they needed at least one healer and Fred's sharp mind could be of some assistance. However, when they returned, laughing and obviously having had a great time, it was Fran who had been a great help, figuring out half of all the riddles. Fred had received new robes, still white but with orange and red fringed edges. If the rest of the group had gotten anything, it wasn't immediately noticeable.

"I've secured the lower beaches, but this threat isn't likely to stop its attempts to wrest it back from us," Galt said, reporting to Alayna. She put a hand on his shoulder to pacify him and I watched them exchange a tender look.

"Thank you for coming," she said, and I felt like perhaps I should leave to give them a moment, but Alayna reached down and gripped my hand tight.

"Anything for you, Lady Alayna," Galt said, bowing his head.

She looked around, saw that we were alone and released my hand to go forward and give Galt a hug. I stepped back, giving them the space they needed. It hadn't been easy for them to find time alone and I'm sure there was much they wanted to speak about, so I slipped out of the tent and stood guard outside it. I would give them their privacy and ensure it lasted as long as possible.

After only roughly ten minutes, Galt appeared outside the tent, his eyes a shade redder than normal, though by his demeaner you wouldn't have guessed he'd been crying or showing any emotion. He reached his hand out to me and I grasped it, each of us pressing with immense power but Galt surprised me by being a match for my strength. He smiled and released the grip.

"You're a good man and I'm glad that she has you by her side. Thank you," Galt said, his powerful gaze washing over me and seeing straight through me. He was a powerful personality and likely an even more powerful *Awakened*.

"You're welcome," I said, not knowing what else to say but it was enough. Galt nodded his head once more, looking as gruff as ever, before moving off to be about his guard business.

A part of me wanted to ask how he'd so easily gotten away or out of Lord Variyn's service or if that was even the case. For all I knew he could be just acting as a Royal Guard for Alayna and using that pretext to take several of his guards along for the ride.

Our time on the first island came to a close hours later, and we were off to the open skies once more. The next month came and went with much happening. We lost an entire ship during a monster raid while searching for outpost survivors. However, the crew survived and joined two others staying behind to cull the monsters. The plan was to set up an outpost, but it seemed foolhardy to me, the monsters were just so overpopulated. At that island we stayed an entire week, killing monsters and hunting out queens.

Now we'd traveled to half a dozen other outposts, and we were down to just a dozen ships still on their way to Avalon, but things weren't looking good. The navigators claimed we should have arrived several times, but our course kept getting messed up. I didn't know the specifics but the way they complained made it seem like purposeful sabotage. Whether or not that was true I couldn't say, but I was eager to arrive as well.

"It's time to turn back, our supplies won't last for the trip back if we don't do it soon," Jorn said, we were in a private meeting with myself and a few others, including a few of the other ships' captains.

"We've got our orders, we are to find Avalon, and nothing should stand in our way," said a gruff captain whose name I couldn't recall. He looked more weathered and older than any other elf I'd seen and even had an eye patch over his left eye from an old wound. "My navigators assure me we are close." He added when Jorn began to shake his head.

"I understand your desire to return to the old lands, but you must see the futile path we walk," Jorn said, shaking his head as if he'd already made up his mind.

"I refuse to give up. This quest we've been given is more

important than just finding old lands. The future of magic and our very lives depend on getting to Avalon," I said, infusing as much conviction as I could into my words. I wasn't sure that I'd gotten my point across, but I refused to yield. "And if you turn around now it will be without me. Ares and I will depart and find out own way if we must."

"That would be suicide," Jorn said, giving me a fatherly stern look. "You've got one more week and if we don't find our way then we must turn back. It isn't just the food supplies, but these engines require an immense amount of mana and essence. We've brought a kingdom's worth of wealth to keep them running, but it won't last forever."

"I can infuse essence into stones, just put us down on one of the monster infested islands and I will give you as much essence as you could possibly want," I countered, a sly smile on my face.

This seemed to surprise Jorn and he looked around the room. "Truly you have this ability?" He asked.

"Truly."

"While this might slow our need, it is still a pressing issue as one man can't truly fill the amount of essence we will need, hundreds of thousand per ship per day." Jorn shook his head again, likely torn with what to do next.

"You know my mind on the matter," said the gruff older elf.

"One more week," Jorn said, sticking to his original time frame.

Five days went by when the black cloud appeared on the horizon. All of the navigators said the island would be just through the cloud, so cautiously we approached, ready for anything.

"Ash Flight are all reporting for duty, something in the cloud that might be a threat," Steph'en said, and I began to prepare, getting my cloak and goggles out. I ran to inform the rest of my group to be ready with their mounts just in case, until everyone was ready to take off.

Making it to the sky I saw that the entire horizon had been filled with black and red clouds, completely and utterly unnatural looking. The wind blew hard in our direction the moment Ares and I were free from the ship's deck. It was as unnatural as the color of the clouds or how high they seemed to be. After weeks of flying this high above the clouds I'd gotten used to breathing the thinner air, my *Awakened* body able to adapt to even the harshest of environments. But rarely had we encountered much if any wind this high, so fighting against it to get a better look at the cloud was wholly unusual.

I watched Steph'en, he gave the hand signal that our squad would be the first to go into the clouds, so I pressed myself low on Ares to make it easy for her against the wind. She sent me an appreciative thought and I send back an encouraging exchange of words to her. Out of the corner of my eye I saw my team take flight around us. The one squad's number had just swelled from six to sixteen, even Kora flew out beside us. What lay in wait in the black clouds better be prepared, because if it turned out to be hostile then we'd surely have the numbers to deal with it.

Steph'en was on point, and I was just behind him, so I

saw the attack the moment it happened. A tentacle larger than Steph'en and his griffin, slammed into him and a moment later he was gone, not even able to make a sound before it wrapped around him completely. Acting on instinct alone I cast a Lightning Strike on the tentacle, diving for it, javelin ready. The large tentacle uncoiled and the limp forms of Steph'en and his griffin fell toward the deadly waters below.

Four of the Ash Flight moved with speed and precision, one catching Steph'en and the other his griffin before they fell to their death, however, with how limp their bodies appeared I was worried. I signaled with my hands to be careful and pull back, but it was too late. Seemingly endless tentacles appeared and began snatching riders from their mounts or crushing them all together. I saw Kora get wrapped up, but she used her ability to turn her limbs into swords and soon she was free.

I javelined a tentacle just as it tried to wrap around Alayna and her mount, just in time to see one reach for Fred. But his fire went white instantly and rushed outward, completely burning away the tentacle. We were dealing with something vastly out of our wheelhouse, and I didn't know what to do next. So I fought, and I destroyed as many tentacles as I could.

All of the remaining Ash Flight were fighting expertly, but most of my time was spent keeping my friends from being wrapped up by the tentacles. I was so distracted that when the black and red energy shot out from deeper in the clouds, I barely avoided getting fried completely, thanks to the skill of Ares. She sensed the energy and forced us downward, barely missing it. However, one of the Ash Flight wasn't so lucky, when the energy cleared, and we traveled above the clouds again I saw nothing left of the rider and one of our ships was smoking from a massive hole in its side.

I made the sign for everyone to pull back, we needed the support of the ships up close and the powerful elf wizards aboard them. Felin took up my call for retreat, signaling it as fiercely as I had. Soon the remaining forces flew for the ships, but I hung back, ready to slow the monster if I could. Fred appeared at my side, his hippogryph screeching in protest.

"Hit it as hard as you can," I screamed the words into the open air and Fred nodded that he understood.

White fire swirled around him like a coiling snake ready to strike. Meanwhile, I began to flood essence and mana into a Fireball that would rock the very foundations of the world around us. I only had half my mana to deal with, but I committed every point of it that I could into a fireball that grew to the size of a small wagon above my head. With Fred's white flame beating back the tentacles as they tried to strike out at us, I let it grow until the very flesh on my arms sizzled and boiled. Then I threw it out into the mass of tentacles where I hoped a face would be.

The moment I released it we dove away, Fred following my lead. We'd need to be as far away as possible, but I looked over my shoulder to try and get an Inspect off, but each attempt failed, as I could only see the tentacles. My attack collided with a mess of tentacles; the flying tentacled monster let out a cry so loud it nearly knocked me unconscious. It didn't end, but we got far enough away that it muted my hearing and no longer threatened to bring me into unconsciousness.

I already had a terrible headache from the low mana, so the sound of the screeching cry only made things worse. Pulling a mana potion from my inventory, I drank deeply, feeling a measure of the tension release as my mana pool began to refill. It was like someone released a powerful vice grip on my mind and I finally snapped back to my usual self.

"Up Ares," I cried, pulling on her reins. I didn't need to be so dramatic about it, as she was connected with me so closely that she reacted before I even spoke. We climbed and saw that my explosive fireball had cleared a measure of the black clouds, revealing what lay ahead. I used Inspect and my jaw dropped open.

Elite Sky Kraken, Level 120

My Inspect didn't give me any health pool information, but just from looking at it I'd say we barely scratched its surface. What could we do against such an overwhelming foe? My mind snapped back to the only other Kraken I'd slain, it had been in a dungeon, and we'd had weapons that did massive damage, the only way we had stood a chance. I prayed to anything listening that the wizards the elves had brought were worth their weight in power.

Why hadn't I insisted that Warrick come with us on the

ship? This was the kind of foe he'd be able to truly match himself against. Maybe I could open a portal and bring him now? It was a plan, but it would take me out of the fight for a while and I wasn't sure that was the right move, for as little damage as I'd done overall, the Kraken now had less than half of its tentacles ready to kill us. I'd blown at least two dozen completely away from the halfway point onward.

The ships were aligning themselves into a loose formation, some higher, some lower, but none too close to each other. The smoking ship held steady in the back, not losing anymore altitude but on fire and at risk. Fred broke off, headed for that ship and I watched, ready to re-engage the kraken to keep it back if needed.

Fred reached the burning ship and suddenly all the fire swirled and surrounded him. I wasn't worried, as his class ability to control fire was one of his most powerful abilities. Soon all the fire had gone out and seemed to disappear into Fred. With the fires out, Fred flew back and joined formation with Fran and the rest of the riders, perched on the deck of the Phoenix's Pride. Felin signaled I join them, and I did so.

Ares cut through the air like we owned the very skies we traveled through, landing gracefully beside a space left open for us beside Felin.

"I've lost six riders in as many minutes." Felin's tone was one that walked the line of rage and calmness. "The ships will come in as close as they dare, and our wizards will call down the elements on this monstrosity. When you were close did you happen to get a read on it, I can't from this distance."

"I did," I said, telling him the name and level I'd gotten, but not a read on its health. He nodded solemnly and sent some of his riders to inform the different ships, each of them flying away. Captain Jorn came up and he relayed what I'd told him.

For his part, Jorn just nodded and spoke with confidence. "I will inform the casters. With our combined might, not even this monster will stand in our way." Then, directed at me as he turned to walk away, he said, "This island better be worth it."

"It is," I assured him, swallowing hard.

There was a part of me that hoped that it truly was and that we were up to the challenge when we finally made it to the shores. If outside the island we were encountering impossibly strong monsters, like this floating sky kraken, then what were the chances we'd be able to face off against the monsters found on Avalon? It didn't seem good, but I couldn't let those thoughts get the better of me right now. I had the power to make a difference, so I would get out there and fight until the bitter end.

I downed another mana potion, needing to top myself off as soon as possible. It helped, bringing me to seventy-five percent and my mana regeneration doing the rest to get me up. My stamina had taken a little hit, but it regenerated so fast that the toll flying took, was barely even registered.

"What's the plan?" Creed asked, his death steed trotting up beside me. "Do we wait for the casters, or should we run interference on those tentacles so they can focus on the kraken's body?"

"I don't know," I said, being brutally honest. I'd waged war and fought battles and dungeons, but nothing prepared me for fighting such an overwhelmingly strong monster. What advantages did we have, what tricks could we play when the foe so wholly out matched us? I pinched my eyes closed as I took everything I knew and tried to figure out how to kill such an impossible foe.

Opening my eyes, I looked out at the kraken and lost what little breath I had left. It's broken tenacles, the damage Fred and I had done, were regenerating. What weakness did this thing have if any? I used my most powerful attack, even infusing it with essence, but all that work had been for naught. It had the ability to regenerate at an alarming rate.

We wouldn't win this fight by chipping slowly away at its health, we needed to deliver a deathly blow. What was the one thing all monsters had that they couldn't do without? Their monster cores, but it would be impossible to locate or reach. Its brain perhaps? But how to pierce its skin and skull to reach its brain? Then an impossible and foolhardy plan formed in my head. How powerful could Phantom Thrust be if I infused it with a ton of essence?

"I have an idea, but it likely won't work and even if it does, I'm going to need a miracle to get away in one piece," I said, everyone was paying attention to me now as I explained my plan.

It was simple, everything had a brain and doing damage to it would end even the strongest of creatures. I knew that as someone who'd passed their second threshold, I could take an arrow to the face and into the brain and likely survive, but if my brains were scrambled, even I'd die from it. So, I would somehow get atop this massive monster, and stab it with Phantom Thrust, then cast Lightning Strike right onto my blade, scrambling what little brains this monster must have.

"That is the dumbest plan I've ever heard, and I've come up with some doozies myself," Emory said, shaking his head.

"We will need to all come in close to deal with the tentacles, but you really think you have what it takes to get through the head and into the brain?" Felin asked.

"I do, but it won't be without risk," I said, then relayed the plan to Ares. She wasn't a fan, and for the moment, was refusing to even consider it. "Not sure I can get Ares on board though." I added, smiling at how much she cared for me.

The captain was less enthusiastic about the plan, instead assuring us that the casters might be able to deal with the threat if we could get the ships close enough. He went on record saying that he didn't endorse my plan, but he needed Ash Flight and any other fliers to deal with the tentacles if his ships were to survive. We committed to keeping them occupied, while the casters took their shot, but in my mind, I knew it would come down to me, as it had so many other times.

My sense of honor and need to do what was right pushed me into knowing this was the only way. Another part of me, newer than the rest, suggested that I was merely insane, but I pushed it down. When given an impossible task, you needed to do the impossible, and likely stupid, thing to see it done. Sure, I didn't want to jump atop a monster the size of a small town, but it wasn't moving and according to the navigators it blocked our passage to Avalon, one such navigator suggesting it was directly over the island.

"Time to deal with some tentacles," I said to no one in particular, but I pet Ares's head as I spoke. "Be swift and deadly. We won't lose any more if we do this smart."

Steph'en was going to make it, but he'd broken several bones and was out of the fight, however, his griffin hadn't survived. A fact that someone had told him and the moan of pain I'd heard from him made me realize just how close I'd come to losing Ares so many times and a part of me wanted to leave her out of this fight. I couldn't bear anymore loss, not from someone so closely bonded to me like Ares.

We took off into the air and I sent out my thoughts to my friends, wishing them the best of luck. The tentacles came swift and deadly, but not as swift as Ares. She dove inward, letting it get close enough that she dug her talons into it, drawing out black blood. As we attacked, I conserved as much mana as I dared, only striking out when I felt it was absolutely necessary. Behind me, on the ships, I felt immense energy being shifted about and I took my eyes off the tentacles for a moment to see what the casters were up to.

Elves, both young and old, stood five to a ship, swirling power around them as they prepared to attack. I could sense barriers being erected around the entire ships and decided that they must have at least two of them feeding it to keep such a huge target shielded. The remaining three per ship called forth lightning, fire, and even ice to do their bidding. Great lances of lightning struck out from one, ice shards as big as a horse from another, and swirling fire to match even Fred, all shot outward.

Each attack was aimed at the kraken's mid-section, right between the eyes. Unfortunately, we weren't disabling enough tentacles, they swarmed in front of the face taking the brunt of the damage. However, the casters weren't done, volley after volley they struck until the tentacles were all disarmed, leaving only the massive bulk of the kraken and its ugly face. Rows and rows of sharp teeth flashed as energy began to form in its mouth.

"Dive!" I screamed, signaling frantically to the riders around me.

As one we dove, and the energy just missed killing over a dozen of us at once. However, the lead ship, Phoenix's Pride, wasn't so lucky. It took the attack straight on, the shell barrier surrounding it shattering on contact, but doing enough that the ship wasn't blown into two pieces right off. Instead, the outer hull, so seemingly impenetrable moments before, now fell apart all over. The fires were put out almost immediately by the fire wizard, but the two that were shielding it had fallen down, each of them unconscious.

The kraken prepared another energy attack, I could feel it drawing in power. If I didn't do something we'd lose the Phoenix's Pride and all hands. Telling Ares my intentions, she agreed, and we used our diving momentum to gain speed and head right for the injured Kraken. I cast an infused Lightning Strike right at the monster's massive eyes, striking on target as I neared. This caused its attention to come right onto me, but I kept closing the distance, casting an infused Firebolt at its other eye. It didn't do as much damage, but I definitely had its attention now.

A line of powerful energy shot out at us, and we dove, just barely keeping ahead of it as it cut a line in the sky. Ares was so precise with her movements that we ensured that the ship wasn't hit despite the attack missing us. Her speed was legendary, and I felt the edges of my vision blur with black as we turned against the momentum we'd gathered.

The energy attack cut off just as a dozen tentacles regrew themselves and it began to move for the first time since we'd engaged it. It was going for the ships, tentacles ready to rip them apart. Another dozen had repaired themselves and the creature pulsed a red haze that hadn't been there before.

This fight wouldn't end well, I needed to enact my plan!

I sent word to Ares, urging her that this was the only way and that I'd be safe. She didn't like it, but she felt the desperation across our bond and we began to climb, the Kraken ignoring us as it seemed unable to catch her and didn't care to waste its time. It was good for us, as everyone else engaged the tentacles and the casters all seemed to be recovering and not attacking.

I'd done the impossible before, I just had to do it one more time. We flew higher than the kraken and my breath struggled to process the thin air. The plan was simple enough, we'd dive straight down onto its head and Ares would escape so that she could catch me once I leapt off. I had no idea if my plan could even work, but we had to try something, otherwise fleeing was our only option.

As if triggered by my thoughts, I saw half a dozen ships break off and pull back out of the fight. The rest positioned themselves in front of Phoenix's Pride, she must be unable to move after the damage she'd taken. This was a last desperate move, so my plan had to work.

Tentacles reached out for us as we dove, but fire, javelins, and more broke them out of our way at the last second. My team fought against all odds to keep me alive, I could do this!

Ares dodged a tentacle and dug her claws into another to help us slow as we reached the massive head. It was so big that I was no more the size of one of its eyes in height. I was so small and insignificant that I wondered if it even realized I was on its head. In answer to that, several tentacles shot out, trying to sweep us off it. Suddenly Fran, Emory, Fred, and Alayna, landed atop the head and cut down the tentacles.

"No!" I screamed as a tentacle swiped for Alayna. But out of seemingly nowhere and atop a black flying pegasus Galt appeared. A spear appeared in his hands, and he cut the tentacle apart as if it was made of nothing. Black thick blood covered him, but he kept fighting, spearing and slashing with the power of a well-seasoned fighter.

I watched preparing myself to strike, in awe of his show of power. Just when I thought all was well, his spear was knocked from his grasp by a tentacle while another came down atop him. Alayna screamed and I looked on in disbelief. Galt had just been crushed, but as I watched, the tentacle quivered, and he lifted it with his two hands. Confident that he was going to be alright, I turned my attention back to my task at hand, but then another scream from Alayna brought me back in time to see Galt flung off the edge, and Kora appearing with wings of glowing energy.

She dove over after him, but he had a head start and you could only fall so fast. I wished them the best, but I needed to act now.

Creed appeared next, each of them fighting on their mounts and creating space for me to work. My heart swelled as Ares refused to leave my side as well, digging her claws into its flesh and taking up a defensive position.

I wasn't alone and I wouldn't need to do this alone. Together we could do the impossible, together we would not fail!

Following my instincts, I channeled even more essence into my sword than it was meant to hold. I felt my attributes swell and the sword felt uneasy in my hands, but I pushed it further until energy cracked all around me. Then I infused my body to the breaking point, energy swelling like a flame around me, all green and blue. Cracks of lightning sparked all around as I gathered every bit of power I could. When I ran out of essence, I pulled from around me and felt some come from my teammates.

Using that raw energy, I focused it into my abilities. Phantom Thrust was my main focus, but somehow, I knew I was also activating Speed Burst, Power Strike, Stamina Surge, Swift Strike, and Force Wave into a single attack. Pulling it all together, I struck downward, ready to channel my spells into the attack the moment I pierced through.

My strike hit and the kraken shook and screeched its mighty cry, but I didn't stop. Blood flowed from my ears and my teammates fell from the attack, but I plunged it deeper until it was as deep as I could go.

Then, pulling even more essence from around me and my party, I cast Blink to bring myself deeper, then while my entire body was inside the soft tissue of its skull, I cast Lightning Strike and felt the power flow through me and into the kraken. So much power and damage flowed through me that I started taking damage, and lots of it.

As I barely held on to consciousness and my ability to breathe in the darkness of the kraken's head, I cast Arcane Missile, Firebolt, then forced my last mana into a Fireball. I don't know when I lost consciousness, but before I did, I felt the greatest wave of essence I'd ever felt before and then everything went still.

CHAPTER 57
DARK NIGHT

The first time I woke up, the air around me was screaming and I thought I saw water below me, but my mind drifted back into unconsciousness a moment later. My dreams were wild and filled with visions of death and destruction. Some part of me realized that if I could dream, even a nightmare, that I was still alive, and this was good. The second and last time I woke up it was on a familiar, yet uncomfortable bed, aboard the Phoenix's Pride.

Looking around, I saw that somehow Ares had found her way down into the lower decks of the ship and laid on the ground beside my bunk. I reached out to her with my mind, and she perked up immediately, letting out a low screech of joy. Her head nuzzled so hard against me that I was sure I'd take damage from it, but my body, despite being in a fair bit of pain, was in solid condition, all things considered.

"Can't a man get a moment of rest after wrestling with

sharks as big as a horse?" A gruff voice I recognized as Galt, sounded from above. He'd been staying in another room all together, so I wondered at why he had been placed with me in here when I realized that we weren't in our normal beds at all.

The gear and storage containers we kept inside, as well as where the window was located was all wrong. I noticed the beds to the left of me were filled with injured elves, one of which I recognized as Steph'en.

Someone attending us must have heard Galt because I heard footsteps and then to my supreme elation, I saw Alayna appear above me, all smiles and red eyes.

"You're awake!"

"I think so," I said, then glancing up toward Galt I added, "Should we go talk somewhere so Galt can rest?"

"He's just grumpy that Kora didn't let him fight the sharks he found in the water, kept saying that he'd brought them low enough that it was his essence to collect. But she scooped him right out and got him to safety. Bless her," Alayna said, glancing over her shoulder.

Kora was there, standing with Fred and Fran by the door, all three smiled in my direction. Fred looked normal enough, but Fran had red around her eyes, and I wondered what had her so upset.

"Did every uhm," I took a deep breath as I suddenly found it hard to breathe and realized that perhaps I was more injured than I first thought. "Did everyone make it? We won, right? The monster is dead?"

Alayna cast her eyes down and I braced myself for bad

news. I sat up and looked all around the room, no Emory, no Zander, no Ismene, no Creed. Were they just busy elsewhere or had something happened?

"We beat the monster, it crashed into the shallows right at the edge of Avalon, but we haven't landed yet. Just rest for now, we won, but not without a high price." Alayna wouldn't meet my eyes, but I needed to know who.

"Who?" I asked, desperation in my voice.

"Creed and Emory haven't been found yet, Zander and Ismene are out helping search parties look. They fell close enough to the shore that they could be down there, but swarms of monsters have come to feed off the kraken and the captain won't land yet. We also lost Felin and half of the Ash Flight, plus one third of the casters that fought in the last push. Your attack injured and killed it but not before it took down an entire ship, all hands lost."

I stood, pain be damned, and Ares stood with me, already knowing my mind. I didn't let anyone stop me and I couldn't look them in the eye. "We need to be looking, all of us!" I said, fury growing in my gut. Not Emory, not Creed, no, no, I can't.

The halls were not meant for griffins Ares's size, but she pushed her way through until we made it to the deck. I checked my status and sure enough, I had several conditions like broken bones and internal bleeding, but I had faith in my body's ability to deal with it. Regardless of what I thought, I used Restoring Light on myself and felt all the better for it. Some conditions just didn't heal well quickly and needed the slower regeneration for the best healing, but

I didn't care at this point. I followed that heal by a Mending Touch and the rest of my group caught up with me, Galt included, and he looked worse for wear, cuts on his face still not healed and a limp on his left leg.

"Let's find your men," he growled, hobbling along. "They didn't tell me, otherwise I'd be out looking, we never leave a man behind." His words rolled out of him like an angry Dire Bear's growls. Then he whistled loud and sharp, his black pegasus flying down from seemingly nowhere.

"I'm sorry," Alayna said. "But we couldn't leave your side, not when you were so close to death. You have to understand."

I did, but the anger that kept me moving wouldn't let me admit as much just yet. Instead, I looked at Alayna and leaned in giving her a peck on the lips. "I need to find my friends, no matter what, I will find them."

I had an advantage that those searching might not have as it was more prevalent in casters. Sensing auras, mana, and essence came second nature to me, and I knew what to feel for with them. I could taste their auras now just thinking about them.

Mounting Ares I called out to the others, "I'm fine, if you want to help focus on their auras. Fred, I know you can do as much, so get out here and help."

He nodded at me and pulled out his figurine of his hippogryph, summoning it forth. Turning away, I urged Ares forward until we jumped off the side, her wings unfurling. It was only then as we were connected that I felt her injury. Both wings had broken bones and flying was as painful for her as it was for me to ride. I used Mending Touch on her, but similar to my own injuries, it was just going to take a little time.

Injured and in pain, we went to searching. I started from the outer edge and deeper waters, looking for even the barest of signs that they were beneath the water, dead or alive. The armor and weapons they had would have the smallest bit of essence to them, but I sensed so much that it was hard to pinpoint anything. Closing my eyes as tight as I could manage, I searched back and forth for them.

I crossed others searching with just their eyes and felt a scornful response toward them, despite them doing their best. Don't the remaining casters have magic to help find lost souls. It was then that I saw them pulling someone up from the water ahead, Ares beat her wings despite the pain and got us within visual range.

It wasn't Creed or Emory, but an elf that must have fallen into the water when the ship came down. They were, of course, searching for their own friends and families as well. That just managed to anger me more, despite my better sense knowing that it wasn't fair. After ten minutes I abandoned the idea of finding them out in the deeper waters and went toward the shallow waters around the shore.

The island, hopefully Avalon, was the biggest of the islands we'd come across so far, sprawling forests and the beach covered in ruins of stone towers and mounds that perhaps would have been buildings. Behind me I saw my companions flying, following my lead.

It was as we got closer to the beach that I began to sense

something faint. Closing in on the feeling, my excitement became palpable as I recognized who I was feeling. Emory, his aura as powerful as ever flared somewhere toward the ruins. And as I focused on him, I caught the barest weakest aura beside him, Creed but he wasn't in good shape. If I didn't know any better, I'd say he was either newly dead or so close that it wouldn't matter if we didn't arrive soon.

I signaled overhead for everyone to follow me, a wasted signal as they were all right behind me, but I wanted them to know that I'd found something. Emory's aura suddenly diminished greatly, and I heard a roar of fury like one I'd never heard from him before as I circled a ruined building of stone. All around a tall stone doorway, trying to force their way in, were green men with crab like skinned armor and bone like weapons, swords, spears, and even maces.

They had shells on their pauldrons and pointy ears like an elf, when I Inspected them, I got the name they went by as well as the level of the one I'd picked out.

Koralent Fighter, Level 39

I had no idea what a Koralent was as I'd never heard of such a race before, but they walked on two legs, used weapons, and spoke a guttural language, so perhaps they could be reasoned with.

Another yell of rage from inside pushed all those thoughts away and I unlatched my belt just as we slammed down amidst them all. Ares lashed out, killing one with a single strike to the neck and turning to slash out at any that tried to approach. I hit one with Lightning Strike, then slashed out with Force Wave, infusing it. The attack cut through three of them before dissipating. Before I could do another attack, my group landed, each of them lashing out with their magic or steel.

The group scattered and ran before us, despite being it being a two to one situation, so deadly was our initial onslaught. I rushed to the door and saw Emory, beaten and bloody, standing over Creed's broken form, ready to fight to the death. He faced off against five of the Koralents but refused to give any ground.

His eyes were practically glowing red from an enrage ability he'd used, when he happened to glance at the door. His aura flared and his voice cut through the din of battle as one of them attacked and he defended.

"Fuck yes!" He screamed, then fell into hysterical laughter. Cutting and bashing away with his shield.

I wasted no time, he'd fought long and hard enough, now it was our turn. Rushing forward I took the head of one unsuspecting Koralent and white flames engulfed the next. To my joyous surprise, Emory yelled at Fred for that, "That was my kill!" He yelled.

Galt limped in, spear ready. He stabbed two in the same amount of time it took me to cut the head off of one and the battle was nearly over before it even had a chance to begin.

I laughed while dancing to the side to dodge a blade strike, while Emory put down the one that dared turn its back on him. The battle was over in seconds, and I hugged Emory, while throwing a Mending Touch on him. Alayna was over Creed washing heal after heal on him, but he didn't stir.

"He's alive, but barely," Alayna said. "We need to get him back to the ship."

It took some work, as Ares and I couldn't take on any extra passengers due to injuries, but we made it back to the ship and more skilled healers than us worked on Creed. They assured us that he would live, but that we were all meant to be resting. My fatigue was catching up to me now that I'd gotten my friends back, and I gladly accepted a bed beside Galt and Emory. The three of us laughed and joked like only those that had faced death together could.

All was coming together, and I finally felt a sense of relief. Even the monsters on the surface hadn't seemed so strong, we truly had a chance. That was when I overheard them saying we needed to make an emergency landing as the stores of essence had been destroyed during the fight on the Phoenix's Pride.

CHAPTER 58
WELCOME TO AVALON

I rested as long as I dared, reports from our landing were not good and the monsters I overheard them speak of sounded much stronger than the Koralent we'd faced when rescuing Emory and Creed. What we needed right now was backup, surely they had casters that could open portals now that we'd arrived at our final destination. That had been the plan after all, both sides bringing in reinforcements to help secure the island once we'd made landfall.

I got out of bed, Creed still sleeping soundly but Emory and Galt nowhere to be seen and I made it to the door without any issue. One of the healers saw me but said nothing about me moving around, my ribs felt much better, and I could breathe without any issue now. I'd returned Ares, despite her protests, to the figurine so that she could heal properly as well.

The ship was a bustle of activity, barrels and supplies being moved here and there as I walked through the main corridors toward the top of the ship. I ran into Ventus on my way up and got him to fill me in as I walked.

"Natives are coming in waves, losses have already begun to mound, several Runeforged have been damaged. I had been sent to fetch you, the spell weavers are having issues opening portals and want you to try. Though I don't know why, the air is so thick with life here that magic flourishes."

"What do you mean, it flourishes?" I asked, as we came out atop the deck, and I got a good look at what lay ahead of us.

It was a battle for sure, lines of elves mixed with Runeforged and even a Rex stood in a line waiting for the forces of Koralent and the monsters that gathered around them, to attack. Among their ranks I saw Naga, giant spiders, mutated looking fire monkeys, and more. From what little I could see from where they formed up on the beaches, there had to be at least five hundred, if not more.

With just a single ship down, the rest still moved above us in the sky, and I wondered why they also hadn't joined us, because we needed the numbers right now. Our measly group accounted for a hundred and fifty strong, the rest going about their business unloading supplies, tending to the sick, or repairing the damage to the ship. A few hundred feet away and halfway washed out into the water was the remains of the Kraken.

It was enormous, most of its body untouched and floating in the water, but its head and a man-sized hole in its head, pointed toward the ship. Its eyes, one ruined and the other whole, looked in my direction almost accusatory as if it was still placing the blame of its death on me. I did a quick check on my essence and gawked at the amount I had, over two million from killing it when I also took essence from my band.

"Sorry, kraken, I'd kill you twice if I had the chance," I muttered. Ventus looked at me but seemed to realize that my words weren't meant for him and so didn't comment. It surprised me at every interaction how much Runeforged grew in their ability to speak and communicate effectively. Whether that was from knowing when not to speak or what to say at the right time, it was truly amazing.

"The spell weavers are just there," Ventus said, pointing at a group of three men in long robes and a few with wispy beards.

I slid down a robe to get off the massive ship and joined the casters as they argued over something I didn't quite understand as they weren't speaking a language that I recognized.

"Problems opening a portal?" I asked looking around the group.

"Ah, Caldor Miles I assume?" The youngest looking of the three said, his voice was a smooth baritone. "I am Sage Paultelluh'ah, but you can call me Paul. It appears that something is blocking our attempts to create portals here and I was wondering if you'd be willing to give it a try. Often how we learn and come about certain spells can be slightly different, but the three of us all learned from the same master wizard, so our methods can't be tested properly, and the other ships refuse to land at the moment."

I listened and nodded where needed, before speaking. "I'll give it my best attempt, but I have to say that opening Portals isn't my strong suit, however I can teleport back to Blackridge and have Warrick come back with me, he's a master at opening portals."

"Warrick?" One of the elderly elves asked. "Sounds familiar, he is human and not elf?"

"Last time I checked," I said, trying to inject some humor into the conversation and failing spectacularly.

"Please," Paul said, smiling gently, "give it a try."

I nodded and stepped back so I didn't accidentally take one of them with me. Focusing as I had done many times before, I reached out and began the spell. I could see the place I wanted to go, felt my magic make the connection, and the last little bit that pulled on me and sent me through began. Then just as quick, it fizzled out, something cutting off my spell just as it was about to activate.

"Huh," I said, looking at the three of them with a perplexed look. "Let me try again."

I tried again, then once more before finally accepting that we were absolutely fucked.

CHAPTER 59
MONSTER INVASION

After much deliberation and orders by Jorn, Captain of the Phoenix's Pride, the other ships landed, and we began to push back the waves of monsters attacking us. It wasn't an easy battle, nor did it come without major losses, mostly elven crew members that were being conscripted into fighting despite not being Awakened. Jorn, myself, and Zander, along with a few others, formed up ranks and assigned proxy level titles to those we could, trying anything possible to help turn the tides.

"If the eastern flank isn't fortified it will break within the hour," Jorn said, gesturing to where a force of five hundred, mostly conscripted crew members with a mix of seasoned veterans stood against hordes of monsters led by the fierce hordes of the Koralent. It was a testament to the power of the remaining casters and their defensive spells that our lines hadn't crumbled the moment these higher-level monsters appeared.

It wouldn't have been so bad if not for the tactical retreats and surges the Koralent kept doing. Their lines were a sea of ever shifting numbers at the edge of a vast ruined city covered in trees. Because of this, they could swell their numbers in random places, pushing hard while the other sides retreated. Normally I'd say this was a good thing, it meant we'd be able to shift down as well and force them to overextend, but with our weakened soldiers we didn't have the punch required to deal with them.

The plan had been simple, when we arrive at Avalon, where we expected resistance of some kind or another, we'd move in military forces and push them back. Without the might of either Blackridge Keep's military or the Elven nation we were just prolonging the inevitable. I so badly wanted to be helpful and be fighting out at the front lines along with my companions, but I knew the importance of having good direction for our forces and if not me, then who?

"Call for the Runeforged to shift to the eastern flank and push hard. They'll be enough to swing the advantage to our side, while forcing the Koralent to consider another area to force through," I said, a runner looked to Jorn, who nodded his assent, and ran off to spread the word.

"We've got a small team of alchemist working on some powerful chemical explosions using some material they've found on the beach; I'm thinking of having the remaining Ash Flight to deliver it on the enemy just as they surge next. Thoughts?" Jorn asked, he really was deferring to my experience which seemed a bit odd to me, but I accepted it for what it was, he was a captain of a ship not a general and I was doing a service for them by commanding the forces.

"I think that would be wise, but make sure they aim for the tree line, I don't want our troops to be entangled in whatever mess is being thrown down. Next, I really think that we should focus on..." my words faltered as troops began to yell from behind us. We held a small reserve force at the water's edge, as well as skeleton crews on the ships to get them to safety if needed.

Ice formed in huge spikes above the ships and began raining down on the helpless crew members. Not a single ship was exempt from this new attack, and I was already calling forth Ares so I could get a better look.

"Pull troops from the front, we need archers to reach whatever is out in the water attacking, it's probably Naga, so be ready for a ground assault as well. I'm going to get a better look."

Jorn nodded and I took off atop Ares. She sent me feelings of comfort and readiness for battle, but I assured her that right now we just needed to see our enemy and get intel. With the Ash Flight cut so thin, a major loss to the Elven nation considering how rare griffins were, it was up to me to get intel from the sea. I'd sent the last of the Ash Flight with bows to pepper the enemy lines until signaled to do otherwise, so me mounting up was the fastest option.

I saw instantly what was attacking us and I didn't even need to use Inspect to be sure. Naga, hundreds of them, their arms held upward and visible in the cool blue water. Groups of two and three Naga worked together to cast the spells that were pelting the ship, I could sense that they were combining their output potential by mixing their auras. If could disrupt even a few of them, it might break off their initial efforts.

That was when I saw several Naga with bows that looked to be made of coral with arrows of sharpened shells. I'd do well to avoid those if I was planning on closing the gap enough to get a shot off. But range wasn't a big issue with my Fireball spell, so I would start with that. From up high I could literally just drop it like a mini explosive on their heads, so I did just that, aiming for the first of ten groupings below.

My spell sparked and flickered, the bit of essence I'd charged into it enough to add insane heat to the spell. I didn't know the exact numbers after infusing a spell with essence, but it had to be at least twice as effective based on the results I'd gotten, which meant for the amount of mana I'd sunk into the spell we were looking at roughly a 1,000 base damage potential. But again, that was based off a hunch with how much increased damage essence caused, it might very well be closer to 3 or even 4 times the damage.

I watched from above as my Fireball hit a barrier below, shattering it the moment my spell contacted it. Just as the ball of fire shattered the spell, it exploded above the heads of the three I'd been aiming for and when the steam cleared all that was left was three corpses floating in the water, surrounded by angry archers. So definitely more than twice the base damage then, more like 5 times to wipe out three at once. Fireball was such a potentially deadly and dangerous spell; I should use it more often.

I had to drink two mana potions, leaving me with only two left, but I ended all ten of the groups of sorceresses. However, it wasn't before they'd been able to do serious damage to all our ships, some having caught fire from damage to the flight systems being breached, most likely. It looked at first glance like we'd lost half our ships' ability to fly, but I couldn't say without speaking with the crews.

Phoenix's Pride had faired best of all, being the first to stop getting attacked when I took out the group of Naga attacking it. Because of the snake like nature of the Naga and their bodies, they didn't seem able to easily climb the sides of the ships and the few that tried were being shot and killed easily by our beach forces. It was because of this I think that they retreated back into the water.

I landed beside Jorn and gave Ares orders to stay high, giving me an arial view of the battlefield. She did so, taking my warning to stay high enough that she was out of arrow range, but not so high that she attracted the attention of a wyvern, or some other flight bound monster. It was a precarious situation flying out in the open, but through her eyes I saw what I needed to see.

"The Naga are amassing for another strike, our beach forces won't hold against the numbers I'm seeing. I'm sorry to do this Jorn, but I have to join the fight if we are going to have a chance." I wanted to stay and help command but with the several hundred coming versus our barely one hundred gathered, we stood very little chance. What was even more disturbing was the Koralent seemed to have found the numbers to surge two spots at once and our front line was buckling from the pressure of it.

"With the damage to the ships, retreat is not an option. I will not leave so many to die here, abandoned by their kin. I will fight as well. I'm only level 42, but I've not forgotten the adventures of my youth and my saber thirsts for the blood of those who dare damage my ships," Jorn said, his countenance changing from a calm exterior to a cunning deadly smile that gave me a chill up my spine.

"Should we bring the ships that can still fly up and out of the water? I'd hoped to use them as a blockade of sorts against sea attack, but these Naga are easily getting through the gaps and having so many openings is just splitting up our forces. If we gave them one larger area to come through, we'd at least be able to funnel them into a large force," I said. What I didn't say was that if we could get them to come together in force, I could best use my Fireball spell to annihilate them.

"We should call for one or two evokers to turn and assist in the beach front attack," Jorn suggested and it was my turn to nod my assent, as that was a wonderful idea.

"Go get two of the casters and bring them here, ask them to bring their strongest evokers as we need explosive power to thin the numbers," I called out to a runner who immediately took off to deliver the message.

"Smart," Jorn intoned, nodding as he watched the runner go. "I will gather together a strike force of *Awakened* and get the troops ready. You," Jorn pointed at another runner, one of the last two, "go and signal for the ships Dragon's Wrath, Golden Lion, and Eternal's Languish to lift off if they can, that ought to give them enough space to funnel in at us."

"I'll attack from the ground at first, but if we get overwhelmed, I'll likely be best mounted so I can rain down hell atop a greater number," I said, waving Jorn off as he left to rally his forces. I'd wait for the evokers to arrive so we could talk strategy, then attack in force.

An elderly elf in red flowing robes leaned heavily on a staff as he approached, alone. I didn't know his name and it wasn't important right now, but he announced himself regardless the moment he came within shouting distance.

"I am high sage Deline Estrawo, wielder of the black flame and evoker of great renown, how can I be of service?" Deline Estrawo asked, huffing and puffing between each word as if he'd just come from running laps.

"I requested at least two evokers, or casters, we are about to be overrun from the water's edge," I said, shaking my head in frustration. I turned to the last runner and was about to give him orders to bring me more casters when Deline Estrawo cut in by clearing his throat then speaking.

His words came out overly emphasized and slow as if speaking to a child that didn't know common tongue. "I am high sage and wielder of the black flame. I am worth a dozen of those casters working to secure your lines and it is only because I wish not to die this day that I chose myself to come assist you. Now quit your prattling and give me a target." With his words said, I noticed he'd summoned black flame at the tip of his staff and though no bigger than the flame of a candle, I could feel the immense heat on my face from five feet away. The last runner took several steps backward, his face red from the sudden flash of heat.

"This way," I said, convinced that perhaps we had a chance after all with a powerhouse like Deline on our side. "I'm going to be fighting to help maintain the front line and lobbing out Fireballs further out when I can, but I'd like you to scorch away their forces as they come out of the water. As many as you can kill and thin the ranks the better. Do you understand?"

"I'll need at least a dozen soldiers standing guard around me if I'm to truly cut loose, I promise not to burn them up, but they will likely become targets when the enemy sees the power I call down on them." Deline, one of the oldest elves I'd encountered so far, cracked his neck to the side and stood up straighter. He even lifted his staff from the ground, not leaning on it for support any longer. "I'm ready."

Just then I caught sight of a small force heading our way and I smiled. "How about instead of a dozen soldiers I give you six powerful *Awakened* to defend you?"

Alayna, Galt, Emory, Fred, and Fran ran right up to me, Fran speaking out first.

"We've all but lost the western flank, we need reinforcements, now! Or we need," she paused, looking around the beach and seeing the ships take off, "to retreat."

"We are being attacked by several hundred Naga from the sea and we've lost half our ships' ability to fly. Retreating isn't an option right now; those ships are lifting up to give space for the Naga to come attack us. Alayna, Galt, and Emory you stay here and protect Deline while he attacks the Naga with his black flame. Fred, you use your white flame to kill as many Naga as you can, same as Deline. Fran, you come with me to the front lines."

Everyone seemed perplexed at best by my orders, but in the heat of battle they'd all learned to listen and accept the orders. All but Emory of course, who'd spent very little time at war.

"What the fuck man, let me come with you into the battle. I'm more use out there than watching over the old guy," Emory said, eager to get back into battle.

Deline mumbled something but I didn't catch it. Looking hard at Emory I sighed, then looked to Galt and Alayna.

"Between Galt's spear and your barriers, do you think you could keep him safe while he rains down fire? I don't know how many will get through, but it could be a fair bit. I'll keep an eye on you with Ares, so if you are overwhelmed just bunker down with your most powerful barrier and I'll get to you. I promise."

Galt surprised me by answering for her. "We've got this," he said, twirling his spear. His limp was barely noticeable now, and he'd been fighting most of the day, so he was healed up enough to be an effective fighter again. This would work, they could do it.

"Not worth protecting, am I?" Deline asked, looking at Emory. "Let me see what you are leaving with me." He focused his attention on Alayna first, scoffed, then regarded

Galt. I'd never been able to get a reading off Galt, but Deline must have because he whistled and nodded his head. "Yes, I think this could work well enough. Go now and let me focus. And you, white flame, keep that stuff away from my fire, it reeks of essence saturation. You'll burn out your soul before this day is out."

I barely heard the last bit as Emory, Fran, and I were running off to join the fight, but I almost turned around when it registered what he'd said. This caster had known what was wrong with Fred at a glance, when Warrick—who'd come up with the same diagnosis—had taken days to figure it out. Maybe it had to do with him being an evoker or his black flame, but I would question him further after the day was won, if it could be won.

CHAPTER 60
FINAL WAVE

We made it to the front line, then promptly ordered everyone back another hundred feet. I wanted to create a dead man's field between the water's edge and our troops, so Deline and Fred could maximize their destruction. I also planned to throw out the occasional spell, perhaps even take to the sky if it called for it, but my Mana was limited when I soaked it all up in large Fireball spells. I would be much more consistently effective on the battlefield leading the troops, or the mix of crew and troops that I had at my command.

Going through the commander menu, I checked what abilities I could activate and hovered over one that would help keep morale high during the incoming devastation, however I didn't activate it yet, instead I'd hold it in reserve for when things really got bad. I'd been using the buffs here and there but made sure I saved a couple daily uses for emergencies such as this.

The enemy hadn't advanced yet, their numbers massing out in the shallow waters, but Jorn's plan had worked. Instead of slipping through the gaps of the ships, they'd chosen to mass together in the gaps created by the three ships taking off. Naga might be intelligent, but they were showing a distinct lack of tactic right now. Surely, they knew we had a plan to deal with them?

It was then that I saw the line of Naga leaving the waters and wondered if I'd made a mistake after all. Huge hulking Naga, brutes they were called, slithered out of the water, each of them four times the size of the already tall Naga. Like giants running to flatten the small folk, the Naga brutes came, nearly a hundred in all. This was going to be worse than a cavalry charge.

I turned to Emory, but I didn't know what to say, we'd just have to fight as best we could but the men beside us stood no chance of surviving this onslaught. I took a step forward, thinking that perhaps I'd meet them in battle before they go to the front line, but a hand grabbed my arm.

Emory looked at me and shook his head. "Trust the man to your left and right, isn't that what you told me? I'm trusting that you will keep fighting at my side and not do something stupid like running out to face the enemy alone. Trust that together we can hold."

I looked Emory in his eyes, his unblinking resolve and serious tone catching me off guard. "Yeah, stand strong at my side and I will do the same."

Fran smiled in my direction, raising her sword above her head and ready to deal death. Together the three of us would bring death to the enemy, but I couldn't help but worry about all the men and women around me who weren't blessed with the powers of *Awakening*. Surely the elves knew the secret to becoming sparked and would have passed it to all those with potential.

Perhaps if I ever find Merlin again, I'll ask him how one prepares to become sparked if they are like Ismene was, unbalanced. If I could get that secret, then spread it far and wide to all those that wished to become Awakened, we'd have a powerhouse of troops to deal with monstrous threats such as this.

"Really wish Merlin was here now, I bet he'd just wave his hand and the monsters would flee at the sight of him," I said, speaking under my breath. Realistically what I needed was the ability to summon a portal or teleport to get Warrick. He would be enough, along with our troops, to turn the tide of this unbeatable battle.

Just as the brutes made it to the halfway point in the dead man's zone I'd created, black fire erupted from the very ground burning them up in moments. I felt the release of essence as dozens fell from the initial attack, but Deline was just getting started. The fire swelled and moved like a cloud of black death, consuming all in its path. But as big and effective as it was, it could only kill so many at once and several dozen still got through.

Two such monsters headed right for us, and I decided to bring that number down to one. Holding out my sword, I infused essence into my Lightning Strike ability, calling down lightning on the bigger of the two's head. Then, as I had about six seconds before it would reach us, I used Arcane Missile, followed by an infused Firebolt. It slammed into the monster with deadly force, bringing it to its knees, but not dead. I Blinked forward and took its head, using Power Strike to aid my swing.

The second turned its head, but didn't stop, instead hissing, it went for Fran. Emory appeared before her, shield held high and energy cascading around him as he activated a skill to repel the giant monster. Fran blurred and moved to the side, cutting out with her blade. Blood spurt out just as the Naga hit the shield, bouncing backward while Emory sunk deeper into the sandy beach.

I hadn't stayed inactive during their back and forth, activating Speed Burst I closed in on the Naga from behind and activated Phantom Thrust, aiming for the base of its spine. The power of my thrust extended out and stabbed right in, delivering a killing blow. I rolled out of the way as the massive bulk fell backward, but the battle was far from done.

All around us the men crumbled under the charge of only dozens of brutes where there had been over a hundred before. We rushed to aid a half dozen soldiers who had expertly stuck a brute with as many spears, however they were about to be flanked by another and crushed. Emory shot through the gap, his charge ending as he collided with the flanking brute. Fran, not to be outdone by me, ran and jumped.

Her foot landed on Emory's shoulder, and she launched herself high enough to get a killing blow on the brute, her sword slid deep into the brute's eye but not before its swinging arm smashed into her, sending her flying. Before I could begin casting a spell, she'd already rolled in the sand and back to her feet not looking any worse for wear.

"Go for the killing blows," I yelled but my words were mostly lost in the din of battle. Our lines had fallen to disarray, but we hadn't been overwhelmed, just scattered a bit. Black and white flames scorched any and all that tried to get to us, and I had to admire how well the two evokers worked.

I looked over the battlefield, then to the shore. A mass of Naga began to chant further down the beach, just out of range of the flames, a quick Inspect showed me that they were more caster types. Charging a Fireball, I decided that with some help from essence in my armband, that I could hit them even from this distance. Four seconds passed and I had enough mana charged into the Fireball, then, flooding my arm I reared back and let loose the ball of flames. It whistled through the air and barely missed a plume of black fire that would have surely detonated it.

This grouping, two shy of a dozen, had a barrier erected like the ones previously. My Fireball hit it, but it didn't shatter on impact, instead it cracked, and a moment later the Fireball exploded. Dust and the spray of ocean water turned to mist, filled the area and the group were lost beneath it all.

Massive ice spikes appeared dozens of feet above our heads, and I knew my Fireball hadn't done its job. But the soldiers, Fran, Emory, and I were fine, these ice attacks hovered above Fred and Deline. I didn't know if Alayna's shield barrier spell would be enough and I looked in her direction just as she activated one of her major spells, a dome of hardened golden light pulsed out, covering them all. She obviously knew her normal barrier wouldn't be enough, but how many hits would this barrier take?

It was a spell I knew she could only do once per day, and it took a major toll on her. I struggled with what to do next, go back to Alayna and help her defend the wizards or try to take out the enemy casters again. I saw through Ares's eyes then and all hope left me. Our back lines were crumbling and monsters by the dozens were making it through. Soon Alayna and Galt would have more to tend with than just ice spears.

The giant ice spears smashed down, and a cloud of blue ice blocked my view. I held my breath, sensing their auras strong as ever. It had held! She was safe for now, but I had to solve one problem at a time. I focused on the grouping of Naga casters and let rip another Fireball, this one bigger than the last by a small margin. It hurt to do it, as my mana pool was dangerously low already, but I stuffed as much mana as I dared into the attack and let it loose.

Before it made impact against the cracked barrier surrounding the monsters, I felt a hand on my shoulder and a voice that I couldn't believe sounded in my ear. "You should focus on fighting and not calling for me while in the midst of battle."

I turned, not caring if my Fireball took care of the threat anymore, because everything was about to change. Merlin stood beside me, all blue robes with stars and planets, his pointy hat tilted back as he held his hand up to his eyes, regarding the battlefield as if it were nothing more than a busy night at his pub.

"Merlin! You have to save us," I managed to say just as my Fireball exploded and rocked the very ground I stood on.

"Save you? How is it you can take down a class A threat like that sky Kraken, nice work by the way. But you can't handle a few low leveled monsters?"

"A few?" I said, looking around at the thousands that overwhelmed us. "It's more than a few."

Merlin looked around, as if just now seeing the horde of monsters that were overwhelming our front lines and the hundreds more beyond the trees. "Oh, well since this is mostly my fault, I guess I can help you this once."

Merlin stood tall, cracked his neck to the side, then expertly cracked his fingers together, before opening his mouth as if to stretch it, he even stuck his tongue out oddly enough. But that was Merlin, everything about the impossible wizard was odd.

Merlin closed his eyes and for the first time since I'd met him that I could remember, I heard him chant the words to a spell instead of just doing it. I listened intently, completely transfixed at the rush of magic I was feeling from him suddenly. It was beyond oppressive, and I fell to my knees before him as he chanted, holding my chest as it felt like it might explode.

"Tempus est omnibus bugging me ex facie mea infernum impetrare!"

It was unlike any runic phrase I'd heard before; the words were so alien and odd. But what happened next was anything if not breathtaking. A burst of power went out from Merlin and the pressure in my chest went away instantly, as well as all the aches and pains I'd been suffering. Soldiers who'd been on the ground, dead for all intents and purposes, stirred and rose up to their feet. But greatest of all was what happened to monsters that touched the pulsing translucent energy.

They simply shimmered and were gone. All signs of them, weapons, dead enemies, everything just gone. I turned to see the wave wash over our broken line, and it was like a mirage of some kind, they just shimmered and disappeared. The half-ruined corpse of the Kraken far down the beach shimmered and left as well when the pulse hit it. Unfortunately, whatever the spell was he used it had an adverse effect on the ships flying above us and suddenly, but slowly, they began to drift toward the ground, one after another cracking against the beach.

The hulls were ruined for sure, but the fall had been slow enough that I was hopeful those aboard had survived.

When it was finally clear that the battle was over, I turned to him, a newfound respect and admiration for the godlike being known as Merlin. Falling to one knee and bowing my head, I spoke to him. "You are more powerful than even the Ordu. I will bow before you, for if there is a god or gods, you walk among them."

"Not yet, but almost," Merlin said, chuckling. "Now stand up before I summon another army and this time, not recall them. All I wanted was some peace and quiet for a few years, but somehow you found me out here. Before I left there were no such flying ships or ships capable of surviving the ocean trip. I even stiffened the borders around the island so that no one could just drop in by portal, but of course, humanity always finds a way."

Several facts hit me as I stood and regarded Merlin. First, had he just said that he summoned that army? And second, how had he blocked portals and teleporting? Neither question came to my lips when I tried to speak to him, instead my mission came forefront to my mind.

"I'm here for the Sword of the Ordu, a Shard of Order," I said, knowing I had to be fast if I wanted Merlin to listen. The frustrated look on Merlin's face as soldiers, Emory, and Fran approached had me worried and I knew by experience that he could be very flighty when he wanted to be.

"Shard of Order," Merlin said, turning his attention back to me, but not before he waved his hand and suddenly, we were elsewhere. "I've heard very few call it by that name. Arthur Pendragon also referred to it as a Shard of Order. You've spoken to one of the first ones, have you? I'd guess it was that Mah'kus fellow. I suppose I ought to help you as I helped Arthur."

I heard what he said, and I was glad, but looking around I was suddenly worried. We stood in a ruin, buildings of stone worn away by time and the jungle reclaiming them, however many scrolls and books had been laid out on a round stone table with a circular bench to match it, most of which was cracked and ruined. But all around us were cats prowling and hissing in our direction. I used Inspect and my butt cheeks clenched.

. . .

Shadow Cat, Level 82

What was worse, is that wasn't even the largest of the cats that moved in and out of shadows, disappearing whenever shadows touched them. I did not feel safe, Merlin or not, but what was I to do?

Finding my wits, none of the cats had attacked yet, so I assumed that Merlin had them under some kind of control, I spoke finally. "Didn't I tell you about Mah'kus, he claims to be a god, but you've done more magnificent shows of power than he ever has, but I think I believe him. He was the one to give me this quest, showing me how I was going to accomplish purifying the Ley Lines before the corruption spread too much."

Merlin nodded knowingly. "Yes, I sensed the corruption before I left, but it would take a Shard of Order to restore it to how it was before, otherwise I'd have seen to fixing it. Those Ordu and their champions, you are a Defender of the Balance no doubt, just as Arthur was. He had a great destiny, bringing our people together in a great time of need. But I've told you that story already, haven't I? You too must have a great destiny ahead of you. But worry not, I might be a bit distracted these days, but I can set you on the right path and do a bit to help you along the way."

"You'll show me where to find the Shard of Order?" I asked, elation filling me as I considered the end of my quest coming so soon after arriving, though it was hard fought to get to this point.

"No," Merlin said, chuckling. "Well not exactly no, but you must prove yourself worthy to me. Just because the remnants of the Ordu have deemed you worthy to be their knight; doesn't mean I think you have what it takes. You will inherit great and unimaginable power if you possess a Shard of Order, more so than the Ordu released when they forged them into simple swords. So, prove to me you are strong enough, smart enough, valiant enough, and worthy enough. Then we will talk."

"But how can I do that, do you not know me well enough to say?" I asked, dumbfounded by the sudden turn of events.

"My judgement is flawed. However, the ancient dungeons are wise, and I will commune with one nearby. He will certainly be able to offer you a suitable challenge, what level are you now. Hmm not very high, however you've got the layout of someone much higher, and that infusion ability is quite the multiplier. I'd say a dungeon around level 65 ought to be challenging enough for you after you spend that massive amount of essence you are holding onto. I'll return in a week, go back to your friends and seek out a Mana Shrine to solidify your power gains. But take care not to venture too deep into the jungle, my army kept back the monsters, so I didn't have to deal with them, but they'll be out hunting now, and I sensed only a handful strong enough to deal with them among your little band of explorers."

"Okay," I said, not knowing what else to say to this

godlike being who had just taken my destiny and fate into his hands as if it were nothing more important than serving a meal at his pub, cool as a cucumber.

"Oh, and put together a team of, let's say, fifteen adventurers around your level. You don't want to challenge a raid dungeon by yourself. Prove yourself inside the dungeon and I will take you to Camelot where you will find the Shard of Order that resides within."

"A raid dungeon?" I repeated, but he'd already waved his hand and I appeared next to Emory and Fran on the beach once again.

CHAPTER 61
RAID PREPARATIONS

"We aren't able to create portals because that blue cloaked god of a man. I just can't get over his raw power. So, he just decided that he didn't want to be bothered. You know we have records going back a thousand years and the name Merlin shows up a fair bit, a common enough name among humans, but there is mention of one such Merlin that did impossible feats such as these. I believe he was killed some time ago if memory serves. How this new Merlin has channeled such power is a mystery that I will see answered," Deline drowned on and on, this latest round just a repeat of what he'd asked, and I'd answered several times over.

"Look, I get it alright. Merlin is a mystery, but he is also the only way I'm going to accomplish my quest now and I will see it through, so answer my question as plainly as you can. Will you join me during this 'Raid Dungeon', or do I need to look for someone else?" I asked as plainly as I could manage and stared right at the wizened old elf awaiting an answer.

He hhmm'd and ahh'd for a few excruciatingly long seconds before nodding. "I will go but keep that white flamed evoker away from me. He can go too, but he steals away all the essence he touches with his parasitic flame."

Now wasn't the time to go into Fred and his ailments, but I hadn't forgotten that I wanted to question him about what he might know. Next, I moved to find the strongest among the elves, wanting anyone and everyone who had levels higher than 50. Unfortunately, I found only eight others like Deline, stronger than level 50, and only three of them agreed to come.

That left me with eleven spots to fill and I knew just the people who I could rely on for the task. Creed was up and about again, having missed the fighting, but he'd recovered when Merlin had sent out his blast of energy or whatever it was exactly. That meant I could rely on Creed, Alayna, Zander, Emory, Ismene, Galt—his limp was completely gone now—, Fred, Fran, Kora, and Beth. Adathin was busy helping in administrative ways and declined joining.

The three unknowns were named Namor, a powerful tank, Estraw, a swift fighter that fought with a thin blade and nearly held the eastern flank by herself, and lastly Belfast, a powerful healer that focused on offense as well as healing.

That filled up fifteen party members, Emory, Galt, Namor would be handling the front line with Fran, Creed, and Estraw taking the melee fighting up close. Next, we had myself, Kora, Beth, Ismene, Fred, and Deline holding the back line with the healers, Alayna, Zander, and Belfast. It seemed like a crowded bunch seeing us all together, but I doubted that Merlin didn't know exactly what he was talking about.

All of us had gathered an immense amount of essence that needed spending, so we used my map to lead us to the closest shrine. It ended up being less than a mile away, further down the beach and just inside the tree line. The strongest four took watch while the rest of us put our hands to stone and increased in level. I'd lost much essence to not being able to hold any more in my arm band and my Core attribute of 91 just not being enough. But I took what I had and leveled all the way to Level 52 from 48, but not a single one of my group made it past level 49, as the essence to do so was over four times as much the previous level.

It was only because of my low cost of purchasing Paragon attributes that I made it as far as I did, that and the millions of essence I'd collected from slaying a legendary Kraken and a horde of monsters around level 45 to 55. For example, it now cost a massive 834,750 essence to get to level 53 plus over a million more to purchase the necessary attributes. This was so level 50 was a soft cap of sorts for most adventurers. The gains slowed down to a crawl and even if you were up for collecting the required essence past 50, most found themselves unable to because they didn't prioritize their Core attribute early enough to hold the required essence to keep leveling.

Sharing your level outside your normal group of adventurers was considered taboo, so I hadn't asked what level exactly the others were, trusting that they were above fifty as they said.

I had roughly half a million essence left over by the time I finished and I found a spell that matched one I'd been trying to learn naturally, deciding to purchase it as it seemed handy. It was called Channel Lightning and it worked similar to my Lightning Strike spell, being an instant cast, but instead of costing X amount it cost 50 mana per second that I channeled it, I immediately paid the essence and reagents to rise it to Rank 2, bringing the channeling cost to a 100 per second. Next, I brought the rest of my newest spells and skills to Rank 2, while bringing my Firebolt, Lightning Strike, Fireball spells to rank 3, increasing the cost drastically, but also the damage potential. Next, I put my Power Strike, Force Wave, and Swift Strike to Rank 3, eating up all but a few thousand of my essence.

Then we took our larger than normal group back to the beach, where repairs and general tasks were being completed by all. I found Jorn preparing the pyres and set out to help him. He already had a team of ten or so, but I began to pick up branches to add to it as the others were until he noticed me.

"This expedition has been one disaster after another," he said, coming in closer to me and speaking in a low voice. "But that friend of yours really saved us from the worst of it. How'd you manage to get him to come here?"

I chuckled, but not out of any sense of humor. "I don't think that I got him to do anything, even now I wonder at the challenges he plans to put me through. It is well within his power to give me what I need and clear the way for you to seek answers about your ancestors but he chooses to play games instead."

"Yet he knows you and he saved us when destruction was all that lay in our future," he said. "Friend he may not be, but I wouldn't say that he is a foe either. Perhaps you might be able to convince him to release his hold on the land and allow us to bring in reinforcements and carry our wounded from this land."

I reached down and picked up a sizable dry branch, adding it to my armful before responding. "I can try, but I wouldn't count on it. I think we need to fix the ships and be prepared to journey back the moment I get what I've come here for."

"A powerful artifact it must be, to risk all that we have and still feel so passionate about retrieving it," Jorn said, his eyes searching me for something, but what I could not say.

I nodded. "It has the power to fix the damage that a Chaos Knight is doing, but I'm hopeful that it will also give me the power to face off against such an impossible foe that slew Bren Variyn with such ease. I can't imagine what wonders the sword will unlock, but I know my duty and I will see it through to the end."

We finished collecting wood, and the teams worked to put together pyres worthy of the fallen. By the time they finished just over a hundred mounds of dirt had been raised, with the centers overfilled with wood, enough to ensure the bodies would be turned to ash or at least that is what I imagined was the goal. What actually happened left me wondering why we'd collected so many sticks in the first place.

Several of the elven casters gathered and began to chant. Flame, orange and red, flowed down from the sky in a swirling pillar, resting over the first pyre and lighting it. Then it dissipated, leaving a roaring fire behind, and the chanting began anew, until each of the pyres had been lit by a fire so hot that I felt it on my face from over a hundred feet away.

I assumed they'd speak over their dead, but what actually happened was more song than speech. Led by Jorn, a song so gentle and soft that it might be confused with a summer's breeze, sounded out over the desolate beach where the fallen had fought and died only hours before. The song spoke to me in ways that words can't communicate. I thought of my ancestors, their struggles against life and taming the wilderness. How so many must have died before the gifts of the Ordu gave us the power to fight back.

I saw images of men, elves, and even orcs fighting for freedom against the darkness and winning the right to stand on their own. For a second, I thought I saw several Ordu in white and golden armor wielding twelve swords, each one unique and powerful beyond measure. I recognized one blade as the sword wielded and tainted by Chaos. What visions I saw as the soft melodic voices of the elves rose from a gentle breeze to a raging storm, my mind reeled from it all.

Then I saw darker images, great vessels of materials harder than Mythril and magic more resistant than the best laid runic patterns. Inside of these massive feats of engineering and magic were dark spots where people had once been. These beings so fully corrupted and given over to a darkness worse than the Chaos. For at least Chaos is natural and must be maintained alongside Order. The darkness they threatened to bring was nothing more than pure and unending evil.

I felt a hand on my shoulder and my visions ceased. Mah'kus stood beside me, saying nothing but looking all around at the pyres and the people watching. Following his gaze, I realized that he was looking at one particular figure in blue robes and a pointy hat. It hadn't been less than a day and already Merlin had returned?

Finally, Mah'kus spoke, his voice comforting against the dark visions I'd been forced to endure. "The time draws ever closer, and I see that your goals are within your grasp."

I turned away from Merlin, he was preoccupied with watching the fires and so far, no one else seemed able to notice him, despite him standing right beside Jorn, the expedition's leader and captain of the Phoenix's Pride.

"Is Merlin like you?" I asked, thinking that Emory, who stood next to me would notice my words and see Mah'kus, but he didn't react at all, instead his eyes closed as he listened to the music of the elves.

"In some ways," Mah'kus said, chuckling. "But no, he is more like you than he is like me. He is old though, much older than any other human that I've encountered."

"He said that you instructed or spoke with a student of his in the past, Arthur Pendragon. How many pawns do you move to accomplish your goals, Mah'kus, dead god?" I asked, letting my sarcasm sink in because of my frustrations with him.

"I haven't yet, but I will have to look into that. Arthur Pendragon, you say? That must be thousands of years ago, what did I hope to accomplish back then I wonder," Mah'kus scratched at his chin as he spoke, looking truly perplexed.

"Did you come here just to warn me that those creatures, so vile and dark, are on their way or did you have a new impossible quest for me?"

"I felt that you'd arrived and wanted to check up on you. I didn't anticipate such powerful foes waiting for you, but I had faith you'd find a way. This Merlin is a useful ally but be wary of those who have lived so long. Often, the price of such an age is your humanity. It is easy to think of others as nothing when you've seen endless years pass by as if in the blink of an eye."

"What of your humanity?" I asked, seeing the way he looked around the funeral of so many elves, it was very similar to Merlin, a look of perplexed wonder.

"I've not had humanity for eons. Make no mistake, mortal, I do what I do for the betterment of my own kind. It is the self-inflicted ignorance of my brothers and sisters that forced me to take actions as I've done, but always I work for the betterment of them. For without humanity and the many worlds that support life, they will lose all sense of meaning, perhaps even allowing the poison of the black dragon to be released. That he had any influence outside his prison at all is evidence enough of our failure to contain him.

But you find me in a chatty mood, and I would depart before I give away all my secrets. Farewell and good luck on your upcoming raid. Remember, when you don't know which path to take, choose the right."

And as fast as he appeared, he was gone. When I looked up, I saw that Merlin wasn't where he'd been either, or perhaps he'd never been there at all, and it was just a trick of Mah'kus. He was, after all, a god. Sure, a dead god by his own admission, but a god nonetheless.

CHAPTER 62
RAID

Two days went by, we continued to prepare as best we could, but the stronger members of the group didn't feel keen on hunting with us so that we could practice working together. That meant that I got two good hunts in with them all and each one was more exciting than the one before. On the first one, Estraw showed me that she was by far one of the strongest melee fighters on the team, by single handedly taking on three shadow cats that no one in the group had a chance to even see until they were already dead.

She was like a rogue and a powerful sword fighter all wrapped into one. Where she was strong, fast, and impossibly deadly, Namor showed in the second hunt what it meant to be a higher leveled tank. Elemental rock golems ambushed us, knocking Emory senseless with a single strike, however Namor appeared taking blow after blow and shrugging each one off, it was simply amazing. Belfast healed Emory within seconds, getting him back to his feet, and

Deline called down his black flame to consume the golems, not to be outdone by Estraw again.

At the end of the second day, Merlin arrived.

"I need to take Kora with me, where'd you go, walking dungeon girl?" Merlin looked around my personal tent where I was currently laying naked next to Alayna, both of us covered luckily.

"Well, she isn't in my covers," I said, mildly annoyed at the sudden appearance of the wizard in my personal quarters. I'd set up, with Alayna's help, several wards and spells that should have kept us protected from intrusions such as this, but of course he hadn't triggered a single one of them.

"Give me a moment to dress and I'll show you to her," I said, pulling the cover aside just enough for me to slip out. Alayna, bless her, continued to sleep soundless beside me and I wanted to keep her that way, so moving as carefully and quietly as I could, I got dressed.

Merlin watched me the entire time, not even pretending to avert his eyes. It was a tad creepy, but Merlin was an oddball and normalcy in any form wasn't something I'd equate to him. I'd just gotten my pants on when Merlin spoke again, but before he could get a word out, I shushed him and for once, he took the hint and closed his mouth. Instead of speaking, he reached out and grabbed hold of something in the air.

To my utter astonishment Fulgar'vi'lectus appeared in his grasp, summoned from wherever it was my bonded weapon went when I wasn't using it. He ran a hand down the blade, it sparked each time he touched one of the runes. I hurriedly finished dressing but kept an eye on Merlin as he fiddled with my precious weapon, the sword that had single handedly made me stronger than most. Not that my gear didn't assist in the rising of my attributes, but the percentage gains was unheard of on most gear.

Fran had a similar sword, but hers increased her attributes a set amount based on her level, giving her plus 20 for level 10 and 22 for level 11, not those figures exactly but it was growth based, which made the weapon extremely rare. What was more, instead of breaking or being worn down the blade had stayed bonded by her father his entire career as an adventurer, so it was as good as new when Fran took it as her bonded weapon.

Normally weapons and armor wouldn't last forever, most adventurers going through several new armor and weapons each year, but bonding weapons created a mystical bond between the bearer and the weapon, making it indestructible. Or in a more real sense, it created an image of the blade and each time it was summoned the blade would be restored to the moment when it was bonded, so my sword and Fran's could break, however we simply need to summon it back and it would be whole again.

I went through all these facts as I finished dressing and to keep me from reaching out and taking my sword back. He was messing with it, adjusting a few of the runes somehow with his finger. It should be impossible, but that word meant nothing when put against Merlin.

"There," Merlin declared, forgetting I'd shushed him apparently, "all fixed."

I pushed Merlin out of my tent, running my hand on the wooden tent frame to deactivate the wards so we didn't wake Alayna as we left, then, reaching in as we left I threw a chunk of mana at it to activate them once more.

"What did you do to my sword?" I asked, reaching out and taking the blade from Merlin. He let the blade go and gave me a perplexed look.

"It had a few limitation runes placed on it that didn't seem necessary. The metal is strong enough to hold much more essence than the limitations were allowing. Now you can get the full benefits of such a wondrous weapon. Just be sure to not fill one channel completely before letting a bit of essence into the others first. Now, where can I find the walking dungeon? She has to be around here someplace," Merlin looked about the camp, scratching at his beard all the while.

I used Inspect on Fulgar'vi'lectus and my jaw dropped open.

Fulgar'vi'lectus

5 Essence Pathways (0/5 Charged)

Essence Pathways: Channels have been cut into the very fabric of the blade to allow for essence to be more artfully charged into the blade. For each Charge that is completed, the weapon will increase its wielder's Base Damage and Attributes. Charges will last ten minutes and increase 125% per filled pathway.

35-53 Base Damage

+20 Strength

+20 Intellect

Durability: 200/200

Rarity: Masterwork Crafted

Item Leve: 40, Level Required to use: Soulbound, Crafted by: Estranel Elladent'ah

The sword had just gone from an amazing to an epic artifact level of usefulness. Instead of a limit of 125% increase in my damage and attributes, it could potentially reach an impossible 625%. How much essence would that require, I wondered, and what were the new limitations of my sword. Suddenly I wasn't so sure that the Shard of Order, the blade I was after, would be a match for my current weapon.

"Thank you," I said, unsure what else to say to the odd wizard who'd so casually just changed the very fabric of my weapon with his finger.

"Kora, her name was Kora, right? Where is Kora?" Merlin asked, not waiting for me any longer he walked right up to a roaming patrol guard and took him by the shoulders. "Have you seen Kora? Pesky thing is able to elude my detection."

"And yet I can sense you just fine," Kora said, appearing from behind a tent. "What does the oldest of meatbags want from me?"

"Meatbag indeed," Merlin said, chuckling. "I need you to talk to a stubborn dungeon and convince him to stop resisting my help, otherwise I might be tempted to shatter his core. Now come on you bucket of bolts, you are needed."

Kora didn't move, instead smiling and put her hands on her hips and sighed. "What is in it for me?"

"We can parley over rewards after you've done your part," Merlin said, stepping forward to reach out for her.

A flash of white light later and Merlin was thrown backward, however, he caught himself before falling. He'd been pushed back a solid five feet and I was looking at Kora with a newfound respect.

"I've got your number," Kora said, walking up to Merlin. "You impress others with your knowledge, but I am just as old as you are, and the stronger I get, the more of my knowledge I can bring to bear. You want my help with another of my kind, then first you will agree to my terms. I want ten bodies made of pure Mythril, use my own form as a template, but don't try and sneak in any runes of your own. I will find them, and you will anger me. You have not yet walked the Path, so we aren't so different, yet."

"What would a dungeon know of the Path of the Titans?" Merlin asked, the area around him suddenly darkening. His tone changed and went aggressive. "I'm no conjurer of cheap tricks," he looked over and winked at me before turning back with the same dangerous tone, "be warned, child of the Wyrd. You may be old, but I saw the birth of the first dungeons, and you were not among them." His tone shifted again, going back to the kind and silly Merlin I'd come to expect. "But I find your terms agreeable, I may not have walked the Path yet, but I've taken enough steps that a small bit of transmutation shouldn't be a problem. Carve what form you want from stone or wood, and I will do the rest."

"Agreeable, take me to my brother," Kora said, reaching out her arm. Merlin took it and in a blink of an eye the two of them were gone.

I was left standing next to a startled guard. Looking at him, I shrugged, "Guess they'll be back later," I said, then turned to find some breakfast in the early morning hours, sun barely peeking over the horizon.

***

The day of the 'Raid' came on the seventh day, two days after Kora returned and flat out refused to answer my questions, neither regarding the frames she'd requested from Merlin nor how the talk with the other dungeon had gone. However, she did inform me that I would have to take Ventus with me, as she'd promised not to interfere with the other dungeon, meaning she couldn't go after all. I took it in stride, as Ventus was a powerful fighter and caster, easily an equal for my friends in power.

Merlin arrived again, this time while I was eating, and happily spoke out to the crowd gathered to eat. "The Raid is ready, come now."

I took one final bite and stood, going out to find the rest of the fifteen that had been chosen to do the raid. We had no idea how long it would take or the dangers that awaited us, so we'd prepared food, supplies, tents, and more.

When we'd all gathered together, Merlin stepped forward and suddenly we were standing outside a massive set of dungeon doors. The runic symbols pulsed and glowed as fiercely as those from the dungeon that had been overrun with essence. I stepped forward, thinking to put my hands on the dungeon wall and feel if it were hot or not, but Merlin grabbed my hand.

"Best not to touch right now. I had to give the poor fellow a good boost to get what I wanted and he's likely to zap you," Merlin said, looking at the dungeon walls as if he were afraid to touch them as well. He stepped forward and the doors swung open, and he motioned for us to follow him down.

When we'd all made it down, Merlin cleared his throat, the dungeon lobby looked just the same as any other except that the water that was usually in the middle was missing and only an empty basin stood there.

"I've prepared a challenge meant to test Arthur...err I mean Caldor, but he won't accomplish much by himself. He needs his faithful knights at his side. Be prepared to sacrifice your lives for him when needed. Oh, and Caldor, you will be tested the same as when I tested young Arthur, do not fail me as he did so many times. My time here is limited, and I wish to see you succeed in your mission. Do well to finish within the month or I'll assume you dead. If you die, this will be the last time I try to help, and down the Path of the Titans I will walk, to see what awaits me." Toward the end he seemed to be talking to himself, his voice lowering and trailing off.

"Path of the Titans?" I asked, my head going to the side slightly as I tried to remember where I'd heard that before but coming up empty. It seemed so familiar and I know I'd heard it multiple times but I couldn't narrow in my thoughts on when and where.

"Enter five at a time, wait a few seconds between each entry and you should be fine," Merlin said. He tapped his finger on his chin a few times as if trying to remember something but shrugged after a few moments and disappeared. His voice lingered and we heard his final words. "Good luck."

"That is one strange man," Emory said, shaking his head and elbowing me. "Should we go first?"

We'd naturally split into three groups, Alayna, Ventus, Beth, Galt, and myself in the first group, Zander, Ismene, Fred, Fran, and Emory in the second group. The third group comprised of the leftovers, Namor, Creed, Estraw, Belfast, and Deline. Being the leftovers didn't hamper their ability though, and they were easily the strongest of the three groups. It wasn't that we feared that the dungeon would split the party, we just naturally gravitated to operating in five-man groups as we'd been conditioned to do so by so many dungeon runs.

But of course, as my vision cleared and I looked around, I saw only Alayna, Ventus, Beth, and Galt at my side, the others had yet to show up. We were in a cave of some kind with very limited light, but I cast Light and Beth pulled out a device that let out an even more powerful glow, sending small orbs of light up to the high ceiling. Several dozen stalactites reached down like the so many fingers, however the cave floor appeared clear several strides in every direction.

We waited five minutes and decided to buff up in the meantime. I refreshed my Arcane Armor and my other buffs, including casting the Light Blade spell on my sword, but dimming it down significantly as my Light globes were doing plenty to light the area. I didn't infuse my blade yet, but it had been such a quick process every time before, that I didn't worry about it. After ten minutes, I decided the dungeon was truly messing with us and turned to my group who'd been chatting quietly with weapons at the ready, Galt with Alayna and Beth with Ventus.

"I think if we want to find the rest of the group we are going to have to venture out and look. Perhaps this is how Merlin planned it or perhaps not, but either way we ought to be ready for anything."

"This place feels odd," Ventus said, looking around as if he could see things I couldn't. Perhaps he could, I didn't know how his vision worked.

"In what way?" I asked, hoping he'd shed some light on what he meant.

He did not, instead, just shook his head in a very human manner. Another reminder of how much he'd changed since Kora first released him from the Runes that held the inner personality of the monster cores at bay.

The cave walls opened in two paths, each one had stone carved doorways lined with runes written in an older style that I almost recognized, but the more I looked at them the less I understood them. I turned to Alayna, but she was already getting close and trying to read them.

"It's a message of some kind," she said, running her fingers across the left one, then moving to study the right.

"What does it say?" I asked after a solid minute of waiting while she studied away, completely enthralled by the chance to look over old runes.

"I think I have the general idea, one door is saying that it is the safe way out of the mountain and the other is saying that the other door is a liar and that it isn't safe, or something to that effect. I'm not a hundred percent sure, it has a kind of poetic phrasing and is hard to understand what meaning the words are truly going for."

"Oh cool!" Beth exclaimed. "It's a door riddle. I think I've done this one before. One is a liar and the other tells the truth. So, we just have to figure out which one is the liar door. I think last time I came across one of these we got to ask a question. Should we ask it a question?"

"Which door leads to safety?" I asked, projecting my voice at the doors. But nothing happened, the light of my spell showed no change on the runes and no voice spoke out to us.

"Let me try something," Alayna said. She pressed her hand on the door to the right and began to speak in a language that I barely recognized as the runic language, but she did it with different phrasing and tone as to make it almost impossible to understand.

Suddenly something happened, the door on the left began to glow a subtle white light. She'd been touching the other door, so I looked at her with a confused expression until she explained herself. I didn't have to wait long.

"I asked that specific door which door would the other door say leads to freedom," Alayna said, as if that put all to rest.

"And that helps us?" I asked, trying to work the logic out in my head.

So, if she asked the liar door what the other door would say is the safe way out, he would lie and say the door that is dangerous. And if it is the truth door and she asked, it would tell us the liar door's pick, which would also be the dangerous path forward.

Alayna went on to explain basically the same, and Galt looked terribly confused and asked the important question.

"So, we go through the door on the right?" He asked, leaning down to look into the darkness, whether or not he had better vision than me, I couldn't say, but I saw nothing when I peered down.

"Yes," Alayna said, beaming.

We went right and after only a hundred feet or so we reached another split. A little work and it turned out to be the same puzzle as before, so Alayna asked her question, and we went left. After three more of these, we reached one that stood in ruins, claw marks breaking away much of the runic doorframe. Alayna tried to communicate to the doors, but nothing. The doors didn't light up or react in any way.

I thought about it for a second and pointed at the door on the right. "We choose the right," I said, shaking my head.

Had Mah'kus foreseen us getting stuck and really just given me the answer beforehand?

"You sure?" Galt asked, leaning heavily on his staff. "Each time we'd chosen the right way, I felt a touch of coolness from a breeze or something, but I don't feel it down the right side, just the left. Perhaps we better follow my gut and go left?"

I looked at Galt, I knew he meant well, but I'd gotten my advice from a literal god and couldn't see Mah'kus pointing us in the wrong direction. "I think we should go right," I said, for some reason I didn't want to explain to Galt, Beth, or Ventus that I was on speaking terms with a god, dead or not.

Alayna gave me a look, then she looked at Galt. I could tell I'd put her in a socially precarious situation, as she likely wanted to support both her father and her boyfriend, but she couldn't do both. "Why are you so sure?" She finally asked, her attention focused on me.

I gave her a pleading look and sighed after a second. "You know how I told you about Mah'kus. Well, he told me, in not so many words, that when we didn't know which way to go we should choose the right. I barely registered the comment until now, but he must have meant this, right?"

She smiled at me, nodding her head. "We go right. Galt, Caldor has had dealings with a being of immense power that appears to be able-"

Galt raised a hand to silence her. "No explanation is needed. I'll lead the way."

He didn't seem hurt, but it made me wonder if he felt

the sting of betrayal or if his emotional hide was as thick as his actual skin. If that were the case, it would take a lot more to penetrate his emotion shields.

The hallway before us was cloaked in the same darkness as before, but Galt was right, there was a lack of freshness that the prior hallways had, though if he hadn't mentioned it, I wouldn't have noticed. In fact, the path forward smelt like death, rotting corpses and a general stench. So, when the path ended, we were all a bit on edge already and the skeletons that greeted us with swords raised didn't help.

"I see no exit," Galt said, while putting himself in front of the group of four skeletons. Before checking the edges of the room for doors, I did a quick Inspect to see what we were dealing with.

Bone Hardened Skeleton Warrior, Level 78

"Shit, they are nearly level 80, get ready for a tough fight," I called out while beginning the process of flooding my sword's pathways with essence. The new openness of them felt strange but I balanced the flow of power and felt attributes swell from the experience. It took a solid three seconds to get them as close to full as I dared, my sword warming in my grip. The blade, already glowing with a soft white light began to glow and spark with blue-green energy. I recognized it as essence escaping through the blade and focused, bringing the essence down just a hair and with it the sparks dissipated.

All the while, I was ready to jump into the battle, but the skeletons hadn't attacked yet. Instead, they stared at us with their hollow eyes, weapons drawn, and heads all pointed at our party.

"Do we retreat?" Galt asked, surprising me as I hadn't even considered retreat.

I searched the edges, cast another Light spell and verified that, indeed, there was no visible exit from this room. The ceiling was odd, only about three times the height as me, much shorter than the starting cave or even the massive hallways we'd been walking in. Despite that, there were also odd holes in the flat stone ceiling every foot or so.

"This is a trap room, everyone out!" I called, turning to see the door that we came through slide shut, despite there having only been an opening and not a door there a moment before.

The room rumbled and the ceiling moved an inch or so, sending dust and debris down on us. Behind the skeletons, appearing as if out of nowhere, appeared a door. The message was clear, kill the skeletons or somehow get around them and you can escape. Based on just the last few seconds we had a minute or two before the ceiling crushed us. I glanced up to see spikes had come out of the holes and I realized that we had a bit less time than I thought, seeing as the four-foot-long spikes would reach us before we were crushed.

"I'll distract the skeletons, you all get out while you still can," I said, accepting in that moment that I was the only one in the room strong enough to deal with the threats, even Galt being as strong as he was, would not be a match for level 78 skeletons.

Galt looked at Alayna and I could see his mind on the matter. He would do whatever needed to be done to keep her safe, it was likely the reason he'd insisted on going with us for the dungeon raid.

"We stand a better chance to move them out of the way together, attack as one and use whatever abilities you have to increase your speed, that is the biggest threat of higher levels, they are too fast," Galt looked at me when he spoke, but he was speaking to everyone.

Ventus rolled his shoulders, a gesture Emory did frequently that he must have picked up. "When I fall, take my core if you can so that I may live again." And with that power began to swirl around him, the wind of his elemental core there to give him speed.

"No," I said, holding up a hand. "Galt is right, we do this together but focus on just getting to the other side. We've no more time to waste, go and stay behind us if you can." I spared a look at Alayna, she was the weakest among us and also the most important member with her heals.

I rushed forward, my muscles bulging as I infused essence directly into them and then I activated Speed Burst, the world slowed but I still moved much faster than I was used to and nearly slipped. Galt and Ventus moved faster than the rest, but not nearly as fast as me. I reached the skeletons and used my 3 seconds wisely, for me they felt like a solid minute of time because of how fast my body moved. The skeletons moved faster than Galt and Ventus, but still slow enough that I could easily move out of their strikes.

Dodging left and then right, and then under, I struck out with my sword. Surprisingly I cut right through the spine of one and it began to crumble as if in slow motion. Turning my attention on the remaining ones I cut and slashed, killing one more before Galt made it to the battle. Fast as Galt was the skeletons were faster, I knocked a blow that would have caught him in the chest, just as my double speed ran out. Suddenly I was only a bit faster than Galt and definitely slower than the remaining skeletons.

We slammed against them, Galt using a shielding ability to block several powerful strikes, then just as the light blue barrier shattered, a golden one appeared over us both. Ventus, on the other hand, moved like the wind itself, cutting and blowing back two skeletons at a time. Beth fired arrow after arrow at the skeletons, but to little effect. The first spikes reached our heads height and we started to crouch, swinging and pushing our way toward the door.

The remaining two skeletons struck back with a fury. Ventus caught one sword strike on the arm in an attempt to block the attack, and it was severed from his body. The sword strike came so fast that it might as well have been invisible. We were nearly to the door when my Speed Burst came off cooldown and I triggered it again. Once more the skeletons slowed to a manageable pace, and I did what needed to be done.

Pushing and shoving I moved everyone close to the exit

and struck out at the final two skeletons, killing one by shattering its spine and disarming the other. However, I'd been fighting hunched and now I'd need to go to my knees, so close were the spikes. I made it close to the door just as the skeleton grabbed my back foot and pulled. I went from inches of reaching the door with the others, to sliding back to the middle of the room. My speed ran out and the skeleton beat down upon me, no weapons but blunt fists doing decent damage.

But I wasn't so far out of my senses not to see the way out. I struck the skeleton with an infused Channel Lighting, the blast of it knocking it back enough for me to activate Blink. With only a foot of space between me and the spikes, I teleported close enough for Galt to grab my shoulder and pull me out of the spike trap room.

"Damn that was close," I said, looking around and realizing that somehow, we were outside in a forest now with no sign of a cave entrance or doorway.

CHAPTER 63
SECOND TRAIL

"It is a shame." A voice rung out and I looked up to see a human with brown hair, a short cut beard, green eyes, and a big frame walking from behind one of the trees. "I'd hoped that each of you would fall prey to one of my trap rooms and this farce could end. But here you all are, safe and sound and ready to start the dungeon challenges that the pesky human wizard planned for you."

Looking around I realized that we weren't alone. The entire group of fifteen had returned, Zander's group was bloody and dusty, where Creed's group barely looked disheveled at all. Only Creed was showing any signs of combat, his full armor up and a massive runed blade in his grip.

"We just faced a horde of monsters," Creed said when he saw me looking, he spoke in his low ethereal voice which meant he had been using a death knight ability recently.

"We nearly got squished," I said, sending him a reassuring smile.

"We had stupid puzzles and riddles," Zander said, almost spitting the words as blood filled his mouth. Then he did actually spit, the brown-haired man making a face at him when he did so. "Each time we got them wrong we had to face monsters that only Fred could kill, I couldn't heal us fast enough and I nearly died. This stupid quest of yours better be worth it!"

Emory was laughing, his left eye black and a gash over it. He'd taken off his helmet and was sitting on the grass. "Those fucking monsters hit like what I expect you hit like when you aren't holding back. Remind me not to pick a real fight with you."

Despite his words, I could tell Emory had likely enjoyed the fight, but only because they made it out alive. Fred's eyes were still glazed over white, and Fran hung on him, favoring one leg and whispering words to him. I cast Mending Touch on her and turned on the newcomer.

"Who the fuck are you and why did you put us through that if it isn't even what Merlin had planned?" My question was laced with accusation and fury.

"I'm the dungeon, and I don't answer questions of lesser beings. You got a taste of what my true dungeon would have been like, it seemed only fair. Now, if you will shut up and get ready, I will give you some directions to the start of your journey."

He looked pointedly at each of us, clearly annoyed at us for surviving.

"Good little meatbags," his eyes passed over Ventus and his ruined arm. "You are one of Kora's?" He asked as he walked up to Ventus, passing right in front of me. His aura was immense this close, and I stumbled back from experiencing it.

"I am," Ventus said, his hand over the ruined arm.

"She told me a bit of what she had planned for your kind. Allow me to fix that for you." He held out his hand and Ventus reluctantly moved his own hand from over his twisted wreck of an arm stub.

A soft white illumination began in the man's hand and suddenly all of Ventus was covered in the gentle white glow. When it finally shimmered to a stop, what was left behind was hardly recognizable as Ventus. For one, he'd grown about two feet taller, easily the tallest of us now, almost like an Ordu in height and slimness. In fact, very much like an Ordu, even the arms were a bit longer just like the Ordu.

"I'm more familiar with the old one's form and I think this will suit you better. I've upgraded the material from the common steel you had to something they call Refined Mythril. I also adjusted some of my little sister's work, you will find you can push more power through your channels now. I even expanded your core a bit, so you aren't the weakest one here anymore." Then he looked at me and raised an eyebrow, "Some of these meatbags can still beat you on power, but I'd wager you are among the strongest beings they have to offer now. Hopefully she will take this as an opportunity and gesture."

"Thank you," Ventus said, his voice a touch deeper than

it had been before. He seemed surprised by this and put a hand up to his throat, then trying again he said, "Thank you." This time it was back to normal, and he seemed pleased by it, his artificial face shifting in ways only Kora had before.

"Anyways," he said, drawing the word out and walking to stand in front of our gathered group. "Your first trial is one of strength and defending the poor people of Camelot against waves of monsters, but I think we can skip that one. You've all proven yourselves to be strong."

He paused and when no one had anything to say he continued, chuckling nervously and looking around as if he expected Merlin might show up and try to rebuke him.

"That means we are on to trial number two, seek assistance from the Lady of the Lake. You will need to show piety, courtesy, and perhaps more, to get her to assist you. She is a master of riddles, but should she choose to give you one, you might have already lost this trial. Travel to the east, be wary of the monsters that lurk in these woods and be quick to gather her assistance."

He raised a finger as if he was forgetting something then added, "Oh, so trial one you would have encountered a powerful witch named Mab who threatens to overrun Camelot with her demonic spawn. You are going to the Lady of the Lake by the request of Merlin the wise wizard to retrieve something to help you defeat Mab, an artifact of some immense power. Not at all how these events truly played out if you ask me, but who am I but an ancient dungeon, I don't know anything."

And with that, he disappeared in a flash and a puff of smoke. I thought I saw him running behind a tree through the smoke, but when I checked behind the tree, I saw nothing.

"At least we've already beaten one trial, did he say how many we had to do?" Beth asked, ever the cheery one, while everyone else looked annoyed at best.

"He did not," Ventus said, taking a few steps up to a tree and punching it.

What happened next surprised me and caused all of us to look at him with a renewed respect. His punch didn't stop, going straight into the tree and blowing out the other side, despite his punch only going about an inch or two into the tree. He turned and looked right at me, raising an eyebrow.

"You feeling alright?" I asked him, as he looked down at his fist and then all around to the rest of our group.

"He has given me an amazing gift. This new body, the power I feel pulsing through me, and the size of my core increased. I shall be a much greater ally in this fight than I previously thought. Thank you for bringing me," he said, looking right at me and if I didn't know any better, I'd say that it was a look of respect.

"Let's move out," I said, walking up to the now taller than me Ventus and patting him on the arm lightly.

Our group took point, with Emory's group in the middle, and Creed's group holding the back position. It was good that we ended up with that layout because the first attack came from behind, swift and deadly.

Two wicked looking beasts laid dead before I even knew

what we were facing. When I rushed to the back to see what had happened, I saw blood on Namor's mace and Estraw's thin blade.

Namor answered my questioning look first, his voice deep and low. "Manticores, level 55. More coming."

Estraw twitched her blade, and the blood came off it. Her voice was sweet and a bit playful. "Best get back into formation and be ready to attack. I feel them coming ahead of us."

I turned and ran back to the front, activating Channel Lightning as five of the ugly human-faced winged beasts appeared. They could almost be compared to griffins in general form, but that is all, because in every other aspect they just looked wrong. Human head, body of a large cat, a tail covered in spikes, and wicked bat like wings. My attack hit the biggest one and bounced to the others around it, doing less damage but stunning one.

I used Inspect on the centermost one and saw that it was going to be more of a problem than the rest.

Elite Forest Manticore, Level 75

"Circle formation!" I yelled as more appeared on our flanks and behind us. I activated Speed Burst as the elite shot out spikes from its tail at me. Still, they moved fast enough that I barely got out of the way, but I was able to catch them on the edge of my blade before they hit anyone else.

The three distinct groups came apart as the healers took position in the middle, the tanks on the outer edge with the melee fighters and ranged fighters circled around the healers. I took up position next to Galt and struck out, wounding the elite in the leg but catching a claw against my chest. My speed ran out and I channeled essence back into my weapon and suddenly I could track their speed once more.

The fight was painful, Creed got knocked out when a poison quill hit him in the neck and Beth was shooting much slower due to getting grazed by another quill. Just as I thought we were making headway with white and black flames ripping apart wave after wave of manticores and the elite finally falling to one of my blows, four larger ones appeared directly above us and landed atop our healers before I could do anything about it.

I activated Speed Burst and cut through the backline within moments, cutting down two of the closest atop Zander, then moving to help Alayna. My sword dug deep, and my lightning struck hard, finishing off the remaining two. However, Alayna was down and not moving, blood pouring from her neck and several quills in her face. I used Mending Touch, poured a healing potion down her throat and used the rest of my heals while I kneeled over her.

Luckily the heals stuck, and I knew she was alive. But still, she didn't move.

"Does anyone have any cure poison potions?" I shouted above the din of battle. The waves were thinning, and I was sure we were close to the end. Zander pushed me aside and his hands glowed as he chanted. Suddenly Alayna began to cough, and I pulled the quills from her face. She blinked, letting me know she was still alive. With no time to waste I joined the front lines again, cutting and lashing out with spells with a renewed vigor.

Galt was the same beside me, he shouted and stabbed and any foe that stood before us died that day. Eventually the battle was won, and we continued on our journey to the Lady of the Lake. However, I noticed that we were getting a fair bit of essence, even despite there being fifteen of us, as we killed at least fifty, if not sixty, manticores. Unfortunately, the normal loot rules must not apply, because we'd gotten none so far.

The forest around us, when we weren't being swarmed by more monsters, was rather peaceful and when we finally reached the edge opening up to a massive lake, I was disappointed. There was something to say about gathering essence and walking through the shade of the trees. We'd faced manticores, mimics that pretended to be trees, trolls twice the size as anything I'd ever seen and dumber than any I'd spoken with, owlbears, and even a giant two headed monster that had used trees as a weapon. Namor had headbutted it directly into its left head and knocked that half of it out. It had been a laughably easy fight after that.

But now we finally stood in front of the lake, we just needed to figure out where this lady was and how to summon her or if she even needed to be summoned. The closer we got the more the path forward became clear. A boat, a very small boat, sat on the water's edge and it was clear, to me at least, what needed to happen next.

Looking out from the edge of the water, I could just barely see an island out in the distance. "I'm going to take the boat and see about finding a lady on the lake."

Surprisingly no one seemed to have a problem with my plan, they all took a seat at the water's edge or on the green grass, only Galt standing watch on the forest edge as if he expected more monsters to burst forth. Not sure how I felt about everyone being okay with me going alone, but I went to the boat and sat down. Before I could figure out how to get the boat to move, it began floating away at a steady slow speed.

"Be safe," Alayna called out, but she was weak from all the healing and one of the first to hit the ground to rest. If we hadn't had three healers and so many fighters, there would have been no way we would have gotten through those woods. I didn't want to think about how tiring it would be to fight our way back to the other side.

The water was still and majestic below me, only the boat's gentle movements causing a ripple to break the surface. I sat, holding my sword as it glowed a gentle blue green, wondering what might lay ahead for me. This trip with the elves had been quite the adventure and I'd lost new friends, but managed not to lose any old friends yet, though it had come close.

I thought about all those I'd lost since becoming an adventurer and had to stop myself. Mick alone was enough to make me want to scream. He'd been such a good friend and a shrewd gambler. I smiled at that. I knew once I'd Awakened that he was cheating most of the time, but I let him, his hands much quicker than they had any right to be. Card games had been fun and reminded me of simpler times when I didn't have all the weight of the world on my shoulders.

Once I got the sword, somehow figured out how to work it and cleanse the Ley Lines, defeated the Chaos Knight and settled the war in the east, I was due some rest. I think I'll take Alayna to the lake where my father often took me and build a small cottage where we can relax for a few years. The world would get along fine without us in it for a little while. The looming darkness that Mah'kus and my nightmares were intent on reminding me about, came to mind.

Would I ever have rest or was my life to be spent in the service of others forever? My father had a wife and children, surely, I was owed that much?

"Rest comes to us all, eventually," a sweet feminine voice said, startling me. I looked up and saw that I had reached the island while I stared out at the water lost in thought. Just off the edge of the island and half in the water was a beautiful woman with silver hair and eyes that glowed a gentle green. She wore no clothing, but her long silver hair did well to cover her breasts. Still, I couldn't help but notice her impossible beauty, unrivaled by any face I'd seen before.

"Is your love not such a beauty, when faced with the grace of unknown splendor?" The lady of the lake asked, and I sputtered when trying to respond.

"I-I only meant, I mean to say, I only thought that you are very beautiful, but your beauty does not diminish her own and I love her still though I see now that she is not the most beautiful creature to be seen." Each of my words sounded trite and wrong, but I pushed along anyway. I only wanted her to know that I was trying to be respectful and of course thought no less of Alayna because I beheld a beautiful face.

"I know, dear child, I know. I am indeed the Lady of the Lake, and it is well to meet one such as you. Very much like the one that came before you, Arthur, I believe was his name. He had a great destiny, and I can see that you do as well, though I worry."

"Worry about what?" I blurted out, still sitting inside the boat and watching her in rapt amazement.

"You wish for a life of simpler means, much like Arthur did and it blinded him to the truth of his life. Greatness like what awaits your destiny is all consuming. You will never have the simple life that you so eagerly imagine. All you can hope for is that you fulfil your destiny so that so many others can have the simple lives that you so wish for."

"I don't wish for a simple life," I said, protesting her assumption based on one daydream. She must know that I've always wanted this life and it truly is everything I've ever wanted and more, but the cost and the weight of it are just hard to bear at times. Surely, she can understand the weight of responsibility when so many speak of destiny and the great things I must accomplish.

"Your mind is open to me, and I do understand now. You are different than Arthur in a few ways, these ways may become your undoing, or they may be the boon that allows you to see your challenges to the end. Only time will tell. Now tell me why you have come to my shores?"

I cleared my throat and averted my eyes as her hair moved enough to show her nakedness, but she made no move to cover herself, so I gathered my wits and spoke. "I am told I need an artifact or weapon that might be used to combat a threat by the name of Mab. Without your help we won't be able to stand against her terrible magic, or so I'm told."

"I've only one weapon against such a threat and it has already been given once and returned. Will you return it to me if I give it once more?" She asked, her eyes going up and down as if taking a measure of me.

"If it is the condition of taking it, then yes I will return it," I said, not hesitating.

"You must remember your promise and not be made a liar, for the gift I give has much power and you will be tempted to take it for yourself, but you must not. You, Caldor Miles, are a great soul and I have faith that you will wield Excalibur with the care and grace it requires." With that, she reached into the water and pulled out a sword I'd seen before, the very same blade that sat on a table so many months ago.

It shone with a light that I now knew meant it was made of the purest refined Mythril and had a blue gem cut in a way that captured and reflected the light from all directions set into the pommel. Over every inch of the polished glowing blade were the tiniest most difficult to see runic formations. Each one so small as to be impossible to read, but somehow when looking at them I could understand the meanings behind each formation. One to strengthen the blade, another to dispel any corruption it might encounter, another to channel life into another being, bringing even the closest to death back from the brink. And hundreds if not thousands of more running across the blade like a never ending story.

I stepped out of the boat and walked up to the sword she held out for me. Gently she placed it in my hands and the moment I closed my hand around the grip everything changed.

CHAPTER 64
THE FINAL TRIAL

I returned on the boat, all the while my eyes unable to focus on all the information I was getting from everything all around me. I knew what the boat was made of, the kind of wood, the methods of its creation, and how really it was all just essence of some kind or another. There were different kinds of essence, and I could feel my own seeping around me. It took great effort but by the time I got back to the shore with my party members, I'd mostly blocked out the crazy influx of information. It was still there, but I was able to focus despite it, kind of like splitting my mind.

"Is that the sword?" Emory asked, he didn't sound impressed. I saw that to most it was just a sword, that they couldn't truly comprehend the power this Shard of Order had to change and alter all around it.

So amazing was the power of Excalibur that I even recognized that this sword was only a facsimile of the real thing, yet its abilities were much the same as the actual blade. Or at least that is the impression I got from the dungeon created blade. Whatever challenges lay ahead for us now, I knew I'd be able to master them. It was a euphoric feeling, and it was slowly overwhelming me. It was like I could do no wrong, lose no fight, defeat any foe.

"It is," I said, holding it out for all of them to see.

"Fascinating," Deline said, reaching out to take it from me. White energy sparked off the blade and burnt his hand.

"This blade is meant only for those select few that have been chosen to maintain the balance and be a champion of Order," I said, my voice felt more powerful, but it could just be my imagination.

"I see, take care that you don't hurt yourself with such a powerful artifact," Deline said, eying the sword with obvious jealousy.

"What do we do now?" Alayna asked, looking at me for answers. I saw the path forward, we had to return to the area we'd last saw the dungeon master, the human created by the dungeon to speak on his behalf.

"Back to where we started. But this time, I will lead the way," I said, feeling the power of the sword pulsing through me. I was unstoppable and no monster could stand in my way, the power of the sword pulsed through me, and I knew with certainty that I was meant to have this power. The surging energy that ran through me gave me the sureness of mind to accomplish anything I required.

Before anyone answered and before half of the group stood, I reached out my hand and created a better path forward for us. Pulsing white energy shot out from the tip of my precious blade, followed by massive crackling green-blue energy. The trees in a massive cone were cleared away, leaving only soft newly upturned dirt for us to walk on. I didn't like that, so I threw down gravity atop it to compact the dirt. The sword answered my call and suddenly we had a ten-pace wide path to follow.

My party said words, but they were lost on me, so intense was the power and euphoria pumping through me. I held the sword against my chest as I walked, seeing all the monsters before they came out to fight against us and undoing each of them with a single thought. This dungeon reality was weakly put together, and it was easy to find and pull the threads. I saw the essence gather and disperse, each of us acting like little funnels scooping it up. That wouldn't do, my blade thirsted for more essence always, so I redirected all the essence from that point onward back into the blade.

With each point of essence and each varied type, I felt my power surge and I knew more and more what I might be able to accomplish. No being of Chaos could hope to match me on the field of battle. Lord Variyn would be an insignificant bug against my power now, oaths be damned. Everything had changed, let those beings of darkness come, let the armies of the beastkin amass, I will defeat all threats and be the better for it.

"Can you hear me?" Alayna asked, she was shouting at me, and I looked up to see her face, worry and concern plain to be seen.

"You need not worry," I said, then taking the blade off my chest I held it out for her to see. "This is the answer to all our problems. We will end this dungeon, and I will claim the true Shard of Order, nothing will stop me now. I am made anew, not even Merlin will be my match."

"We're here and the dungeon man is trying to talk to you, he says if you don't listen soon, he'll just leave," Alayna said, pointing to the tall brown haired large human, his piercing green eyes cocked into a look of amusement.

"Oh, I will take care of him," I said, bringing the power of the blade to bear and pressing its power against the dungeon master.

He scrunched his brow, but otherwise nothing happened. Wait, why had I just tried to attack him, is he a threat? No...no I need to talk to him.

"Where next?" I asked, finding it hard to not lash out at him with my newfound power.

Chuckling, he cleared his throat before he spoke. "You've done well, time for your final trial." He clasped his hands together and looked oddly satisfied. "Listen carefully, because I will only tell you once. Your next challenge is to go to Camelot and place the sword into the stone you will find in the throne room. It will activate the city's defenses and your trial will be over. Can you do that?"

I wouldn't.

No.

This was my sword, and the power inside was mine.

"I will go to Camelot and defend the city, the stone is not needed," I said.

Yes, that would work. Just a compromise and the same outcome. The blade was mine and no one would take it from me. Surely, they didn't expect me to do such a silly thing as giving away the tool of our salvation?

My father's words, varied and wise, filled my head. It wasn't my sword or my power. No, this power was so absolute that it was corrupting my very thoughts. My father's voice filled my mind, though these words were new and not ones I'd heard him say to me before.

Be strong my son, fear not the power. Master it, do not let it master you. You have strength beyond the power that the blade promises. Shrug it off and make me proud.

"Father?" I asked looking around, tears beginning to form in my eyes. A surge of strength of mind came upon me and I knew what I had to do. "Gather close and I will end this dungeon."

Without question and a touch of fear on their faces, my party members came in close. I gripped the sword and willed it to do as I wished. A flash of white later, and we stood in a mighty throne room grander than any I'd ever witnessed. But I paid no mind to any of it but the stone, roughly the height of a man some dozen paces from me.

Each step was harder than the first, as if the very fabric of reality willed me to fail and take the power within myself. But I refused such enticing thoughts, instead I stepped once, twice, three times.

Four, five, six, my knees nearly buckled under the strain.

Seven, and I could taste blood in my mouth.

Eight, and I could see the end, I was so close, but the pain of losing the power worked hard against me.

Nine, and ten, and the very fabric of the dungeon

quaked from the unleashing of power as I struggled to maintain control of myself.

Eleven, and I could hear Alayna screaming my name as the very armor I wore, and flesh began to burn away.

Twelve and I was close enough to plunge the blade into the stone. I knew where to place it, I knew that this would give the city the defenses it needed against the wicked Mab, but I also knew this was all just a test.

A test I was failing. Clutching hard onto the blade I fell to my knees and crawled the rest of the way up the stone. My entire body burned a white flame, and I felt my own spark, deep within ignite around my aura to protect me.

I thought then, in my most desperate moment, that my father's hands, strong and sure, lifted me back up and together we plunged the blade into the stone.

All at once, every ounce of my energy left me and a great force blew me backward into the arms of my friends, who stood all around me. They were beaten and bloody, Emory had lost half his face from the intense power but somehow, he was still alive, they all were. It hadn't been my father that had helped me after all, but my friends. With their help, even at the risk of death, I was able to take that final step.

The dungeon was over. We received no rewards, loot, or essence. Instead, a door appeared and we left. Merlin awaited us outside the dungeon.

"You did it! I knew you had it in you. Are you prepared for such power now?"

"No," I said, shaking my head and wanting nothing to

do with the immense power and responsibility that came with it.

"Good, you shall have it!" Merlin exclaimed, clasping his hands together we were swept away and appeared in the same throne room the dungeon had depicted, but this one was in ruins. The ceiling caved in and debris everywhere.

"Who is that?" I asked, looking to the massive throne where a ten-foot tall, armored man sat with Excalibur sitting across his lap.

"That?" Merlin asked, squinting. "Oh, that's Arthur, he didn't have it in him to return the sword to its resting place. Good luck getting it from him."

CHAPTER 65
CAMELOT

"You've got to be kidding me?" I asked, the armored figure didn't move, and we were in no condition to challenge anything right now.

"Oh, you are all looking pretty rough, here, let me fix that and don't worry so much. I have faith in your abilities," Merlin said, a wide smile on his face as he adjusted the brim of his hat and chanted a few quick words I didn't catch. A pulse of energy, smaller than the first one, pulsed out and our wounds cleared, and I felt refreshed like I'd gotten a week's worth of sleep. Whatever spell he was using it was one I needed to learn.

"How can that be Arthur?" I asked, getting a good look at the ancient armor and the oversized sword he carried. The sword I recognized, it was a larger version of what I'd had in the dungeon, but the armor looked odd, with gears and such at the joints. "Is he some kind of Runeforged?" Suddenly it became clear what he must be, and I looked to Ventus wondering if he could confirm, but he just shook his head.

"What? No, he's had a bit of work done, a new leg here, a few organs replaced, most of his face, both arms. Okay he's a bit more machine than man, but I'm pretty sure he is still alive. Otherwise, I've been talking to a dead man for the last few weeks." Merlin was ranting at this point, and I decided to try something.

I walked toward the armored figure, Arthur, and made it within five paces of him, but still nothing happened. Turning back to my party, I raised my hands and spoke. "I think whatever it was, it isn't alive anymore."

As if in response to my words, the room shook, and I heard the grinding of metal on metal. Slowly turning back toward Arthur, I gulped. He was standing now, and he wasn't quite ten paces tall from this close, the throne making him seem larger than life. However, he was an impressive foot or two taller than me.

"You seek to carry my burden?" A voice asked, it was gravelly and rough, probably what I sounded like after not drinking water for a week.

"I do," I said, taking a measured step back and summoning my own sword into my hands, immediately filling it with essence. My body responded instantly, my vision growing sharper, my muscles bulging slightly with new growth, and best yet, my senses went into overdrive. I could now hear breathing from the armor, slow and raspy.

"I sense the Ordu chose you to be their agent," Arthur said, his shoulders rolling as he adjusted himself, the sound of metal on metal grinding into my ears. "Prove to me that you are worthy by sending me to the grave. I can no longer bear this burden."

"You would duel me for Excalibur? I don't wish to take your life, but I must have that sword if I'm to fix the wrongs committed by agents of Chaos," I said, maybe he'd see reason and just give me the sword?

"Single combat. We fight to the death. Prove yourself worthy."

Great, this guy wanted to die, so it might not be so difficult after all. In answer I raised my sword, but Arthur was faster. He thrust forward his blade in an almost casual way, and Excalibur cut right into my bicep muscle, forcing me to drop my sword. He pulled his sword free, and only then did I see the state of my armor, pieces were literally hanging off in places and would be providing very little by way of defense.

I activated Speed Burst and used Blink as a strike came for my face. With my speed increased, I moved at his same speed, but he was clearly an expert swordsman and his sword cut into my thigh a moment after I Blinked. My helmet hadn't been so lucky, somehow it didn't Blink with me and I saw it had been cut nearly in half. This fight was not going well.

It didn't matter, I would have to figure it out. My friends had put their lives on the line for me and I couldn't fail here at the very last step. I urged essence into my very muscles until my body started to move close to his speed, though I was far more clumsy than he was and it showed at the higher speeds.

He slashed again, this time to take my head clean off. I ducked the strike and used Phantom Thrust to get my first strike. Surprisingly the area in his gut where I hit blew apart in a spray of gears and blood. He hunched over suddenly, coughing and wheezing. Feeling bad about it, but needing every advantage I could get, I struck for his head, using Power Strike and activating Speed Burst again.

Suddenly he held out his hand and lightning came down from above, striking me and throwing me back. My muscles seized and I realized I was stuck in a stun. However, he didn't take advantage of it, instead he was chanting words while holding his side. Several chunks of metal flew to him from across the room until he stood up straight again. Red blood poured out of his side, but he'd stuffed the area with metal gears and shards, for what reason I couldn't say.

If he meant that to be a heal, it wasn't working. The blood continued to flow, and the metal looked painful as hell. Holding out my sword I cast Lightning Strike, but before it could hit, Arthur raised his sword and caught the blast. He let out a satisfied sigh and his bleeding stopped.

"Your attacks are laced with so much essence, it's like taking a cool drink of water after years of walking in a desert. Thank you," Arthur said, his voice slightly less gravelly than it had been before.

Note to self, do not infuse my attacks with essence.

I shot out a Rank three Firebolt and it struck him full in the face, blowing off a part of his helmet and revealing an elderly man's face. Around his forehead was a small band of gold, like a crown. Even from this distance I could see the runes that glowed on its surface, they seemed to pulse along with his raspy breaths.

Arthur came at me then, roaring and posed to take my head off again. I Blinked, but this time had my sword up, ready to block the attack I knew would be coming. I caught it just as it would have sliced one of my legs clean off. Instead, I used Swift Strike to turn his sword into an awkward angle and knock it from his hands.

He turned, lightning crackling up his hands and shot off two separate lines of lightning at me. I activated my Mana Shell, throwing mana and essence alike into it. A moment later the attack struck me and shattered my barrier, but it managed to block the attack. Before he could get to his sword again, I ran forward, activating Speed Burst and chopping down with Power Strike as he reached for his sword.

I took his right arm off just below the elbow, but I didn't stop there, I couldn't with a threat like Arthur. My Phantom Thrust ability activated as I stabbed for his exposed face and I felt it sink into flesh, he'd moved, and I'd hit his neck instead.

Then I reached down and picked up the massive Excalibur, pointing both blades at Arthur, as he struggled to breathe or speak. He fell to his knees before me, and I thought I saw relief run across his face as he stared up at me.

"Set him free," Merlin said, his voice more somber than I'd ever heard before.

Putting the two swords on his shoulder, crisscrossing

them, then shutting my eyes from having to see it, I took his head clean off. Once more I'd had to result to taking lives. I opened my eyes to see what I'd done, but I blinked, confused at what I was seeing.

Motes of light poured out of the armor and there was no sign of Arthur, just his armor and metal bits. On the other side of the room Merlin held a stone as it collected the motes of light until there were no more. Not knowing what I'd just witnessed and not caring if I were being honest, I stared at the armor on the ground. Perhaps he had gone someplace better, I knew little of the afterlife, but this is what he wanted.

I had Excalibur, the Shard of Order, the Sword of Truth. I felt my quest completing and it pressed against my mind to be acknowledged, but I ignored it. If I waited until after I visited a Mana Shrine and got rid of all this excess essence, I'd be able to collect a huge bounty from the quest.

Something was bothering me though; the sword wasn't reacting like it had inside the dungeon. I had no sense of things, no immense rush of power, no ability to turn the very fabric of reality against my foes.

"Merlin, I think something is wrong, the sword isn't working," I said, and Merlin looked up from his gem. He was petting it and whispering to it now, so odd this impossible man.

"Nonsense, it's just a bit dry. Give it a few million or so essence and you'll begin to wake it up again. Takes a bit of work to get it back to full strength, old Arthur liked to starve it so he could keep himself in check. How'd you think you beat him so easily? Hah."

"How much essence did you say I needed, just to wake it up?" I asked, shaking my head. It was never easy and after so much growth and power leveling now, the sword wanted essence too?

But I had essence, and if it wanted some, I would give it all it could take. I began to channel essence into the sword and suddenly it shrunk, becoming the ideal long sword length for someone my size. Still, I felt nothing from it, but the runes on the edges shimmered and moved as it drank in several hundred thousand of my essence. But still, it was only the tip of what it required.

"Now, if you are all done bothering me, I am sending you and your friends home. Do not return to Avalon for at least another ten to twenty years, or perhaps two weeks, I don't know how long this process takes, but I am putting three krakens in the sky this time, so don't even think about it!" Merlin was ranting and I barely listened to him, as I walked over to Alayna with a smile on my tired face.

I picked up my helmet and a few pieces of my broken armor, then suddenly white light flashed all around and I stumbled forward like I'd been pushed. Looking around I gasped, I stood outside Merlin's Pub and by my side was Alayna, Ismene, and Emory, they'd been the closest to me a moment ago. I looked all around, sure that this was just some kind of illusion. But suddenly the door swung open, and Mab appeared.

"That pesky little turd. Come in and get a drink. He

should know better than teleporting mortals so far against their will. You will need a drink, please come in, come in."

I looked to Alayna, then to Ismene, and lastly to Emory who said, "Fuck it." And followed her in. I shrugged and did the same. I needed a drink and for someone to explain to me what the hell had just happened and where everyone else had gone. But I'd settle for just a drink and conversation with close friends.

LEAVE A REVIEW

Thank you for reading. Please leave a review at, My Book.

Check out my website at AuthorTimothyMcGowen.com

If you really liked the book, please consider reaching out and telling me what you enjoyed about it at, Timothy. mcgowen1@gmail.com.

Join my Facebook group and discuss the books at: https:// www.facebook.com/groups/234653175151521/

Join my Patreon at: https://www.patreon.com/ TimothyMcGowen

ABOUT THE AUTHOR

Timothy McGowen was born in Modesto, California. His journey into stories started with reading the Goosebumps books. Later he read a novel by Terry Brooks and became hooked on fantasy/scifi almost instantly. Shortly after that he was given a school assignment to write a 5 page fiction story, and 25 pages later his story was half done. He hasn't stopped writing since.

His popular Arcane Knight series has sold thousands of copies in both ebook and audible so far. Consider signing up for my newsletter for news on book releases as they become available.

facebook.com/timothym.mcgowen

twitter.com/TimothyMMcGowe1

instagram.com/timothy.mcgowen1

LITRPG GROUP

Check out this group if you want to gather together and hear about new great LitRPG books.

(https://www.facebook.com/groups/LitRPGGroup/)

LEARN MORE ABOUT LITRPG/GAMELIT GENRE

To learn more about LitRPG & GameLit, talk to author and just have an awesome time by joining some LitRPG/Gamelit groups.

Here is another LitRPG group you can join if you are looking for the next great read!

Facebook.com/groups/LitRPG.books

List of LitRPG/Gamelit Facebook Groups:

- https://www.facebook.com/groups/LitRPGReleases/
- https://www.facebook.com/groups/litrpgforum/
- https://www.facebook.com/groups/litrpglegends/
- https://www.facebook.com/groups/LitRPGsociety/
- https://www.facebook.com/groups/AleronKong/

Made in the USA
Thornton, CO
08/03/23 21:57:21

97dca0db-1f4d-431f-a52e-e15732113c6dR01